I0722451

DREAMING ABOUT THE BOY NEXT DOOR

MOST LIKELY TO ★ BOOK TWO

SARAH SUTTON

DREAMING ABOUT THE BOY NEXT DOOR

Copyright © 2022 Golden Crown Publishing, LLC

All rights reserved. No part of this publication may be reproduced, stored or transmitted in any form or by any means, electronic, mechanical, photocopying, recording, scanning, or otherwise without written permission from the publisher. It is illegal to copy this book, post it to a website, or distribute it by any other means without permission.

This novel is entirely a work of fiction. The names, characters, organizations, businesses, places, events, and incidents portrayed in it are either the work of the author's imagination or used fictitiously. Any resemblance to actual persons, living or dead, events or localities is entirely coincidental.

For information, contact:

http://www.sarah-sutton.com

Images © DepositPhotos – Vadymvdrobot, Asier Romero Carballo & bloomua

Cover Design © Designed with Grace

MORE BOOKS IN THE MOST
LIKELY TO SERIES

Teaching the Teacher's Pet

Dreaming About the Boy Next Door

Rebelling With the Bad Boy

To anyone who's ever rocked out to
"Best Friend's Brother" by Victorious Cast

And to my grandmother, who is my #1 fan.
Love you to pieces.

I didn't realize how much I relied on Dad to wake me up in the morning until he moved out.

Well, really, I relied on his relic of a coffee maker, which, in tandem with the rising sun, stirred the house with a scream. As ear-piercing as the bean grinder had been, it'd been a steady thing to expect every morning, more effective than any alarm clock.

Mom, a late-riser, had given him more than one ultimatum about the thing—either he threw it out or she'd do it for him.

That ultimatum might've been why three weeks after Dad took the coffee maker and moved into an apartment downtown, I woke up late for the third time in the past week.

First period at Brentwood High started in eight minutes, and I could already envision Mrs. Winston's wrinkled scowl. At this point, I didn't have many excuses left to give her. Since it was only the second week of my senior year, and last week—due to Labor Day—we'd only had class for four days, she had to see right through the excuses, anyway.

The first time it happened, I told her I overslept. The second time, I told her I had to talk to Mrs. Diego about a math problem—which was risky, since Mrs. Winston easily could've called to fact-check me. Today, I was fresh out of excuses.

All that was left was the "my parents are getting a divorce and I can't sleep" card, and with the attention *that* would bring me—attention that probably would involve a trip to the guidance counselor's office—I couldn't imagine playing it.

Snatching my phone up from my nightstand, I hurried to dial a number I knew by heart, turning on speaker.

"Hey," Rachel said on the second ring. "Why are you calling me? Aren't you—"

"Are you at school already?" I asked, barely looking at the T-shirt I picked out of my dresser before throwing it on. Backwards. The tag tickled my throat, a little *hello, I'm not supposed to be here*, and I tucked my arms back in with a growl. "Please, please, *please* tell me you haven't left your house yet."

"Hate to be the bearer of bad news, but I'm already in homeroom." She paused. "Wait, are you running late *again?*"

"I keep snoozing my alarm in my sleep." I shrugged on a random pair of shorts too short for dress code, but at that point, I was picking the lesser of two evils. Short shorts over being even later, risking the dragon breath of my ancient teacher. "Stop by the English room and spin me a sob story for Mrs. Winston, would ya? I'm not sure my puppy dog eyes will cut it this time."

"Ooh, I'm on it. I'm sure Maisie and I can make something up. I'm in drama for a reason, you know."

If there was anyone who could sell a convincing lie, it was Rachel.

I dashed across the hall to the bathroom, giving my teeth a rushed, painful scrub—my gums would hate me later—and then giving the rat's nest on my head a painful grimace.

My hair was knotted from a night's worth of tossing and turning, and there was no salvaging it in the two minutes I had before I needed to be out the door. That was the problem with the cheap store-bought pink hair dye mixing with my restless sleeping habits—the color was pretty, but my bleached hair was *so* not a fan. Smoothing down the bumps as best as possible, I wound my hair into a bun at the top of my head.

Whatever. Not like I had anyone to impress.

As I snatched up my backpack, my phone let out a chirp in my pocket, a text message blinking. I stuffed my feet into a pair of sneakers as I read it.

Dad: **Hey, kiddo, I hate to start your morning off with bad news, especially on a Monday, but I have some.**

The dean is sending me to a guest

lecture Saturday morning at a college in Westview, so can we push your weekend with me until next weekend? Your mom will be ok with it, right?

With now six minutes left until classes started, I had no time to waste on the disappointment, nor a text back. It would come later, in full force, on the fact that once again, he'd put off my weekend to come visit. In the three weeks he'd been out of the house, I hadn't seen his new apartment once.

When I picked up my house keys from the side table near the door, I couldn't help but notice how empty it looked. Dad's car keys were gone, but he'd left the keychain picture from our last family vacation on one of the hooks. We were all smiling wide, unaware that in a year's time, the happy expressions would disappear. I was surprised Mom hadn't taken it down yet.

Before I turned toward the door, my gaze caught on the mail on the table, catching on the red, bold letters stamped across the envelope that sat on top.

Overdue Payment—Final Notice

Five minutes until class started. I didn't have time.

Fumbling out into the heat—was it seriously over seventy degrees before eight o'clock?—I picked up my bike where I'd left it leaning against the front porch railing. Mom's beat-up sedan was in the short driveway, but I wasn't surprised—no doubt she was still asleep. She never put anything on her schedule until after nine.

Though it was against Brentwood's city ordinance, I biked on the sidewalk. It saved me time of stopping for road traffic. I barely slowed as I turned off Walnut Street, standing up to pedal like mad onto Main. For the third time in the school year, I thanked my lucky stars for living two roads down from the school—luck had been on my side when Mom and Dad had chosen that cute, three-bedroom house.

And then luck said "psych" when it allowed Dad to leave with the coffee maker.

The pedestrian crossing light for the sidewalk began blinking its countdown as I neared it, and instead of squeezing my handbrake, I cut the curb to swerve back onto the roadway. My bag slammed against my spine, and the front tire threatened to give way beneath the rickety suspension. The quaky landing stuck, and I blew past the *Do Not Cross* sign and turned onto College Avenue. I could see the school's spires from here. I was going to make it.

With two minutes left until the bell, I didn't bother locking my bike to the rack when I got to it. I tripped as I hopped off, sprinting to the doors. I was going to make it.

The hallway was empty as I ran down it, sneakers slamming against the linoleum, my laces flicking off the ground as they fell out of their knot. One minute.

Mr. Pieffer, the science teacher, walked out of the men's restroom where we nearly collided. I swiveled at the last second, sneaker letting out a screech. Or maybe it was him. "Ava Jenson, we do *not* run in the hallways!" he yelled, but I didn't slow, huffing as I propelled myself up the west side staircase.

Literally a millisecond before the bell rang, I sailed through Mrs. Winston's open classroom door. I skidded to a full stop with my palms slapping against Nina Haven's desk, causing her to lurch away.

"Nice of you to make it, Ms. Jenson," Mrs. Winston said with a voice that was absolutely *not* pleased. She probably had already checked me off as tardy and now had to change it. "Glad to see your *sprained ankle* is doing better."

I lifted my hands from Nina's desk to look over at another one, finding my other best friend, Maisie, sitting in her seat. Her expression was a twist of *oops*, and she winced as she raised her narrow shoulders in a guilty apology.

"Please take your seat." Mrs. Winston walked over to her door and shut it with a hard shove, causing the glass in the pane to rattle. She lifted her ancient gaze to mine, promising nothing but suffering. "And see me after the bell rings."

"So, what did she end up saying?" Rachel asked as I followed her through the lunch line. My own packed lunch dangled from my fingertips, and I gripped my lit phone in the other hand. "Maisie said that you actually ran into the classroom. So much for our excuse."

I cringed. "Yeah, as much as I appreciate it, maybe next time you shouldn't lie."

"Now she tells me."

"She let it slide one last time." Mrs. Winston's reprimand hadn't been that severe—riddled with the "just because it's your senior year doesn't mean you can slack off" speech—but it had been laced with a promise. One more tardy, and I had a one-way ticket to my own seat in detention.

I'd never had detention in my life, and here I was on my last warning. Only a week into the school year.

As Rachel picked out her food, I scrolled through my inbox with laser-eyed concentration, skimming the subjects of submissions to my school-centric gossip website, Brentwood Babble. For a Monday morning, when people had all weekend to do gossip-worthy stuff, tips were seriously lacking. **I saw Jade and Connor at the Wallflower this weekend** or **Ashton drunk texted Riley Friday night** or **Someone on the football team is getting held back.**

I mean, the tips were *okay*, but not something someone would sneak a peek at their phone under their desk to read. Nothing "drop everything and share with your top three closest friends" worthy. A few people might be drawn in by the juicy key terms, but the submissions weren't exciting enough to capture the attention of the masses.

And since it was the beginning of the school year, capturing the attention of the masses to regain my relevancy was key.

We sat down at our lunch table, where Maisie had already claimed residence with her homework sprawled around her. Giving my burning eyes a break, I blinked up from my cell screen to the occupants of the lunch table. Rachel Manning, best friend since diapers, sat at my right. She'd loosely pulled back her brown curls with a scrunchie, letting a few pieces frame her face. Maisie had collected most of her math worksheets now, pushing her glasses up higher on her nose with her knuckle. Across from me sat Alex, Maisie's boyfriend.

They were talking about football when Rachel dropped her voice. "I've been holding off saying it," she said, attempting to scoop up her spaghetti, but it kept slipping onto her tray. Ugh. No one could've paid me enough to risk Brentwood's lunch food. "At least until, like, it was legit. Until he confirmed it with me. Reed quit the football team."

The hand holding my phone spasmed as I gasped. Her twin brother, Reed Manning, was one of the defensive linemen on the Bobcats team, and last Friday, the first game of the season, his jersey never popped up on the field. Everyone had been confused—including his sister. She must've confronted him about it over the weekend.

I waited, but Rachel didn't follow her words with a

punchline. "But your brother was one of the best players! Was it because he was passed up for quarterback?"

I remembered the submission to Brentwood Babble that'd come in two weeks ago, announcing the coach's decision for quarterback. And it *hadn't* been Reed, who'd been gunning for the top-spot his entire football career. Quite honestly, a lot of seniors had. Everyone thought the title was going to go to Connor Bray, practically the best player on the field, but a different senior, Landon Settler, had snagged the title.

But even though Landon was chosen as quarterback, Reed and his dad had been living and breathing football since the two-hand touch days. And yet, Reed just *quit*?

"Is it okay if it put in my blog?" I asked Rachel, already loading up the *add a new post* screen. *That* was exactly what I needed. *That* was "drop everything" worthy. And if I posted it before the end of the school day, everyone would be buzzing about it.

"Yeah, go ahead. I doubt he'll be mad about it, since he already skipped last week's game. Rumors are already flying, I bet. I don't know *why* he quit, though. He won't tell me."

Suspicious. Selecting the bold-face text option, I got to work, forgetting about the world around me.

Another Football Player Bites the Dust???

Everyone at Brentwood High knows

*that being on the football team is prestigious, but what would you think if I told you someone *willingly* left the team? Well, my sources tell me that Reed Manning did just that! Before the game last Friday, he turned in his shoulder pads, hung up his jersey, and called it quits.*

Tell me below: what do YOU think would've caused him to walk off the field?

Weird, weird, weird.

"Maisie," I said as I looked up from the screen. "Can I send over an article for you to proof after your tutoring? Just about this month's school events."

Sometimes when I finished a longer article, I'd send it to Maisie for her to look over. Sometimes. There were times I didn't. Like when it was on a topic I knew she'd roll her eyes at—and that was usually when I covered things involving someone's love life.

She nodded, but before she had a chance to respond, her boyfriend made a noise. "So, you're starting up your tutoring? We've only been in school a week. Who needs tutoring already?"

Maisie barely glanced over at him. "I told you I was Friday at lunch."

"No, you didn't."

"She did," I said, turning to my phone screen in an attempt to stop my eye roll. "How else would I have known?"

I wasn't Alex's biggest fan, but it was a secret that I strived to keep, for the most part. Telling Maisie that I didn't approve wasn't going to help anyone. And it wasn't like Alex was a bad person, but he was more caught up in himself than Maisie. Which, when you're in a relationship, the scales should be a bit more balanced.

Or at least that's what I thought. Not that I had any experience of my own. Lately, I'd come to the conclusion that relationships were...messy. Scary. I didn't really want one, anyway. The butterflies in my stomach were practically mummified, and I was okay with that.

Before I had a chance to press *post*, sending the football article to the unsuspecting eyes of Brentwood society, my phone buzzed. The telltale staccato vibration of a new Babble submission. With a tilt to my head, I opened it.

And then sucked in the world's loudest gasp.

The four words in the subject line were *everything* when it came to all the jaw-unhinging, world-stopping, "drop everything and share to your top three closest friends" sort of blog posts. And someone submitted it to *me*.

The Most Likely To List

Here's the link to this year's MLT list. Wanna post?

Everyone at my table—and even the table beside ours—stared at me. The gasp I'd pulled in was startlingly loud. I was surprised I wasn't hyperventilating yet. "Someone sent me the link to the Most Likely Tos. To Babble. The submission asked if I could post it."

Rachel latched onto my arm with a screech, craning her neck to peer at my screen. "Post it, post it, post it!"

I didn't even waste a second of this golden opportunity, and with my heart practically seizing in my chest, I sent the link school-wide. A cascade of musical chimes echoed through the cafeteria and a burst of pride swelled within me, knowing those people had notifications turned on for my website.

The Most Likely To list was one of the most exciting things about the back-to-school season. It was a list of superlatives decreeing who in the student body was most likely to do certain things. Most Likely To: Get Held Back. Most Likely To: End Up Alone.

The list usually consisted of seniors, since their names were more easily recognized, but there were a few underclassmen trickled throughout the fifty labels. Anticipation and dread mixed in my chest, causing my fingers to tremble as I clicked the submitted link.

No one really knew who created the list, though everyone suspected it was the Top Tier—the popular clique of Brentwood High. The jocks never got a label on the list and were never subjected to that kind of negative attention.

However, I had to admit, whoever created the webpage this year definitely could've used some pointers from me; their graphic design was a mess. Horrible color palette, ugly fonts, corny clipart. And dear God, was that Comic Sans?

Despite its ugliness, I was an eager bobcat, ready to clamp down on the fresh meat. The list meant that my week of Brentwood Babble content was *made*.

With hungry eyes, I scoured the lines, screenshotting the most shocking ones. I stopped when I got to the next name, the next tag. My stomach dropped when I read the label first, knowing that one did not go without the other.

MOST LIKELY TO: MARRY A MATH BOOK
Maisie Matthews

My first instinct was to play it off, to not tell her. But I didn't even have a chance to decide. Alex passed his phone to her, and Maisie looked at the screen with a scowl that would've sent a kindergartener running. Her eyebrows ducked down beneath the rim of her black glasses, lips pressed into a line.

That was Maisie, though. This kind of stuff didn't hurt her feelings—it made her *angry*.

If I was being honest, I didn't really get why. Gossip was fun to read about, but it wasn't that big of a deal. It rarely lasted beyond the week. It wasn't anything to get that upset over.

At least, I thought so until I saw my name.

I'd scrolled past it before it registered. *Ava Jenson.* The realization came accompanied by a swift stab in the stomach, one that almost sent my cell tumbling.

MOST LIKELY TO: NEVER HAVE THEIR FIRST KISS
Ava Jenson

The name almost didn't even look familiar. *Ava Jenson.* They couldn't mean *me.*

I blinked once, twice, but it didn't change.

When I looked up, Maisie had already gathered her things and walked away from the table, leaving Alex, Rachel, and me all engrossed in our phones. In my chest, my heart pounded erratically, following a beat to a heavy metal song or something. My insides had the screaming part down. "I'm on the list," I whispered, but my words boomed in my ears.

"You are?" Rachel squinted closer. She must not have gotten that far yet. "Oh. Wow, they gave you *that* one?"

"What other one would they give me?"

"I mean, I can't believe they put you on the list at all. You can post anything on your blog, and since the whole school can see it, you'd think they'd treat you like a queen."

Like a queen. *Ha.* I'd started Brentwood Babble

because I'd thought it would help me break into the Top Tier. They collected only the coolest kids at Brentwood High, the way one collects rocks, and though the clique mostly consisted of jocks, they weren't *all* into sports. When I'd started the blog my sophomore year, I'd thought I'd be part of the exception, and they'd welcome me in with open arms.

Nope. Instead of treating me like a queen with her cell phone shaped scepter, they treated me like I was the court jester.

The cafeteria started humming with voices, the gossipy whispers that hinted I'd have a busy night ahead of me wading through email submissions. I wondered which label captured the most attention this year, *who* they were talking about the most. Usually, the relationship-centric ones got the most hype. Labels like Most Likely To: Fail A Class or Most Likely To: Get A Ticket weren't sensational enough to linger on for long.

Most Likely To: Never Have Their First Kiss was a relationship one, which meant that everyone would be talking about it. Talking about me.

But why would they vote *me*? I smacked my lips together, but they didn't feel chapped. My teeth weren't perfect—my two front teeth were slightly bigger than average, an insecurity I'd long since gotten over. Well, for the most part. But they weren't abnormally big. Not big enough to prevent someone from wanting to kiss me.

Right?

Rachel, sensing my tooth-related crisis, reached over and rubbed my arm. "It's okay, Ava."

No, *okay* was being voted for something stupid, like Most Likely To: Break Their Wrist. *Okay* was not being on the list at all. "What about me is unkissable?" I demanded, staring straight into her dark brown eyes.

"Apparently, your mouth," Alex replied, and when I went to shoot him a glare, he was too busy engrossed in his phone.

"Ava. Seriously. They probably heard you haven't had a kiss yet and put you down."

Yeah, fine, it was true that I'd never had my first kiss. Not that opportunities hadn't risen. I'd almost had it in the second grade when Cameron Gilson wrote me a note and told me to meet him at recess for a kiss behind the slide. Of course, I'd never gotten the chance to decide whether or not to go through with it. My mom found the note and called the school, who then had a teacher monitor follow both of us around for the next week. By then, Cameron had moved on to Riley Huntington.

Your first kiss is special, Ava, Mom had said then. *You can't waste it.*

So, I took the advice to heart. Kept the first kiss protected like it was worth a million dollars. And now here I was, a first kiss-less senior, and the entire school knew it.

"They said *never*, Rachel," I said, shaking my phone at her for emphasis. "Never is *forever*. I'll *never* have a kiss?"

She rolled her eyes at my dramatics. "Of course, you'll have your first kiss. It'll happen when it's supposed to happen."

That sounded like another way of saying *don't hold your breath.* I pressed my fingertips to my frowning lips. I was the opposite of Maisie. This kind of stuff might not have hurt her feelings, but it absolutely decimated mine.

And her next words, though I was sure she meant them as comforting, only caused my skin to grow cold. "Stop worrying, Ava. You'll have your first kiss, and it'll be magical, and you'll fall deeply in love. It'll happen, trust."

I stared at my best friend as she resumed trying to eat her pasta, horrifyingly afraid of her being right.

My phone started buzzing, the emails and comments and opinions already pouring into Brentwood Babble, so fast that I had to switch it on silent mode. Two years of constantly refreshing my inbox in hopes for the next juicy gossip thread, and here I was, purposefully putting my phone on silent. For the first time since the birth of Brentwood Babble, I couldn't even bring myself to look.

Rachel's bedroom was the definition of organized chaos.

The space looked like our favorite antique store, Timeless Treasures, threw up in it. Knickknacks littered every surface. An old stained-glass lamp sat on her desk, surrounded by little figurines that a grandma would collect. She even had a shelf in the corner of her room for creepy, probably possessed dolls.

And then her bedspread was bright blue with little daisies and rainbows on it. Darkness to sunshine. Balance.

But it wasn't just the knickknacks taking up space. Her closet had exploded onto the floor in front of the double mirrored doors, and it looked like she'd attempted to sort things into piles, but got distracted halfway. Or bored.

When I looked up from my laptop, I could've sworn one of the piles moved. "Is there a mouse under there?"

Rachel, who stood on her tiptoes to look on her closet's top shelf, said, "Could be."

"I could help you clean your room, you know. For a fee."

"Let me guess—all I'd have to do is ask Reed why he quit the football team?"

Now that she brought him up, I realized it wasn't a half-bad idea. "Where is he?" I asked, casting my gaze once more to my screen. "I haven't heard his monster steps in the house yet."

"Connor's, I think." Rachel gave a little sigh. "I can't believe my brother's friends with Connor Bray. The wrong twin really got all the popularity and saved nothing for me."

"It's because Reed's prettier than you."

Rachel flipped up her middle finger.

The webpage I'd been designing for the past two days was almost finished. Two new moms had bought a web address to announce their new baby, and their theme was woodland animals. From the instruction email, they wanted a mix of script fonts for the headers and a cute, rounded font for the details. I'd done a handful of baby announcement pages since offering web design, but this was my first woodland theme.

Babble was one of my biggest accomplishments, and it'd been what had led me down the web design path in the first place. Finding the perfect color palettes, creating the prettiest loading screens, even down to creating a custom cursor—I loved it all.

"Rach." I maneuvered the laptop to face her. "Yea or nay?"

"If I say yea, you'll put the laptop away?"

Okay, fair enough, this *had* been taking up most of my concentration since coming over to her house, but it was mostly a desperate distraction attempt. However, now that Rachel's words created a crack in the dam I'd carefully crafted, there was no stopping the flow of thoughts.

The overdue payment notice. When I'd gotten home from school, it was gone from the entryway stand, disappearing to wherever Mom put it. It wasn't the first of its kind. The first had been Mom's credit card bill. The next had been a notice from the mortgage company. This one, if I was remembering the company name correctly, would've been her car payment.

I wasn't sure if Mom forgot about the bills or if she didn't have the money. Either option made me feel sick.

"It's the first client I've had in two months." I shut my laptop and laid it on her nightstand. I had to shove aside cables and random scrunchies, but it fit. "I was hoping if I finished a few days early, they might leave a tip. It's nice side income, you know? But I'll put the finishing touches on it tomorrow."

I fell against her pillows, staring at the glow-in-the-dark stars she'd stuck on her ceiling in the eighth grade. Whatever tape she'd used clung on faithfully. It'd probably survive World War III. She'd gone as far as to put them up into actual constellations, and I eyed the medium-sized Dipper, thoughts quickly devoured by the absolute insanity consuming my email inbox.

Earlier, I'd finally gotten up enough courage to peek at the Babble submissions. Finally worked up the energy to write an article, even though I'd typed it up mindlessly. I remembered mentioning the new labels—Marry A Math Book, Stay A Prude, and Peak in High School—and touched on a few of the relationship ones, but the specifics of my phrasing muddled together like alphabet soup.

As I'd written, there was no escaping the hypocrisy that itched at my skin like fire ants. I tiptoed around a truth that everyone knew, but was too embarrassing to talk about. "Are you sure I can stay the night?" I asked.

"You know my mom doesn't care. As long as we're sleeping by eleven. Or at least look like we're sleeping by eleven. Are *you* sure your mom won't care about you staying over on a school night?"

It was a legitimate question, since this wasn't something my parents allowed too often. Maybe once a quarter. They definitely would've said no, given how fresh we were into the school year and the fact that I was already three tardies in, but Dad was no longer around to ask for permission, and Mom had been swept up in her own little world. She'd been out most nights with her best friend, Lindsey, while I stayed home, unable to fall asleep until her car pulled into the drive. When I'd texted her to let her know my plans, I was surprised I even got an acknowledgement. "She's cool with it."

Rachel glanced back, taking in my expression in all its complicated glory. "Are you thinking about the Most Likely To list again?"

For that brief second, I *hadn't* been, but that conversation seemed a lot easier than the truth. "Yeah."

"Look at it this way—yours isn't the worst label on there. You could've gotten voted Most Likely To: End Up Alone. That's brutal."

I couldn't even remember who'd gotten that title. Someone had pressed the *delete* button on all the information in my head once I saw my own name. It was a surprise I remembered how to breathe. "I need to focus on building Babble," I said to her ceiling. "Who cares that I've never been kissed? I'm a nobody. I need to focus on other people's love lives. To hell with mine."

"You're being melodramatic. I'm glad it's just me seeing this side of you. I'd be getting secondhand embarrassment."

It was my turn to flip her off, but only her shoulder blades saw it.

In all honesty, I couldn't even pinpoint why the label bothered me so much. The probability—Maisie would've loved me taking this from a mathematical perspective—of me never having my first kiss was practically nonexistent. I was only seventeen, after all. Plenty of time for these lips to get to business. From a realistic standpoint, being on the Most Likely To list was something I should've rolled my eyes at.

But being on the list for that specific label felt like someone pressed their fingers into a bruise on my side. It was embarrassing, yes, but also highlighted a new insecurity.

"Ah! Found it!" With a little hop, Rachel yanked something off the top shelf of her closet, falling to the floor with a thud. She brushed the dust off, and when she turned to me, I realized she held a book. "Scooch over."

I wiggled to the very edge of her bed, giving her ample room to flop down on her stomach beside me. "Are you going to read me a bedtime story?"

"Better. We're going to find you a guy to kiss."

"In a book?" I peered at it closer. "Wait, you spent the last twenty minutes digging around for last year's yearbook?"

Rachel flipped through the long, glossy pages until she got to the class line-up, going straight to our grade. "In a class of three-hundred and twelve, there's got to be a cute guy you could kiss. Would you be willing to kiss an underclassman? Because then your pool is even wider."

I rolled over onto my stomach too, digging my elbows into the firm mattress. "You're seriously looking for a guy this way?"

"Uh, do you have any other suggestions?" She slammed her finger down on a portrait, poking his laminated cheek. "What about Aaron Keesler? Look at those eyes. *So* blue."

His eyes *were* blue, almost vividly so. He was cute. His hair was cut short and looked a little spiky, but as my eyes trailed to his lips, I winced. "Is his mouth too small?"

"Small?"

"Like, his lips." I pressed my fingers to my lips again, tracing their shape. "Are my lips too big?"

"You're thinking about this too much," she said with a sigh, flipping a page. "Ooh, what about Justin Rothford? He's got normal-sized lips."

Justin was the opposite of thin-lipped Aaron, with dark eyes and long brown hair. It nearly touched his shoulders, which were covered by a goldfish-printed shirt he wore for picture day. There had to be fifty small goldfish all over the fabric. Questionable choice. "He's got braces."

"So?"

"What if our teeth get stuck together?"

"Ava, *you* have to have braces too for that to happen."

I guess that made sense. She flipped through a few more pages, pausing long enough for me to scan through the portraits, but each time I tried to imagine actually kissing any of them, my stomach tied up in knots so tight that I almost thought I'd puke all over her duvet. What did she expect me to do with these guys? Waltz up to one of the guys in the halls and plant one on them?

The idea had me nearly breaking out in hives.

Kissing seemed...weird. Like it involved a lot of chapped skin and saliva. Don't get me started on *tongues*.

With a groan, I buried my head into my arms. "It's no use."

I heard the soft *thunk* as Rachel shut the yearbook. "You're taking this more seriously than I thought you would, honestly."

"I guess I feel embarrassed."

"Trust me, you're not the only senior who's never had their first kiss. It's not something to be embarrassed about." She nudged me, but I refused to lift my head. "It's just a list."

"Easy to say when you're not on it."

I regretted the words as soon as I said them. Not because they were biting, but because they instantly made me feel pathetic. And I didn't want to be that person. I *wasn't* that person, but it was hard to not feel self-conscious when a personal detail was put on blast like that, for everyone to judge and see.

Everyone would be looking at me, whispering about me. I'd never been the one on blast before, and I hated it.

Again, I was fully aware of how much I, the owner of the Brentwood Babble domain, was a hypocrite.

"I need to take a page out of Maisie's handbook," I said with a little shake of my head, trying to clear out the thoughts circulating like a never-ending merry-go-round. "She brushed off her label so easily."

"That's Maisie. She doesn't care about any of the popular stuff."

That was true. Popularity, sports, who's-dating-who—Maisie lived her life as if none of it existed. As if none of it could touch her.

"You shouldn't put too much energy into it, anyway," Rachel went on. "You're hot. It'll happen eventually. And don't worry, I'll be your wing-woman and keep an eye out for potential mouths."

I couldn't help but snort and laid my head down on my folded arms. Despite her teasing, I felt uneasy, like instead of laying on her soft mattress, we were on a bed of nails. If I shifted too much weight in one direction, the points would stick into my skin.

My thoughts went back to who might've put me on the list. Who saw the label Never Have Their First Kiss and immediately thought "oh, yeah, Ava Jenson." Maybe I'd posted an article that ticked one of the Top Tier members off. Maybe I didn't post about them *enough*.

Dang it, there I was going again. Spiraling down the rabbit hole of obsession.

"You know," Rachel murmured, flipping another page. "You could use this for a spread on the Most Likely Tos."

I peeked my head up. "What do you mean?"

"Like, take a picture of everyone who's on the list this year and upload it to Babble with their label. The webpage for the Most Likely To list this year sucked bad, but if you uploaded a prettier post of your own, it'd be memorable. People would be talking about it."

Yeah, because the thought of having my picture plastered on Babble with Never Have Their First Kiss underneath was exactly what I wanted. However, from a blogger's perspective, it annoyingly wasn't a bad idea.

"You know, it's weird that so many in the Top Tier are on the Most Likely Tos," Rachel said as she scrolled through the list. "Landon, Madison, Nate—that's not normal. Especially Landon and Madison. The quarterback and co-captain of the cheer squad on the MLTs?"

I glanced over at the yearbook to find Madison Oliphant's photo, the co-captain of the cheer squad. Her bright pink-lipped smile stared back at us. Her hair was expertly coiled, the perfect picture of popularity. And yet, she'd gotten a label of her own this year. "That is weird," I agreed. "Populars are never on it."

"Times are a-changing."

Before I had a chance to respond, someone from the other side of Rachel's closed door banged against the wood, startling the both of us. Being on the edge of the bed meant that when Rachel jumped, she ended up knocking into me, and my lack of balance sent me careening onto the floor with a considerable *thump*.

Rachel's voice rose a decibel. "Jeez, *Reed!*"

The door cracked open, and a face poked between the jamb, one instantly recognizable. The signature amused grin, too, was familiar, one that he and Rachel shared. "I'm home," her twin said cheerfully, finding me on the floor. "What are you doing, Paparazzi?"

Yeah, *ha*. Witty nickname there. Reed had assigned it to me since the dawn of Babble— "Paparazzi" since I took photos and posted them. "Checking for dust bunnies," I muttered, rubbing my elbow where pain had lanced up my funny bone.

"You didn't have to knock on the door so hard. I'm surprised you didn't put a hole in it."

"I'd be the one fixing it," Reed replied dully, and then receded into the hall. That was Reed—as little interaction as possible with this sister and her dweeb friend suited him best.

But before he had a chance to fully close the door, Rachel called after him. "Hey, hey! Where were you so late? Were you really at Connor's, or were you at Kelsey's?"

I swatted at her thigh, whispering, "I thought he was talking to Jamie from sixth period?"

"No, that was last week."

Reed opened the door wide enough to scowl at us, letting more of Rachel's bedroom light out into the hallway. It reflected in the gold strands of his hair, making it look even lighter. "Nosy much? Do you really want to know or do you want to post it on Ava's blog?"

"As if her blog would care about your love life," Rachel piped back. "You might be in the Top Tier, but you'll be old news soon since you quit the football team."

"Why don't you two worry about your own love lives?" Reed suddenly gave a theatrical, mocking gasp. "Oh. Wait."

Rachel wasted no time in launching a pillow from her bed at her door, but he'd slammed it shut at the last second. "You want a brother?" she asked me. "I'm selling mine. I'm getting a hamster instead. They might smell the same, but at least the hamster won't leave his underwear in the middle of the bathroom floor."

"Tempting," I snorted, crawling to where the pillow had fallen and swiping it up. "But I'm going to have to pass. I think he would drive me insane within the first day."

"Likewise, Paparazzi!" he called back through the wall, voice a bit too clear for my liking.

"Quit eavesdropping!" Rachel banged against the wall and then slumped against her headboard. "I should've consumed him in the womb."

I laid back down beside her, picking the yearbook up, tracing my finger along the laminated pages. "Missed opportunity."

I laid on Rachel's hard floor with my eyes open, unable to close them for more than three seconds. The air conditioning kicked on and rattled the vents, and there must've been a screw loose from how loud the noise was. And then, when the air-con kicked off, the quiet was *too* quiet. Rachel's nasally inhales, the scrape of her duvet as she shifted every five minutes—it was all enough to keep me wide-awake.

The air conditioner turned on again, wheezing out cold air, rattling that dang screw.

As quietly as I could, I pulled back the blankets from my makeshift bed, getting to my feet. My ninja-like stealth was pointless, though—Rachel could've slept through a bomb dropping. Her gaped mouth and heavy exhales hinted how deep into dreamland she was.

I tugged on the hem of my pajama shorts as the cold air brushed across my bare legs and squeezed out into the hall.

Rachel's house was a layout that I knew like it was my own from years of spending time within the walls, so even though the hallways were dark, I knew exactly where to step to avoid end tables and bookshelves. I knew exactly when to take each step down her stairs, when to turn the corner into the kitchen. I also knew which cupboard had the cups, and I pulled one down to fill it with tap water.

A large bay window let in the orange light from the streetlamps, and I peered through the wavy glass. The image of Walnut Street was sleepy, all the surrounding homes slumbering with their lights off. The house across the street, too, was dark, hinting that if anyone was inside, they were already turned in for the night. From this view, it almost looked haunted, with too many shadows dancing across the yard. It looked cold. Empty, as if it was a dollhouse and someone had reached in and taken all the pieces out.

My gaze lifted to the upper left window as I took a sip of my water, wondering if Mom was truly asleep or if she wasn't home yet. Her car was in the driveway, but that didn't mean anything. One of her friends could've driven. She'd never stayed out this late before, especially not on a weeknight, but lately she'd been coming home progressively later.

Dad leaving had hurt her deeper than it'd hurt him— at least, so I thought. It wasn't like either of them had talked to me about it.

"Are you sleepwalking, Paparazzi?"

The suddenness of the steady voice and my stupid nickname, so loud in the bubble of silence, had me jumping, and half of the water from my cup sloshed onto the floor. When I turned, I found Reed Manning standing behind me. Barefooted. Bare-chested. Even his pajama pants were hanging low enough on his hips that I could see the band of his boxers. His golden hair appeared mussed from sleep, but his eyes were wide awake.

"Jeez, sorry." He grabbed a dishcloth from where it hung off the oven handle. "I didn't realize you'd be so jumpy."

"I didn't realize you'd come up behind me like a creeper," I shot back, heart still trampling in my chest. "What are you even doing down here? You should be asleep."

Reed dropped the towel on the floor and pressed his foot into it, mopping up the water. "Perks of being the only man in the house. I get to inspect the scary noises, like someone rummaging around in the cupboards like she's *trying* to wake up everyone on the block."

I made a face at him. The "only man in the house" thing reflected back to a topic that was as touchy as could be in the Manning household: Mr. Manning's infidelity. Last summer, Rachel and Reed's father moved out. Or, rather, their mother kicked him out after he came clean about his affair.

"What are *you* doing awake?" Reed asked, leaving the towel on the ground to walk over to the cabinet. He withdrew his go-to *Super Mario Bros* mug, but instead of opting for tap water, he pulled out a pitcher from the fridge. The soft blue light filled the space as he opened the door, glinting off his canvas of bare skin. "Can't sleep?"

I looked down at the cup in my hand. "Not really."

He leaned against the countertop and brought the mug to his lips. "You want to talk about it?"

Even though we were in the same grade and he was Rachel's twin, I'd never been close with Reed. People always assumed that twins were always super closely bonded, but it wasn't really the case with Rachel and Reed. Growing up, he had always found us annoying with our dolls and the way we liked to reenact our favorite movies out in the backyard. When we got into middle school, he'd started up sports and never had time to be annoyed by us. And then, when we started high school, he'd quickly risen to the Top Tier, ditching Rachel and me in the dust. For how little our paths crossed, it was easy to forget that he was even Rachel's brother.

The idea of divulging any of my secrets to him fell into the category of *never gonna happen*, but I knew he was just asking to be polite. Then again, how polite could one be after scaring the bajeezus out of his sister's best friend in the middle of the night while half naked?

I'd seen him shirtless before after years of hanging around the Manning house, but it felt awkward now with all the lights off. Like I needed to avert my eyes from his pointy-looking collarbones. And those grooves by his hips... "You care?"

"Not really, but listening to you might help me fall asleep."

I glared at him as I lifted my cup to my lips, swallowing a snarky reply.

"Is it about the list?"

"You know I'm on it?"

"I did not. Not until just now, anyway. I'm an awesome guesser." Reed arched an eyebrow. "What's your label?"

I squeezed my eyes shut, hating my cheeks for the wave of heat that swallowed them. I shouldn't be embarrassed, but, well—whatever. "Never Have Their First Kiss."

Reed didn't respond right away, and I refused —*refused*—to check out his expression. For all I knew, the loser was probably fighting a smile, and I well and truly would've died inside. Nothing stroked a girl's ego like her best friend's brother laughing at her love life.

"You seriously haven't had your first kiss?" he asked, and when he finally spoke, his voice sounded normal. No trace of humor.

Still, I didn't risk looking. "I know that's surprising to *you*, Mr. Lip-Lock. I just...I'd grown up thinking I wanted to save it for Mr. Right. Which is ridiculous. I'm not going to end up marrying the guy I have my first kiss with. This isn't a movie." I lifted my chin, as if I could make that decision right then and there. *This isn't a movie.* "I overthought it my whole life. It's not that big of a deal."

If I'd kissed Cameron Gilson behind the slides, I wouldn't be in this situation. I wouldn't be overthinking. I wouldn't be waiting on some fairytale. Mom thought she found Mr. Right. She and Dad had their first everything's with each other. Now look where they ended up.

Reed didn't hesitate. "I mean, it's whatever. I'm sure there's a lot of seniors that haven't had their first kiss."

When I finally opened my eyes, Reed's expression was neutral, like he truly didn't have an opinion on it. Or it was neutral because he couldn't have cared less about this conversation. It was kind of strange how close he'd come to repeating what Rachel had said verbatim, but then again, they *were* twins. They looked nothing alike, though. Rachel's hair was dark brown and curly, a trait she'd gotten from her father, where Reed's hair was more of a golden color, not a wave in sight. I knew Rachel had brown eyes, but I didn't know what color Reed's were. It was impossible to tell in the lighting.

"You've had your first kiss," I informed him, as if he didn't know. "You've kissed, like, twenty people."

"Twenty-one," Reed deadpanned, a glimmer of his usual grin peeking through.

And just like that, Rambling Ava entered the chat. "Were you nervous your first time? I'm nervous, but I don't want to wait on it anymore, you know? I don't want to build it up so big in my head anymore. But, like...I mean, what do you even do with your mouth? What if I'm a horrible kisser? What if I'm a horrible kisser and word gets around? No one would ever want to kiss me again. Although people are probably already suspicious."

The small smirk that had begun forming on Reed's lips stretched wider, a surprised humor dancing in his eyes. "You've really been stressing about this."

"It's not like I haven't thought about it before the list came out." In fact, it'd been something that'd bounce around in my head. When would I have my first kiss? Who would it be with? What if I was bad at it? "But now I've made the decision that I want to get it over with. Take the pressure off."

Yeah, that sounded right. Rachel and I looking at guys in the yearbook seemed awkward earlier, but now I felt confident about it. Go up to someone and—*bam.* Make it happen. Rip the Band-Aid off. I would stop stressing about it.

"So, kiss someone." Reed shrugged lazily, slouching lower against the counter as he stretched his feet out before him. "First kisses aren't that big of a deal. They're usually awkward, too. I'm sure if you put out an ad on Babble, you'd have guys lining up."

"An ad? Because *that's* not skeevy at all."

Reed reached out and put a hand on my shoulder, giving me a shake. "Well, until you find someone, you can practice on your pillow."

With his heavy touch, something else sunk into my bones. He was a blockade of skin and abdominals, but for some reason, staring at his bare collarbone caused me to stop. Inspiration. It struck like lightning, electrifying my thoughts.

I tilted my head up, half-hating him for the height difference. His eyes *were* brown, like Rachel's, but much, much brighter.

He had his mug half raised to his lips but stopped, instantly suspicious. "Why are you looking at me like that?"

"I should kiss *you.*"

"*Me?*" Reed, jerking his hand away, sounded horrified, and his expression morphed to match. It was all arched eyebrows and saucer-wide eyes. "Why me?"

"I said I wanted to get my first kiss over with, and I'd rather it be with someone I like—"

"You *like me?*" If possible, he sounded more alarmed. His face became thoroughly freaked out-looking, like I'd proposed to him more than just a kiss.

"Ew, not like that!" In fact, I'd never thought of him as kissable before this moment. Yeah, he had a nice mouth—plush-looking lips that would've matched mine—and he was attractive, but since he was Rachel's brother, he was strictly off-limits to think about in that way. Rachel would smother me with a pillow in my sleep if she thought I had a crush on her brother. "Someone I like, but won't *fall for*. If I have my first kiss with you, I'm safe from catching feelings."

The list of why I'd never fall for Reed Manning was *long*. I didn't have enough fingers to tick off the reasons. I saw him in his awkward, long-limbed phase in elementary school, and the phase in middle school where he put on way too much body spray and tried to grow out a mangey mustache. And even now, senior year, I dodged him for obvious reasons.

"It's just a kiss," I added. "You kiss people all the time."

A fact, too, especially if he's already over Kelsey and onto someone new. He hadn't used to be a serial dater, but it seemed that ever since junior year, he'd turned into Mr. Player. Never stayed with one girl longer than two months. He was definitely not the boy next door.

"Don't you and Rachel have a rule?" he asked, making a face. "Like a 'no dating my brother' rule?"

"How do you know about that?"

"Rachel used to suck at hiding her diary."

Okay, that unlocked a whole new level of discomfort. If he knew about the rule, what else did he know about? I shook the thought from my head before I had a chance to spiral. "We wouldn't tell her." That part seemed self-explanatory. Rachel finding out would be the equivalent to a hydrogen bomb dropping on our quaint little Brentwood street.

"Jeez, you're too calm, you know that? It's like you're asking me for five dollars instead of kissing you. You'd be great at poker."

"You're the one who said kisses weren't that big of a deal." I smiled when he looked away from me, knowing he was eating his words. "One peck and then it's done. You'll show me how to do it, I'll have officially had my first kiss, and then—ta-da. Over with. Like getting a shot at the doctor."

"Except doctors always give you lollipops, and kissing you would give me hell with my sister."

I stared up at him, my determination starting to morph into an offended shock. "Oh, you don't *want* to kiss me, is that it?"

Reed squeezed his eyes shut. "Jeez, Ava—"

"Forget it, forget it." Insecurity wiggled in to take its place, and then a nice little dose of shame. It could've been because he didn't want to risk the wrath of Rachel, but it could've been because the idea of kissing *me* grossed him out. I took a step back, my butt hitting the countertop of the island. "It's not like you could keep a secret from her, anyway. Don't you have twin telepathy?"

Something about that made him sigh, a sound that seemed to echo in the dark kitchen. "I keep secrets from Rachel all the time."

"Like with the football team?" Reed's expression turned into something that was considerably less romantic. Not that he'd really looked romantic before. "Why did you quit?"

At first, I wasn't sure he was even going to answer me. "Maybe I wanted to try a new hobby instead of practicing all the time. Videogames, maybe. Collect rocks. Comic books always seemed cool."

The flippant response made me sigh. "Why quit something you've been so passionate about for the last six years?"

"Are you asking because you care or because you think *Babble* will care?"

"You can't deny that it'd make a good article. Everyone's probably dying of curiosity. You practiced all summer and you quit before the first game of your final season? Something smells fishy to me."

"Don't." There was zero humor in his voice. Instead, he'd filled it a with warning that took away any traces of levity from a few moments ago. "I mean it, Ava. You can post about everyone else, but put me on your blacklist."

"I don't have a blacklist," I replied, but it was more or less a lie.

And Reed knew it. "You never post about your friends. Rachel, Maisie, Alex—they've never gotten an article. And you never post about yourself. That's a blacklist."

It was true that I'd never posted about my friends, and I didn't post about Alex by association. Rachel and Maisie didn't have the kind of draw the Top Tier had. I loved them to death, but they weren't "drop everything" worthy. If most Brentwood High students saw the article title, they'd say "Rachel who?" Which tanked likes and comments, and no likes and comments equaled less visibility. I needed that engagement, and the Top Tier guaranteed it.

It wasn't a topic I wanted to talk about anymore, especially not with the judgey eyes Reed gave me. Plus, there was an awkwardness between us now, one that had been conjured by my embarrassing proposal and his firm rejection. Suddenly feeling bone-weary tired, like the rattling of a screw couldn't stop me from sleeping now, I pushed away from the island. "We should get to bed. It's already after midnight, and Rachel's alarm clock is always a rude awakening."

Before I could get more than two steps away, Reed's hand curled around the spot above my elbow, halting me. The judgey eyes were gone, replaced by something that brightened his gaze like before. I could've sworn there was curiosity there. "So, after that pep talk, you're not going to follow through?"

"On what?"

"Our kiss."

For no reason at all, my heart fluttered in my chest. Instead of letting my surprise shine through, I put a hand on my hip. "I thought you couldn't kiss me."

"I didn't say it was a good idea," he said, shooting me a look that matched his words. "But if you want to get it over with, and you feel...comfortable with me, I can—I can do it."

"Jeez, take one for the team, why don't you."

Reed smiled, and despite his hesitance, it was real. I couldn't remember the last time I'd seen him smile without some sort of sarcastic amusement or malice.

Like all the other times a kiss was a possibility, my stomach flipped over, desperate to escape the nerve-wracking situation. The floorboards underneath my feet grew warm and stuck to my toes. I wiggled them, freeing them from the suction. "Maybe...maybe it's not a good idea."

"No, you wanted your first kiss." Reed took a step toward me, and suddenly his body was all imposing lines and warm skin. "Don't worry, I'll give you a good one."

I bit down on my lower lip, recalling how many Babble submissions I'd gotten about Reed's kissing skills. I'd read enough to know he was good at it.

Just a kiss. It was the key to unlocking all the nerves in me. I could get rid of this pesky first kiss, and then I could stop overthinking it with any other guy that came across my path. I wouldn't be able to tell anyone about it, least of all Rachel, but really, this kiss was for me.

"Run me through the basics," I instructed, brushing my hair from my eyes. This was no big deal. "Like...what do I do with my hands?"

Reed came close enough to plant his hand on the counter behind me, and we were suddenly closer than we'd ever been before. It was...weirder than I expected it to be. Not necessarily *wrong*, but awkward enough that I held my breath. I came face to face with that prominent collarbone, his body heat threatening to swallow me in a warm embrace. "Whatever feels natural."

Of course, with our height difference, Reed looked down at me, most of his face hidden by the darkness of the kitchen. "Um, okay."

"Make your kissing face." I wanted to point out that I didn't have a kissing face—Ms. Never Been Kissed over here—but instead I pursed my lips into what I *thought* was right. Until Reed snorted. "A little less of a duckface."

"A duckface," I muttered, offended, but relaxed my lips to the point where they were barely pursed. It must've been exactly what he was looking for, because a second later, he was slanting forward. "Whoa, wait!" I yanked my head away while he jumped. "Uh, which way are you leaning?"

"Leaning?"

"Yeah, like...are you going left? Should I lean left, too? Or are you leaning right?"

"You're overthinking this."

"I don't want to mash my nose into yours."

He chuckled but never answered, leaving me to

watch which way his chin tilted. When the shadows shielding his expression began to clear as he drew nearer, a new thought zipped through me.

"Wait, wait," I rushed to say again, pressing my palm against his skin to stop him. His bare skin. His *hot* bare skin. I tugged my hand to my chest. "What—what do I do with my tongue?"

Reed choked on the breath he drew in. "*Jeez*. Keep it in your mouth. We're not using tongue."

Why'd he say it like *that*? "Why not? The idea of my tongue freaks you out?"

"It's going to be a five-second kiss, Ava. Max. My mouth will just be touching your mouth. We're keeping this PG. No tongue."

No tongue. Not that I wanted tongue in the first place. Less saliva, less...strangeness. "So, hang on, am I supposed to—"

"Ava?"

I swallowed. "What?"

The sort of half-tugging grin he gave me then was one that would've made anyone's toes curl, eyes simmering like coals over a hot fire. He looked like he was about to share with me the dirtiest sort of secret. It was in that second, as the air shifted and my blood pumped warmer, that I realized I was in way, way over my head. "I'm going to kiss you now," he murmured, taking my chin in his hand. "So shut up."

Sucking in a sharp breath, I squeezed my eyes shut, my thoughts a dizzying swirl. *This was really happening.* In the three seconds that Reed hesitated—most likely debating, one last time, whether this was a good idea—my heart pounded so fiercely that I was sure I was on the brink of passing out. That, or it was on the brink of bursting in my chest, the anticipation building and building until—

Reed kissed me.

I never thought my lips would be so sensitive, but the second Reed's touched mine, the pressure was enough to send a tingle down my spine. Through my whole body. I could feel where his bottom lip ended and where his skin began. The fingers holding my chin in place slackened for a moment before sliding up along my jawline. It was a butterfly touch along my skin, something I hadn't expected to feel so...good.

I tried to remember every movie I'd seen that had a kissing scene, but my body took over, instinctively knowing what to do. It turned out that I didn't have to think about where to put my hands. Of their own accord, they rose to rest over Reed's collarbones, pressing into the ledge of the bone. His skin was fiery to the touch.

Those five seconds came and they went, and now I knew for absolute certain that I really, *really* liked it.

The five seconds came and went, and...neither of us pulled away.

Reed's fingers inched toward the back of my head to wind in my hair. His fingers squeaked against the countertop as he gripped it, arm stiffening against my side. One of his bare feet made a sound on the floor as he stepped closer, filling the two-inch gap that had existed between us before. His lips brushed my bottom lip, trailing his teeth along it in a sensitive caress, and I swallowed a gasp.

All those Babble submissions weren't lying. Reed Manning knew how to kiss.

I'd gone my whole life thinking that a kiss just involved lips, but it was so much more than that. It wasn't only Reed's mouth on mine, but his fingers stroking my skin, his little inhales as he pulled away and kissed me again. All of it created a moment so electric, so perfect, that I couldn't have dreamed of this if I'd tried.

Reed's hands found their perfect spot on my hips, and without breaking away, he lifted me up onto the countertop. Our mouths were level now, my world enveloped by a moment in time where nothing existed beyond this. There was no Most Likely To list, there was no house across the street, and there was no Rachel sleeping upstairs.

There was me and there was him, taking my first kiss and blowing it out of the water.

Oh, no, a small part of my brain whispered, one nearly drowned out by the dizzying tilt-a-whirl happening with my insides. *Oh, no, no, no.* I ignored it, curling my fingers into his hair to draw him closer.

Until something loud slammed in the hallway, followed by a string of high-pitched, sleepy curses. There *was* no Rachel sleeping upstairs—she was about to stumble into the kitchen.

I shoved Reed away from me with a gasp, and when he drew his hands back, he took some of the fire with him. He didn't stop, though. Instead of waiting for his sister—with the looks on our faces that would've no doubt exposed what just happened—he flung himself behind the breakfast bar and into the darkness.

And no sooner had he ducked out of sight did Rachel step into the dark kitchen. "Ava? What are you doing?" she questioned, her robe tied around her. "Uh, why are you on the countertop?"

Like a deer in headlights, I froze. I was about to be run over by the oncoming car, but I couldn't bring myself to move. "Um...I was...thinking. What are you doing awake?"

"I got up to pee, and you weren't there. I thought you might've gone home, but I thought I heard something in the kitchen." Rachel scrubbed a finger against her eye, looking very much so like a toddler. She didn't realize how frantically my insides were shaking, and it took everything in me to keep my breathing from reaching hyperventilation levels. She had zero idea that Reed was crouched on the floor just a few feet away. "Were you thirsty?"

"What?" I followed her gaze to Reed's *Super Mario Bros* mug he'd left on the counter. "Oh. Yeah."

"Reed's going to be mad at you for using his mug."

I couldn't think clearly enough to respond, not for the longest moment. Fog had infiltrated my head the second Reed had kissed me, and it had yet to dissipate. Channeling my normal Ava self was impossible with my lips tingling like they were about to fall off. They felt swollen. "Oh."

"Mom must've forgotten to close the curtains,"

Rachel said, and took one step toward the window, toward the corner Reed had ducked into.

That finally cured me of my paralysis. "*Wait!*" My thighs squeaked as I slid off the countertop, practically shoving Rachel backward to get between her and the window. "I'll do it, I'll do it."

Rachel gave me a funny look. "Okay, sheesh, you don't have to yell. If you wake Reed, I'll never hear the end of it."

This situation was *not funny*.

And I'd been right in my assumption that Rachel closing the curtains would be a bad idea. Though Reed was crouched on the ground, pressed up to the kitchen island cabinets, he was still visible even in the dark kitchen. He had his hand over his mouth, and from the split second of looking at him, it didn't look like he was breathing. I didn't let myself stare long. Before he could meet my gaze, I turned to the window and tugged the curtains shut. Then I moved to grab Rachel's arm. "Let's go back to bed."

"Hey." She stopped me from tugging her out of the room, and the look she gave me had me freezing. *She knows*, I thought, a desperate edge sinking its teeth in. *She took one look at me and she knows.* The Reed-induced fog made it impossible to think of an apology other than bursting into tears. "Watch, tomorrow, no one will be thinking about the list. At least, they won't be thinking about *you*. No offense, girl, but you're not the most shocking one on there."

Rachel was my best friend, but she wasn't a mind-reader. Of course, she'd be able to see that something was wrong, but she couldn't always tell what. And Reed was right. They must not have twin telepathy, otherwise she'd be able to sense him cowering in the dark. "You're right," I said at last, clearing my throat. "It's—it's dumb to put so much on a stupid kiss."

"Hey, my first kiss wasn't bad. Think of the spit like moisturizer."

An hour ago, I probably would've been thoroughly grossed out. I might've laughed. Now, still reeling from what had happened less than ninety seconds ago, I could only draw in a shaky breath.

Rachel patted my hand and started to walk with me into the hallway. "But I've got faith. With you, I bet your first kiss will be magical."

Magical. I cast one last glance into the dark kitchen, but there was no movement. *Magical.* Like my palms smoothing over Reed's bare skin. His hands grasping my hips, hoisting me up to give himself better access. His lips, a determined pressure against mine.

Oh, no, indeed.

"**Y**ou look tired."

Alex stood with me by the lockers while we waited for Rachel and Maisie to show Tuesday morning, but the clock was ticking closer and closer to the top of the hour, which meant I'd have to head to class soon. I might've lucked my way out of a detention with Mrs. Winston yesterday, but I couldn't toe the line any further.

Then again, I wasn't sure I wanted to wait around to face Rachel. I'd ducked out of the Manning house in the wee hours of the morning, unable to face either twin.

Alex surely wouldn't be waiting much longer, either. In fact, I was surprised he was sticking around instead of heading to class, making lame small talk. "I'm fine."

"I know no one likes coming to school and hearing they look like crap, but—"

"I said I'm fine, Alex."

"I remember how I felt when I got put on the list last year. I couldn't sleep either. It's kind of a double-edged sword, you know?" Alex rocked on his heels, gazing down the hallway. "You feel important, because someone in that group must've noticed you, but it's for an embarrassing reason."

I gripped my phone in my hand, imagining it was a stone I could smack into his forehead. "I'm not embarrassed."

He nodded his chin, as if saying *uh-huh, sure.* "I was embarrassed."

That was because his label had been Never Get A Girlfriend. Coincidentally, he asked Maisie to homecoming three weeks later, the day before the dance. And *that* was why I didn't trust him. I couldn't tell if he asked her out because he wanted to or if he asked her out to scratch his name from the list. Sure, they'd been together for almost a year now, but that fact always lived in the back of my mind.

I blinked down at my phone, hoping it would have the effect of a door slamming on *that* conversation. I loaded the Babble webpage, instantly soothed by the familiar blue and gold layout. Something about it made me feel less on edge. Maybe it was because each time I looked at it, I was always transported to the days I spent building and perfecting the webpage, gleaning any ounce of information that I could from articles and YouTube videos.

And now, here we were, two years later, and I was just beginning the journey of doing web design professionally. It made my coder heart squeal with joy.

Loading up the Most Likely To post, the one with the

yearbook-like layout, I balked at the statistics. "Last night's article got a hundred and seven comments!"

"Lemme see." Alex craned his head closer, nearly knocking into mine. "What do they all say?"

I fought the urge to pull away from him while I opened the comment box. An array of usernames greeted me. That'd been a huge engagement boost when I first introduced it—up until then, people could only comment or submit tips using their email address. Now they could be completely anonymous if they chose.

Which was a good and bad thing.

"Ouch," Alex hissed, pointing at my screen. "That one's brutal."

*ForgetForever: **Notice how she didn't mention her own tag? Awkward!!!***

*Hunt4Bulldogs: **I wouldn't either— she's never been kissed?!***

*JeffBoy22: **I call cap on that. I saw her kissing someone at a party over summer***

*Hunt4Bulldogs: **nah, look at her. Never been kissed? I can believe it***

"What's *that* supposed to mean?" I demanded aloud. "What does *Hunt4Bulldogs* look like?"

"Probably a football player," Alex replied, reaching out and scrolling through the comments. "Bulldogs? That's Jefferson's mascot."

This time, I did jerk my phone back, scowling. "I know that."

"Good morning, you two."

I lifted my head to find Reed standing before us, bag hanging loosely. He wore a Bobcat graphic tee that they sold at the school spirit shop, two sizes bigger than he really needed. It swallowed his frame, obscuring all the muscles I'd had a front-row seat to last night.

My brain liked to test its recall, because for a split second, all it did was conjure the image of Reed shirtless. *Not now!*

Looking at Reed, there was absolutely no indication that we'd made out last night. Not in the glint of his eyes, not in the tilt of his lips. It was almost as if the kiss hadn't happened. As if the hand lazily slung off his backpack strap hadn't threaded through my hair last night.

Don't think about it.

"Wow, hey, Reed," Alex greeted happily, literally getting stars in his eyes. "What are you doing over here?"

Reed gestured at me with one finger, sending a flurry of exclamation points down my spine. "My locker. I need my history book."

Right. Right. I edged away from Rachel's locker, which was next to Reed's.

I had the urge to stare at his profile like a creeper while also running away like a little girl. Once Rachel had led me to her room, I'd laid in my sleeping bag with hyperawareness, but I couldn't hear him tiptoe his way to his room. Which was saying something, because he usually walked like he was trying to knock a floorboard loose. I'd avoided him this morning, but maybe I didn't have to. Here he was, going back to pretending I didn't exist like he did since I became friends with Rachel.

It had me second-guessing my sanity a little. The kiss...it *had* happened, right?

Reed didn't glance up as he asked, "How are you doing this morning?"

"Ava's upset that people are posting about her on her blog," Alex crudely filled in for Reed. "It's karma, Ava. It was bound to come and bite you sometime."

"People are posting about you?" Reed asked while shuffling through his locker. For the second week of school, his metal box was already a pigsty, with pieces of notebook paper along the bottom. "What are they saying?"

Alex opened his mouth to reply for me, but I cut him off. "I can handle online criticism. If I couldn't, I wouldn't have started Babble."

"Don't let them get to you, Paparazzi." Reed looked me in the eye as he shut his locker door. It wasn't the first time in the whole interaction, because apparently eye contact was easy-peasy for him after such a personal encounter, but it was the first time I didn't look away. "You'll have your first kiss eventually."

The words were a joke and only the two of us knew the punchline. It grated against my skin.

"I don't want to rush it," I said, even though my brain

yelled at me to keep my mouth shut. "I think I'd regret it if I rushed it."

He still wore his easygoing expression, but his eyes narrowed ever so slightly. He cut a quick glance to Alex, who was looking up at Reed like a little fangirling puppy.

"Move, move, move," Rachel huffed as she rushed up to her locker, fumbling for the combination. Her high-end boots slipped a little as she came to a halt. "I didn't realize how late it was."

Alex watched as Maisie trailed behind at more of a languid pace. "You have five minutes."

"Yeah, but *somebody—*" Rachel shot me a look, and then shifted it to Reed. "Didn't wake me up this morning. *And* he left without me. My whole schedule is off."

"Not my fault if you didn't set your alarm," Reed replied, reaching out and rubbing the crown of her head, messing up her hair. "I figured you were taking one of your mental health days."

"The second week of school? Mom would kill me, and you know it."

Reed raised his eyebrows at me in an expectant way that had me freezing. "If you want someone to blame, blame Ava. She didn't wake you up either."

I started blinking seventy times a minute. "I—I went home early. At, like...five. Too early to wake you up."

"Dang." Maisie gave me a sympathetic frown. "Five in the morning? That's early for you."

Yeah, well, I didn't get much sleep, anyway. Apparently kissing your best friend's brother worsens your insomnia. "Uh-huh."

Reed wasn't even bothering to fight his amusement. "Well, I'm off to homeroom," he said, edging away from us. With Alex now perfectly distracted, there was no one to catch Reed tip his head quickly to the side, eyes holding mine all the while. "Have a good day, Rachel and Rachel's friends."

Awesome. Demoted to Rachel's friends. Reed walked away, but before he turned the corner, he caught my gaze one last time, doing that head-jerking thing that made his intentions clear. I swallowed hard.

"I'll—I'll meet you in homeroom," I told Maisie, squeezing her arm before taking a step. "And I'll see you at lunch, Rach."

"Don't be late!" Maisie called after me, and I threw her a thumbs-up.

Yesterday, when I'd been racing down the hall, there'd been not a soul in sight. However, today, with five minutes still until the bell, everyone was taking advantage of the opportunity to get more gossip in. As soon as I turned the corner Reed had disappeared down, all hope of finding the boy was lost in the sea of students. Especially with my height deficit, standing on my tiptoes didn't even help.

There was no way I was going to find him—and talk to him—before the bell.

No sooner than I'd had the thought did a hand wrap around my upper arm and tug me to the side, fishing me from the flow of traffic and pulling me into an empty classroom. It was Mrs. Oakley's classroom, the senior US History teacher, and since she had first period as her free period, she didn't come in until the second class of the day.

With the lights out and my steps off-balance, it was impossible to orient myself.

At least, until Reed pressed me against the wall beside the door, easing it shut behind us. I swatted his hand off my arm, giving him as strict of a glare that I could muster. "Jeez, are we in a spy movie or something?"

Reed's easygoing expression was a bit different than it'd been a second ago; less guarded, more intense. He'd put on a bit too much of his cologne this morning, the green apple and jasmine scent making my head swim. With him so close in the darkness, this felt like an echo of last night. Enough for a stab of déjà vu. "We should talk about last night."

"Now?" I demanded, glancing around the room. The desks looked ghostly. "Class is literally about to start, and if I'm late again, I'm getting detention."

"Fine, I'll make it quick, then." Reed folded his arms across his chest in a macho-man look, but it struck me distinctly as the way a brother might look at his sister when she annoyed him too much. "Don't get any wrong ideas about last night. The kiss didn't mean anything to me."

The subject shouldn't have come as a surprise. Reed spent the last ten years barely acknowledging I existed. The way he spoke now was no different from how he'd been speaking to me my whole life. Except despite how blunt his words were, I struggled to comprehend their meaning. "I—you—excuse me?"

"Just because we got carried away doesn't mean it meant anything. It was a good kiss." He tilted his head to the side. "You know, honestly, for it being your first, I expected it to be worse."

I opened my mouth to say something, but stopped at the last second, gaping like an idiot.

"It was a good kiss," he repeated, "but it didn't mean anything to me. I want to be sure we're on the same page. Let's forget about what happened, okay?"

Oh? I wanted to say, to channel even just an ounce of confidence that he practically oozed. *You kissed me like that and you didn't feel anything at all?*

Because even though I wasn't sure what I felt, I knew it'd been something.

The way he spoke sounded like he was talking about something else. The dinner he had last night, a piece of candy he'd never had before, or a new soda he'd sampled. *It was okay, but I wouldn't try it again.*

"You pulled me aside just to make sure I hadn't gotten *butterflies?*" I demanded, crossing my arms across my chest and mimicking his stupid stance. "Your ego's bigger than I thought. Not everyone wants to date you, Reed. In case you forgot, we already agreed that it was a one-off thing. It didn't mean anything to me either."

The words didn't sound like a lie, but they tasted like one. Admitting anything different to Reed, though? Now? It was the equivalent of standing in front of a crowd in my underwear. I'd scrub the kiss from my brain, scrub the feel of Reed's hands along my body along with it, and start fresh.

It seemed possible enough...right?

"Glad we got it cleared up," Reed said, and his expression *looked* glad. It almost stung how relieved he sounded. He took a step back from me, and then, without warning, he smacked his palm against my arm. "Like I said, Paparazzi, you did good."

And then he left. He sauntered out of the classroom like he was giving me a sports pep talk instead of telling me that despite how heated the proposed timid kiss got last night, he wasn't attracted to me in the least. I stood there exactly as he'd left me, jaw dropped, eyes wide, asking myself *did that just happen?*

The tardy bell rang out like the slamming of a court gavel, sealing my fate. *Yes, yes it did.*

My blue-light blocking glasses gave the webpage in front of me the faintest tinge of yellow, but a smidge of a headache was inching its way through after hour three of staring at my computer screen. After school, I sent in the baby announcement webpage for client review—which got a 5-star approval and a $10 tip—and began working on a site mockup. I offered the mockups on my website so clients could see what my range of abilities were, and partly because I was addicted to the site building process.

This one was a bit of a bigger build, with a five-page design and custom HTML. I created the mockup with the idea of it being a culinary blog. Using mocha brown, olive green, and bright orange color scheme, I established the contact page with clean and professional fonts, the 301 redirects, and created a faux blog post with a recipe I'd gotten from one of Dad's cookbooks he'd left behind.

Probably more in-depth than it needed to be, honestly, but once I got started, it was hard to stop.

It was also the sort of mind-numbing work that I could do without my thoughts straying in a million other directions, which was fitting for the current state of my life.

The coffee shop in Jefferson, the next town over, was abuzz with the after-school rush, but I'd successfully claimed a table by the windows, and the one that had the working outlet. My computer chugged the electricity like it was its own brand of espresso. I had my earbuds in so the amount of people filtering in and out wouldn't disrupt me too much, but in the three weeks that I'd been coming here, I'd gotten good at tuning out the noise.

My phone pinged with the staccato vibration of a Babble submission, and I dropped my coding to snatch up the latest tip. **Chelsea Milton got cut from the volleyball team!**

Despite the intriguing subject line, my heart gave a sigh of relief. All day, I was so afraid I'd open Babble to find a bomb waiting for me. **Reed Manning and Ava Jenson made out!!!** Not that Reed was much of a gossip—the exact opposite—but the paranoia of it getting out was enough to make me jumpy.

And just like that, the heat of the kiss resurfaced like

a pool float, bringing along a stinging flush across my body. I lingered in that forbidden territory longer than I should've, replaying the kiss over in my head, curling my toes inside my sneakers.

The bubble popped when I recalled his response. *Don't get any wrong ideas about last night. The kiss didn't mean anything to me.*

Even now, I could've wrung his neck. It ticked me off that he pulled me aside for that pointless—and a bit hurtful—conversation. Mrs. Winston hadn't been as forgiving a fourth time, and I'd been smacked with the big Detention card.

I put my phone down, rubbing my forehead. God, what was I thinking, asking Reed to kiss me, anyway? *Reed?* It was a moment of pure idiocy. Weakness. Desperation. The true depth of the consequences hadn't really hit me. But now, as I went on the rollercoaster again, recalling the high of the kiss and the low of his 'it didn't mean anything' spiel, I realized how stupid I'd been.

A tanned hand fell across the chair across from me, and through the soft hum of my earbuds, I heard, "Is this seat taken?"

I schooled my features into annoyance, prepared to scare off the stranger who couldn't come up with a unique pickup line. "Yeah, actually, it—" I looked up and stopped, the sentence dying off in a half-finished breath.

Mr. Jacob Manning was a man I'd grown up not really paying much attention to, mostly because he was rarely home. He was usually at work or out golfing during the times Rachel and I hung out. If he was home, he paid more attention to Reed while they ran football drills in the backyard. There were times that they'd be up before the sun even rose, and Mr. Manning's shouts at his son were loud enough to wake us up in Rachel's bedroom.

And after Mrs. Manning kicked him out last summer, I hadn't seen him since. And to my knowledge, neither had his kids.

He looked a lot like Reed, with the strong jawline and same build, but I could see more of my best friend when I looked into Mr. Manning's eyes. "Hi," I said softly, blinking up at him as my body locked in place.

"So, this seat *is* taken?" he asked with a small smile on his mouth, one that looked about as plastic as the keys on my keyboard.

"Oh, um, no. Go ahead."

Mr. Manning needed no more persuasion. He slid effortlessly into the seat across from me and set his to-go coffee cup on the table. "You look different from last I saw you," he said kindly. "Your hair is pink now."

"Uh-huh."

"I bet your father fought you tooth and nail on that."

Dad probably would've, if he knew about it. I hadn't seen him since I dyed it two weeks ago. Mom had rolled her eyes when she saw it. "*Ah, you're entering your rebellious phase.*"

"I heard you're designing websites now," Mr. Manning said as he took in my open laptop, turning his coffee cup from side to side. "That's pretty impressive for someone your age, you know. Starting your own business is a big accomplishment."

"I offer the service through a third party," I said, and now I did close my laptop. It was impossible to feel comfortable in his presence, given what happened. "Like a marketplace for clients to find designers. I do it for cheap—cheaper than most people on the site. I'm trying to gain experience now, build reviews, that sort of thing. I wouldn't necessarily call it my own *business*."

Mr. Manning nodded as I spoke, listening intently. "That's still very interesting. Quite ambitious. Have you worked with any big companies yet?"

"No, no, mostly people who want their website updated or tweaked. Small-time bloggers, announcement pages, that sort of thing."

Mr. Manning took a sip from his coffee, and while he did so, I was able to notice more about him. His hair, chocolate brown, was cut in the same style as always. It was the same way Reed used to cut his hair before he started growing it out. Mr. Manning wore a striped button-up shirt, no tie, with the top button undone. I couldn't help but look at his left hand. No wedding band.

"Ava." The name was startling, because though he must've said it before—knowing him for ten years, surely he'd said my name once—it sounded so foreign. Like a stranger was calling me. "Can I ask you a question? I'll understand if you don't want to answer, but...well. I'd really like to know."

I tried to give him a polite expression. "Sure, what is it?"

"How are Reed and Rachel?" He let out a soft breath after the words. "Like I said, I understand if you don't want to share. They haven't spoken to me in such a long time, despite me trying to reach out. Just...is there *anything* you can tell me? How's Reed doing?"

I looked down at my laptop, fixing my attention on the hairline scratch on the corner of the lid, fighting the push and pull of guilt from either side. From the best friend standpoint, I knew Rachel wouldn't want me to say anything, but then again, my heart squeezed painfully at the predicament Mr. Manning found himself in. That, and the man had a really good puppy dog face.

"They're doing okay," I began slowly, not convinced this was the right move but unable to stop myself. *Keep it vague.* "The school year just started, so they've been busy."

"Yeah?" The happiness in that one word was enough to ease my conscience, if only a little. "I couldn't make it to last week's football game, but I'm excited to see Reed play his senior year. I don't know how he'll feel about me showing up."

I tensed up as soon as he brought up football. It made sense that if he hadn't spoken to either twin, he wouldn't know that Reed quit. Heck, *Rachel* didn't find out until last week. Reed had gone to all the practices before the first game of the season. I definitely didn't want to be breaking that news to Mr. Manning.

"Ava, did you know that I own my own construction company?"

I blinked. "Uh, yeah, I knew that."

"Ever since I found out you design websites, I've been thinking about mine. It was made ages ago by someone who probably didn't even know what they were doing, you understand. I'd be interested in hiring you for a site makeover, if that would be something you're interested in." Mr. Manning raised his eyebrows. "What do you say?"

It felt like I was walking along a war-torn desert, and suddenly—*click*. I stepped on a landmine. There was no reversing off it. If I could, I'd have packed up my laptop an hour early. I never would've come to Expresso's at all. I never would've let myself get into this predicament.

I bit down on the inside of my cheek. "Mr. Manning, I don't... I don't know—"

"I'd pay you well," he hurried to add. "I'm sure a bright teenager like yourself has something she's saving up for, right? A car? College tuition?"

I pictured the envelope on the front entryway stand in the house. *Shutoff—Final Notice.* The whole reason I'd begun scrambling for more website gigs these past few weeks, why I'd been building templates and tweaking HTML. All for a paycheck that would take some of the weight off my mother.

As soon as Mr. Manning mentioned money, my throat closed up.

"You know, if you were to work with me—and do a good job—I can recommend you to a few friends of mine. Have you heard of Pilar Start-Ups? It's a company based in Bismarck solely dedicated to helping small entrepreneurs start their business ventures. A buddy of mine is one of the CEOs. I could pass your name along to him, and he can promote you to a whole slew of people who need sites designed." He sat back in his seat and smiled broadly, the plastic replaced with something much more genuine. Maybe it was because he felt more comfortable with me now, the stiffness of striking a conversation gone. Maybe it was because he knew he was dangling a carrot in front of me. "With companies like these in your portfolio, you wouldn't have to do projects for cheap anymore. It'd be the best of experience, with the best kind of references. I don't have to tell you it would look fantastic on scholarships and college applications, right?"

My eyes fell once more to my closed laptop. One of the biggest things with web design was getting my name out there. With hundreds of thousands of other people designing websites out there, as soon as people realized how old I was, clients ran for the hills. Experience was hard to garner. Sure, when the occasional YMCA-goer asked for their baby announcement site done, I was over the moon, but otherwise clients were few and far between.

And here Mr. Manning was, offering to give me the experience I needed. More than that. Offering a way to help Mom keep her head afloat. With Dad's loss of income, and not many houses to sell, it was clear money was tighter. This could keep her from taking on another job to pay the bills, or doing the unthinkable, selling the house.

Even working with him alone would be enough. In Brentwood—heck, in the entire county—Manning

Construction was one of the biggest construction companies. Whenever anyone had remodeling done, the business would stick a sign in their yard. Signs were all across Brentwood and Jefferson, proudly displaying their social proof.

"I appreciate the offer," I said slowly, speaking to my computer. "But I'm not sure it'd be a good idea."

"Why don't you sleep on it?" Mr. Manning leaned forward and withdrew his wallet, slipping out a white and beige business card. "My email is on the back. Talk to your parents, think it over, and email me."

I shouldn't have taken the card. I'd like to say it was the respect that my parents instilled in me that had me accepting the matte thing, but really, it was something else. Something...selfish. What if I worked with him, just this once? I'd design the website, he'd recommend me to his friends, and it could help me gain more popularity. The money would help Mom pay her car bill. Rachel wouldn't even have to know. It wasn't like she checked my personal webpage, anyway—if I listed Manning Construction as a client, she'd never even know to look.

Mr. Manning rose from the table, offering me one last nod before he took his coffee and departed. I turned the card over, studying the email. The longer that I sat there, the stronger the sinking feeling got that it wasn't a carrot he'd dangled in front of me. Instead, it was a worm on a hook, and I was a fish stupid—*desperate*—enough to take the bait.

The uneasiness followed me the entire night. I couldn't settle my nerves down enough to lie down, so I worked on the finishing touches on my website template. Around eleven-thirty, nearly an hour past my usual bedtime on a school night, and an hour after Mom had gone to bed, I started my routine.

What was nearly as stressful as thinking about Mr. Manning was thinking about his son. As I brushed my teeth and changed into my pjs, I couldn't get what had happened twenty-three hours earlier out of my head. "You kissed him," I told myself, and that was the first sign I was losing it. I was starting to talk to myself. "You kissed him. It happened, so move on. It was nice, sure, but that's only because kisses *are* nice. It wasn't nice because it was *Reed*. That would be..." *Weird, weird, weird.*

As I stepped out into the hallway, I heard Mom's voice filter from her bedroom down the hallway. At first, I thought she was talking to me. I stepped further down the dark corridor, and the closer I got, the more I realized she *wasn't* talking to me. However, it was what she said next that had me listening, anyway.

"We split the bills evenly, and they're *still* this high." Mom sighed, and it sounded shaky. "Yeah, I know. It's my credit card payments, the mortgage, and my car payment. I don't know how I'm going to pay it all, Lindsey. I know,

I know. When he...left, the last thing I was thinking of was how I'd pay for all this."

A sickening flutter took root behind my rib cage, buzzing like I was about to throw up. I hugged my arms to my chest, knowing I needed to walk away but was unable to get my feet to move. The need to hear the conversation to completion was overwhelming.

"I can't. I *won't*." Mom's voice became fierce. "He hasn't even seen Ava since he left—I can't ask him to help me."

For some reason, the day I came home to Dad's packed suitcase came into mind. Dad, resting one hand on the handle, touching my cheek with the other. "*I'll see you soon*," he'd said. "*I love you, kiddo. You know that, right?*"

"And maybe...maybe it is time. Maybe you're right." I heard Mom sniffle. "I mean, I'm sure I'd get enough for it if we sold now. We could move into a smaller house, pay off some of the debt. Ava will be off to college next year, and I can't imagine living in this house alone, you know?"

Boom. That was the bomb my body instinctually knew to wait for, and it exploded through me. The dark hallway seemed to sway like I was in a funhouse, and if I hadn't been leaning against the wall, I would've stumbled. She couldn't mean... Of course, she couldn't mean—

Mom danced around the words, but in the end, she added, "Yeah, I don't think it'd be hard to sell this house. But I don't know. I just don't know."

No. It was the one word ringing in my head, a clear denial that refused to negotiate. Just—no. Selling this house, the house I'd lived in my entire life? The house right across the street from my best friend? Absolutely not. I wanted nothing more than to barge in there and tell Mom exactly that, but my feet refused to move.

Rationale crept in slowly. Mom was only wanting to sell the house because she couldn't afford all of her bills. The shutoff notices were just pressuring her. I knew things were tough, that was why I had been trying to scrounge up extra client work. But the few and far between projects weren't enough.

Mr. Manning's offer. The money he'd pay me to work on his site, and the recommendation to others who needed a website. That would be enough. I'd just have to compromise my morals to do it.

Work with Mr. Manning or lose my childhood home?

Mom and Lindsey had switched to talking about Lindsey's kids, and my legs carried me to my bedroom before I knew what was happening. My mind was whirling, but everything else felt numb, like I'd crossed into dreamland. The unthinkable—but it wasn't anymore. Mom thought about it. I just had to keep her from pulling the trigger.

I'd figure it out. I'd have to.

I flipped off my overhead light, letting my night light illuminate the room. I walked over to my window next, ready to pull my thick curtains together.

As I clenched the fabric, my gaze snagged on movement across the street. The Manning's front door eased open, revealing the object of my incessant thoughts as Reed crept out onto the front porch. He had on dark clothes but wore a pair of his brightest sneakers, and the reflectors on them caught in the lamplight. For a wild second, I thought he was going to cross the street and come to my house, but Reed only ducked his head and started off down the sidewalk.

I watched him until he moved out of view, and even then, I debated pulling on a pair of sweatpants and following after him. Where was he going so late on a school night? I wracked my brain, but the possibilities offered more questions than answers.

$\mathcal{E}$ven though we were supposed to be working on our worksheets in the last ten minutes of Physics, I sat at my blacktopped desk and fiddled with my fingers. I could never focus in class. It was the second to last class of the day, which meant my brain was ready to check out, and there were too many distractions. Florencia Rodrigo gossiping with Devin Lepper at the table behind us, for example. The fact that Mr. Pieffer was playing *Galaga* on his computer, with the sound on. And then there was Reed, who sat two rows behind me. Who, I was trying to convince myself, wasn't staring at my shoulders, though it felt like it.

Attempting to focus was useless.

I also had to fight the urge to pull out my cell and check my inbox. Even though Mr. Pieffer was playing his own computer games, he wasn't too hip on students using their phones in class. He was one of the few teachers who actually enforced the rule.

Rachel was being the dutiful student and going through her worksheet, and I distracted myself by watching her write out an answer on her worksheet. She held her pencil loosely in her left hand, angling so she wouldn't drag her palm against the graphite. She was left-handed—was Reed lefthanded too?

Stop, I scolded myself and the way my thoughts casually drifted to the wrong twin. But looking at Rachel now, I couldn't help but imagine how the conversation might've gone if I told her the truth. *The other night, I asked your brother to be my first kiss, and he said yes. And, well—it was really good. Are first kisses supposed to be that good?*

If Rachel didn't stab me with her pencil, I'd be surprised.

It wasn't the threat of violence that kept me quiet. The longer I kept it to myself, the more I could play it over and over in my mind and no one would have any clue.

"So, have you seen your dad's apartment yet?" Rachel asked after a moment, cutting off my train of eye-stabbing thought. "Hopefully he's at the nice complex with the elevator."

"I haven't been yet." The day they'd announced the separation was fresh in my mind, even though it happened weeks ago. The way they'd delivered the news had been flat, emotionless, like they were talking about splitting the last cookie instead of splitting up. The words *moving out* and *apartment* had lost their meaning. "I think he wants to surprise me. Surprises are what they do best."

"You mean about the divorce? Hey, at least your dad

didn't cheat on your mom with some woman from Jefferson."

Once more, I fell silent, watching her work. At first, I thought the sudden mention was because somehow, she found out about yesterday, with her dad finding me at the coffee shop. But when she didn't follow up, I realized that was her response to me talking about the divorce.

When I'd first told Rachel about my parents' separation, that'd been her response nearly word for word. *At least your dad didn't cheat.* As if that somehow made the prospect of my parents falling out of love more bearable. As if it made the fact Mom cried herself to sleep less heartbreaking.

"I'm still surprised he came clean about it, you know," Rachel went on, but her voice sounded different. Stiffer. "My dad, I mean. And like you can't believe your dad got a new place? I can't believe mine ruined our whole family."

I thought of Mr. Manning's sad expression from the café yesterday, and with the thought came the ugly confliction. Whenever Rachel looked at me like that, my stomach twisted painfully. "I, uh, I had someone reach out for another website design."

"Look at you, my techy best friend." Rachel beamed, and just like that, the conversation was once more in neutral territory. I wasn't so easily put at ease, given the new topic I shifted to. "You should start a business and Maisie can be your math financial person."

I snorted at the clunky title, but it sounded off-key. "I feel a little weird about doing it."

Rachel didn't look up at me, but I could tell she was interested in the way she tipped her head closer. "Why not?"

I chewed on the inside of my cheek, watching as she began flipping through her Physics textbook. "Uh, the job is kind of big. Bigger than I've ever done before." It wasn't a blatant lie, but the way I danced around the truth made me uneasy.

She lifted her head to peer at me. "Do I know them?"

I wedged my fingers underneath my legs, pinning them to the seat, forcing them still. There was no dodging this one now—it was either tell the truth or tell a lie.

"Hey." Two hands suddenly appeared on the blacktop table, and I traced the arms up to find Reed leaning over me, his gaze on his sister. He kept his voice low, letting it mix in with the murmuring of other students. "Quit gossiping, yeah? I can hear you two tables back."

His hands were inches from where mine rested on the table, his arm close enough to my face that I could see the freckles dotting his skin. And don't get me started on the way he *smelled*. Jasmine and green apple. Clean, sharp, intoxicating.

Stop smelling him!

"Mind your own business," Rachel told him. "Everyone else is."

"No, they're waiting for Paparazzi to share a Babble submission she hasn't posted yet," Reed replied, tipping his head at me without looking over. Like he could talk *about me* rather than *to me*. He turned to the table behind us, to Florencia and Devin. "Am I wrong?"

Florencia gave a weak chuckle, whereas Devin ducked his head.

My tolerance had reached its peak. Reed's indifference prickled to an undeniable point. Resting my elbow on the back of my chair, I told the pair, "Reed quit the football team."

Their reaction was instant, with wide eyes and dropped jaws all around. Because even though it was suspected, no one had confirmed it yet. Not the coach, not any player from the team, and not Babble. "We—we were wondering," Florencia gasped, leaning forward. "You weren't in last week's game. Why, Reed? You were always so good at football. You were even better than Connor."

"Flo!" Devin sounded horrified.

Now Reed looked at me, and I felt a surge of triumph. I'd take the angry-eyes too. He looked a lot like Rachel had a few moments ago, but instead of shying away like I'd done with her, I found myself smiling up at him. "You only said I couldn't post it. I didn't."

"It's obvious at this point," Rachel said, taking my side as she returned to her Physics sheet. "I don't know why it's that big of a secret."

"Even if you didn't know why, it *was*." Reed leaned down further, putting his face more at level with mine, sending my heart into cardiac arrest territory. "But then again, you have a knack for posting about people's private lives, right?"

My jaw dropped open. "I post *submissions*—and it's probably *them* submitting it!" I'd found it out more than once that a few students wanted to hang their own laundry out to get people talking. Mostly Top Tier. I didn't care one way or the other. Either way, it made for great content. "If you don't want your life on Babble, you shouldn't be in the Top Tier, then."

"I have a few secrets of my own I could share, you know."

I narrowed my eyes at the threat, even though I knew it was a bluff. He wouldn't tell Rachel about the kiss. It wouldn't be just me she'd stab with that pencil.

Mr. Pieffer's landline suddenly began to ring, and I turned to see him debate on ignoring the call, in favor of the *Galaga* game. In the end, his ship ended up exploding, and with a grumble, he swiped up the receiver.

And then he looked in our direction. "Ava, you're wanted in the principal's office. Reed, is there a reason you're standing at that desk and not working on your homework?"

"Just had a question, Mr. P," Reed returned.

Rachel frowned at me. "What did you do?"

"No clue," I said, gathering my things and getting to my feet. Reed took a step back, but I had to brush past him, my shoulder clipping the very edge of his.

I'd only been called to the office twice before—once in elementary school, once in high school. The time in elementary school had been a massive misunderstanding involving two boys and four handfuls of mud. The misunderstanding had come in on their end because they thought they could throw my winter hat in the mud without retaliation. I'd thrown two handfuls of mud at them—bullseyes both times—and they each threw a handful of mud back—which, with their abysmal aim, they both missed—and all three of us were prohibited from playing at recess for a week.

And the other time was last year when the IT guy asked me to help redesign the Brentwood Bobcats webpage.

"Who's our next one?" Principal Oliphant, a tall and sleek woman, asked one of the secretaries when I walked in. "Oh. Hi. What's your name, dear?"

"Ava Jenson."

She gave a bright smile, one that looked effortless. "Perfect! Come into my office. We'll chat there."

I'd never had the pleasure of personally meeting Principal Oliphant before. She spoke at pep rallies and things like that, but I never looked closely at her before. I knew a couple things about her. She was one of Brentwood's biggest sports fans, attending all the games to cheer on her Bobcats. Football was her preferred sport, and then cheerleading was second. I also knew that she was also the mother of Madison Oliphant, a cheerleader high up in the Top Tier.

And being a huge sports fan as well as the mother of one of the most popular girls at the high school, I also knew there were times where she turned a blind eye to questionable actions of the jocks and the Top Tier.

"Have a seat," she said kindly, gesturing between the two chairs opposite of her large desk. There was a picture frame on it, but angled so I couldn't see the photograph. I sat down on my hands, keeping them from trembling. "I'm not sure if word's gotten around yet, but I'm meeting with each individual whose name appeared on the Most Likely To list this year."

"That's a lot of people."

"Fifty labels, fifty students to speak to, yes," she agreed with a nod. "As the administrator for this school, I want to check in with you, Ava. I can see how something like that might be hurtful, and I want to extend a personal invitation for you to talk about your feelings."

Her words sounded rehearsed. I wondered how far down on her list I was, if she had time to memorize the whole spiel. "Talk about my feelings with you?"

Principal Oliphant shifted. "Well, I'd set you up to meet with our school's counseling office."

If I was being honest, I hadn't realized that Brentwood had a counseling office, but I didn't say that to her. If only I'd gotten a chance to meet with her Monday. I might never have kissed Reed. "I'm okay. It's not that big of a deal."

"What was your label, Ava?" she asked, glancing down at her paperwork. "I can't find—"

"Most Likely To: Never Have Their First Kiss."

She lifted her chin, a true curiosity lingering in her eyes. "You don't find that offensive?"

Well, I did, but I've already gone ahead and fixed that problem. "I mean, it's a little rude, sure. But I've dealt with worse."

Most of the submissions to Brentwood Babble were

way worse than the List. Like how last week, someone had submitted all the juicy details of Nathan Tulane's possible cheating.

"How are things going at home, Ava?"

Principal Oliphant was smiling, but the subject change caught me so off guard that I actually jolted in my seat. "What?"

"How are things going with your home life?" She checked the paperwork again. "Jenson, right? Is your father Howard Jenson? I went to high school with him, and with your mother. They were high school sweethearts."

I knew that story. Dad was on the football team, line-backer of the Bobcats, and Mom had been a cheerleader. The clichéd school couple, except they lasted more than a week after homecoming. They lasted twenty years. They used to have pictures of their golden days framed in the hallway, Mom decked out in her sweater cheer uniform, Dad in his cheap-looking shoulder pads.

That photo disappeared before Dad even moved out, and in hindsight, I should've realized that'd been a bad sign.

"Ava, Mrs. Winston says you've been showing up to class late."

When Mrs. Winston would've had the time to tattle, I had no idea. But I had a lightbulb moment. "I've been having a tough time transitioning back into the school year," I said slowly, thinking it through as I spoke. "My dad's...shift at work changed, and he's been gone. A lot. It's been rough."

It was sort of a lie, sort of the truth. As long as they blended together smoothly enough, it would be okay.

Principal Oliphant nodded thoughtfully. "The beginning of the school year can be quite tough to get back in the swing of things. Especially when the home routine is also tumultuous."

"I have a detention for the tardies." I looked down at my lap, pinching my leg until my eyes began to sting. Rachel was the performer, but maybe I could pull it off. "I just—do you think I could get one more chance? I promise, I won't be late again."

"Tell you what," she said, leaning her elbows onto the desk. "Since it's the beginning of the year, we can let this slide. Especially since things have been so tough as of late."

I clamped my teeth together to keep from sighing in relief.

"Well, if you ever want to speak with the counselor, please let me know." She straightened the papers on her desk, straightened her pen, and then rose to her feet. "About the Most Likely To list or about anything else. Okay, Ava?"

The way she kept repeating my name almost felt as if she was trying to hypnotize me or something. Like if she said it enough times, I'd suddenly spill everything out. She'd *definitely* rehearsed this routine. I felt sorry for anyone who came after me. "I'll keep that in mind."

Principal Oliphant beamed, as if that bogus answer was a satisfactory one in disguise.

She walked me out into the main office area, keeping

that smile in place while the secretary wrote me an excuse note. Last period had already started, which meant I'd have to sneak into class late.

"Have a great rest of your day," Principal Oliphant called as I opened the door out into the hallway. As it was shutting behind me, I heard her voice once more. "Okay, so who's next?"

Since my parents' separation, I'd gotten used to having dinner on my own.

We'd never really been the type of family to eat dinners together, anyway. Dad usually stayed late at the college grading papers while Mom normally ate dinner with her clients or coworkers. These past few weeks, though, I'd been taking my meals much earlier, mostly because I found myself wiped out around ten o'clock. For a girl who used to love pulling all-nighters, it was insane.

I stirred my fork through my pasta. I'd overcooked it this time, leaving my penne noodles all mushy and depressing. The sauce was the only thing saving it.

While forcing myself through the soft and squishy meal, I checked my inbox for any new articles. A lot of them mentioned the list somehow, but the idea of writing an article about the Most Likely Tos turned my limbs to lead. For the school to finally drop the topic, I'd have to stop writing about it.

The overall vote of the comments was that they liked

the sort of yearbook spread I did with everyone's head-shots tied to their labels. There were a few who didn't have photos that I could find, and it'd been mostly freshmen who'd unfortunately made the cut. Despite everything—being on the list, kissing Reed, and Rachel's father trying to solicit me behind her back—that was a much-needed ego boost.

I opened up my inbox, staring at the email I'd drafted with a sick feeling lingering in my throat. I blamed it on the pasta. It definitely wasn't because the subject line read **Ava Jenson — Manning Construction Website Design Proposal.**

Even though I'd had a conversation with her earlier, I wasn't stupid enough to think that Rachel would be cool with this if she knew the truth. Her encouragement would've drastically changed if she knew that the person who wanted to work with me was really her father. But still, it was such an opportunity. Experience gained, money earned for Mom's bills, and Rachel would never have to know. Right?

That seemed to be my mantra lately.

If you have to keep secrets from your best friend, my brain said, *you're doing something wrong.*

Yeah, thanks, Brain. Wasn't aware.

But I needed this. Mom needed this. If Rachel had to choose between me moving away or me working with her father, she would've picked the latter. That was what I told myself.

As soon as I clicked the send button, the sick feeling in my throat traveled down to my stomach, twisting severely. It was necessary. The more I mulled it over, the more I realized it. In order to help Mom out, to keep her from considering selling the house, this was a necessary evil. It would all work out.

It had to.

"Hopefully it's not too much work." Mom's voice carried into the house from the direction of the front door, her realtor voice in full blast. She must've been on the phone. It was early for her to be home—I wasn't expecting her arrival until closer to six or even seven. "But there are a few things needing fixed. Small things, of course, nothing too crazy."

I'd put a forkful of pasta into my mouth when a new voice—a deeper voice—responded. "I get what you mean, Mrs. Jenson."

"Ah, well, call me Kelly, Reed."

Reed.

I choked on my bite of food, the mush having no mercy as it slid down my throat. My fork clattered against the ceramic bowl as I dropped it, creating a noise almost as loud as my cough. "Ava?" Mom called. "Are you okay?"

"I'm—fine!" I gasped, fighting for some semblance of sophistication for when they walked around the corner, and hopefully not looking like I needed the Heimlich maneuver.

By the time they came into the dining room's archway, I was breathing normally, but my face burned something fierce.

"Hey, Paparazzi," Reed greeted with his normal

smirk, though it seemed a touch more well-mannered in Mom's presence. I'd seen him only a handful of hours ago, but he looked different now. He'd changed out of his jeans, wearing a pair of black sweats. His golden hair looked mussed, as if he'd taken a nap since school had gotten out. "Forget how to chew?"

I narrowed my eyes at him before sliding my gaze to Mom. "Why is he here?"

"He's going to help with some last-minute projects around the house," Mom said, venturing deeper into the dining room to lay her briefcase down on the table. She unzipped it and sifted around the contents. "I'm booked up with showings and paperwork these next few weeks, and he's much cheaper than hiring a contractor for these tiny little tasks."

"I worked summers with my dad at his construction company," Reed told me like it was new information. He leaned against the archway and folded his arms across his chest. "What are you eating?"

"Uh, pasta."

"Is it any good?"

I stared down at the overcooked noodles caked in an unhealthy amount of parmesan cheese. "Michelin star quality."

"So, Reed," Mom said, finding a piece of paper she'd stuffed in her case, and she pulled it out. "I made a list the other day, but tell me if there's anything you don't want to do, okay?" And then she cleared her throat. "There are two treads on the back porch that are rotted. I think Rick replaced them once upon a time with untreated wood, so those will need replaced. There are a few holes in the drywall in the basement that need patched over. Ava's bathroom showerhead makes this God-awful screeching noise whenever she uses it."

The corners of Reed's lips twitched, but he kept his mouth shut.

"Why are you doing this?" I asked Mom, frowning. "I haven't heard you talk about any of this."

"I'm tired of living in a dump, that's all." She gestured at me. "That being said, clean your room, you hear me? Deep clean it. It's starting to get a funky smell."

It was *not* getting a smell, but seriously—did she have to say that with an audience present?

Mom looked down at her cell phone. "Oh, shoot, I've got to take this. Ava, show him around the house, will you? Show him what needs to be fixed? I'll be back in a minute."

Reed straightened as Mom brushed past him, already pressing the phone to her ear. With her gone, Reed looked drastically out of place in the dining room, standing with his hands folded stiffly in front of him. It was like he was wearing clothes that were two sizes too small; the Jenson kitchen was two sizes too unfamiliar.

"Go ahead and finish eating," Reed said as he walked further into the room. He peered at my bowl. "Isn't it a little early for dinner?"

"Never too early for carbs." My politeness came in a belated, awkward nod of my chin. "You can sit down if you want."

It seemed to be the invitation he'd been waiting for.

He slipped into the chair across from me stiffly. The table was relatively free of clutter—a surprise, given Mom's love for leaving papers scattered everywhere. There was a happy vase of daisies in the middle of the table, hinting at a cheery household that'd been absent for a while. "So, what's with the home projects?"

"It's news to me." I stabbed a piece of pasta. "A lot of things are, lately."

"Does your dad not have time to fix these things?" He quickly lifted his palms, slouching back. "Not that I care about doing it. Just curious."

For a moment, I didn't trust myself to speak. So, instead, I shoveled more pasta into my mouth. It was cold now. Cold and mushy. *Yum.* "He moved out three weeks ago."

Saying it aloud never got easier, even though I'd been living the new reality for nearly a month.

"Three weeks?" The words shocked Reed more than I thought it would've. "Does Rachel know? She's never mentioned it."

"She knows, but we haven't really talked about it. I think it's hard for her to talk about it...after everything with your dad."

His dad, who I agreed to work with literal minutes ago. Reed's hand fisted on the table, fingers curling into a white-knuckled grip. The fist oddly juxtaposed his expression, which belied mostly confusion. Something hot stirred in his eyes, though. "Did your dad do the same thing?"

"No, he didn't cheat." It was an ugly word, and I found myself unable to look at Reed. Despite the line of awkward I was tiptoeing, the desperate urge to talk about it rose up again. Reed. He was one of the only people who would understand. "Uh, it's nothing crazy like that. They fell out of love, I guess. Fell in love with their careers, fell out of love with each other."

From what I gleaned from the rare arguments I heard Mom have over the phone, it all came down to this: Dad and her settled down right out of high school, and they were each other's firsts. First significant other, first kiss. Their *only*. And Dad, twenty years later, couldn't get past that *what if?*

I'd spent so many nights trying to pinpoint when things had changed, flipping through my memories like I was sorting through a filing cabinet. I'd finally narrowed it down to one defining moment—when Mom quit styling hair in our basement and got her realtor's license. That was when she'd started being out of the house more, staying out later, getting dinner on her own. Dad, in turn, started putting his own time into his career.

Love was a fickle thing. The risk versus reward didn't seem worth it.

"Okay, enough depressing," I said, pushing to my feet. I hadn't finished my bowl of penne, but my stomach felt too tight and unsettled to keep eating. "Come on, let's go look—"

Reed grabbed the fork from my bowl before I could pull it away and carry it to the sink, and before I could protest, he stabbed a penne noodle and popped it into his mouth.

There were only two thoughts in my mind: *he's eating my cold, mushy noodles* and *he just wrapped his mouth around the fork I'd been using.*

I watched him try to fight a grimace. "This is..."

"Fantastic? A culinary masterpiece?"

Reed swallowed hard, gently placing the fork into my bowl. "I'm thinking you don't know what Michelin stars are."

An odd feeling stirred in my chest, a buzz like electricity. The bantering was weird. I wanted to laugh—I nearly did—and I wanted to return a witty retort of my own, but either option seemed...strange.

I walked toward the sink and heard his chair screech as he stood up. "Ava. Have you been talking to someone about all this?"

"What do you mean? Like Rachel or Maisie?"

"Like a therapist."

Instinctively, my nose wrinkled. "No."

"Therapy isn't a bad thing. We went when we found out Dad was cheating."

I remembered that. Reed and Rachel's mom had signed them up for a few therapy sessions in Jefferson after the discovery, hoping they'd be able to work through their feelings. Rachel had complained about it the entire time, but then again, she had been a human-shaped bundle of anger then, a dragon ready to breathe fire over the slightest thing. Growing up, she was a total daddy's girl, and the complete betrayal had left her broken.

"I'm okay," I told Reed, scraping the noodles into the garbage disposal. "But if I need to talk to someone, I'll stop by the counselor's office."

Principal Oliphant's words from earlier resurfaced. *If you ever want to speak with the counselor, please let me know. About the list or about anything else.* I wondered if she gave out the offer to everyone or if I looked especially burdened.

When Reed spoke again, his voice was so much closer, so much softer. "You can talk to me, you know. I've got a lot of free time since quitting the team, and...I'm a good listener."

Okay, now the buzzing became stronger, like instead of electricity, it was actually a hive of bees hidden inside my ribcage. I braced my hand on the porcelain edge of the farmhouse sink, the line of my shoulders stiff. "Why would you even want to?"

Reed propped his arm on the counter beside the sink, leaning down until he could see my face. The sun shined through the window, sifting through the sheer curtains, catching him in his eyes. "You're Rachel's best friend. It's the least I could do."

His face was probably a foot and a half away from mine, far enough for the space to feel casual, but close enough for me to imagine what it might be like to kiss him again with the sunlight shining on our faces. In the light of day instead of in the gloominess of night. "Just because I'm Rachel's best friend?"

"Yeah, you're like a sister to me."

"Ew, don't say that—you kissed me!" I couldn't keep

my hands to myself this time, and I shoved at his chest. Hard. Harder than necessary. But the word rocked me to my core. *Sister.* He might as well have said "you're one of the people on the planet I'm least attracted to."

"About that," he murmured. "I think I came across harsher than I meant to yesterday."

My insides tensed, and I fought to remain casual. Calm. "I have to say, you're playing it cool a lot easier than I thought. It's almost like it truly didn't happen."

"I didn't mean to hurt your feelings."

His words didn't make sense until they did. "You thought *that* hurt my feelings? You know what, fine." I turned to face him head-on, forcing my eyes on his and not letting them wander anywhere else. It was easier to look him in the eye now than I expected, easy to force a level voice. "You're right, it was a good first kiss. I wasn't sure what to expect of my first kiss, and it was good. You're really good at kissing." *Too good.* "But, for the sake of being transparent and being on the same page, let's be clear that it didn't mean anything to me either. *I* used *you*, remember? That was all it was to me. And you didn't hurt my feelings."

The words were the only armor I had, a shield to deflect what could've been an awkward conversation with these bizarre feelings left in pieces. Better to nip it in the bud now.

For a moment, we looked at each other in silence. Monday night, he'd been close like this, but it'd been too dark for me to fully discern the finer details of him. Like how he had a tan freckle underneath his left eye, right below his waterline, or how the bridge of his nose curved ever so slightly to one side. His eyebrows were darker than his golden hair, the same color as his lashes.

"I'm thinking about asking Cindy LaVore to homecoming," he said, unflinching. "You wouldn't care?"

"Why would I?" My voice was a challenge. "When have I ever cared about your love life?"

I held my breath while waiting for his answer, my lungs aching after a stretch of silence. Twelve inches between us, *maybe*. One second of a sudden movement would be all that it'd take.

No. My thoughts were a tangle, but my moral compass wasn't. It was strong enough to remind me that this wasn't a good thing, and *I* was strong enough to listen. Barely.

Ultimately, it wasn't even me who pulled away first. Reed straightened from his leaning position. Without warning, he took my pasta bowl from me and flipped on the faucet, pumping a dollop of soap into the ceramic. He washed the bowl without a word, head tilted down as he worked, hair slipping a little into his eyes. I stared at him with my throat tight, curling my toes.

Once clean, he picked up the dish towel draped across the oven handle and dried the bowl off. "You're pretty good at playing it cool, too, you know."

If only I was as good at pretending as him. If only the kiss meant as little to me as it did to him. I took the bowl from him and carried it to the appropriate cabinet, and without looking at him directly—because I had a feeling the look in my eyes would give something away—I gestured down the hallway. "Come on, let's go look at the things on Mom's list. I'll show you the basement first."

"This is Josh. He's five-foot-nine, has brown hair, likes to listen to rap music and country —which are two opposite ends of the spectrum, so I'm impressed—and he has two dogs. *Two.* You've always loved dogs."

"Josh sounds lovely," I responded, not turning around from my locker, not looking at whatever photo was no doubt on her phone screen. I knew exactly where her thought process was, too, and didn't miss a beat. Instead, I loaded up my English and Science books. "Does Josh have thin lips?"

"I don't think so. Look for yourself."

The way Rachel rattled off characteristics of this *Josh* had me assuming she was reading from her phone. At least, I assumed that until I looked over and found a five-foot-nine boy standing beside her.

In her rapid-fire list, Rachel had left out one thing: Josh was the owner of the world's deepest dimples. They indented into his cheek even when he wasn't smiling. Like right now, even though his lips weren't curved, the dimples were visible. He looked well-mannered. Friendly.

Maybe a wee bit uncomfortable.

"Uh, hi, Josh," I said slowly, turning my wide-eyed gaze to Rachel.

"We have last period together. We got to chatting, I asked him if he was single, he said yes, and here we are." Rachel leaned around to inspect his face. "His lips are average-sized, I'd say, wouldn't you?"

I smacked Rachel, but the poor guy quirked his average-sized mouth into a small smile. "Thanks. I pride myself in my ordinary lips."

Whoa. His voice was *beautiful.* It was low but velvety smooth, like he was trying to record a podcast or something. Maybe he was a podcast host. If he wasn't, he should be.

"My introductions have already been had, but I'm Josh."

He extended a hand to me like we weren't in the high school hallway, the gesture reeking of a middle-age business meeting. Still, I slid my hand into his. "My name's Ava."

"I know," he said, and then sucked in a breath. "That sounded creepy as soon as I said it. I mean, I know because you run Brentwood Babble. Which someone told me the other day, so it's not like I knew of you long. And..." He drew in a breath through his teeth. "I'm rambling. Sorry."

"I'm a rambler too," I told him, shutting my locker. "But it's nice to meet a fan."

"I *am* a fan. It's like I'm talking to Gossip Girl in the flesh."

I raised my eyebrows. "You've seen *Gossip Girl?*"

"I'll shamelessly use the excuse that my *sister* watched, and I happened to be in the room for every episode."

We laughed together, and Josh's laugh was as deep as his voice, catching the attention of some of the students around us. It was then that I noticed Reed further down the hallway, in the M section. Since I was in the J's, we weren't far apart. He leaned against his locker with his eyes on his cell, scrolling. He was propped in the same way he'd been Monday in the kitchen, with his feet crossed in front of him. He lifted his attention from his phone and met my gaze.

Inwardly cursing, I forced myself to look at Josh, hating that I'd gotten caught with my staring problem.

Rachel stood with her arms folded across her chest, looking satisfied. And then, at normal volume, she nonchalantly dropped a bomb. "I thought Josh could be a good pick for your first kiss."

I sucked in a gasp and whirled on my friend, horrified and furious all at once. "Rachel!"

"What?" she asked, playing all innocent. "He's totally kissing material."

It was physically painful to look at Josh with my embarrassment no doubt on my face, but I shot him an apologetic look. "Please excuse my best friend for corralling you for her sinister and very embarrassing purposes. She was dropped as a child."

Josh pointed a finger at his chest. "It's okay. I'm Most Likely To: Be Forgotten After High School, so I totally get the idea of wanting to use the list like a bucket list."

I winced at his label, the harshness of it all. I remembered the label, but I didn't remember his picture in the yearbook. "Are you a senior?" For some reason, with the softness in his cheeks, he struck me more as *sophomore* material. The way his hair was styled, with the front pieces fanned through with gel, also made him look younger.

"I have a baby face," Josh said, reading my mind with an understanding nod of his head. "I get it all the time."

As nice as Josh seemed, I couldn't help but feel a bit wary of him. How had Rachel approached him, anyway? "*Hey, my bestie hasn't had her first kiss yet, and she needs someone to mack on*"? And what had been Josh's response? "*Hey, okay*"? I didn't know a guy at Brentwood High who *would* turn down such an offer.

That was basically how the conversation with Reed went, only with a little more coaxing.

But if Josh's only hopes were of being my first kiss, he was going to be disappointed.

I turned toward Rachel, giving her a glare. Josh was close enough to hear, but I hissed, "You can't go up to people and ask them to kiss your best friend."

"Why not?" she whispered. "You said you wanted to get it over with."

"That's not why I'm here," Josh hurried to interject, raising his palms like one of us pointed a gun at him. "I mean, I'm not here thinking I'll get a kiss out of it, I just—"

"Well, that's a relief." Reed stepped up beside Josh, cell still in his grip, the other hand tucked into the pocket of his jeans. "You should at least buy us dinner first."

I stiffened at his approach, even though he barely even spared me a cursory glance. He focused on Josh way longer than he lingered on me, and then he dropped back to his phone.

"Butt out, Reed," Rachel snapped, turning to Josh. "Ignore my brother. I do."

I expected Reed to walk away at that, to take his languid posture and go out to his car. He didn't. He didn't even look up from his cell.

Though Josh kept up his smile, it was clear that he was uncomfortable. From his posture alone, it was easy to tell. "It was really nice meeting you," I told him, squeezing my backpack strap. "Maybe I'll see you around?"

Rachel chimed in. "You should give him your number, Ava."

I could strangle her. My hands weren't very big, so maybe I'd use my backpack strap. Whatever it was, my best friend seriously needed to be strangled. It wasn't that I *minded* giving Josh my number, but I definitely didn't need prompting, especially not with an audience.

It seemed like Josh was the one to notice my discomfort now, because he said, "I'm sure we'll see each other around."

I risked a glance at Reed, but he was looking at his

phone. Totally disinterested. Like he wasn't listening. I didn't know why that propelled me forward, why that spurred me on, but it did. "Do you have your phone, Josh? I can give it to you now."

"Oh, yeah, yeah." Josh tapped his front pockets before finding his cell in his back one, quickly unlocking it. "Go ahead."

Rachel peeked over Josh's arm as he was ready to key in the numbers, but it was her twin I looked at. He'd stopped scrolling, as if his focus had sort of stalled on the dimly lit screen. Like he was listening now. I recited my cell number quickly, feeling a surge of triumph for no reason at all.

Josh's dimples pressed in deeper. I had to admit—he *was* really cute. I wasn't normally a dimple girl, but wow. "Cool. Well, I'll text you and maybe the three of us can hang out or something."

Three of us. Noticeably not the two of us. Noticeably not the four of us.

"See you tomorrow, then, Josh," Rachel said to him happily, and then latched onto my arm to tug me away. Judging by her wide, nonchalant expression, she obviously hadn't picked up on the weirdness of the whole situation. That was made especially clear when she leaned closer as we walked out of earshot, asking, "I told you I'd find someone kissable. He's cute, right?"

My mouth felt dry. *Kissable. Cute.* Reed walked behind us, slowly enough that he wouldn't walk *with* us, but close enough that he could hear. Probably. If he cared to even listen. Which he probably didn't.

But still. "I can't believe you. You really had to do that in the high school hallway? With your *brother listening?*"

"Please, if we have to hear about every girl he's kissing through Babble, he can listen to us talk about it, too. This is revenge for that detailed novel Grace Hockessin sent in last year."

For the first time, I couldn't blame anyone for wanting to gush about their kiss with Reed. If I had someone to gush to, I'm sure I would've written a novel, too.

I fought the urge to look behind me. "I guess, yeah, Josh seemed nice. Perfectly..."

"Kissable?"

"Yeah. Perfectly kissable."

We made our way outside, and Rachel walked me to where I'd locked my bike up that morning. The leather seat was blistering hot when I pressed my palm to it.

"I was thinking, before going to Allen's Alley, we could meet up and stop by a few of the shops on the main strip," Rachel said, watching as I flipped my backpack around to search through the pocket. "I'm in a shopping mood."

"When are you not?" Reed asked. I hadn't realized he'd followed us over. "You haven't unpacked from your last mall trip."

Rachel held a hand up to silence him. "I'll text Maisie to see if she wants to come."

"We can see, but I don't know when she gets out of tutoring," I reminded Rachel.

My bike lock key had gotten buried beneath my books in my bag, and when I tugged it out, the lanyard strap snagged on something at the bottom of my backpack. I fumbled with it, and the strap ended up slipping from my grip. My keys clattered onto the ground on the opposite side of my bike, just out of reach.

Without having a second to react, Reed bent down and swiped them up. He jingled the keychains before offering them to me on one long finger. We locked eyes.

Absolutely nothing about the action was sentimental. Not a single thing, but something about it shocked me enough that it took me a second to take them from him.

"I'll pick you up around five, okay?" Rachel said, causing the world to veer back into focus, the white noise of the outside resuming.

"Who said you're taking the car?" Reed demanded, but Rachel was already walking away. For a beat, Reed lingered, almost like he would say something more. He never would've lingered before. He probably never would've picked up my keys before, either—he probably would've joked about me being klutzy, or even kicked them further out of reach.

Then again, it was probably me reading way too much into everything. I was doing exactly what I never wanted to do.

I threw my leg over my bike and used my tiptoes to keep me off the hot seat, readjusting my backpack. "See you later," I told Reed.

"Bike safe," he responded, and we parted ways like that. On an awkward, stilted sort of goodbye where we couldn't quite look the other in the eye. Among the consequences I should've thought of before kissing Reed, I never realized not being able to talk normally with him would've made the list.

Jefferson, though it was rival territory, was home to the best antique shop in the surrounding area, Timeless Treasures. It was a place Rachel, Maisie, and I frequented as often as we could. The store's aisleways were narrow, lined with displays of costume jewelry, vintage silverware, rustic signs, and many more knickknacks. I loved combing through everything. The whole store smelled like wood, lacquer, and paint, and it was a comforting mix of scents I'd grown to love. The shop owner, Mrs. Hewitt, went to a convention every Saturday to find new objects to stock, and each time, she was on the hunt for something specific for a special customer.

"Sorry, Rachel," Mrs. Hewitt said as soon as we walked in, the bell on the door ringing a dull note. She looked up from her spot at the register, giving us a warm, wrinkled smile. "No new dolls for you. There was one, but it was a modern-day American Girl Doll."

My best friend sighed, settling in her disappointment while Maisie and I started browsing the store. We'd pushed back our usual bowling time so that she could finish tutoring and come with us. Alex had picked her up from her house and brought her here, and as a hater of all things antiques, he stayed out in the car.

"This is new," Maisie said to me, picking up a cigar box from one of the shelves. The red wood it was made out of was scratched beyond belief, the logo illegible, but it had a pretty gold latch. "I could keep my protractors in this."

I squeezed her arm affectionately. "I love that you have enough protractors to fit into a container."

"I'm like the Girl Scout of math lovers—always prepared," she said with a wink, moving on.

The floorboards creaked as we meandered through the shop, alerting Mrs. Hewitt to the exact square foot we were standing on. "That's such a bummer," Rachel was telling her, and I glanced up at her through the stacks of books and other odds and ends. "Do you think next week's swap meet will be better?"

"Next week's is more jewelry based, I'm afraid, but I'll keep my eyes peeled. I'll make sure my granddaughter, Rosie, is paying attention, too."

After years of coming to the store, we knew that Rosie was Mrs. Hewitt's granddaughter, and a junior. I thought she went to Jefferson, but I couldn't remember. She sometimes helped man the place if Mrs. Hewitt was busy, and though she was quiet, she was always nice.

One of the tables in the center of the shop housed the more expensive things, things that Mrs. Hewitt could easily see from her spot at the register. I looked at a quill pen and inkwell in the center, and I found my feet dragging as I moved past it. The thought was intrusive, and though I was torn on the *why* behind my actions, I pulled out my cell and snapped a photo.

> Me: **Look at this. Made me think of you.**

Not even ten seconds later, my phone dinged.

> Dad: **Neat!**

It was more than what I thought I'd get, but less than what I'd wanted. He hadn't texted me since Monday when he canceled our weekend plans, and this one-word response did nothing to ease the ache inside me. On the other hand, I kicked myself for wanting his attention. He was the one who sent our household into a tailspin—he should've been the one texting me "thinking of you," right?

"I should probably pick something up for Alex, shouldn't I?" Maisie asked as we trailed deeper into the store. "I feel bad that he's waiting for me out in the car."

"He could've come in," I pointed out.

"This really isn't his thing." Maisie trailed her fingertips along a hand-carved dresser with white paint that had begun to chip. The vintage appearance of it was to die for.

I followed Maisie to the library section of the store where Mrs. Hewitt kept all of her books stocked and away from the sunlight to reduce fading. Something on the floor caught my attention. A wavy, worn-down cardboard box was pressed underneath a shelf, looking like it'd once been water-logged and dried in the sun. The words scrawled across the front were faint, but readable. *Comic Books. 50¢ each.*

Maybe I wanted to try a new hobby. Comic books always seemed cool. It'd been Reed's response when I'd asked him why he quit football. A flippant answer, of course, but my mind snagged on it now. Maybe it *had* been an offhand remark, the first thing that came out of his mouth, but what if it was something that would interest him?

Yesterday, Mom finished her phone call after I led him outside to see the rotten porch steps, and with her presence, we dropped the kissing subject. Obviously. Mom did not need to be privy to that information. But still, Reed and I hadn't really left things on great terms. Not bad terms, but also not get-him-a-gift terms.

Never in my life had I purchased something for Reed, except on his birthday when I always got him a gift card to Dick's Sporting Goods, and yet, here I was, thinking of him when I wasn't supposed to. When it wasn't allowed.

Bending down, I slid the box into the light and thumbed through the slick comics. Most of them were well-loved, with their stapled covers sliding off or torn at the corners, but to me, that made them even more special. Most were titles I didn't recognize, a few about super-heroes, a few actual manga graphic novels. I picked up the ones with the most interesting covers.

"Since when are you into comic books?" Maisie asked

as she bent down beside me, clutching a dark brown book close to her chest. No doubt a classic Mrs. Hewitt had found. "Not that I'm judging or anything. They look pretty cool."

"Right?" I found another one that was mostly in good condition, trailing my fingers through some accumulated dust. "I was just looking. The superhero ones look pretty cool."

"Oh, yeah?" Maisie studied them closer. "Maybe I should get Alex one. I'm more of a superhero movie watcher, but you'll have to let me know if they're good."

Biting down on my lower lip, I got to my feet, holding the comic books to my chest the same way Maisie clenched her newest find. Like it was the most important thing in the world. "I'll let you know."

"You're up, Maisie," Rachel said as she sauntered back from the bowling lane, smirking. She'd gotten a split, but it brought her nowhere near my epic, strike-filled roster. I prided myself in my extraordinary bowling skills, mostly because that was one of the cooler things about me.

Maisie got to her feet with a nod and turned to Alex, who stared down into his pop like he saw a bug swimming around with the ice. "Wish me luck?" she asked him.

"Good luck," he returned, the words seeming pulled out of him.

I stared at him and at his lack of interest, as if my looks could turn him to stone. *I don't like you*, I thought at him. *I really don't like you.*

He did a double-take at me. "Why are you staring at me like that?"

"Like what?" I asked innocently, but didn't lessen the death glare.

Alex didn't answer, but took his straw between his

teeth again and turned to watch Maisie bowl. *Yeah, be intimidated,* I wanted to tell him. *I might be small, but I can rip you to shreds.*

Rachel put her hand on my knee and squeezed, and I thought that was her way of trying to call off the attack dog in me until I looked at her. She stared off toward the doorway, and when my gaze followed, I stiffened, too.

Brentwood High's Top Tier just walked into Allen's Alley.

Though the Top Tier was a pretty big group, comprised of mostly jocks, there were those who were higher up in the pyramid. Connor Bray led the pack, because though he wasn't the quarterback, he *was* the most popular guy in school. Easily the cutest. His girlfriend and co-captain of the cheer squad, Jade Dyer, stood behind him with her second in command, Madison Oliphant. Landon Settler, quarterback and Most Likely To: Never Get A Girlfriend, stood chatting with none other than Reed Manning.

I stiffened at the sight of Reed, but maybe my reaction had more to do with the girl by his side. The girl with her hand wrapped around his.

My first thought was that she was so pretty that it wasn't fair. Her deep skin was flawless, and she had a chunk of her curly brown locks wrapped up into a bun, the rest flowing over her shoulders. She wasn't Top Tier, but she definitely looked like she belonged in it.

And ugh, her boobs were even nice. I had the chest of a sixth grader.

"What are they doing here?" Alex asked, the disbelief

palpable in his voice. "I can't imagine Jade bowling, can you?"

It was an understatement, even judging by Jade's mini-skirt and perfectly coiffed blonde hair. Her wearing bowling shoes? Definitely not. Then again, I couldn't picture Madison bowling either. They seemed too haughty for something as fun as this.

Rachel leaned her head into her palm. "Absolutely not. But Connor? Yeah, I can imagine him bowling. God, he's probably so good at it."

Though my mind reeled all over the place, it had snapped to enough awareness for me to grab my phone. I clicked on the camera app, zooming in past the bald man in an orange polo getting them their shoes. "Probably not the only thing you're imagining. What's a good headline?"

Once I got the picture, though, I didn't load it imme-diately into Babble. Instead, I found myself analyzing the shot. Connor was smiling at something Landon must've said, but it was Reed, who looked directly at the camera—at me—that had me swallowing hard.

"Rach," I whispered, leaning closer. "Who is that girl with your brother?"

"I think her name's Cindy. Reed's latest fixation."

Cindy. As soon as she said it, I could've smacked myself over the head with how obvious it was. *I'm thinking about asking Cindy LaVore to homecoming. You wouldn't care?*

I didn't care. So didn't care.

"Hey, Bobcats," Connor greeted when he got to the

table beside ours, his features a mask of pleasant surprise. I forced my gaze on my phone. An article would keep me occupied. Would keep my attention on something *other* than the couple who sat down to put on their shoes.

ALERT THE MEDIA—It Must Be Date Night!

Brentwood's Top Tier was spotted having a date night at Allen's Alley tonight! Our favorites, Connor and Jade, were accompanied by Reed Manning and his new beauty, Cindy LaVore. Can I just say they're sooooo cute?! What better way to spend date night than bowling at Allen's?

Madison and Landon tagged along, too, suspiciously empty-handed. But I did get some interesting tips earlier—something about a potential babe for a certain Mr. Settler? More deets to come!

I attached the picture to the blog post and sent it off into the Babble atmosphere, not bothering to read it over.

"It's Ava, right?"

I looked up at my name, finding Landon standing

above the empty metal chair beside me. The six-foot-something guy loomed like a building next to me, looking—uncomfortable. "Hey, that's me."

"Can I sit here?"

"Oh my gosh, yeah, yeah, sure." I hurried to nudge aside our drinks on the table, clearing a space for him.

Landon was a bulky guy, tall with tons of muscle. He dwarfed the chair and smoothed his hands down his knees, as if trying to smooth out his nerves. Though he wasn't as popular as Connor, he still was cute with his side-parted reddish-brown hair that curled at the ends. The timidness about him was also kind of adorable. Someone in the Top Tier, *shy*. Go figure.

"Um, I heard someone submitted a tip about me to your website." He studied the lanes, watching as Reed set up the names. "About me and my...girlfriend."

My insides perked up at the word, latching on like a dog with a bone. "So, it's true?"

"Yeah. It's true. And recent."

"Do you want me not to post about it?" I asked, trying to read between his lines, deflating a bit. It wasn't often that people asked me not to post about things submitted about them, but I always respected the request. Even if it sucked sometimes. If Landon asked me not to post, I wouldn't, even though I'd be dying to share.

But he quickly sat up a bit straighter. "No, no. You can. I figured you might have questions. About us. And I could answer them. For your blog, I mean."

Wait, he was offering me an interview with him about his new relationship? I glanced around, but Rachel was too busy staring off after Connor to notice. Alex was finishing up his second attempt to knock down all the pins, failing miserably. Reed and Cindy were setting up the names on the scoreboard, but before I had a chance to look away, he caught my eye.

Crap. I tried to play it off like my gaze had just been roaming, but I'd been caught. Again. As nonchalantly as I could, I poised my phone so I could type out some notes. "So, what's her name, Landon? The submission didn't say."

"Lacey," he answered. "Lacey Churchill."

Churchill. The last name was familiar, but distantly. "How'd your paths cross? Was it by chance?" I went into full-on interviewer mode, mentally searching for questions I knew readers would be most curious about.

Landon's lips twitched a little, as if he thought about smiling. Or grimacing. "You could say that. We, ah, hit it off, I guess. She's a great girl."

"Why isn't she here tonight?"

"She doesn't like bowling." His expression deepened as soon as he spoke, which made me realize that it *had* been a grimace. "Well, she actually doesn't like this alley, she said."

I nodded as I typed out his responses into my Notes app, and when I glanced up at our lane, I found my name blinking on the TV screen. Dang—not nearly enough time. "Thanks for giving me the info," I told Landon as I pocketed my cell phone, even though we'd barely scratched the surface of the plethora of questions I wanted to ask. Like, who asked out who? Had they gone on their first date yet? Were they going to homecoming together? But I held back, because even though Landon had offered, judging by his posture, it was obviously too new for him to talk freely about. "Can I ask one more question?"

Landon nodded.

I laid my arms on the tabletop and leaned in, getting as close as possible to lower my voice. "Do you know why Reed quit the team?"

"Reed?" Landon's gaze moved to the ball return, hesitating. "He didn't really say, honestly."

"He hasn't told his best friend?"

"If you know Reed, you'll know he's not really a 'talk about your feelings' kind of guy."

Of course, he was right.

"Ava, it's your turn," Alex said as he sat down beside me, picking up his drink with the expression of a pouty toddler.

My bowling shoes slipped a little on the carpet before I stepped to the clanking ball return, trying to ignore everyone around me. I reached for the orange ball, but at the same time, a tanned hand stretched out as if to grab it first. Our fingers collided, and we both froze at the contact.

I looked up and locked onto Reed's gaze, which was inches from mine, directly on me. He pulled his hand away, but the tingling sensation remained. "Go ahead," he said while tipping his chin at the ball, selecting a different one.

"I didn't think you liked bowling," I said as I walked

to the mouth of my lane, staring down at the array of pins at the end.

Reed walked up to his lane beside mine. "Why wouldn't I?"

"You've never tagged along with us before."

"Maybe that says more about your merry band of friends than bowling." His eyes glistened with amusement. "Bumpers?"

I hugged my orange ball closer to my chest, refusing to feel embarrassed. "It's for Rachel. My ball doesn't even touch the sides."

That made Reed smile, wiping away the embarrassment trickling through my veins. A thrill replaced it, like I'd stuck my finger in an electrical outlet.

I swung my arm back and let my ball fly, and it clattered into the pins. My strike streak was ruined—my ball only knocked a path through the center of the pins, making it impossible for even a split.

I blamed it on the boy at my side, whose mere presence proved to be a distraction. I watched Reed get into position, lining up his ball, posture perfect.

"Guess your reign as Bowling Queen has ended, huh?" Rachel teased as she walked past me, and normal Ava would've scoffed, maybe rolled her eyes. She would've responded with something witty. Now I was wound too tight to banter properly with her.

I jumped as Cindy began clapping for Reed as he made his way to their table. "Aw, you were one away from a split. Good try, babe."

Babe? They were already at the babe phase?

Chill out, Ava. One stupid kiss didn't give me any sort of territorial claim over him. I didn't *want* any claim over him. But these feelings and thoughts—they swirled around me like fog on a dark night, impossible to see through.

Maisie tapped her fingers against her soda, condensation rolling down the side of the glass. "He's giving you a run for your money, Ava."

The screen blinked happily as Alex sauntered back from the lane. "Yeah, yeah," I muttered. "One strike doesn't match my level of awesomeness."

"It comes close," he retorted, but I wasn't listening anymore. Right before my eyes drifted down to my phone, I caught Cindy walking from her lane, eyes alight as she cleared all the pins. Reed slapped her hand in a high-five, but she surged forward and pressed her mouth to his cheek in a chaste victory kiss.

And hello, my insides *did not* like that.

"I'll be right back," I announced to no one in particular, or at least I thought I said it—either way, my legs jerked me up from the chair and carried me straight to the entrance of the building.

From the outside, Allen's Alley wasn't exactly the cleanest establishment. The trash cans were overflowing, and the front patio smelled distinctly like fish, even though it wasn't on their menu. Since it was an alley *and* a bar, its clientele catered more toward adults who liked a drink or four rather than a family-friendly atmosphere. As soon as I stepped through the front doors, I was greeted with a cloud of smoke from the people huddled around the outdoor ash tray. I moved past them and their quiet chatter toward the corner of the brick building.

The sun was almost entirely set, with only a sliver dancing above the horizon. The colors lit up the sky, creating an orange-y glow. Even with the sun nearly tucked out of sight, it was hot, warm enough that even in my short sleeves, I quickly missed the AC of the alley.

Okay, Ava, it's time to get a grip. I pressed my palms into my cheeks, forcing my lips to pucker. Seeing Reed with a girl wasn't anything new, but these sticky feelings were. I was in quicksand, struggling to get free only to sink further.

If I had known kissing Reed would send my thoughts and feelings into a tailspin, I never would've done it. Or I would've stopped after the four-second mark, where it was still a casual peck. Because yes, that part of the kiss was *nice*, but I would've stopped thinking about it after a day. I would've thought "hmm, wow, what a normal first kiss." I would've thought "yeah, I guess that's kind of what I expected it to be."

But the innocent kiss it'd started out as had transformed into something that contained more pressure, more hands, more tongue—hello, merry-go-round memory.

Kissable Josh. If I kissed him like I'd kissed Reed, would it elicit the same feelings? Probably. I mean, before Monday night, I'd never, *ever* thought of Reed that way. I could appreciate his football player body, sure, but it never stirred butterflies before. So, if I kissed Josh...would it be the same?

I didn't really know Josh—aside from the fact that he was five-nine and had two dogs—but he was already a better choice. He had Rachel's stamp of approval. He wasn't going to homecoming with someone else. He wasn't a player. Best of all, he wasn't Rachel's twin. Major points there.

And besides, I didn't *want* to be feeling this. I'd just wanted my first kiss, not the strings attached.

"Is the reception better out here?"

Reed had silently approached during my lip-lock-related spiral, and I didn't notice him until he stood a few feet away. Though he had his hands in his jeans' pockets, attempting a look of cool-boy nonchalance, his expression was uncertain, like he might turn around and hightail it inside any second.

I was so wrapped up in my thoughts that I didn't get it. "Reception?"

"For your phone." Reed gave a half-hearted chuckle. "It was a joke, Paparazzi."

"Oh—I needed air." It was a crappy lie. There was certainly less oxygen out here than there was inside—the sweltering heat had absorbed it all. Apparently, though, my brain cells went along with it. "I'll be inside in a sec."

Reed cast a glance over at the group that smoked by the door. "I'll stand with you."

"What, you think they're going to bother me?" They hardly even batted an eye when I walked out, probably because my height—a squat five-two—and Brentwood High mathletes tee—curtesy of Maisie Matthews circa two years ago—stuck me obviously in the *underage* category. I lifted my fists. "I think I'll be okay with these bad boys."

Reed put his warm hands over mine and lowered them. "I don't think your toddler-sized knuckles are something to brag about."

Narrowing my eyes, I punched him in the shoulder, hard enough for him to sway back on his heels.

Despite the slug, he smirked. "Was I supposed to feel that?"

I went to hit him again, to pack all my power into it, but he caught my fist. And held it. His palm was warmer than my knuckles, and the heat felt like it traveled all the way up my arm to pump into my heart. His fingers were calloused from the near decade of playing football, and his thumb trailed along my skin. Despite the summer sun, goosebumps rose on the back of my neck. "Has Kissable Josh texted yet?"

I ripped my hand away from his, scowling. "Don't call him that."

"Why not? I thought he was *perfectly kissable*."

The two words were more than mimicking mine from after school—they were infused with enough scorn that it made my ears pink. So, he *had* been listening. "It's none of your business, either way."

"It's ironic that *you're* saying that." The way he looked at me made me want to squirm. "Hey, I'm all for your interest in him. He seems more your speed."

Now I really wanted to hit him again. I curled my fingers, still able to feel the tingle of his skin against mine. "Did you ask Cindy to homecoming yet?"

"Why? Waiting to post a Babble article?" I braced myself as Reed took a step closer, close enough that his silhouette mixed with mine on the sidewalk. His eyes softened. "I shouldn't have said what I did about you posting about people's private lives. You don't post hateful things."

"What, did you read my blog or something?"

"Yes."

Back up the truck, he went through my blog? I tried to imagine Reed opening up Brentwood Babble, reading through *my* articles. It was stupid—the idea of hundreds of Brentwood students reading my writing wasn't embarrassing, but Reed? It felt...different.

"You're a good writer, you know. You do a good job at making your blog posts feel exciting. And the fact that everyone follows your blog proves it."

"Oh, I know," I said, lifting my chin, fighting to *not* let his compliment get to me. *Heel, butterflies, heel.* "See, I told you it wasn't as bad as you made it out to be. You should've listened to me."

"Last time I listened to you, I ended up kissing you."

Well, that nonchalant mention did nothing to improve my lack of oxygen. I wanted to look away. I should've looked away. Focusing on his brown-eyed gaze and his hair that shifted in the wind was so not helping. My body had its own ideas, and the memories he conjured just by looking at my mouth had me freezing. "Whatever."

"I know we're not talking about it," he went on, letting the *it* linger in the air for a moment. A strange quality creeped into his words then, a curiousness that almost sounded plaintive. "But we can be friends, right?"

Friends. It was a neat, orderly category. Like the box at Timeless Treasures, *Friends* was scrawled clearly across the front. It fit me in with Landon, Connor. It didn't fit me in with Cindy and the other girls he'd kissed in the past. To throw off the scent of my utter shock, I forced myself to scoff. "I'm Rachel's friend."

"Why can't you be my friend too?"

Why not? Because in all the years that I'd known him, he was always Rachel's twin. Never my friend. Never the person I'd confide in, never the person I knew more than a handful of facts about. He was always *there*, the way Rachel's father was *there*, but I'd never stopped to get to know him.

"The better question is, why do you want to be *my* friend?" I replied, blinking expectantly. "I've always been the annoying girl that hangs out with your sister. Why change your mind now?"

"You don't talk to Rachel about what's going on at home," he said simply. "You should have someone to talk to. I can be that person."

Once again, his words knocked me off balance. What would being friends with him entail? Sharing secrets? Saying hi in the school hallways? Getting each other gifts once in a while? I thought about the comic books that were currently in my purse. If we were friends, could I give them to him?

I opened my mouth to respond, but I realized

someone was walking up behind him. It took me a belated second to place the face.

"There you are." Cindy came up behind Reed with her full lips twisted into a little frown. "I didn't realize you came outside."

Reed took a step away from me once he saw her, putting six feet between us. Enough space that it could've looked like we were two strangers standing together. "Just needed some air."

Cindy's attention wandered past him to me, and she did one of those up-and-down scanning looks, but it was accompanied by a friendly smile. "You're one of Rachel's friends, right?" she asked. "Reed said you were both on the list. So, which one are you? Marrying the math book or never having their first kiss?"

A part of me wanted her to guess, but my ego probably wouldn't have been able to take it. "Never have their first kiss."

"Ava," Reed added. "Her name's Ava. Rachel's other friend is Maisie."

"You're the one who runs Brentwood Babble, right?" She placed her hand on Reed's back and leaned into his side. I hadn't noticed how tall she was before. Even in her bowling shoes, she was only an inch or two shorter than him. "I think that's so cool, you know. You must feel so powerful to have all the dirt on everyone."

It was true that I had tons of info on people in Brentwood, not even just Top Tier. Even if things never got posted, I read every submission, even all the scandalous ones. "I wouldn't say *powerful*."

"For running the school's gossip column, I wouldn't have thought you'd be on the Most Likely Tos. So, you haven't had your first kiss yet? Kind of rude someone thinks you won't ever have one."

This conversation was rapidly inching up on *awkward*, especially with Reed pointedly not looking at either of us. "Yeah, kind of rude, but most of the labels are," I replied, trying to keep my voice lighthearted.

"Have you thought about just kissing someone random to get it over with?"

Funny story, Cindy… "Uh, no. Not really."

"We should go inside," Reed said, grabbing Cindy's hand and giving it a tug. "It has to be our turns by now."

"You guys go," I said, fishing out my cell phone and holding it up. "I need to call my mom really quick."

Another lie, one that had to be painfully obvious too. But the reason I'd fled the alley in the first place had only followed me outside, and I needed to reorganize my thoughts before facing Rachel and Maisie again. I was sure that if I walked in now, my feelings would have to be written all over my face. Unease and uncertainty in equal measure, leaving my heart pattering unevenly as they turned away.

Reed turned once before they disappeared inside, and in the second that our gazes locked, I had one single thought: *what's high school without a little drama?*

Initially, I'd been fully present in the conversation with my best friends Friday afternoon. Maisie was sitting on my bed and hugging a pillow to her chest, and Rachel was rummaging through my closet in search of...something. I couldn't remember. As soon as I glanced out the window, I was lucky to remember my own name.

I'd lived across the street from the Mannings for all of my seventeen years. Seventeen summers where their lawn needed mowing, and not once—*not once*—had I really paid attention to who mowed it.

But now, what was supposed to be a quick peek out the window, turned into me totally ensnared by Reed Manning's naked chest, by the way the sun glistened off his skin, by the way his forearms flexed as he pushed the mower in horizontal lines across his yard.

White earphones hung from each ear, the wires drawn to his pocket where his phone presumably was. He pulled the mower toward him, pitching it on two wheels to angle it around and start back across the yard, the movement so fluid that I couldn't look away. And I so wasn't looking at the machine.

Reed *did* look hot. *Warm.* Maybe he needed someone to bring him out a glass of water.

"What are you looking at, Ava?"

I jumped at Rachel's question, dropping the curtain. My expression had to scream of guilt, but her attention had already been drawn to the mirror and Maisie's was on the pillow she clutched in her lap. Thank *God.* "Guy outside running," I said, voice shrill to my own ears. "Shirtless. He was...ugly."

Maybe *I* needed a glass of water.

Maisie beckoned me over to her, patting the bed. "Here, let me draw your pawprint."

Right, my pawprint. I'd finished drawing a Brentwood Bobcat's essential on Rachel's cheek a few moments ago, preparing for the football game tonight. It was an away game, which meant we had to deck out in as much pep as possible when we invaded enemy territory. The school sections were always a bit less crowded, but those who did show up were required to ooze school spirit. Pawprints were something Rachel and I did for every game—go Bobcats!

"Should you practice first?" I asked Maisie as I sat down on my bed, watching her squint behind her black glasses. "Not that I don't think you'll do a great job. It's just that, out of your family, you're not the most...artistic." The opposite, in fact.

"You were the one who drew a pawprint with only

three toes," she replied, catching the face paint marker when Rachel tossed it at her. "I've got this."

"I wasn't done yet," I grumbled.

Maisie propped her hand on the side of my head to hold me steady. I watched the concentration settle over her face, the look she normally got when she was trying to decipher her impossible math problems. They weren't impossible for her—she was a whiz at that kind of stuff.

It was nice to know the Most Likely To list didn't get to her. *Marry a math book.* Even when mentioning it tonight, she'd brushed it off easily. Then again, *was* that an insult for her?

"How has everything been lately?" Maisie asked as she worked. "Is everything...okay?"

I smiled a little at her tiptoeing. "Are you talking about my dad leaving?"

Maisie readjusted her hold on the pen. Before she began tracing the print, she looked me in the eye. "You haven't really said anything about it recently."

"I mean, there's not too much to say," I said, once more trying to keep my voice cheerful. The last thing I wanted to do was to weigh the conversation down, weigh the mood down. "It sucks, but it is what it is. I'm hoping to visit him soon."

Rachel turned around from the vanity to look at us. "We should do something after school next week. Maybe get lunch. We haven't done that in forever."

"I'll be tutoring until five," Maisie said with a little shake of her head. "But I could do something after."

"Wait, *all* of your tutoring sessions last until five?" I

scrunched my nose. She tapped my cheek so I'd stop frowning, giving her a smooth canvas. "Why so late? Mrs. Diego should really start paying you minimum wage."

"One of the students is on the football team. He has to wait until after practice ends, which is usually around fourish. And before you ask, no," she rushed to add. "I can't tell you who it is."

Ah, right. Tutor-tutee confidentiality. "You should get paid for staying at school so late."

"I don't mind." Her voice went soft as she focused on my cheek, the cool felt tip of the marker gliding across my skin. "There. I think I did okay for my first try. Go look in the mirror."

I obeyed, rolling off my bed to step up beside Rachel. She'd finished finalizing her makeup—a glittery blue eye look with a strip of yellow underneath her lower lash line —and with the headband she'd borrowed from my closet, she was perfectly peppy. I smiled at my pawprint, which took up a small section of space on my left cheekbone. "It's so cute," I said, poking at the still-drying face paint. "It's perfect."

I plopped down on to my bed, bouncing Maisie in the process, and stared up at my ceiling. Even though the window was closed, I could hear the lawnmower from across the street, and even though I wasn't looking anymore, I could see Reed in my mind's eye. The sun glinting off his skin, his forearms...

The hormones my first kiss awakened were going to drive me insane.

"Oh my gosh," Rachel said suddenly. "Maisie, have we told you about Josh?"

Maisie glanced between us tentatively. "Josh?"

"He's the guy Rachel thinks I should kiss," I told her, already shifting uncomfortably at the subject. Couldn't we go back to talking about pawprints? "Kissable Josh is her target."

"*Kissable Josh?*" Rachel squealed. "Is that what you've been calling him in your head?"

It didn't occur to me until Rachel repeated it that I repeated Reed's nickname for him. *Kissable Josh.* "No, I swear."

"Uh-huh."

Maisie reached out and started playing with the ends of my hair, angling the pink-dyed tips into a heart on the duvet cover. "What do you think about him? Can you see Josh being your first kiss?"

I closed my eyes deliberately in case they were more expressive than I realized. I couldn't tell them I'd already had my first kiss—the number of questions would be never ending—but then again, if I did kiss Josh, and if whatever these feelings I had for Reed were transferred to him, I could pretend he *was* my first kiss. No one would have to know. And besides, if I stuck with Josh, Rachel wouldn't bring another unsuspecting student to me.

"I haven't decided," I said finally. "But I don't think it's as big of a deal anymore. My first kiss, I mean. I'm... over it now."

"Good. It's lame to stress about things like that,

anyway." Rachel's voice lowered into a more scandalous tone. "Speaking of first kisses, Reed and Cindy totally kissed last night."

"Ugh, I don't want to talk about last night." Maisie groaned, sneaking her fingers underneath her glasses and pressing them hard into her eyes. "I can't believe Alex spilled soda all over my pants. And they were *white*."

"But Connor Bray gave you his sweatpants—*swoon*. I'd keep them forever."

I was slow to keep up with them. "Reed—Cindy—*kissed?*"

Rachel wheeled my spinning chair closer to us, propping her feet on my bed. "Well, I think so. You didn't see? He walked her to her car, and I could've sworn I saw him lean in. Have I mentioned how unfair it is that he got all the cool traits? Flirtatious, popular, athletically inclined. Whoever was divvying up the genes between us sucks."

Heat bloomed behind my ribs, and the breath I drew in burned. I'd half expected to feel some sort of sadness, but this emotion was definitely harsher, hotter. "It's so easy for him to kiss people," I muttered, a disbelieving scoff escaping. "He's so...so..." *Annoying, infuriating, ridiculous.*

"Maybe he should give you pointers," Rachel said, knocking her socked foot against my thigh. "With how many relationships he's been in, he should offer a kissing course."

Again, the universe was cosmically *not* funny.

Without thinking about it, I pressed my fingertips to my lips, tracing the outline of them. Reed kissing Cindy.

I hated the mental image with a passion. Was it quick? Longer than five seconds? Was it like ours?

My kiss with Reed felt like a lifetime ago. And though we were in this back-and-forth game of tug-of-war, being friends and then struggling with the whole "being friends" thing, if we stuck to our agreement, the kiss would soon change to a faded memory. I needed to bury it so deep that it would soon fade away.

In my pocket, my phone gave a shrill ping, loud enough for Rachel to hear it from the desk. "Ooh, a new Babble submission?" she asked, expression lighting up. "What does it say?"

"Maybe you should be my Babble secretary," I said with a little smile, loading up my inbox. "You can vet all the posts and I'll—"

My words died off as soon as I spotted the email's sender. *Jacob Manning.*

Hello Ava,

Your proposal sounds great, and I'd be more than happy to triple the payment you requested. From the mockups you sent, you definitely should be charging more. A professional should take pride in their work and charge what it's worth, don't you think? I'll be attaching a ZIP file that contains our logo, brand colors, and other

*details you'll need for this
assignment.*

*I hope all is well. How are the
twins? Is Reed gearing up for the
big game tonight?*

*Please email me back once you've
received this so I know it didn't
go to spam.*

*All the best,
Jacob Manning*

When I got to the line about Rachel and Reed, the sick feeling had returned to my stomach, churning like my after-school snack was going to make an appearance. It was hard to pretend that this was just some client, not their father, when he asked about them.

"Is it bad?" Maisie leaned forward, trying to catch my eye. "Your face looks pale."

I looked at Rachel first, but her attention was back on herself in the mirror, wiping away her eyeshadow fallout. Oblivious to my apparently pale expression.

"It was a spam email," I got out with a forced laugh, locking my phone before pressing it against my thigh. "Bummer."

In the distance, the lawnmower shut off, sending me back into a full spiral.

Away games weren't as exciting as home games, but there was something to be said about spreading school spirit in enemy territory. Not our *true* enemy, of course—that title belonged to the Jefferson High Bulldogs—but Chesterville was a formidable opponent. The stadium lights blared down on the players, illuminating them as they ran around in the grass. It was the fourth quarter, and both teams were already starting to slow down. Thankfully, Chesterville more so. Their defensive linemen started developing cracks in which our offense blew holes right through.

I couldn't care less about watching a random football team on TV, but when it came to the Bobcats, I was dedicated.

With seconds left on the clock, Landon pulled back from the line of scrimmage to find a player to throw the ball to. It cut through the air cleanly, its target already waiting in the endzone. "And the pass is complete to number 22, Connor Bray!" the announcer called into the microphone, though his voice was nearly lost in the eruption of the Bobcats student section. "That puts the Brentwood Bobcats at a 6-point lead, taking home the victory!"

The electric excitement that ripped through everyone in the away side's bleachers was definitely my kind of high.

The final score on the board blared a solid 40-34 win.

Rachel's cheer blended in with mine, both sounds lost in the crowd as the team celebrated on the field. The perfect way to end the night, and the perfect end to a busy, crazy second week of school.

My feet ached from standing the entire night, and I stretched my arms overhead. Clattering filled the air as people started making their way toward the exit, the metal bleachers echoing from each footstep. "That was such a good game," I said, shuffling through the crowd with Rachel clasping my upper arms. "A little too close for comfort, but they came through."

"How epic would it be if we had a no-loss season?" Rachel asked, jostling me excitedly. "We'd go to playoffs!"

I couldn't help but laugh. "This was just the second game, Rach, but I like where your head's at."

It wasn't unheard of for Brentwood to make it in the playoffs—up until two years ago, the team made the cut for five seasons straight. Brentwood making it to the play-offs, especially for our senior year, would be absolute insanity. I could imagine the Babble articles I could write.

But thinking about the playoffs and the football team had me thinking of a certain ex-player, one who would be missing out on such a huge accomplishment.

The crowd dispersed as we moved toward the parking lot, headlights flashing in the dark sky as car after car began pulling out. Rachel squeezed my arms once more and then let go. "I chugged my slushy too fast," she told me, taking a step backward. "I don't think I'll make it home. Can you wait here for Reed while I run to the bathroom really quick?"

"By myself?" I scanned the busy parking lot. "I'll come with you."

"You can head to the car once he gets here," she said, waving me forward. "He'll be ticked if he has to wait on us, so this way you can distract him."

I opened my mouth to protest further, but she took off in a jog toward the outdoor bathrooms, leaving me in the dust at the edge of the sidewalk.

I wrapped my arms around myself as person after person walked past me toward their cars, carrying their stadium seats under their arms. There were a few football players, too, but none of them were Bobcats—after away games, Coach Gardner corralled the players onto the bus as quickly as possible, trying to avoid the bombardment of people trying to talk to the team.

It was strange to think that this time last year, Reed was someone that people tried to pull aside and talk to. It was kind of funny—as diehard of a fan as I was, I couldn't recall him playing for the life of me. The only thing I could remember was Mr. Manning yelling from the sidelines.

I winced, tapping my phone against my opposite hand. The email sat like a ticking bomb in my inbox. *Please email me back once you've received this so I know it didn't go to spam.*

Tomorrow, I'd start on his website redesign. *It is just a job,* I reminded myself. *And once it's done, you never have to think about it again.*

Except the last time I listened to that mentality, it hadn't really worked in my favor.

My phone began chiming in my pocket, and I hurried to fish it out, peering at the screen. *Speak of the devil.*

"I had to park all the way in the back of the lot," Reed said as soon as I put the phone to my ear. "I think I can see you on the sidewalk."

I lifted my head, but couldn't see anything beyond a kaleidoscope of headlights and taillights. "Wait, where did you park?"

"Walk straight," he said. "You'll see me."

"Rachel's in the bathroom." I glanced behind me toward where the public outdoor restrooms were, only to find a long line stretching from it. About three-quarters from the front stood Rachel, doing a teenager-rendition of a potty dance. "Or, well, she will be in probably five minutes. The line's long."

"You're going to stand on the curb waiting for her, then?"

I hesitated, rubbing the edge of my sneaker against the concrete. *You can distract him.* "Um, no. I'll come now. My feet are killing me."

Reed didn't hang up as I started in the direction he'd instructed me to go, instead letting out a soft breath on the end of the line. "Good game?"

"Great game. Landon threw the ball with seconds left, and Connor was waiting for it in the endzone. I swear, I think he made a deal with the devil for that playing arm."

Reed's snort was loud in my ear. "I'll tell him you said that."

"You should've come to watch and support them." I

stuck to the very edge of the parked cars, keeping an eye out for any cars that decided to reverse. "They *were* your teammates for all those years after all."

"It would've been weird to just watch the guys play," he said nonchalantly. "Do you see me yet? Straight ahead?"

I squinted, looking for the silver sedan, but there were streetlights in the lot, leaving the area drenched in darkness. "Uh…"

A pair of headlights in the back corner of the parking lot flashed their brights on and off twice, drawing my attention to it, and a second later, I spotted Reed rising out of the driver's seat. He had his cell phone pressed to his ear, eyes directly on me. "Now?"

Instead of replying, I ended the call.

He stuck both of his hands into his pockets as I approached, giving me a moment to look him over. The red t-shirt he wore was two sizes too big, a trend for him, but the joggers he wore fit just right. They had to be too warm for a summery-feeling night like tonight, but he didn't seem to care.

"What was the final score?" he asked once I got close enough, craning his neck to try to see the scoreboard. They'd already turned it off.

"40-34," I told him, slowing until I was a few feet from him. "Connor ran the final touchdown."

"Nice." Much like I'd looked him over, Reed scanned me then, from my face all the way to my sneakers. I held perfectly still until his eyes came to mine, oddly breathless. I blamed it on the humidity. "Did you have fun?"

"It's impossible to *not* have fun at a Brentwood football game."

Reed just smirked, leaning against his closed car door.

It was a subject I'd attempted to broach with him several times only to have it backfire, but I couldn't help myself now. My curiosity was starved, not satisfied until it had an answer. I took a step closer. "Wouldn't you have had fun if you came? *Played?*"

"Do you think I can't see through your prying tactics?" he asked me, but there was an amused glint to his eye. "What makes you think I'll tell you now?"

"We're friends now, aren't we? Don't friends share secrets?"

Reed was in the middle of considering me when a car zoomed down the parking lot aisleway, its tires popping on the gravel. Without warning, Reed's hand shot out around my wrist, jerking me into him, away from the roadway. His personal space suddenly became my personal space as I latched onto his shoulders, and even through the bagginess of his T-shirt, I could feel the firm muscles from years of sports. My world was off-kilter for more than one reason, especially as I inhaled his jasmine and green apple scented cologne.

"People shouldn't drive so fast in a parking lot," he muttered, looking down at me. He brushed his thumb along my cheek. My body gave a small jolt at the gentle trace that swiped underneath my cheekbone. "Your pawprint smudged a little."

The touch, as featherlight as it was, did wonders on

obliterating all logical thought. My tongue became a deadweight in my mouth, unable to conjure a single response. I did, at least, have the wherewithal to drop my hands from his shoulders.

The corner of his mouth he'd been biting a second ago tipped up as his hand fell. "Would you believe me if I told you that I hated football?"

"No." My answer, as embarrassingly breathless as it was, came immediately. "You've played tackle since the fifth grade. You even played on the community teams out of season. If you hated football, you wouldn't have been so dedicated."

"My dad never gave me a choice."

His expression tightened a bit at the mention of his father, something that Rachel's did as well whenever the topic came up. It happened around the mouth and around the eyes, and try as the twins might, they couldn't fully hide the reaction.

"He wouldn't let me quit before," Reed said, easing the hand that'd touched me into his pocket. "But...I can quit now."

I had the strongest urge to put my hand back on Reed's shoulder, to grab his hand, to do *something* as my chest squeezed. There were these snippets in time that Reed seemed different. No longer the grouchy brother, but more vulnerable. He put on a brave face, but there was something simmering underneath the mask of expression, something that the longer I looked at it, the more it broke my heart.

"I didn't know," I said lamely.

"You wouldn't have," he replied, shrugging. "Some things don't need to be talked about."

"If they bother you, you should talk about them."

"How about you, then?" He tilted his head to the side, placing his hand on the edge of the car behind me. It only succeeded in bringing him closer. "Anything bothering you?"

I'd run out of fingers if I tried counting everything that had been bothering me lately, but right now—in this moment—I couldn't think of a single one of them. I took a step back, sneaker turning over gravel. I knew just the thing to change the subject, and swallowed hard. "I did—well, I got you something."

"*Me?*"

I avoided his eye as I unzipped my crossbody bag, moving fast before I chickened out. Earlier I'd been too much of a coward, but now, with no one around, I could do this.

Careful not to tear the edges, I pulled three comic books out of my purse, patting the covers in a nervous tic before offering them out to him. "Ta-da."

Ta-da. What was I, five?

Reed eyed the books as if they were a live animal. "What are these?"

"Books." *Duh.* "Well, comic books. You said you thought reading comic books could be a good hobby to replace football, so I picked some up. I mean, I *saw them* and picked them up. I didn't go out specifically to buy them for you."

Why did it seem like I was always only rambling with *him?*

In a panicked half second, I thought he was going to continue to stare at the books, or even turn them down. Slowly but surely, Reed lifted his hand to take the small stack from me, angling the covers to read the front. "Where'd you get these?"

"The antique shop over in Jefferson. The one where Rachel gets her dolls." Reed still eyed the comics with that strange expression, in a way that planted a seed of insecurity behind my ribs. "Don't worry about it if you don't read them. You can throw them away if you want. They were, like, a dollar."

Reed's head lifted, and the insecurity swelling inside me vanished with just one look. His gaze was light, and lips pulled into a soft smile that knotted up my stomach. "No, I love them. Thank you, Ava."

Ava. The paparazzi nickname had always grated on my nerves, but I didn't realize until that very moment how much I liked it when he called me by my true name.

"Jeez, that line was stupid freaking long," Rachel grumbled, and we both jumped at her sudden presence. She noticed too, because she squinted between us as she approached. "What? Why are you two just standing here? Why aren't you in the car?"

"We wanted to make sure you'd see us," Reed replied evenly, the look gone in a flash, replaced with the casual look he always shot his sister. He'd expertly hidden the comic books out of view. "Took you long enough."

"Uh, yeah, I could see you. What were you talking

about?" Rachel narrowed her eyes between us. "You better not have been talking about me."

I tried to imagine what she might've seen as she walked up. Had she seen him touch my cheek? "I asked him if he kissed Cindy," I told Rachel, but even though I was focused on her, there was no missing Reed's steady intake of air. "The people of Babble have to know."

"You totally did, right?" Rachel asked, starting around the front of the car to the passenger's side. "See, Ava, I called it, didn't I?"

I stepped past Reed and his stiff spine, opening the door directly behind his. He wrapped his hand around the top part of it, trying to catch my eye, but I slid into the backseat. "You did."

Before I had a chance to shut my door, Reed ducked in and slid the comic books in the pocket attached to the back of the driver's seat. He moved so quickly that Rachel, who was in the process of twisting her long hair into a ponytail, didn't notice. When he glanced at me, all I could see were his eyes, brown framed by black lashes, and the little freckle below his waterline. So many details all at once that, even in the dim light, I could see clear as day. "You two are so annoying."

A shrill, eardrum shattering sound had me bolting awake, and my first thought was *Dad really needs to fix that coffee machine.*

But with the thought came reality, crashing into me like a wave. My lungs clenched as if they'd filled with water. As similar as the sounds were, it couldn't have been Dad's coffee maker acting as an alarm. I might've been still waking up, but I was lucid enough to know that if Dad was making coffee, he was making it at his apartment.

I blinked at the sunlight filtering through my curtains, but the sound never came again.

So, we were starting Saturday morning off with hallucinations. Awesome.

Despite the age-old advice of never looking at your electronics when you first wake up, I reached for my phone anyway out of an impossible-to-break habit, checking the comments on my last post. I'd announced the final score of last night's football game, and the comments were in typical Brentwood Bobcats fashion.

BundlesOfBobcats: woohoo, let's go number 22!!! Look at all of those touchdowns!

GirlWithBangs: thanks for reporting on this! I couldn't make it, but with all the pictures, it feels like I was there! Xoxo

MrTwister123: Missed Reed on the field. Or maybe I missed looking at those pants… ;)

BundlesofBobcats: @MrTwister123 You SO aren't alone in that!

I smirked at Reed's little fan club before moving over to my inbox to see if I'd gotten any submissions overnight. Nothing too crazy—unless you counted Riley Huntington's house getting TP'd—but as I scrolled, I found the message from Mr. Manning again, opened but unanswered.

Please email me back once you've received this so I know it didn't go to spam.

With a deep breath, I worked painstakingly through a response.

Hi Mr. Manning,
Thank you for sending over that ZIP

**file—I'll get right to work! Since
it's a redesign and not a full
build, it shouldn't take too long.
I'll have everything for you to
review on homecoming!**

Reed and Rachel—

I stopped. That topic of conversation was outside the realm of professionalism, which meant I probably didn't *have* to answer, but how could I just ignore him? I couldn't even imagine what he must've been feeling anyway, not being able to check on his kids. That was the deciding factor. I'd be vague, but still answer.

**Reed and Rachel are doing well.
Rachel and I went to the game last
night and cheered on the team. Go
Bobcats! I'll get started right
away and update you when I can.**

There. Short and sweet and sufficient. Vague enough, but not rude. Right?

Before I could second guess any of it, I pressed send.

A sudden banging sound had me jumping, and it was almost like the sound of a hammer striking down. Throwing my covers off—and throwing the comfortable warmth with it—I pulled on a sweatshirt and padded into the hall.

And found Mom, rubbing her eyes like a toddler woken up from a nap. "Morning," I greeted, eyeing her up and down. "Did the sound wake you up too?"

"*Mmm.*" She sounded less than enthused. Actually, she sounded less than awake. "I didn't realize he'd get started so early. It's not even nine o'clock. On a Saturday."

"He?"

"Reed. Sounds like he's out replacing the porch steps." Mom gave an obnoxious yawn, shuffling past me. "Go ask him if he'd like anything for breakfast, will you?"

"Why can't you?" I called after her, but her silence was the only reply.

After an internal battle, I ducked into the bathroom and scrubbed my teeth like my life depended on it, because there was no way I was walking up to Reed Manning with morning breath. My hair was still in the two braids I'd woven it into last night, so thankfully not a knotted mess, but they were chaotic enough that I untwisted them.

"Who cares what you look like?" I asked my reflection, shaking out the poodle-like curls. The pink was fainter after last night's shower, but the dye clung on faithfully. "It's just Reed. He's made it perfectly clear he doesn't look twice at you."

I grimaced, my pep talk doing the opposite of pepping me up.

When I got outside, I found that Reed had already pulled up the treads of the steps, but instead of stopping at the two bottom ones, he'd pulled up all four steps, leaving them stacked in the grass. He was in the process of hammering down the tread closest to the landing, and as I slid open the door, he looked up. "Did I wake you?"

He had on a loose T-shirt and a pair of dark blue work jeans. Strands of his golden hair were stuck along his temples in a way I was horrified to find attractive. "I normally get up at this time."

Reed looked at me for another beat before turning to the stairs, twirling the hammer. "Your mom said the bottom two were rotted, but once I replace those two, they wouldn't have matched the top ones. I figured since I had enough wood, I'd just redo them all."

I tugged at the hem of my sleep shorts, desperate to make them cover as much leg as possible. "Hopefully she's paying you for all this."

"She is, but it's not like I have anything better to do."

I chewed on the inside of my cheek, thinking about the comic books from last night.

Reed dipped his hand into a tin can filled with nails, positioning one over the step. His hammering took away any opportunity for more conversation, at least until the nail was flush with the board. I took a step closer and crouched at the edge of the step. "Do you want any breakfast? Bacon? Pancakes?"

He ducked his head, but I could see the smirk stretch across his lips. "Not if you're the one making it. No offense, but I barely survived your bite of pasta. If you can even call it that."

Even though he wielded a literal weapon, I reached out and smacked him for the dig. Since I was crouched so close to the edge of the porch, leaning forward caused me to lose my balance, and there was nothing to brace myself on.

The hammer clattered on the step as Reed dropped it, his hands catching me by the waist instead. Ten points of pressure caught me from tumbling, and for a moment, I was suspended over the torn-up steps, arrested in his grasp.

"Should've been voted Most Likely To: Break Her Neck," Reed murmured, taking a short step closer. "First you almost get hit by a car last night, now falling off the porch—"

"I just woke up," I said defensively, fighting to keep my voice level. "I'm allowed to be off-balance."

A corner of his soft lips flicked up, and with it, so did my heartrate. "I wondered why your hair looked like you hadn't run a brush through it."

Even once I felt stable again, Reed didn't let go right away. One of his hands reached up and brushed a lock of hair behind my ear. The involuntary breath I drew in got stuck in the middle of my windpipe, and I held perfectly still. He was close enough that I could see how each strand of his hair was a different shade, and I knew if I used the color picker from my web designing site, each would read with a different Hex color code. On my hips, his fingers pressed down ever so slightly, enough that, for a split second, I thought he was going to pull me into him.

"I'll take pancakes," he whispered with that same sort of smirk. "Extra syrup. I like things sweet."

And then, once he made sure I wasn't going to face

plant again—which could've been possible; my knees were wobbly once more—Reed pulled back. He took the dull, fuzzy feeling of warmth with him, and the world lurched into its normal clarity. His attention on me had dropped as he went back to the task at hand, hammering in a new board with a loud *thud, thud, thud.*

Instead of smacking him again—because trust me, the urge was strong—I trudged into the house, muttering under my breath all the while. "Yeah, yeah, you could use some sweetness."

"Rachel, you have to get it on my *hair*, not on my forehead!"

"Yeah, well, if you'd stop squirming, maybe I could!"

I stared at my reflection in the mirror Sunday afternoon with a growing horror, one that built as my forehead progressively got pinker and pinker. Rachel, who was freely wielding the hair dye brush, couldn't care less about precision. It wasn't her friend. That's why my forehead, the tops of my ears, and the white sink counter before us were all splotched in pink hair dye. It looked like a unicorn had been assassinated in the Jack and Jill bathroom.

"And you want to be a hairdresser after high school," I muttered, fully knowing that the quip would earn me a punch to the shoulder.

And it did. She also lifted the hair dye brush up

threateningly. "I can leave a massive dye-free spot on the back of your head. I'd be nice to me."

I readjusted the towel around my neck, making sure it fully covered my top. "I'm sure this is all a part of your...creative process, oh wise one."

She punched me again.

The smell of hair dye was enough to burn a third nostril, probably because we had the doors shut. She'd fought me against it, but the idea of Reed walking in while I looked like an Easter egg was not my idea of a fun time. I wasn't sure there was a less attractive version of me if I tried.

And then my thoughts supported up my craziness with logic. *Not that he finds you attractive, anyway!*

I was still self-conscious, Thoughts. Sue me.

"This is going to look so good, you know," Rachel said reverently, parting my hair to the side. "It's going to be the perfect refresh for homecoming. What color is your dress again?"

"It's white with gold sequins." I tilted my head to the side, trying to imagine my hair in its final state. "You don't think it'll be too vibrant?"

"Nah, pink and white will look perfect together. Here, grab my phone from the sink and send a picture to Maisie. See if she wants to swing by."

With nothing to do but obey, I followed her orders. When I picked up her phone, a text was waiting for her. She had the settings where the texts only loaded once she unlocked her cell, since Reed used to have a bad habit of snooping, which meant I only could see who the sender was.

And it caused me to frown. "Josh texted you?"

"He had a homework question." She nudged me with her hip. "Don't worry, I won't steal your man."

"He's not *my man*. I've spoken to him once." I rubbed my shoulder absently. "And I don't really mind. He just hasn't texted me yet."

"He's probably nervous," she murmured, flipping over to the last section and coating it with the dye. "You weren't exactly your warm and bubbly self when you two met."

"Yeah, because my best friend brought up kissing him within minutes of me learning his name."

Rachel just rolled her eyes.

I watched her work in the mirror, and I thought of the first time we tried this a little over two weeks ago. It'd been a spur-of-the-moment impulse, one that came about during a two-day sleepover with both Rachel and Maisie. We'd relied on the poorly written instructions on the box as well as a few YouTube tutorials, and miraculously my hair ended up *not* fried to high heaven with the bleach, and it held onto the hot pink we'd gone with.

She didn't let the Josh subject go. "Maybe you two should get lunch or something. Get to know each other a little, and then *bam!*" She gave a dramatic air kiss.

"I still can't believe you actually asked him to be my first kiss."

"I'll always be your wing woman, girl." Having finished up the last little bit of dyeing, Rachel pulled off her plastic gloves and tossed them in the trash. "So, do you really think Jannor broke up?"

Brentwood's hottest couple, Jannor—Jade and Connor. "Who's to say?" I murmured, tapping my cell. "I got a lot of tips, but no concrete proof. They were together Friday night."

The tips I'd gotten were vague to say the least, but all surrounding an argument that seemingly went down at the Wallflower diner in Jefferson. From what I saw—and what my armchair reporters sent me—they hadn't spoken today, but he did sit by her at lunch.

Rachel waggled her eyebrows at me. "Maybe I've got a chance."

I couldn't help but chuckle. "Keep those fingers crossed."

"Does it feel sad that this is your last year reporting on Babble?" She swiped up her cell phone and began typing on it. "The last year reporting on Jannor, the last year talking about the Most Likely Tos. It feels strange for me, so I can't even imagine how it feels for you."

Using the edge of the towel, I wiped at some of the pink dye on my forehead. "I haven't thought about it much. I've had a lot on my mind."

"Like?"

I didn't feel like getting into the whole divorce talk again, the mere prospect weighing me down. "School and web designing and stuff. Nothing too major."

Rachel bobbed her head slowly, biting the corner of her lip in thought. "So, have you gotten any...crazy clients lately?"

I practically hiccupped on the breath I tried to draw in. "Not really. Things have been pretty slow after the baby announcement."

There. I played it cool, I was sure of it. In the mirror, I saw Rachel fold her arms across her chest. From the stiff line of her posture, it was clear something was bothering her, but I waited it out, let her work it through first. "I'm worried about Reed."

"Why?"

"He's been acting different lately." She was quiet for a long moment. "He takes late night walks sometimes. Which is weird, because he's never done that before. I don't know why, but sometimes he won't come home until after midnight."

Even though I hadn't been moving before she spoke, I stilled. The other day, when I saw him leaving his house—was that what he'd been doing? Sneaking out to go on a late walk? *Why?*

"And...it's weird that he quit the football team without telling me or mom about it. That he practiced all summer and then never showed for the games. That's not normal for him. I've asked him about it, but he brushes it off."

The exact expression Reed wore when he told me that he hated football was practically burned into my memory, and I thought of it now. Him hating football didn't make much sense, but him not talking to Rachel about it was even more confusing. They weren't the closest of siblings, despite their twinship, but I would've thought that something that major would've warranted at least a brief convo. "Maybe he just wants to do something different for his senior year. Maybe he feels freaked out by it being our last year, too."

Her voice dropped to a near whisper, almost like she didn't want to be overheard. "I think Dad cheating really affected him. I think that's why he's dating around and never settling with someone for long."

"We *are* in high school," I pointed out, this conversation inching into strange territory. It made my skin itch. "Long-term relationships are rare." And not even that realistic.

Rachel leaned against the edge of the sink, but still didn't look at me. Almost like everything would be all right as long as we didn't make eye contact. She could hold it all in as long as she didn't look. "Sometimes I think..."

"What?"

"I think..." And then she stopped. Blinked. I saw the resolution settle over her, the thought of *never mind* slide across her expression. She gave her head a shake and attempted at a bright smile, finally looking over at me. Her brown eyes were shining. "I think you're right about us being in high school. Reed's no different than Ashton or Collin or any other senior at Brentwood. Dating around, I mean."

I chewed on the side of my cheek, wishing I had the right thing to say to her. I'd never had this issue before, blanking on words of comfort. It was usually my job in our friendship, but when it came to her brother, I was afraid something I'd say would sound *too* concerned, and it left me silent. But it was clear it weighed on her, and for some reason, she didn't want to splurge on all the details.

So, I reached for her cell again, offering it to her. "Should we ask Josh if he wants to meet at the Wallflower for lunch?"

She raised her eyebrows. "Should we?"

Getting out of the house to meet Josh would lift her spirits, for sure. I nodded, turning to my reflection. "Once it's time to wash this out, we should go."

And the suggestion did the trick. Her eyes lit up, and she clutched her phone with a tight urgency. "I'll text him then pick out an outfit for you. Ah, this is perfect! I'm sure he'd totally be down for a date."

I started to nod when her words actually hit me. "Wait, a *date*?" I demanded, but Rachel opened her bedroom door and disappeared, leaving me staring after her.

hen I'd offered us to meet at Wallflower, I definitely meant for Rachel to tag along. I didn't mean this as a date. Him and I, us two, *alone*, date. Didn't want that at all. But here I was, wearing one of Rachel's sundresses that was too long on me, walking into Wallflower without Rachel by my side.

Chill, Ava, I'd told myself. *Treat it like you're out to dinner with Rachel.*

I had found Josh easily in the sea of filled booths and tables, all because of the brightly printed Hawaiian shirt he wore. A sweet ballad played over the antique jukebox in the corner, though it was barely audible over the sound of conversation and forks scraping against plates. He'd managed to snag a seat against the wall during rush hour, and he'd lifted his blonde head as soon as the door chimed, lifting an arm into the air. His grin had been easy, dimples and all.

From there, it was clear to see I'd worried for nothing.

"Okay, I think it's ready." Josh leaned back into his

seat now, dusting his hands and gesturing toward the spread in front of us. "It's ready for us to dig in."

A bowl of mac-and-cheese ordered with a side of chicken tenders, which he cut up into fine chunks. He mixed it into the macaroni, and even though that alone sounded weird, he threatened to ruin it entirely.

He ordered a fried egg on top.

"This *can't* be good," I muttered, staring at the mixture with a warring sense of disgust and anticipation. "I can't imagine it tasting good."

"Trust me, it's life-changing." He gestured to it. "Try it. You'll be amazed."

I stared at the lines of hot sauce across the top, and at the oozing fried egg mixing with the cheesy macaroni. The chicken—that made it bearable. "You better be right," I told him, picking up my fork and rubbing my napkin across it. "I've been promised life-changing, and I am expecting life-changing."

Josh swiped up his fork, too. "Make sure you get everything in one bite. Mac, chicken, egg, hot sauce—the whole shebang."

"Yes, sir."

Not even fighting a grimace, I loaded up my fork, dipping my collection in a bit of the hot sauce. Josh hovered his fork over the bowl, gesturing it toward me. "Cheers."

I tapped my fork against his and took the big bite. I chewed, waiting for the disgust to hit me. "I can't even taste the egg."

Josh dropped his fork and made a *boom* gesture.

"Amazing, right? Now you'll always order it this way. Michelin Star quality, I'd say."

I smiled a little, thinking back to my conversation with Reed. Maybe it was more of a grimace than a smile. "I don't know about *that*." Despite that, I went back for another bite. "Chicken and hot sauce, maybe. The egg? *Ehh*."

"Trust me. Three days from now, you'll find yourself hungry and this sudden thought will come up: Man, I could go for macaroni and eggs right now."

Shoving down another laugh, I went in for another bite.

My nerves had somewhat disappeared now, almost like the mac and cheese had been the perfect icebreaker. Talking to Josh was easier than I thought. He had the kind of personality that easily should've been in the Top Tier; easygoing, charismatic, funny.

"You dyed your hair again, right?" Josh asked, stabbing a piece of macaroni and tender. "The pink is brighter. It looks good."

I touched the wet braid over my shoulder a bit self-consciously. Once I rinsed the dye out, Rachel didn't even let me wait until it air-dried before she started weaving it off to the side. "*You'll thank me later*," she'd said as she braided, ignoring my protests. "*I know you will*."

Rachel probably thought she was being a great wing woman, getting me an in with Josh, even though I hadn't asked for one. But then again, maybe this was okay. He *was* Kissable Josh. But I realized something as we joked and chatted—this *was* comfortable. Easy. He was great company, and the more I hung out with him, the less Rachel would be on my back about finding someone for me to kiss. It felt like a win-win scenario all around.

"Thank you," I told Josh, twisting my fork. "So, uh, tell me about yourself. Do you play sports?"

"Nah, not since elementary school. I'm not really a competitive person."

That explained his anonymity a little. Still, it was weird that, before last week, I'd never met him. "Are you in band?" When Josh shook his head, I said, "Sorry for all the questions. I'm wondering how our paths had never crossed before."

"Well, Brentwood *is* huge," he said, tapping his knuckles on the tabletop to the music coming from the speakers. I recognized the fast-pace beat from a frequently played one on the radio. "But I'm actually new."

"*New?*" I raised my eyebrows, but he didn't elaborate. "Like, you just transferred?"

"Yep. From Clinton Prep. Would not recommend transferring to a massive school your senior year, but here we are." He gave a small, deprecating smile, his dimple becoming a firm indentation. "The tuition got too sky-high."

My fork clinked off the ceramic bowl between us. "I bet it's been so hard learning everyone's names. I've had three years to memorize, and I *still* see people I don't know." There were four middle schools within the Brentwood School District, and five elementary schools, so it was easy to have never crossed paths with any students before. "Wait, you've only just started here and you got on the Most Likely Tos?"

"Impressive, right?" He pretended to dust lint off his shirt. "I've caught the eye of someone. I'm quite proud."

Most Likely To: Be Forgotten After High School. It made so much more sense now. I leaned my chin against my fist, letting him take a few bites because I was scarfing down the mac-and-cheese mixture. It *was* good. "It's not as offensive as it sounded before."

"Never have their first kiss, though...that's hurtful."

Now it was my turn to shrug, wishing I could turn the conversation around. I couldn't think about *that* without thinking about Reed. More specifically, Reed's mouth. "I've never really been interested in anyone enough to kiss them, I guess."

"Honesty hour?" Josh leaned across the table once more, like we were sharing a secret. "I haven't had my first kiss yet either."

"*Really?*" I narrowed my eyes at him, looking for a trace of deceit, but his features were so baby-like and innocent. "Don't lie to make me feel better."

"Cross my heart. I paid more attention to academics than to relationships. Practically everyone at my school was the same way. But turns out Brentwood's academics aren't quite as, ah...*advanced* as Clinton Prep's were."

I nearly snorted. "So our easy classes open up some time for relationships?"

His cheeks pinked for the first time since I'd met him,

and I was struck by how cute it made him look. "Maybe a little."

I studied him from across the table, especially as he started carefully avoiding my gaze. That took my initial first impression of him and dashed it against the ground. He wasn't looking for someone to kiss—this was a boy new to the whole relationship scene, like me. Having that understanding erased some of the tension that clung to me, tension I hadn't even realized was there until it vanished.

"You know, Rachel...she made it sound like I'm ready to go kissing anyone. I'm not." I watched his expression, but he didn't have a reaction. No surprise, no disappointment—he was just listening. "I don't really care about being voted that for the list." *Not anymore.*

"I'm not here because I thought you might kiss me," Josh said, and his words made *my* cheeks heat now, but I blamed it on the hot sauce. "You seem like a cool person— you and Rachel both—and I'm looking for some friends."

Once more, something about his words gave me a huge sense of relief. I raised one eyebrow. "So, this *isn't* a date?"

Josh's lips twitched up. "Not unless you want it to be."

Smooth, I thought with an inward chuckle, loading up another bite of macaroni and chicken. "So, you said you had a sister, right? The one who watched *Gossip Girl?*"

Josh nodded. "Step-sister, actually. My mom married her dad about...five years ago now? Time flies." He paused, thinking. "Rachel's parents are divorced too, right?"

I nodded, and words were on the tip of my tongue. *So are mine.* Except that there was no way I'd say the words aloud. "Yeah, hers split up last summer."

"I remember her saying something about it. So, she lives with her mom but visits her dad on the weekends?"

The first part of his sentence had tripped me up—Rachel had told Josh about her parents' divorce?—that it took a second for the second sentence to fully register. "Oh, uh, no. They're no-contact with their dad." Where would he even have gotten that from?

Josh bobbed his head to a slow beat. "That was how it was with me at first. My dad moved across the country after they split, so I didn't even see him until he came to visit a year ago. It's crazy how the dynamic flips."

I couldn't feel what my features morphed into, but I hoped my expression was more polite than pained. Rachel had no contact with her father, and Josh had been in the same boat—was I next in line to join the club? The idea made me sick.

Before I had a chance to come up with a response—and rescue the conversation from the bottomless pit it'd fallen into—Josh's phone went off with a low chime. He fished it from his pocket, shaking his head. "Speaking of the sister," he said, thumbing through the text. "She wants me to order her a piece of chocolate cake. Have you ever had it?"

"I have, and it's *delicious.* Triple-layer goodness that they make every day."

"We need one of those then," Josh said, rapping his knuckles once more on the table before getting to his feet. "I'm going to go ask our waitress for two."

This time, when I smiled up at him, I knew it was genuine. *A pleasant surprise,* I thought, watching him walk up to the area where the waitress was leaning, chatting with one of her other coworkers. His low voice reached me even from this distance. *This was a pleasant surprise.*

"Mom?" It was ten minutes before eight o'clock when I got through the door. I tapped my fingers on the to-go box, listening to the hollow sound inside. Josh gave me the slice of cake to go, and though I'd tried to split it in half, Josh sent the rest home with me. Secretly, I was grateful—I had a midnight snack for later.

Her car was outside, but the only response I received came by way of the air conditioner's hum. I checked the kitchen, the laundry room, and even the bathroom, but she wasn't there. I poked my head into her bedroom, but no mother in sight.

The house was quiet in a way that I hated. Dad should've been home watching TV. Eight o'clock was when his favorite crime drama came on, and he would've already been in his recliner at this point, feet propped on the coffee table even though Mom always yelled at him for it.

A thick lump formed in my throat. "Mom, are you home?"

Nothing. Did she go out again with her friends? It was possible, but she almost always left a note. Always texted. I sat down on the edge of her floral quilt and pulled out my cell phone. Instead of calling her, I opened up my Friend Finder app, waiting for it to load. She'd made me download the app my freshman year under the guise that she liked having *her* location tracked because of all the open houses and tours she did with people.

I hadn't asked, but I knew that was probably her way of tracking me without an objection on my part.

Blue words flashed on my Friend Finder app. *Cell phone not found.*

When I called Mom, her phone went straight to voicemail, her chipper realtor tone greeting me. "Hello, this is Kelly Jenson—"

I hung up, letting out a slow breath, and dialed another number. Rachel took a few moments before answering. "Oh my gosh, *hey*! I've been waiting for you to call! Did you just get home? That's a good sign, right? How did it go?"

"Before we jump in," I said quickly, trying to cut off her excitement, or at the very least curb it for five minutes. "Have you seen my mom at all since I left your house? Like, going out with a friend?"

"Uh, no. Why?"

As I got up, I saw Mom's nightstand and the tissue box sitting on it. There were several tissue wads surrounding the surface, and I tried to think if I noticed Mom's allergies acting up. "She's not home."

"Hmm. Well, that's okay, isn't? I mean, old people

can have social life too, right?" Rachel hummed a little, sounding suspiciously like the *Jeopardy!* theme song. "Can I ask about the date yet?"

I puffed out a breath and padded my way to the bedroom, carrying my cake with me. As I eased open my door, I turned the call on speaker mode, wanting to fill the house's silence. "It went okay."

"Just okay? Come on, Ava. Gimme all the deets. I won't interrupt."

The familiarity of my bedroom created an instant calm. When I turned thirteen, I'd been allowed to paint my room for the first time. Mom, Dad, and I taped lines across my boring white walls and as a family, went to work filling in the geometric shapes we'd made. Teal, pink, light blue, light green—it'd been a fun experiment, and a memory that I could recall with perfect clarity. The geometric lines doing wonders to quell the building heaviness in my body.

That, and Rachel's voice, drawing me to the moment. "Uh, it was...good. It didn't really feel like a date. There wasn't any pressure."

"That's good! He seems like he'd be super easy to be around. Did you end up getting food?"

"Yeah, he ordered something kind of weird, but it was fun trying something new." I walked over to where my computer sat on my nightstand and flipped the lid open, transferring it to my bed as I sat down. "He's nice."

"Ah, my matchmaking is top-notch." Rachel gave a contented sigh. "Did you kiss him?"

I opened my mouth to answer, but stopped short. A

part of me wanted to lie to her because I knew that if I told the truth, a swarm of questions would follow. *What? Why didn't you kiss him? I thought you said you were comfortable? Did he not want to kiss you?*

A soft *knock-knock* had me jerking toward my doorway, and upon spotting a figure looming there, I screamed.

Halfway through the scream, I realized it wasn't an axe murderer—it was Reed.

"*What?*" Rachel shrieked, echoing me. "What, what's wrong?"

My heart raced in my chest, slamming against my ribs to break out. "I, uh—I saw a bug," I rushed out, swallowing past the new tightness in my throat. "A really big, ugly bug."

Reed scowled.

"I'll talk to you tomorrow, okay?"

Rachel gasped. "*Tomorrow?* Ava, you're going to leave me hanging until morning?"

In a terrible sort of way, I *really* wanted my best friend to shut up. At least while she was on speakerphone. "Leaving you in suspense," I said with a sort of humor I didn't feel. "Love you."

"Ava—"

I hung up, and once again, the house's white noise filled the space. Reed wore a pair of work overalls, but instead of having his arms through the straps, he knotted them like a belt to keep the pants up. The black shirt he wore was smeared with what looked like white paint, and even from here, I could see the substance dotting along his cheek. "You're jumpy," Reed said.

"I didn't know you were here, lurking in my house like a ghost," I said defensively, swallowing hard. My racing heart refused to calm down. "*Why* are you here?"

"I was patching up the drywall in the basement," he replied, and he took a step deeper into my room, his socked foot causing the floorboards to give a small creak. "I heard you walking around."

"So, you came up to say hello?"

"Or came up to kick a potential robber's ass, but sure," he murmured, adding, "We'll go with your answer."

My phone buzzed in my hand, alerting me to a new text from Rachel. I was half-surprised she hadn't called me back.

Rachel: You suck. Just so you know. At least tell me if you kissed!!!

She had to know that if I hadn't said anything, it obviously hadn't happened.

"Do you know where my mom is?"

"She texted me earlier. She said she was getting drinks with a friend, but she told me where the spare key was so I could let myself in." Reed nodded his chin at my bed. "What's in the box?"

"Cake from Wallflower."

"Ah, so that's where you went on your date?" Reed

gave an easy smile when my head jolted toward him. "You had your phone on speaker."

A weird twisting feeling wrung out my insides as I studied the Styrofoam to-go box. Okay, so he knew I went on a date. Not that he'd care. He probably thought it was *cute*. "Yeah, that's where I went. Do you want some?" I tapped the lid of the box.

"You can't keep giving me presents, Paparazzi. I might start to think you have a crush on me."

Playful banter was a staple of Reed Manning's, and usually I was able to dish it right back. Now, his words caused too many thoughts to surface, and I desperately wanted to jump to a denial, but knew I couldn't object *too* much.

Then again, the comic books *might've* been too far.

I settled with making a face at him. "No wonder you've had so many girlfriends. You think someone's trying to come onto you when they're being nice."

He laughed, but instead of coming closer, he showed me palms. They were smeared with spackling, too. "How about I wash this off and we split it?"

It was decided. Reed ducked into the bathroom across the hallway of my bedroom while I went into the kitchen to grab forks, blood doing a strange dance to the techno beat of anxiety. *It's just cake,* I reasoned with myself. *I mean, we probably could eat it in the kitchen. I should tell him we need to eat it in the kitchen.*

And I would've, except when I returned with the forks, Reed was already sitting on my bedspread with the cake box open on his thigh.

"You're lucky," he said when he looked up at me. "Any second longer and I would've dug in with my hands."

"Uncivilized," I scolded, fighting a stupid grin. He had one leg pulled up on the bed, and I sat cross-legged beside him, close but not too close.

Reed dug into the chocolate frosting first, scooping up the little chocolate chips pressed into the side. With it balanced on his thigh, I was careful not to tip it over when I got my small bite.

"So, your date," Reed said around his piece of cake, already analyzing his next forkful. "Who was it with?"

"Josh Geller." I studied his expression, but recognition didn't flare. "Rachel introduced us the other day. After school."

"Did you kiss him?"

"You're as bad as your sister."

"Hate to break it to you, but I'm totally invested now," he said, casting me a smile. It was one of his normal, nonchalant ones, like he was truly unbothered. "Rachel might've set you up with him, but I'm over here waiting for my caterpillar to turn into a butterfly."

I went to break off another piece, but Reed blocked my fork with his, getting it first. "I've already turned into a butterfly." My cheeks felt hot, hot, hot, but I forced myself to look at him. I wouldn't shy away from it. From *him*. "Remember?"

Reed's gaze was warm, but it had me fighting a shiver. The way he watched me now was too reminiscent of the night we kissed. I drew in a breath, but I shouldn't have; it smelled like *him.*

He ducked his head toward the cake box, and as soon as there was a break in the connection, everything logical flooded back. *Rachel. Josh. Cindy. He kissed her—he's going to homecoming with her.*

"You're home alone a lot." Reed glimpsed around my bedroom. "Do you ever go to your dad's?"

"I haven't yet. I don't even know what apartment complex he's at."

"You haven't seen him since he left, then?"

Like Rachel had done earlier, he didn't look at me when he spoke. This time, I was thankful for it. I understood my best friend a little better now. It was easy to talk about hard stuff when eye contact wasn't involved. "We've texted here and there. Enough that it doesn't feel like he completely abandoned me." The last line unwound itself from the tangle of my thoughts and slipped out, causing my skin to flush. "I mean, of course he didn't abandon me. Not like...not like—"

"It's okay," Reed said. "I don't have the market cornered on dads who walk out."

We lapsed into a cake-eating silence, each of us taking smaller and smaller bites to get the piece to last longer. I scraped as much of the frosting as I could off the bottom, even though that was my least favorite part.

"My mom..." I began, and despite the chocolate cake, the words tasted bitter. "She's behind on some of her bills. Apparently, all of them are coming due at once. I'm afraid—" This time, I cut myself off, unwilling to speak the words aloud.

I could feel Reed looking at me. "Afraid...?"

"I guess I'm afraid she'll do something drastic."

He didn't ask me what I meant, even though it could've been so many things. *Drastic.* In my head, there was only one terrible choice for her to pick: selling the house. Mom talking on the phone with Lindsey was still crystal clear in my memory.

But that's why you took the job from Mr. Manning, my brain reminded me, trying to soothe the storm before it brewed inside me. *It'll all be okay once that's finished. Hang in there.*

Reed readjusted his grip on the Styrofoam container, and then, after switching his fork to his other hand, he touched his fingers to where mine were on the bedspread between us. The tentative touch felt more like a whisper at first, a hesitation, like he expected me to jolt away. Quite the opposite happened, really—I didn't move.

I stilled, but I didn't shut up. "You know what my dad told my mom?" I finally looked up at Reed. "That he regretted marrying so young. That he couldn't shake the thought that he wanted to experience life without her. That he wished he'd dated around more before her."

Reed's long lashes swept down across his cheekbones in a slow blink, like he took the blow of the words. "That's...brutal. Seriously."

"That's why I wanted to kiss you. Or kiss *someone.* Someone I could get it out of the way with. To get the early relationships out of the way, I guess. After putting so much pressure on the kiss, I was afraid I'd get too swept up in it. And now, I won't ever wonder *what if*." I chuckled a little, one that absolutely lacked any trace of humor, and looked at the cake box. Only a little sliver remained. "I think it's good that you date around a lot. Truly. You'll never have to wonder 'what if' either."

I'd grown up my whole life wanting a love like my parents—high school sweethearts, football player and cheerleader, cute house with a picket fence—but now I saw the beauty, the necessity, in Reed's lifestyle. Now my parents' love story terrified me.

"I can kind of see what you mean," he said slowly, twirling his fork. "I mean, I guess that's why I can never get...comfortable in a relationship. It's scary putting so much time into someone if it doesn't work out."

The seriousness in his tone had me peering up at him, but there wasn't a trace of teasing in his expression either. His actions suddenly made so much sense, like someone flicked on a light switch over. That had been why Reed dated Jamie and Kelsey and Cindy, why his relationships didn't last longer than three months. Heck, maybe that was even one of the reasons he agreed to kiss me. "Why didn't you say that when Rachel and I poked fun about you dating around?"

"I guess I never cared to correct you before."

"But you do now?"

Reed glanced at me from the corner of his eye, but it was the briefest peek that I couldn't even begin to translate what it meant. "Cindy. Friday night, you said something about me kissing Cindy."

Nope, nope, didn't want to hear about any of that. Pretending I wasn't affected would only get that much harder. "It's really none of my—"

"I didn't kiss her." He broke off a chunk of chocolate but didn't bring it to his lips. "She leaned in, but we didn't kiss."

"Why are you telling me?" I asked, quirking an eyebrow at him. It was a bad sign that my insides did a little jump for joy, though. I'd deal with that later. "You should've kissed her. You've never held back before."

"You're right."

His words were low, low enough to tickle my ears and send goosebumps down my spine. My next question felt like it was nearing a line I shouldn't cross, but I found myself toeing it, anyway. "Have you asked her to homecoming yet?"

"Not yet. I think she knows it's coming."

Of course she would've. When Reed set his sights on someone, it was obvious. And with him sauntering into Allen's Alley holding onto her hand, that'd been a declaration. He'd chosen her. Before, I never really paid much attention to Reed and his girlfriends—sometimes Rachel and I would bet on how long they'd last—but now I couldn't help but feel a wiggle of concern. *What if she's the one that lasts?*

I swallowed my last bite of cake and licked the remaining frosting from the fork. There was one small sliver left now, but Reed could have it. "I know we joked about it last time, but you should let me know when you ask her. I'm going to do a compilation post of all the homecoming proposals, and yours...would be a good addition."

And I'd rather hear it from you than from a submission.

When he didn't say anything, I looked up and found him staring at me with an intensity that caused my throat to close. No, with how close he was, I could tell he wasn't staring at *me*—he was looking at my lips.

Something about his eyes had my insides somersaulting. The bed underneath me suddenly felt much softer, the distance between Reed and me much shorter. In a different universe, I'd reach up and wipe my lips, because he was no doubt staring because I had frosting smeared across my mouth like a toddler. If I had a grip on my sanity, that's what I would've done. Instead, I let my thoughts get away from me.

Kissing Reed felt so long ago now, and even though I thought the memory had been branded in my brain, I desperately wanted to remind myself of what it felt like. What he tasted like. If I kissed him now, he'd taste like chocolate. The frosting I'd licked off the fork—he'd taste like that.

I let my eyes dip to his soft-looking lips, and the charge of energy I'd felt the first time we kissed kicked back with an electric thrill, skittering along my skin. In that moment, I wanted. Too much. To throw all the pretending out the window, to throw caution to the wind, and just—

"Knock, knock."

We both jumped a mile at Mom's soft voice. It startled Reed badly enough that he nearly upturned the box on his thigh. He grabbed it at the last second and put it on the bed, hastily shoving to his feet. We both whirled to find her in the doorway with her purse slung into the crook of her elbow, her gaze a little glassy. "Sorry, I thought I heard voices."

"I—I thought you were getting drinks," I gasped out, clenching my fork. "You're home early."

"Lindsey's son had a stomachache, so she went home." Mom flicked from me to Reed standing a good three feet from me to the Styrofoam box on my bed, and I knew that if she hadn't been drinking, her expression probably would've been a little more confused. If she were sober, she would've asked what we were doing here. In my bedroom. Alone. "Ava, I thought I told you to clean your room."

My room wasn't that dirty, in the grand scheme of things, but not really my biggest concern at the moment.

"I—I finished the drywall downstairs," Reed said, and if I didn't know any better, I would've thought his voice trembled. He distinctly didn't look at me. "Let me show you."

Mom allowed him to corral her from my bedroom, and I knew I should've gone with them. I couldn't move, though. There was no facing Reed now, either. Not after staring at his mouth like a pervert, thinking what I thought, and freaking him out enough to send him fleeing.

With a soft groan, I fell onto my pillows, and though Reed was gone, it took my pulse a long, long time to die down.

It rained Wednesday morning, which meant I had to park the bike for the day and let Mom drive me to school. Normally, I would've carpooled with Rachel and Reed, but her text this morning totally wiped that off the table.

> Rachel: **Hey, I'm staying home today —cramps are terrible. Come over straight after and tell me more about the date!!!**

Yeah, carpooling with Reed? It was a two-minute drive, but no, thank you.

However, it meant that when school let out and it was still raining, I was in a pickle. I'd have to wait until either it stopped or for Mom to finish her work day to swing by and pick me up.

I pulled out my notebook and Physics textbook from my locker, shoving it into my pastel blue JanSport, right beside my laptop. Working on Mr. Manning's website would serve as a good way to pass time.

Sixth period hadn't been the same without Rachel and her quips to get me through Physics and Mr. Pieffer's monotone drawl as he talked about kinematics. Brentwood Babble was suspiciously quiet today. I wondered if the lull was a sign that soon something bigger would come across my inbox, and couldn't help but cross my fingers. It'd been a week and a half since the Most Likely To list came out—things were already slowing down. I stopped getting whispers as I passed in the hallways, which was great.

I lifted my head from my locker, turning to the M section. There were too many people filtering through the halls for me to pick out a tall, golden-haired boy.

"Thank God, the school day's over," a voice said, and when I turned around, I found Josh approaching with his backpack tight against his spine. He gave me his dimpled, welcoming grin. "Did today drag on, or was it just me?"

"Definitely dragged. I thought I was going to fall asleep in Physics." I shut my gold locker door and leaned against it, looking once more down the hallway.

"So, uh." Josh chuckled lightly, maybe even a bit awkwardly, and slipped one hand into his pocket. "It's raining."

I smiled a little. "I gathered that when the PA system announced football practice was canceled."

"Do you need a ride home today? I'm assuming you didn't ride your bike. I doubt those space buns would've survived the downpour."

I reached up and touched one of the knots on the top of my head instinctively. All the bobby pins I'd stuck into it this morning had done well to keep them secured. "I was actually going to camp out in the library for a while," I told him, hoisting my backpack strap further up on my shoulder. "Utilize the free Wi-Fi while I have it."

I hadn't gotten much progress in Mr. Manning's site last night, so I'd need to make great strides today. Mom had taken the bills off the side table by the front door, but I knew they were around somewhere.

"You want company?" Josh's dimple pushed in deeper. "I have homework I can do, so we can just...work together?"

"Paparazzi."

We both turned toward the new voice and shadow looming across our conversation. Reed had approached silently, stopping beside us with only a textbook under his arm.

Josh's posture stiffened a bit. "Hey, Reed."

Now it was my turn to glance between them, a little confused. I hadn't realized they knew each other. Reed would've known Josh's name by our conversations, but would Josh have known Reed's name? After a few weeks of being at Brentwood?

Reed, though, didn't seem like this was anything out of the ordinary. Instead, he gave Josh one of those bro chin-nods before turning to me. "Do you need a ride home?"

It was almost painful to hold his gaze, my insides squirming under the embarrassment of the last time I saw him. Staring at his lips like a crazy person, mere seconds away from leaning forward if Mom hadn't intervened. It was like my brain had shut off, and all thought of consequences went out the window.

Then again, Reed was acting...cool. Maybe he hadn't picked up on the fact that my heart had been racing out of my chest last night. Maybe he hadn't picked up on the fact that if Mom hadn't walked in, I would've kissed him.

Or maybe he *had* picked up on it, but was being uncharacteristically gracious enough to let it slide.

"Do you two live near each other?" Josh asked before I opened my mouth to answer.

Reed nodded. "We live across the street from each other."

"You do?" Josh turned to me. "I didn't realize. That's cool."

I imagined the scenario like a movie, the one where I went home with Reed instead of going to the library with Josh. Reed would no doubt ask me *why* I hadn't taken up Josh's offer, and what kind of answer would I give? It wasn't that I didn't want to ride with Josh—it was just that between the two, I wouldn't have picked him.

It's because you're not as comfortable with him yet, I told myself. *And you'll never be comfortable if you don't try.*

With that thought steeling me, I turned to Reed. "I'm going to work in the library," I told him, forcing myself to not look away. "With Josh."

"That works for me," Reed said, pulling his car keys from his backpack pocket, letting them clatter noisily. "I was going to swing by Landon's for a bit, and now I don't have to drop you off first."

"Sounds perfect, then," Josh said cheerfully.

"I'll see you tomorrow," Reed said to me, tipped his head once more to Josh, and pivoted on his heel. My fingers curled as I watched him dissolve into the bustle of students leaving for the day, his backpack getting lost among many.

And it was exactly how it was supposed to be.

Josh and I set up our little station at a small, two-person desk near the windows, with him pulling out his Physics textbook and me withdrawing my laptop. There were a few kinks I wanted to work out with the site. When I opened the Contacts tab on my phone, the loading rate was an awkward, stilted progression throughout the page. I wanted it to be a bit smoother, with each textbox loading in the correct succession.

There were a couple other things—like one of the links on the About Me page had a broken progression and Mr. Manning's picture on the page was a bit bigger than the rest of the employee's headshots—but nothing too major. I had a few other pages to redo entirely.

Josh bent down to grab something from his backpack when his gaze slipped across my laptop screen. I had the webpage loaded, but the HTML box open over most of it. "Whoa, are you a coder?"

"Not in, like, a hacky way," I told him, scrolling through the layers of code until I found the spot where the Contacts page was affected. "I design websites. Or, well, sort of. This one's a redesign, but I'm trying to build my portfolio."

"That's the coolest thing," Josh said with awe in his voice. "I swear I'm like an old man with technology. I can barely figure out my email."

I snorted a little as I worked, reordering the HTML structure. Once that was finished, I closed out the box and picked up my phone, hoping that those tweaks caused the webpage to load smoother.

Josh eyed my screen closer. "Ah, Manning? Are you working on Rachel's and Reed's dad's site?"

I actually jumped at his words and the realization that came with them. My dirty secret was now known by a third party—a third party that seemed to have interactions with both Reed and Rachel. He shared last period with Rachel, and somehow, he knew Reed, too.

"T-They don't know," I stuttered, the breathlessness hitting me fast. "Can you—I mean, would you mind not telling—"

"Hey, hey." Without hesitation, Josh mimed the act of zipping his lips shut, tossing the key over his shoulder. "Your secret's safe with me."

His words came as an immediate assurance, but they didn't pacify me enough. I clutched my phone tighter in my hand, wondering if I should say something else, make him pinky swear or something.

Josh laid his hand on my arm, the warmth of his fingers seeping into the bare skin below my elbow. I looked down at the touch. "I promise I won't say anything, Ava. But that's a big job. I mean, everyone knows Manning Construction. I'm sure they'd be happy for you."

No, I thought. *They absolutely would not.* But then again, Josh knew nothing about the situation with their parents.

"Wait, so you designed Brentwood Babble all on your own?" he asked, withdrawing his hand. "Dang, I assumed you'd hired a professional. You're just *that* good?"

"Your flattery is appreciated," I said, and though I tried to fight a smile, it came through anyway. "It'll be sad once senior year is over. Babble is like my baby, and it'll be heartbreaking to retire it."

It was something I'd thought about more and more lately, especially since Rachel brought it up. This time next year, things would be drastically different. Hypothetically, I could still post tips people submit, but I wasn't even sure what those would look like. Most of the Top Tier was graduating this year. Brentwood would look entirely different in a year from now.

It left me in a brief, anxious stage of crisis, wondering what I'd be doing if it wasn't Babble.

Josh made a soft *hmm* noise as he studied my computer screen. "I'll brainstorm some ideas. Just because you have to retire Babble doesn't mean you have to give up blogging entirely."

"If you think of anything, I'm all ears." I gestured at his textbook. "But stop letting me distract you."

Even after Josh bent his head, I studied him for a moment. Rachel did pick a good guy, even if he missed out on being my first kiss. He would've been a good candidate for it. I didn't know him very well, but what I did know about him, I liked. Patient, kind, caring.

Things Reed Manning didn't exactly excel in.

We worked for an hour in the library, but even while I finished up the things on my list and drafted a check-in email to Mr. Manning, I couldn't stop wondering whether Josh would've been a better first kiss than Reed. It would've been less complicated for sure, but on the idea of him being *better*, I guess I'd never really know.

The school library closed at four, so we packed up our stuff then. I'd sent the email to Mr. Manning, and until he responded, knots would live in my stomach. It was that way with every client, waiting for approval, and even though this was only a checking in point, I felt nervous.

It probably had to do with who he was.

Josh led the way to one of the side entrances closest to the senior parking lot. When we got to the double doors, we found the rain splattering off the overhanging roofline, creating a line of dampness on the concrete. Josh lifted his jacket up over his head, peering down at me. "Come closer and you won't get wet."

It took me several seconds to actually put two and two together, but I hastily stepped into the pocket of warmth between his body and jacket. I had to huddle tight to his side to fit under the canopy he'd created, giving me a distinct whiff of what he smelled like. Almost like laundry detergent—maybe it was.

"Ready?"

This was totally a kissable moment. When I looked

up at him, it brought our faces within inches of each other. All I'd need to do was turn a bit more, tilt my head, surge up on my tiptoes. It was a strange thought, knowing that I could be kissing someone if I made one sudden move. Josh's lips were very pink, and the side where he had the dimple curved up in an innocent smile.

Anyone else would've called Josh the safe option, but then again, what was wrong with being safe?

The moment, as fleeting as it was, came and went in an instant, bubble burst by a boy and girl coming out of the double doors. The girl with a long skirt opened up a yellow umbrella, but the boy, decked out in black, merely bent his head against the rain. They walked past us, leaving Josh and me alone once more, but the tension had walked away with them. I merely pressed as close to Josh as I could, giving a nod. "Ready."

"You'll turn left at the next stoplight. It's the fourth house on the right."

Josh made a soft sound. "You and Rachel both live so close to the school. No wonder you bike every day."

I tapped my sneakers together. "I have to find some way to sneak some exercise in."

"We didn't really get much of a chance to talk," he said, flipping on his blinker and slowing for the yellow light. Rachel would've gunned the acceleration for the yellow, and I'd braced myself for Josh to do the same, but was pleasantly surprised when he slowed. *Good driver*, I thought appreciatively. *Good sign*. "Here I was, hoping for a long drive where I could get to know you better."

"You're very honest," I told him, dancing my fingers along my backpack. "Get to know me...like in a friend way?"

Josh nodded. "I never thought it'd be hard to make friends in a school this size. I figured I'd meet *someone*, you know? Except everyone already has their friend groups, and it's like they're not open to adding one more."

Instantly, I understood. There was no hope of infiltrating the Top Tier as a new senior, but even in other cliques, everyone would've already closed ranks around those they knew best. Rachel, Maisie, and I were probably one of those groups. Even including Maisie into Rachel and I's duo had been tough, and that was just freshmen year. But now, senior year, when everyone already had a tight bond with their friend group? "I could see how that'd be hard. Brentwood is known for its cliques."

"Which is probably good for Brentwood Babble." He cast me a sidelong glance as the light flicked green. "Makes it easier to choose which group to talk about."

"I guess."

Josh found my house quickly and easily, pulling into the slanted driveway and pausing a few inches from the garage door. His windshield wipers made a harsh suction noise as they swiped along the glass; now that we weren't moving, they didn't need to be on such a high setting. "Do you want to do something?" Josh asked suddenly, planting his elbow on the center console between us. "We could go see a movie. Or we could watch a movie at my place. My mom is home," he rushed to add, cheeks pinking. "So, I'm not, like, inviting you over for anything weird."

"Weird?" I raised a playful eyebrow. "Weird how?"

That pink flooded into a beet red. "Like...uh, never mind."

I leaned into the seat with a small smirk, grabbing my backpack straps. It was fun to tease him, to see how flushed he could get. "I should check on Rachel. She's been home sick all day."

The windshield wipers made one last squeaking shriek before he turned them off. "Maybe some other time?"

My phone chimed in my backpack's side pocket, and though my fingers itched to snatch it up, I forced them into stillness. It wasn't the quick staccato vibration that I'd programmed for Babble, but the chime I used for a text. "Will your mom be home tomorrow? We could watch a movie then."

"Should be. She's normally home this time of day."

I popped the passenger's side door open and slid out of the low seat, turning to duck my head into the cab. "Tomorrow, then?"

Josh reversed out of my driveway with both hands clutching ten and two on the steering wheel. I hesitated by the edge of the sidewalk, taking the drizzling rain like a champ, and pulled out my cell phone.

Rachel: **KISS HIM!!!**

I looked up, finding the little peeping Tom in her upstairs bedroom window, her face practically plastered against the glass. Even from here, I could see her livid frown and the thumbs-down she gave me.

"There's such a thing as privacy," I said as I let myself into Rachel's bedroom, dropping my damp backpack on the floor. She left her blinds thrown wide, not trying to hide the evidence of her spying at all, even though she'd jumped back into bed. As I stepped over the threshold, I could smell the peppermint scent of her heating pad. "What are you, my paparazzi?"

"I need photos to print out for your wedding," she said with an exaggerated wink, and then fell deeper onto her blankets. "Ugh, I feel like I'm dying. For a girl who never wants kids, this whole monthly thing feels like a sick joke."

"You're lucky your mom lets you stay home."

"Yeah, *lucky*. Where's Reed? I thought he'd drop you off."

I gave her the rundown of how the whole carpooling situation came to be, where Reed said he was going, and the possibility of tomorrow. The *likelihood* of tomorrow. She seemed excited at the prospect of another outing, but wanted to dive in and rehash the first.

"Sooo, yesterday. At Wallflower. What'd you two talk about?"

My brain suddenly emptied, like someone pressed the delete button on the memory of yesterday. All pathways to Wallflower and the conversations we had there came up as dead ends. "I...can't really remember."

"You can't remember? You were there for two hours, weren't you?"

Two whole hours and I was sluggish to recall the information, like the interaction had happened in a dream and not in real life. "We talked about how he came from another school."

"Which one?"

Crap. "It was a private school."

"*Ava.*" Rachel pulled a pillow over her face, her dramatic sigh muffled but audible. "Are you even trying? I mean, if I went on a date with him, I'd be talking about more stuff than school. And I'd *remember it.*"

No kidding. Was something wrong with me? I mean, I could remember topics we'd touched on—school, his relationship past—but why couldn't I remember the actual words? It wasn't like I didn't have a good time. For a first date with a guy who was practically a stranger, I had fun. And here I was, feeling neutral, bizarrely blanking on seventy-five percent of those two hours.

Rachel peeked out underneath her pillow. "Don't you think he's cute?"

"I do," I rushed to say, putting as much emphasis into my voice as I could. "I think he's really cute."

"So?"

So, it's that when I look at him, I think about my kiss with your brother. I dug my fingers into my knees. "There is no 'so.' I had a nice time. We're going to his house to watch a movie tomorrow. That's all."

Rachel peered at me closer, probably analyzing my words, my tone. I hadn't snapped at her, but the tension in my chest came out in my voice, all the thoughts bouncing around enough to drive me crazy.

Without saying anything, I crawled onto Rachel's bed further and dropped onto the pillow beside her, cozying up on the daisy and rainbow duvet. She looped her arm around mine, joining me in staring up at the ceiling, and asked, "How's everything going with your parents?"

"The same, really." Mom's schedule was completely booked this week. Open houses, showings, finance meetings, drinks with clients. Which was a good thing, of course. If she could sell a house, maybe there'd be less of a pinch for money. We were running dangerously low on groceries, so that might've been something to put on my list of to-dos. If I ran out of my sugar O's, I was going to riot. "I'm going to Dad's this weekend." Maybe. He hadn't canceled yet, at least.

Rachel leaned her head against my shoulder, her curls scratching against my cheek. "Do you believe in love, Ava?"

"*That* was a random segue."

"It was a random thought."

I made a soft humming sound under my breath, giving it a dedicated thought. Love. Rachel wasn't a serial dater like Reed, but she'd had a few short-term relationships. Three, maybe four in her whole lifetime. They mostly stemmed from dates to homecoming and holiday flings, not anything long-lasting. I couldn't remember one of them getting the big L word.

My entire life, I'd grown up thinking my parents embodied love. I thought they were in love. I thought they'd always be in love. I'd always thought Rachel's parents would last, too. And yet, life threw curveballs.

"I think I do," I answered finally, the words coming out in a push and pull. Slow, like I wasn't sure they were the truth. "People fall in love all the time, so I think it exists. I just think making it last...that's rare."

"Is that why you're not so worried about your first kiss anymore?"

Among other reasons. "I don't know. I guess maybe. A kiss is different than love, though. Before my parents' marriage fell apart, I would've said I believed in it."

"My dad told my mom that he loved her up until the truth came out," Rachel said, now rendering me silent. "Like, the day before he told her, he bought her a cake for her half birthday. Her *half birthday*. Who celebrates that?"

I didn't say it, but I thought, *someone with a guilty conscience.*

"But it was all a lie, you know? He'd been with that —" her voice hitched. "—horrible woman for a year at that point. *A year*. We went on family vacations in that year, and he lied through all of it. And they're not even together anymore. He threw everything away for something that didn't last."

My eyebrows drew together. "How do you know they're not together anymore?"

She coughed. "Social media stalking, duh."

I leaned my head against hers and reached over to pat her hand, striving for any sort of comforting gesture. "To be fair, not every relationship is like that. My parents—"

"You don't know what it's like," Rachel said, and suddenly sat up to stare down at me. Her curls were mussed and her gaze was fiery, looking like a lion in her cluttered bedroom, but her expression lacked the anger her words held. Her eyes were wide, glassy, like they were about to fill with tears. "Your dad didn't cheat on your mom. You should feel lucky everything is as civil as it is."

I tried to draw in a breath, but it stuck in my throat.

As soon as she finished speaking, it was obvious that the words had come in an emotional rush, that the balloon of feeling had been expanding and expanding until it finally popped. Heat burst through me, pooling in my cheeks, a buzzing bundle of emotions stirring in my chest. I couldn't pinpoint a single one, but the sensations of them all made me sick. "I—I know that."

The tension in Rachel eased ever so slightly, and she turned her face away from me. "Sorry. I'm sorry. I just don't feel good."

I sat up too, folding my legs over the side of her bed. Her once welcoming and warm bedroom now felt cold, and even with the blinds open, the rain clouds didn't allow a ray of sunshine through. Her rainbow printed duvet seemed less lively, and I felt more so like one of her dolls in the corner—silent, unmoving, only there to witness the world around it. Even though it was silent, Rachel's intense voice rang in my head. *You should feel lucky.*

Rachel pulled her knees underneath her, turning toward me. "Let's talk about something else," she declared, shaking her head as if to shake off the tension. "Want to go watch TV?"

The buzzing feeling still consumed my chest, like bees were hard at work to build a hive in my ribcage. My hands were shaking, trembling, hinting at a balloon of my own threatening to pop. I curled my fingers, desperate to force it all down, put it all at bay. "Sure."

I imagined my feelings like one large filing cabinet. Whenever something bothered me, I took that piece of emotion and filed it away. The only issue was that now the drawers had a hard time closing, too full of things unresolved. But who could I share them with? My parents' divorce was too touchy of a subject with Rachel, and my parents were too busy with their own lives to listen. And the kiss...my thoughts about Reed...I couldn't talk to anyone about that. I'd have to take it to my grave.

I rested my head on the arm of the Manning's living room couch, viewing the TV from the slanted angle. My fingers still quivered as I pressed them underneath my cheek, and I hoped it'd die down soon.

I woke up to the familiar staccato vibration of a Brentwood Babble submission coming in rapid succession. At first, I ignored it, wanting to sink further into the heat that bundled my body. The fact waded slowly into the fogginess of my brain, the impromptu mid-afternoon nap leaving me disoriented. I couldn't even remember what day it was, and it took me several moments upon opening my eyes to remember *where* I was.

Until I looked around. One of the Manning's blankets had been thrown across me, creating that cocoon of warmth. Rachel was no longer in the chair she'd sat down in, nowhere to be seen, but Reed lounged on the other end of the couch.

And my legs were across his lap.

One hand held the remote, and his other laid on my shin. All of him looked totally comfortable with the predicament. Through the blanket, I could feel each of his fingers, could feel where the backs of my calves rested on his thighs.

My stomach flipped over like a boiling pot of water, and heat rushed through me.

Reed noticed me stirring, glancing away from the TV. He'd changed the channel from our Netflix show to watch a football game. "Well, good afternoon, sleepy-head. I was wondering if your phone would wake you up. It's been going off for a few minutes."

"I—I didn't mean to fall asleep," I said, or whispered really, because the air seemed really thin. "Where's Rachel?"

"In the kitchen talking to Mom."

She was one room away, could walk in at any second and see us doing...*this*. And maybe it wasn't weird, maybe it was totally normal and my twisted brain made it more than it needed to be, but panic sank its teeth into me. Like if she saw my feet in her brother's lap, she'd somehow find the truth about everything.

When I tried to pull my legs away, Reed held fast, settling deeper against the couch. "You're warm, you know."

"*Reed.*"

He patted my shin and lowered his voice. "Rachel was in here when I sat down. It's fine."

When he sat down. So...what? Had he sat down and I shifted my legs onto his lap? Or had he been the one to pull them there? My phone vibrated again. I patted the couch cushions but came up empty. "What time is it?"

"About five-thirty."

Jeez, so that meant my little "shut-eye" turned into a nap an hour and fifteen minutes long. "There goes getting into bed by a decent time," I groaned, giving up on my cell phone search and slumping against the couch arm. "You weren't at Landon's for very long."

"He and his new girlfriend had plans." Reed tilted his head and gave me his sole focus, those brown eyes searching my face. Even though the kitchen was a few rooms away, I could hear Rachel's voice, could hear the low mumble of Mrs. Manning's reply, but they were both background sounds. Everything else seemed blurry under Reed's stare. "Your hand left an imprint on your cheek."

Spell broken. "Great." I reached up and fiddled with one of my space buns, pulling out bobby pins. "I'm sure my hair looks crazy, too."

"I think it looks cute."

I forced myself to take a deep breath and not to over-think it. Instead, I made a neat little bobby pin pile in my lap, unwinding the hair I'd twisted into the bun and letting it loose. It had an awkward kink in it, not some beautiful curl like the movies, but the sensation of letting my hair down after a whole day of it being up made me sigh. So much better.

"How was the library with Kissable Josh?" Reed asked, tracing his fingers over my shin, making a path in the fuzzy blanket.

I pressed my palms over my ears, unable to fight the outward cringe. "Please stop calling him that."

"What should I call him, then?" He pinched my calf lightly. "Dimples?"

I leaned forward and squeezed his forearm. "*Stop,*" I

told him, but it was through a burst of laughter. "Oh my gosh, stop."

"He really only has one dimple, doesn't he? So, he'd be *Dimple*. You could call him blue eyes. *That's* super romantic."

Without thinking, I put my hand over his mouth. My world became a moment of fracturing seconds of his soft lips against my skin and my fingers on his cheek. His brown eyes were all melty and totally latched onto mine, and they were all I could see. My breath hitched in my throat, and I dropped my hand as if it burned. It didn't take away the sensation—it was like his lips branded onto my palm.

I tried to pull away again, ready to bolt, but Reed locked onto my legs once more. Refusing to let me move, refusing to let me go. The tumbling sensation in my stomach came again, stronger this time. I wanted to lean closer, to put my hand over his mouth once more, to put my lips there. The fierceness of that longing almost made it hard to breathe, especially when Reed Manning looked at me like *that*. Like he wasn't Rachel's brother, like he wasn't going to ask some other girl to homecoming, like I wasn't planning to kiss another boy.

Reed's fingers on my leg moved slow as they curled around my calf, and my mind went into overdrive imagining how it would've felt if the blanket hadn't been such a cruel barrier

"Oh, you woke up?" Rachel sauntered into the living room like a cool breeze chasing away the summery warmth. This time, when I jerked my legs away, Reed let them go. "I couldn't believe how fast you fell asleep. It was barely ten minutes into the episode."

My heart trampled like a racehorse in my chest, but I scrubbed my fingers through my hair, desperate to play it cool. "I've been really tired lately."

Somewhere in the unknown, my cell buzzed again. I pulled up the couch cushion, searching between the cracks, when I found it. It'd fallen between the arm and the sofa structure, and the glowing screen of notifications illuminated its position. Brentwood Babble notifications piled up, filled with exclamation points and caps-lock. "Whoa."

"What?" Rachel wedged herself into the cushion between Reed and me, tilting her head to see my cell. "Something with Babble?"

"You two and that site," Reed muttered, swiping the remote to turn up the volume. "I swear."

"You're jealous no one talks about you," Rachel quipped. "Reed Manning is fading into nothingness."

"Thank God."

Once my inbox loaded, I nearly dropped my phone at the first submission.

CONNOR WAS CAUGHT HOOKING UP WITH SOMEONE OTHER THAN JADE!

"*What!*" Rachel screeched, the sound piercing in my ear. On the other side of her, Reed jumped a mile, the remote clattering to the floor so hard that the batteries popped out. "He moved on already? What the heck! I didn't even get a chance!"

As I scrolled through my inbox, I quickly discovered that the flood of staccato pings were all relating to that topic. Tips and submissions about Connor Bray weren't anything out of the ordinary—people sometimes even sent things in regarding what energy drink flavor he was trying that day—but this...this was huge.

"Fine, I'll bite." Reed sighed, glancing over. "Who moved onto who?"

"Connor was caught in the hookup closet," I said, scrolling through the paragraphs of misspellings and fangirling. "Apparently, he left and then some girl walked out a few minutes later."

"Is there a photo?" Rachel pulled my cell from my hand then, scrolling through the submissions. "Darn, no photo. But someone said she had brown hair. You think it could've been Kirsten Oldham?"

Reed rolled his eyes. "Do you know how much of Brentwood High has brown hair, Rachel? You have brown hair. Maisie has brown hair. Practically 80% of people at school have brown hair."

Rachel gave a little sigh as she passed me my phone. "I wish it was me. How come you haven't put in a good word for me, Reed?"

I scrolled through the submissions quickly, watching as they devolved into "*I heard Connor was caught in the closet!*" and "*Someone told me about Connor!*" Which was a bad sign for me. If people were spreading rumors and information outside of Babble, my relevancy? *Poof.* Gone.

The idea had me scrambling up from the couch. "I have to get on this before it spreads any further."

"Find out the truth for me, though," Rachel said as she plopped into her chair, trying to snatch the remote away from Reed. "I'm going to be really sad if someone already beat me into winning Connor Bray over."

As I started upstairs to grab my backpack, I called to her with absolute certainty, "Not that you'd really want to go toe to toe with Jade Dyer!"

Brentwood Babble was one thing that stayed consistent when everything in my life was upending in turmoil. The familiar blue and gold color scheme of the dashboard screamed of countless hours of researching how HTML worked and painstaking patience to get everything perfect. There was only the main blog as well as a search bar, and a landing page for returning users to login to submit new tips and comment.

At the top of the page, navy paw prints worked their way across the header, with *Babble* scripted across them in glittering gold.

With the blog page loaded, I opened up a new thread, cracking my fingers once before setting to work.

Jannor On the Rocks?! Connor Bray already moving on to someone new?

My sources tell me that Connor was allegedly caught in the equipment closet after school today, and he wasn't alone. Though no one caught a glimpse of his closetmate, his girlfriend, Jade, was at practice when this occurred. What do you think? Is Jannor officially over? Is Connor Bray a cheater? Say it isn't so!

Let me know in the comments below: who do you think could've captured Connor Bray's attention, and his heart?!

I sat back against my headboard, stretching my toes in front of me. I didn't usually have so much trouble writing Babble posts, not for the most part. Normally, the lines flowed because I could practically imagine how people would react. But writing this one felt...different. I'd been meticulously working my way through the article, writing and rewriting dozens of times. When I glimpsed out of my bedroom window, I found the sun already dimming in the sky. I'd been at this a while.

Without allowing myself to overthink, I copy and

pasted the article and sent it to Maisie for proofing. I normally wouldn't have had her proofread relationship-related posts, but this one was major. Probably the most important one Babble had seen in a while, aside from the Most Likely Tos. It needed one more set of eyes.

I set down my phone and rubbed my hands across my forehead, trying to ignore the building tension in my chest. Almost like someone was gradually squeezing my heart tighter and tighter.

With my eyes closed, I pictured the moment on the Manning's couch. My legs in Reed's lap, his hands on my shins. My palm over his mouth.

I lowered my palm from my forehead to press against my own lips. *Pathetic.*

My cell split the silence in my room, and if my heart wasn't already beating fast, it would've frantically skipped a beat then. I pulled it out of my pocket and eyed the screen before answering. "Was the article riddled with mistakes? Or are you calling because you don't have time to proof it?"

I tried to interject levity into my voice, but there was no missing the nervousness in Maisie's. "Y-You know, it's kind of an invasion of privacy, isn't it? The whole article, I mean. That's why I'm calling. Like...who really cares who Connor was spotted with?"

I couldn't help but chuckle as I stretched up from my bed. "I love you, but I totally get that the gossipy stuff isn't your thing. I just can't believe he'd move on so quickly, can you? This is big news, Maisie. Like, imagine if the world discovered that 2+2=5 instead of 4."

I paced back and forth across my shag rug as I spoke, lulled by the movement. It wasn't enough to fully dismiss the anxiety, but enough that I had something else to focus on, at least for a moment.

Until Maisie drew in a breath. "Ava, writing an article like this without proof would be horrible. What if it's not true? You know how the gossip mill at school works. An article like this could really hurt him."

My pacing stopped right in front of my window, stomach tensing as if she'd dealt me a blow. Her objection to it felt like sandpaper scratching across my skin. Rachel had called me her little paparazzi, and Reed wielded the nickname with sarcasm, but I could never be a writer for a tabloid. Petty gossip was fun, but Maisie was right—this was too big to post without proof.

It might not have been something I'd have thought about before the list. I didn't even think of it now, but even if Maisie had pointed it out before, I might not have done a full-stop. But this was post-Most Likely Tos. This was after I knew how it actually felt to be gossiped about.

My insides deflated like someone had let go of the opening of my balloon.

My train of thought started zooming down a different track. How many times had I posted something without proof? Had it ever hurt anyone? Embarrassed them? Once more, my stomach cramped as unease tore through me.

Against my ear, my phone gave a soft chime with a new text message, and I pulled it away, pausing the white static on Maisie's end to read it.

Reed: **I forgot to ask earlier. DYHYFKY?**

I nearly dropped my phone, but halted in the process of wearing a path on the floor. "Hey, I have to go. My—uh—mom got home. I'll see you tomorrow."

I pulled my phone away before Maisie had a chance to say goodbye, drawing in a deep breath as I sat down on the edge of my bed. The ground was way too unsteady to stay standing.

Me: **Am I supposed to know what that means?**

Reed: **Did You Have Your First Kiss Yet? It's a well-known acronym. Maybe you should brush up on your internet slang ;)**

Was it stupid that, despite my bleak mood, a freaking winky face lifted my spirits? Probably.

Me: **Oh, yes, silly me to have forgotten DYHYFKY. Should I even call myself an internet blogger? I guess I have much to learn from you**

Reed: **You've already learned one thing**

The hands holding my phone faltered, fluttering thumbs coming to a full stop as I read and reread Reed's message one, two, twenty times. *Surely, he's not talking about the kiss. He's probably talking about something totally, totally normal and I'm zeroing in on that one thing.*

That really amazing one thing.

> Reed: **Sooo...is my caterpillar a butterfly yet?**

> Me: **Someone's a nosy Ned. I didn't ask you when your first kiss with Cindy was**
> **And I don't want to know**

> Reed: **What can I say? I'm emotion- ally invested.**

> **And I'm not the type to kiss and tell. Not sure if you knew**

I bit down hard on my lower lip. I was playing with fire—I knew that from how flushed my cheeks were feeling—but I couldn't bring myself to step away from the flames. This flutter in my chest... The kiss had sparked it all, and now I was addicted to the way it felt.

If only I could feel it with someone other than Reed. That sobering thought doused a bit of the heat, splin- tering the magical feeling. The flutter in my chest dulled.

And then my phone lit up again, this time with an incoming call. *Reed.*

"Hello?" I whispered into the phone, like a teenager afraid of being caught talking to a boy past curfew. Which was ridiculous.

"Why are you whispering?"

"No reason." I cleared my throat, but the ache didn't dissolve. "Your, uh—your voice sounds different on the phone." The lilting tilt to his vowels, the soft way he ended a sentence. It made my skin shiver. *It sounds so different directly in my ear.*

"Really? Yours sounds the same. What does my phone voice sound like? Super macho and mysterious?"

"High-pitched and crackly."

He made an offended noise, but didn't try to quip back. "Did you finish your article yet?"

Reed asking about Babble had my guard up, since I knew his stance on the site. But, too, after Maisie's call, the article would most likely go into the trash icon. "Why? Got any insider info for me?"

"You wish." He paused then, but I could hear him draw in a breath. "Are you in your room?"

"Yeah. Why?"

"Go to your window."

I had been expecting to see something on the lawn, maybe, or even something on the windowsill itself. Something to explain why Reed wanted me to stand there. And once I parted the curtains, I spotted the house across the street with its lights on. One specific light in particular that was in a bedroom upstairs, the room beside

Rachel's. And, like the subject in a painting, Reed stood in plain view.

The sun was quickly setting, casting a warm glow on our street. The lawn stretching between Reed and me felt more like inches instead of so many feet; I could see his expression so clearly. A slight tilt to his lips, eyebrows raised.

"I feel like we're in a music video." Reed started casting glances around his bedroom, ducking his head out of the window for a second. "Should I hold up a sign?"

There was something about watching his lips move but hearing his voice directly in my ear, as if he were leaning into whisper himself. Goosebumps crawled along my skin. "Wow, was that a Taylor Swift reference? I'm proud."

Reed ducked his head for a second, but when he tilted his chin back up, he gave me the world's most brilliant smile. One that rivaled the brightness of the setting sun.

There it was again. Playing with fire. Juggling it like I knew what I was doing. Like getting burned wouldn't be a bad thing. Because at any moment, Rachel could look out the window or could walk into Reed's room or my mom could pull into the driveway.

At any moment, he could pull away from me, just like he always did with everyone else.

This wasn't a game to him—for it to be a game, he'd have to be playing. We'd both made it clear that the kiss meant nothing, but in moments like this, gazing at him across the yard, caught in a universe of him and me, it was impossible to keep the lie. Reality was cruel, and quickly set in.

"I'm going to Josh's tomorrow," I told Reed, pinching my curtain tightly, the sheer material grating underneath my fingertips. "We're going to watch a movie."

"Oh, yeah? What movie?"

I wasn't sure what I'd hoped his voice would sound like, but I hadn't been hoping for the nonchalant tone. "I don't know yet. But maybe...maybe then I'll kiss him."

"There's really no rush anymore, right?" Reed asked, but his tone became more serious. "Do it when *you* want to. When it feels right."

When it feels right. Like how kissing *him* felt right? With his hands on my waist and my hands in his hair? His bare collarbone, sharp and protruding through his skin, but so delicate to the touch? *That* kind of, right?

"Do you think I should've waited?" My voice dropped to a whisper. "To have my first kiss, I mean. With someone...else?"

Reed barely moved across the street, almost like time had frozen. So many feet separated us, but it was almost as if we stood right in front of each other. Yesterday, with him in my bedroom, tiptoeing that dangerous line had been thrilling. Now, looking at him this way, it felt *scary*. A part of me wanted to hang up before he answered.

"Honestly?" It was only one word, but it gave so many things away. His hesitancy. The way the word pitched up at the end hinted at the uncertainty. "In a selfish way...I liked being your first kiss. That I was the first person to know you that way."

I was dead. Totally dead, and someone was pressing paddles to my chest and shouting *clear!* Tingles tore through my body, potent as electricity, enough that I nearly dropped the phone.

Maybe I was looking into his response more than I should have. Maybe I wanted it to mean more than it did. All I knew was that here I was—struck with the reality that despite my best efforts, this boy had my butterflies at his beck and call. And it terrified me. "Reed—"

"Rachel's coming upstairs." His words were a quick rush as he turned away from the window. I hadn't even had a chance to see his expression. "See you at school."

And with that abrupt goodbye, the connection between us ended, illustrated even further by his curtains swinging shut. Even with him gone, I stood in the window for a moment longer, unable to pull my cell from my ear, if only to prolong the illusion of him about to say something else.

Don't play with fire, my thoughts murmured, a sympathetic voice in this self-destruction. My phone chimed, and before my heart could skip a beat, I saw that it was from Maisie. *Don't get burned.*

I already knew that it might've been too late.

"So, my mom actually has a doctor's appointment today," Josh said as he let us into his house, glancing quickly over at me. "But I told my sister about today, and she said she'll be home. I don't want you thinking I was trying to trick you or anything. I want you to be comfortable."

Josh's level of overthinking almost rivaled mine. It nearly made me laugh. "It's fine either way. Really."

Since I was going to Josh's after last period, and maneuvering my bike into the back of his car would be tricky, I'd opted to walk to school today instead of catching a ride with Rachel and Reed. It seemed like the safer, wiser choice. Once school had gotten out, Josh waited for me by my locker, twirling his car keys.

"Have you thought about what kind of movie you're in the mood for?" he asked, shutting the side door behind us. "Comedy? Horror? Rom-coms?"

"You watch rom-coms?"

"Hey, I have a varied taste."

This time, I did laugh as I took residency on the L-shaped couch, right in the corner seat. It swallowed me like a hug. "Surprise me."

"Got it. Popcorn?"

"Of course. Do you have extra butter?"

Josh's dimple deepened further. "I'm not a monster."

As he ducked into the hallway, I was once again struck by how easy things felt with him. Comfortable. Like we were friends—had been friends—for a while. It seemed like a good sign. The level of familiarity took away any tension that might've lingered from going to someone's house for the first time. As I settled deeper into the couch, pulling a throw pillow into my lap, I felt perfectly content.

Josh's house was pretty clean, but looked well-loved. Nothing looked brand new, but everything had that homey feel about it. It made me think about the overdue bills Mom had. Of course, we wouldn't lose our house—I was sure Dad wouldn't let us dig that deep of a hole, despite not helping financially—but I struggled to push down the *what if* thoughts. What if Mom did sell the house? All of our lived-in furniture would be dragged out piece after piece. The bones of that homey feel would be transported to a new house, but there'd be no duplicating the comfort of Walnut Street. The memories I'd been building there for the last seventeen years would be handed over to a new owner who wouldn't cherish them like I did. They'd paint over those memories, knock them down, renovate them until nothing old remained.

I shoved my hands underneath my legs, forcing the trembling to a standstill.

With the scent of buttery goodness in the air, Josh hurried back into the room. He sat down on the cushion to the right of me, creating a wave of movement along the old sofa springs, a large ornate bowl of popcorn cradled in his arms. He tipped it toward me, giving me easy access. "Thanks," I told him, grabbing a handful.

"Can't have a movie without popcorn."

Josh shifted close enough for me to burst into hyper-awareness. His face was angled at the TV, but it gave me a clear view of his profile. His nose was smaller than Reed's, lips fuller, and the cheek that I could see was the dimpled one. When I'd kissed Reed, my fingertips had brushed his jawline. How would it feel to touch Josh there? To be close to him that way?

The corner of Josh's mouth suddenly tipped upward. "Do I have something on my face?"

My cheeks burned hot. "N-No."

"Ah. Just admiring then?"

"Honest *and* full of it," I said with an eye roll, but his teasing attitude loosened a bit of my tension. "I was thinking."

"About?"

There was something about the openness of his expression that nearly had me being honest, if only to see what his reaction would be. *I was thinking about kissing you.* "Well—"

The side door Josh and I had walked in from shuddered open, making me jump. A girl hiked up from the little steps that led out into the garage, and she shrugged her backpack straps off. It took me several embarrassing moments to realize who I was staring at.

Cindy LaVore.

"Oh, hey," she greeted, stepping away from the door without shutting it. Her curls were pulled off her face by an elastic today, a bright pink one that I caught a glimpse of as she bent to unlace her shoes. Even coming from a seven-hour school day, she looked pretty. I usually looked like I'd gotten hit by one of the buses. "I didn't realize you guys were here already."

She's not surprised to see me, I thought, even as I gaped at her like a fish out of water. *There's no way—no way—that she's—*

Josh's voice cut through my stuttering thoughts. "Great, you're home. Ava, have you met my step-sister, Cindy? I know Brentwood's a big school."

"We've met," Cindy answered quickly, offering me a smile. It did nothing to soothe me now. *Cindy* was Josh's sister. It made sense, then, why Reed and Josh acted as if they knew each other, even a little bit. Because Reed was hanging out with Josh's sister.

More than just "hanging out." They were going to homecoming together. Despite Reed's denial about the other day, they'd probably kissed at least once. Maybe even more times. *Don't think about it.*

"Hey!" Cindy turned toward the side door and raised her voice. "You coming? You're letting out the AC."

"Coming," a familiar voice answered, and my blood turned to ice.

Oh, heck no. No way. I forced my attention to the

black TV, staring at my reflection inside it. It wasn't just mine that I could see—Josh sat beside me, his head turned toward where Cindy stood at the edge of the couch, and the reflection clearly showed another person walking into the frame.

"Hey, Paparazzi," Reed greeted, coming up to the couch and stepping into view. "Fancy seeing you here."

I wasn't sure whether to feel annoyed or alarmed.

"Sit down, guys," Josh said cheerfully. "I made popcorn. Do you want your own bowl?"

Alarmed. Definitely alarmed.

By way of an answer, Reed sat down on my left side, on the side that faced the TV straight-on. He was so close that not even my backpack would've fit between us. "I'm down for popcorn," he said, reaching across me to grab a handful of popcorn from the bowl Josh had brought out for us. "There's enough to share, right?"

"I'll grab us a bowl from the kitchen," Cindy said, and Josh stood up, too.

"I'll just make another bag," he said, tapping me quick on the shoulder. "I'll be back."

And that left Reed and me in the homey living room with the TV reflecting back at us. Reed grabbed another handful from the bowl in my lap, and when I smacked it away, kernels went flying. "Are you serious?" I hissed.

"Hey! Don't waste the extra butter!"

"What are you doing here?" I held the popcorn away from him, glaring. "You're—you're interrupting."

Reed tilted his head in that annoying way of his. "What, exactly, am I interrupting again?"

"*Reed.*"

He popped a piece into his mouth, awaiting my reply with a smirk.

I gritted my teeth in frustration, because any second now, my voice would pitch high enough that it'd definitely be audible from the kitchen. It didn't matter, anyway. Cindy came back into the living room with a bag of shareable M&M's. "He'll bring in the bowl when it's done," she said, sitting opposite of Reed. Without hesitation, she laid her legs across Reed's lap, sinking low into the couch and getting easily comfortable. "We can watch whatever, but if it's a superhero movie, count me out."

The déjà vu of the moment hit me with the weight of a freight train. I wondered if Reed's mind took the same route that mine was—yesterday, we'd been in that exact position. My legs in his lap, his hands tracing patterns on the blanket covering my shins. If I concentrated, I could almost remember what that fingertip felt like, how something so silly and small could take my breath away.

Except there was no blanket on Cindy's legs—his fingers were on her skin.

It also made me remember how I'd pressed my palm to his mouth, to his lips. My hands now were fisted in my lap, containing the emotions inside me.

After coming back into the room, Josh loaded one of the streaming sites and picked a movie easily, tilting the popcorn bowl closer to me for easier access. "Don't fall asleep," he warned with a glint to his eye.

Yeah, with Reed at one side, inches away, and Josh on the other? "No chance of that."

As the movie opened, my phone gave a soft buzz in my pocket.

Ava,

Oh, wow, what an improvement already!

I noticed that the images in the About Me section are sized a bit differently than previously. Can you make my image a little larger than the rest? I do own the company —might as well stand out when possible, ha-ha! But overall, so far, I'm very impressed with your work. I know my employees will also love it.

I did have a question for you—I noticed Reed didn't play the game last Friday. Do you know anything about that? I know school has just started, but I hope the twins are enjoying their senior year. How is Reed feeling about it so far? Do you know?

I look forward to your response!

All the best,

Jacob Manning

I swallowed hard as I read through the last paragraph. Again, he brought it back to Reed. In a way that asked for more detail than before, too.

I made my bed, though. I knew why I did this. Even if he'd ask about them, I needed this gig. The money for Mom. The recommendation on college applications.

I glanced over at Reed, whose profile was in broad view as he focused on the TV. After what he told me about his father forcing him to play football, Mr. Manning's question about Reed not playing seemed to weigh heavier.

Reed caught me looking from the corner of his eye, and he raised his eyebrows at me, almost like a *what's up?*

"The movie's starting," Josh whispered to me, as if we were at an actual theater instead of sitting on his living room couch. He drew my attention off of Reed and to the screen.

"Sorry," I mumbled, locking my phone and sliding it once more into my pocket. Even though my thoughts were elsewhere, there was no forgetting the email, and there was no forgetting the boy beside me.

Over the hour and forty-five-minute film, it became increasingly hard to pay attention. Cindy had scrolled through her phone the entire time, text chime after text chime cutting in between the action scenes. Josh tapped his fingers on the ceramic bowl throughout the movie, even after the popcorn was all gone. And Reed—halfway through the film, he'd draped his arm on the back of the couch, and it was a constant fight to *not* lean backward and touch my neck to his forearm.

By the time the credits rolled, I felt wound tight, a rubber band about to snap.

"I should probably head out," Reed announced to no one in particular, pulling his arm back. "I've got a mountain of math homework."

"Maybe your sister's friend can help you," Cindy replied as we all got to our feet, pocketing her cell. "Hey, Ava, I meant to ask you—how come you didn't post that Connor thing yesterday?" She folded her arms across her chest and blinked innocently, but the action itself reminded me too much of the Top Tier, especially Jade. "A few of the girls in my homeroom were talking about it. I was waiting for you to cover it on Babble."

For some reason, the question caused a burst of anxiety to bubble within me, and maybe it was because I was suddenly aware of everyone looking at me. "It'd already spread around school without Babble," I told Cindy. "It was kind of old news when I got to it."

I could've been honest, that I wasn't comfortable posting without proof, but I was afraid that'd introduce us down a new rabbit hole. *Have you ever needed concrete proof before?*

"Do you know who it was?" Cindy leaned closer. "The girl caught with Connor, I mean."

"No one named names."

"Yeah, but do you have any ideas? Has there been any tips before involving him and someone else?"

Her words had me hesitating. Absolutely nothing had come in about Connor with someone else before yesterday, which was odd. No photos, no rumors, nothing. Him hooking up with someone else wasn't just out of character—it was way out of left field.

"Cindy," Josh groaned. "Lay off with the gossip. Don't turn into one of those people."

"Don't be rude," she snapped, glaring at him. "*She's* one of those people."

I wasn't sure the atmosphere could get any more awkward. Truly. The tips of Josh's ears were consumed with red, as obvious as a shout. *One of those people.* For the first time since starting Babble, I felt embarrassed.

I took advantage of the lull in conversation. "Can I hitch a ride with you?" I asked Reed, picking up my backpack where I'd left it against the wall. "That way Josh doesn't have to drive all the way into town."

Reed gave me a nod, and we made our way to the garage. They'd left the garage door open, and as soon as I stepped down onto the concrete floor, I could see where Reed had parked in their sloping driveway.

Cindy wrapped her arms around Reed's neck and pulled him in close, and before I had a chance to turn away, I could see how firmly they pressed together. She was touchy-feely, but then again, could I really blame her?

As she coasted her hand up his back, I realized yes, yes, I could.

Josh slid his hands into his pockets and hovered on the threshold of the side door, tapping his socked feet. "Well, uh...I'll see you at school tomorrow?"

This was the moment I'd been prepping for, coming to pass in an almost ironic way. Josh was looking down at me a little tense, on the balls of his feet as if he were thinking the same as me. As if at any moment, one of us was going to lean in for a quick goodbye kiss. A quick *close your eyes and pucker your lips* of a moment.

But Reed was already pulling back from Cindy and she was pressing her mouth against his, and every past instance where I'd dodged kisses came rushing to the forefront of my mind. Like when Levi Trevino tried kissing me after a basketball game last year, and I leaned away at the last second. Or in the ninth grade, when Michael Christianson leaned in during a slow song and I ended up stomping on his foot. Even all the way back to Cameron. The fluttery, anticipatory moment had risen several times, but I could never follow through.

Except only once.

I stepped backward from Josh, heart racing as if I were about to pass out. "I'll see you tomorrow."

By the time I settled into the passenger's seat of the Manning Twins' shared car, my brain ran a mile a minute, flooded with unease and anger and relief and all the emotions in between. I didn't kiss Josh, but Reed kissed Cindy, and the whirlwind of *something* tasted bitter in my mouth.

Not betrayal. Not jealousy. Definitely not either of those.

There was no ignoring the tip of a dagger pressing into my chest, though, not when the pain was so piercing. Not when my fingers still trembled where they were pinned underneath my thighs.

It wasn't until we were down the road that the ticking timebomb finally detonated, and I snapped. "It wasn't cool that you showed."

Reed glanced over as if to confirm that, yes, my glacial tone had been directed at him. "What do you mean? I was invited, same as you."

"But you knew I'd be there. What I was there trying to do."

"You mean kiss Josh?" Reed pulled his visor down, glaring into the sun. "You still could've, Paparazzi."

"Not with an audience! I'm not like *some people* who are so willy-nilly with their kisses."

"She kissed me, for the record—"

"Oh, like you would've objected if she'd asked! You don't object if anyone asks, right?"

"Which part are you mad at? The fact that I showed up or the fact that I kissed Cindy?"

I swallowed my answer, swallowed the truth, because his question was a strike-anywhere match, nearly producing a flame. "Why didn't you tell me that Cindy was Josh's sister, anyway? Don't you think someone should've told me that?"

"They're step-siblings, first of all. Second, I didn't even know Josh existed until he transferred this year. I only just found out myself."

But even then, that gave him so much time to have said *something*. And it didn't answer my whole question. "Does Rachel know?"

"I told you, twin-telepathy isn't a thing. I don't know what she knows."

I tugged my hands through my hair, fingers getting knotted up in the dyed and split ends. "Cindy inviting you—is that the only reason you came?"

Reed squeezed the steering wheel, not looking over. "What other reason would there be?"

He was everywhere, a looming figure that just when I'd stopped thinking about him, he'd pop up. Stealing my attention and scrambling my thoughts. I'd seen more of him in the past two weeks than I had in years. Maybe I was more aware of him now, but there was no ignoring him, not when he wasn't ignoring me.

"Is that why you were pushing me to get closer to Josh?" I asked Reed, turning to face his profile. He had his jaw clenched, eyes squinting at the brightness. "Because you were trying to pawn me off on your girl-friend's little brother? Because you were worried I was still thinking about what happened with us?" My words came in an undammed flow, like someone had shattered a glass fish tank, the shards biting as water poured out. As soon as I'd said it, too, I realized how true it rang. "So, I'd forget about our kiss?"

Reed drew in a slow breath, shoulders rising and falling with the soft sigh. He started braking for a stop sign, and when he spoke, his voice sounded completely normal, as if it were an honest question. "What kiss?"

The Reed in this car was nothing like the Reed from last night, smiling at me from his bedroom window across the street, sending me semi-flirty texts. It was like they were two different people.

"I can't believe I wasted my first kiss on you," I muttered, and yeah, it was petty, but being petty was the only way I could keep from melting into a puddle of absolute mortification.

"If I'm remembering correctly, *you* were the one who asked *me*."

"Yeah, and *I* was ready to walk away." And it was *his* hand that caught me around the elbow. *So, after that pep talk, you're not going to follow through?* "You should've let me. But you wanted to be *selfish*." The word he'd used last night took on a different meaning now.

Reed frowned, looking so much like the grumpy brother I'd known him as. The one who would roll his eyes when we asked him to play in elementary school, the one who would hog the TV in middle school, the one who pretended we didn't exist in high school. When he spoke, his voice was frigid. "If I'd known it was going to get this complicated, I would've let you walk away. You never should've asked me in the first place."

I let out an abrupt breath and directed my gaze out

the side window, glaring at the scenery passing us by. "You're right," I said finally, clenching the material of my backpack, the dagger in my chest sliding to the hilt. It pierced me through and through, popping the bubble of anger, allowing for a rush of pain. "I shouldn't have."

Normally, football games did a fantastic job at brightening my mood, but as the clock ticked down toward the end of the fourth quarter, I found myself eager to go home. Or really, go to Dad's apartment downtown. He was supposed to pick me up at the end of the fourth quarter, the first time I'd see him in weeks, and I'd *finally* get to see the space he'd been living in. I'd be able to wake up with the coffee maker again.

I felt *exhausted*, like my energy reserves were fully running dry. Distantly, I realized I'd been feeling this way often. So often that I'd almost come to expect it. I used to be the girl who pulled all-nighters binge-watching Netflix dramas, and here I was, ten minutes to ten at night, feeling like I was about to fall asleep standing up.

It wasn't just being sleepy, but a sort of exhaustion that left me absolutely drained.

The game had dragged out as the Haven High Ravens fought tooth and nail for the victory, even though they should've known it was pointless. At this rate, I wouldn't get to Dad's house until after ten, and with my energy levels rivaling a grandma's after nine-thirty, I'd be bolting to bed.

"You look like you're about to fall asleep," Maisie said as she looked over at me, and even though I'd been standing beside her the whole game, it was still a shock to see the blue and gold Bobcats colors adorning her normally anti-school spirit self. She even had a pawprint on her cheek, looking cuter than ever.

"It's been a long day," I said, trying to appear somewhat less zombie-like by blinking my eyes and stiffening my spine. "I didn't really get much sleep last night."

Of course, I hadn't, because how was I supposed to sleep when each time I tried to count sheep jumping over a fence, they turned into little Reed Mannings doing mundane activities, like mowing the lawn, watching a movie, and making my heart race? *What kiss?* And then the not-so-awesome ones that followed. *You never should've asked me in the first place.*

I also couldn't forget that *another* Manning man made things hard. Mr. Manning's email asking about Rachel and Reed had sat in my inbox until Friday after school, where I used homework as an excuse for a late reply. Totally not professional, but he'd started it first.

And I'd closed it out with a simple *happy to be working with you*, not talking about Rachel or Reed at all. He hadn't sent a reply yet, which made me feel icky with nerves. What if I upset him?

Chill out, I told myself sternly, ignoring the building

buzzing sensation in my ears. *Stop stressing about everything. Stop worrying. Focus on the game.*

"Ugh, I can't believe I have to babysit after this," Rachel muttered, and when I turned toward her, her gaze was locked on her cell phone. "At least he *should* be in bed when I get there."

"Babysit?" Maisie echoed. "It's, like, ten o'clock."

"Oh, well, the parents went out of town, and I'm filling in for the day babysitter," Rachel replied quickly. "I have to spend the night there."

"You're getting paid to sleep?" Maisie asked. "I'd love that job."

The crowd behind us erupted as a football player started pressing toward the endzone, students rallying as if their volume would propel the player across the line. The colliding bodies made it hard to read the jersey number, but I thought it might've been number twenty-two. Connor Bray's number. They didn't even need this touchdown, really. We were ahead with a fourteen-point lead with four minutes left on the clock. At this point, running down the timer was a formality.

"I can't believe nothing came of the tips about Connor in that closet," Rachel said loudly, catching the attention of some students around us. "But it looks like him and Jade are still together, doesn't it?"

I hadn't really been paying attention, but I did see the two of them talking near the water bottle station earlier—and they seemed normal. Maisie had been right to talk me out of posting about it. The rumor was nothing but.

"Did you ever get to the bottom of why Reed quit football?" Maisie asked. "Did he ever tell you, Rach?"

"Nope. He tells me to drop it every time I bring it up."

"Weird." Maisie cast a sidelong look at me. "Have *you* heard anything?"

She was only asking because of Babble, not because she had an inkling of Reed and I's super-secret friendship. Not that it really existed in the first place. I gave him comic books. He gave me ulcers. Wasn't really a fair trade.

I had to lie, but no guilt followed; I felt too numb for that. "Haven't heard a thing."

"Homecoming is next week," Rachel said, leaning her head closer to me and giving me a smirk. "You think Josh is going to ask you?"

This year, it seemed like homecoming was approaching way too quickly. It was a busy time of the year with Babble. Submissions had already come in about who asked who to the dance, how they asked, and things like that. Each time there was a dance, I was more overwhelmed with tips than worrying about who I'd go with. "He might," I said, but even as I said it, I found myself shifting uneasily. "Maisie, has Alex asked you?"

Maisie drew in a short breath. "We're dating—does he really need to ask?"

Rachel and I both answered at the same time: "Yes."

Maisie laughed, but there was something about her expression that seemed forced. "I'm fine with how it is, seriously."

"Mom's making Reed bring Cindy to the house for photos," Rachel said, sensing the need for a subject change. "Well, if he mans up and actually asks her. So, if we want pictures, we should do it at one of your houses. And if Josh asks you, you have to tell me, because I'll find a date too."

My cell started ringing, the tone barely heard over the roar of the student section. When I pulled it out of my pocket, my dad's cheery face from the Florida family vacation grinned at me, sunburn and all. "I'll be right back," I told them, hurrying to move away from the noise. The bleachers were filled to the brim, and I had to *excuse me, excuse me* my way through the student section to the stairs. "Hello?"

"Hey, kiddo," Dad greeted, and I relaxed instinctively at his warm tone. "How much longer is left to the game?"

"Only a few minutes, I think." I stood on my tiptoes, but I couldn't see the scoreboard from here. "Have you eaten yet?"

"I have," he began, but the tone of his voice had me stopping my back-and-forth pacing. It'd been the same tone he'd used weeks ago when he announced he was moving out. The same tone he'd used the first time he'd postponed me coming to visit him. He probably would've used the same tone the second time, if he'd called me instead of texted. "Listen, Ava, why don't we meet up tomorrow for breakfast instead of meeting tonight? I'm just feeling so tired, kiddo. I wouldn't make good company."

Digging the toe of my sneaker into the trampled over

grass, I let my other hand dangle at my side, fingers twitching like they wanted to curl into a fist. *How many times does this make?* I wondered distantly, between the ramble of my father's excuses and the football announcer in the background. *How many times has he avoided seeing me?*

"Ava? You there? Did I lose you?"

I let out a soft breath between my teeth. It was okay. Dad being tired was okay—I was tired too. A few minutes ago, I was envisioning the quick tour of Dad's apartment and then falling onto whatever bed he laid out for me for the night. It'd been a long week for me—it'd probably been a long one for him, too. "Y-Yeah, tomorrow would work better for me. Maybe we could meet at the Wall-flower at ten?"

"That sounds great," he said, and if I hadn't known any better, I would've thought he sounded relieved. My stomach tied up in knots. "I'll see you tomorrow, okay? Love you."

"Love you too," I said as the buzzer sounded, signaling the end of the game.

The uneasy feeling didn't disappear even after I lowered my phone, and even though I tried, I couldn't really place *why* I felt edgy. I checked my cell, but I had no text messages, no new Babble submissions. In the middle of the grass behind the bleachers, watching person after person shuffle toward their car, I felt lonely.

This time last week, Reed had been driving Rachel and me home from the away game. I'd given him the comic books. He'd told me about quitting the football team. And now, here I was, not sure if we'd ever talk again. Maybe that was for the best.

Who was I kidding? It *was* for the best. Better to cut ties now before too much got ruined.

Rachel and Maisie came down from the bleachers a few minutes later, and by then, I'd managed to pull on a semblance of a nonchalant expression. If I couldn't tell them the whole truth, no way I was going to bother them with my crap. And in that moment, I wouldn't have been able to take it if Rachel said something about things not being as tough because someone didn't cheat. Fake a smile and let it loose when I got home—that's what I'd do.

We ended up parting our ways quickly, Maisie sticking around to wait for Alex, and Rachel and me heading toward her car.

"You going to tell me what's wrong?" Rachel asked as she eased her seatbelt over her chest, starting the engine. "Because you've been pretty quiet tonight. You didn't do hardly any of the cheers."

"Just tired," I told her, leaning my head against the seat.

The past few times I'd been in the car, Reed had been the one driving, and I'd forgotten how terrible Rachel's driving was. She either slammed on the brakes or the gas pedal, the ride a jerky start-and-stop mingled with the hottest pop station filtering between us.

I sat quiet in the passenger's seat, staring at the glowing dashboard, trying not to remember yesterday in this very same spot. *What kiss?* After that, we'd driven in silence, the kind that was choking instead of comforting.

And now, forced into the spot that I'd been hurting in yesterday, the sensation began to build again. "Can I ask you a hypothetical question?"

"Ooh, fun. Sure."

"How do you know if you like someone or if it's just your hormones?"

Rachel snorted. "You sound like an old lady, blaming feelings on hormones."

"I can't tell."

"Wait, wait, wait." Rachel stepped on the brakes and caused the tires to squeal in protest, jarring me forward against the seatbelt. "You're crushing on someone?"

"It was a hypothetical," I said, rubbing where the belt dug into my neck.

"And I'm hypothetically asking if my best friend has a crush," she replied, foot not easing from the brake. Even in the dim lights, her eyes were two circles of excitement. "Come on, you haven't had a proper crush on someone in *ages*. Give me all the deets!"

I winced a little at the way her voice pitched up at the end, heart already pounding fast. I shouldn't have said anything, but the black hole yawning beneath me had begun to swallow me whole. "That's what I'm saying. I don't know if it is a crush, or..." *Or if it's me fixating on one thing that happened between us.*

A wave of headlights from behind us filled the cab, triggering Rachel to accelerate past the stop sign. "Is it Josh?"

It made sense that her mind went to Josh. "I plead the fifth."

We journeyed the remaining minute from the school to her driveway in utter silence, my best friend processing my hypothetical with a semi-remote expression. Her eyes were wide, but I couldn't glean a single emotion from them. At least until she turned off the car and turned to me.

"You can tell me if it's not Josh." Her brown eyes were wide, and though the cab was dark, her expression was clear. "We're best friends. We tell each other everything."

Was that true, though? It had been at one point, I guess, but now, did it still hold? There was so much I had kept from both Rachel and Maisie the past few weeks, and it was one thing stacking on top of the other. Like each thing was a brick crushing my chest flat, knocking any and all remaining oxygen from my lungs. I couldn't tell them any of that. *I* was the strong friend.

"I kissed him."

"*Josh?*"

"No, it...it wasn't Josh."

Panic chased hot on the heels of my words, and if my brain had feet, it'd be kicking me for opening my mouth. Rachel's reaction was about what I'd expected it to be, gasping and wide-eyed. "Ava! You—you kissed someone? When? Who? How am I finding out about this just now?"

"It was impulsive," I told Rachel, and through the racing pulse roaring in my ears, I could barely hear myself. "I—I did it without thinking. I didn't tell you because I was embarrassed, so please don't ask who it was. I'll tell you...one day. I just...I regret it."

"That's why you got over the whole Most Likely To thing so quickly," Rachel realized, slumping in the seat with her thoughts obviously racing a mile a minute. Then she turned to me. "Was it a bad kiss? Is that why you regret it?"

My experience with kissing was limited—I'd had exactly *one*—but how was I supposed to tell her that it exceeded every single expectation I had built up in my head? Years and years of thinking about my first kiss, and my fantasies never had been able to come close to the reality. But if I told her how good it was, she wouldn't stop until she got the guy's name, age, and street address.

And she'd have a heart attack when she realized how many of those things she had in common with him. *Manning, seventeen, 304 Walnut Street.*

"I liked it more than he did," I said, feeling pathetic as soon as the words were out. "And I hate that I liked it, because I don't think he's thought twice about it."

"Screw him, then," she said simply. "If a guy can't see your worth, he's obviously blind."

Her words were probably meant to be comforting, but there was something shallow about them. They did nothing to burrow in deep and chip away some of the anxiety, and maybe it was because I knew she didn't know the whole story. If she *had* known the whole story, I knew without a doubt she'd be changing her tune. I might've been her best friend, but Reed was her brother.

Blood. If anyone was going to get forgiveness, it would be him.

I regretted saying anything, for drawing any sort of attention to me at all. "It's not that big of a deal," I said, tipping my chin up and drawing in a deep breath. "You're right. That guy's definitely blind."

Now it was my words that felt shallow, hollow. Spoken with little to no conviction, but Rachel bought them, and reached over to squeeze my hand. "Josh isn't blind. He's so into you. Shift your sights from your bummer of a guy onto Josh and things will be much better. Promise."

I wasn't sure what "so into me" looked like, or how Rachel would know, but I didn't ask. I popped open the car door at the same time Rachel did, both of us standing in her ghostly driveway. The streetlamp nearest to us had burnt out, casting the yard in blue-ish shadows.

"I'm going to grab my overnight bag," Rachel said, and then pointed a finger at me over the roof of her car. "Next time, tell me when things are bothering you. I mean it."

With how much I'd been keeping bottled up, the idea of confessing any ounce of it felt impossible. Even still, I nodded.

After waving goodbye, I walked across the dark street with my arms wrapped around my middle. As I stepped onto my driveway, I noticed for the first time that Mom's car was absent from it. I double-checked the garage in case she'd decided to park in there, but it was lacking her sedan. Nerves stirred in me. It was after ten—why wasn't she home yet?

My thoughts launched into overdrive, assuming the worst. Her car was broken down on the side of the road. She'd gotten into an accident and was passed out, unable to make a phone call. One of her showings today had gone crazy and was holding her hostage in the house's basement.

Without letting myself fall into the rabbit hole—too deeply, that is—I pulled my phone out and checked out Friend Finder app. Her little dot popped up, and she was on Main Street, right around the corner.

So *not* currently in a basement being held hostage. Good to know.

I changed out of my Brentwood gear quickly and scrubbed off my makeup, wiping away the black pawprint on my cheek. Before bed, I'd have to hurry and post the score for the game. I was happy that I'd drafted most of the post earlier before the game had actually ended. All I had to do now was put in the final scores as well as Connor's last touchdown. And then—sleep. Blessed, blessed sleep. Hopefully tonight I'd be able to fall into the blissful oblivion without picturing Reed Manning mowing lawn.

After buttoning up my sleep shirt and shrugging on the matching shorts—a blue gingham print that was the cutest thing in the world—I finally let my space buns down from their headache-inducing death grip. My scalp sighed in relief.

But as I swiped up my cell, ready to post the game's

updates, my gaze caught on my bedroom window. My blinds were down—no one was getting a free peep show —but something drew me to them anyway, like a magnet attracting a sliver of metal.

And I honestly wasn't sure what I'd been expecting, because when I pried the blinds apart, there was no one outside. I couldn't stop myself from looking at Reed's bedroom window, but he wasn't standing in the frame of it. His room was dark, like he'd already gone to bed. Doubtful, for eleven o'clock on a Friday night. Maybe, like Rachel had said, he'd snuck out again, disappearing off to who knew where. Maybe he was sneaking off to Cindy's.

I tried to rationalize what harm one text would do.

But then again, what would I say? After yesterday, what was left *to* say?

To distract myself, I went into the kitchen to grab a glass of water. Mom had left a stapled stack of paperwork on the counter, one that I nudged aside so that it wasn't so close to the sink. However, the ink slowly registered, and I scanned the lines.

Pre-Sale Inspection for 305 Walnut Street Brentwood, CT—drywall issues in basement, rotten porch steps (back of house).

It went on further with realtor mumbo-jumbo that didn't quite make sense, but then again, the fact that it was *our* address on this made even less sense. Pre-sale inspection?

I picked up the stapled stack and flipped through it.

There were a few printouts of comp houses in the area, selling prices, and then—*boom*. There was an exterior picture of our house staring back at me, with Mom's handwriting scrawled along the bottom. *Possible listing prices. Updates that will improve cost of home: repair steps, fix drywall, update outdated bath fixtures, new paint. Pre-sale inspection—check. Open house* 10/08.

The shallow breaths I pulled in did nothing to calm my racing thoughts, ones that made me dizzier and dizzier with each passing second. This wasn't happening. There was no way. No way. Mom wouldn't sell our house. Not without talking to me, not without talking to Dad. No way.

But then...why would she schedule an open house for it?

All the repairs, making sure the house was clean—this was why. A reason I was afraid of, but I never believed it would actually happen.

The front door opened, but I didn't fully register it until I heard Mom's shocked voice. "Ava? What are you doing home? I thought you were going to your dad's this weekend."

I whirled around with the stack of papers, chest rising and falling fast. "What's this?"

It was clear Mom had been caught off-guard. With it being so late, she wouldn't be coming from work. No doubt she'd gone out with her friends...again. "Where did you find that?" she asked me.

"You left it out." My voice sounded wavy, like I was

speaking through water. "Tell me you're not selling our house."

Mom looked away from me then, pinching her lips together. "Sweetheart."

"Tell me you're not selling our house," I repeated, firmer in the pronunciation, but my voice seemed to shake. "We've—we've lived here my entire life. We can't just *move*."

"I found a great house over in Jefferson—it's practically a *dream* house, Ava. It's a little smaller, but my God, you have to see it." She put as much excitement into her voice as possible, but even she had to be able to tell that she sounded more desperate than anything. "This is too much house for us, sweetie."

I drew in a sudden breath, swaying as if her bomb-like words jostled the earth too. "You—you didn't even tell me. You didn't even *talk* to me."

There was no missing the dissatisfaction that cracked through her expression. That was the perfect word. *Dissat-isfaction.* Her forehead wasn't wrinkled with sadness and her mouth wasn't twisted with anger. She looked dissatis-fied with my response, like someone had told her that the investment she made ended up losing money. "Ava, like I said, it's the perfect opportunity. The perfect house for us. We can't let this opportunity pass us by."

She wasn't listening to me, but ever since Dad moved out, that had been the new normal. It was like they were acting on autopilot. *Get through the day.* But this? This was *not* autopilot. I'd already had to swallow their marriage breaking up—now they were taking the house too?

I was shaking all over, as if an earthquake was happening only within my body, the epicenter just behind my ribcage. *This is not happening*, I told myself, trying to calm down the storm swallowing me whole. *This is not happening.*

"Rachel lives across the street," I said. I honestly knew that it wouldn't have been the reason she'd change her mind. She wouldn't go "hmm, you're right, Ava, we need to keep you within fifty feet of your bestie" but I hoped it'd at least make her stop and talk to me about it. Have a discussion.

But it didn't. "You can see Rachel every day at school, Ava. And she has a car. She can pick you up and you can still hang out."

No, *Reed* and Rachel had a car. A joint car. And since Reed was Mr. Popular with places to go and girls to see, he called dibs all the time. "Is this about money? About the bills? I've—I've been taking on more website design projects, but I could get an actual part-time job. I could save up some money and pay rent. I'm sure there are places hiring high schoolers—"

"Ava." Mom looked up at me finally, turning those almond eyes to me. Her complexion looked especially washed out in this light, her blonde doing her no favors. It cast a shadow on the perfect image she was desperate to portray. "I'm sorry that this is so sudden. I'm sorry this is upsetting you. This is the way it needs to be."

Flat. No room for debate or negotiation. No room for discussion at all.

It reminded me of the day Dad decided he was moving out. Realistically, he'd probably made the decision weeks earlier, since he already had a new apartment downtown lined up. But they didn't tell me what was happening until I came home from Rachel's to find a suitcase in the hallway with a duffle bag on top of it. It was funny, even though Dad had lived here for the past nineteen years, he could fit his entire life into two bags.

"We've decided on a separation," they'd said. "I'm sorry if this is hard for you, but we've put a lot of thought into it, and this is the way things need to be."

It seemed like Mom and Dad had a catchphrase.

"Nothing's even packed." The kitchen was filled to the brim with knickknacks. Mom's giant China cabinet was still shoved into one corner, more of a dust collector than anything else. The giant oak table was a monster and a half and took up most of the dining room, and Dad had always joked that they'd never move because trying to take the table with them would be a nightmare.

"I have movers coming soon to help with the packing. We'll need to downsize, so you need to go through and make a list of things you want to keep, Ava. Anything else will get donated."

Downsizing. Moving. Divorce. Change, change, change.

"I have to get out of this dress," she said with a little huff, but her voice sounded different. Thicker. She avoided looking at me. "We'll talk about it more tomorrow."

And then she left me and the paperwork in the dark kitchen, thoughts crashing down around me mercilessly. I'd been shoving down all the truths for so long that they reemerged with a vengeance, leaving me neck-deep, threatening to swallow me whole.

A robotic, panic-induced shuffle brought me to my feet, carried me to the hallway and out the front door. I knew I needed to get a grip. *Boo-hoo, Ava Jenson, you have to move houses. Big deal.* I couldn't get my thoughts to calm down. It was always like this. In some distant part of my head, I *knew* I was spiraling, but my body was too concerned with getting myself out of the situation.

I felt the grass between my toes before I even realized I was outside, and then crossing the gritty roadway to help myself onto the Manning's front porch. My hand wrapped around the doorknob, but the deadbolt was unforgiving, creating a loud noise of denial instead of swinging open.

It was a small thing, their door being locked, but I had to bite down even harder on my lip to keep from making a sound. My phone was in my bedroom; I couldn't even call.

Without warning, the yellow door swung inward, revealing a shirtless Reed Manning holding his *Super Mario Bros* mug in his left hand. His eyebrows shot up as he realized who exactly stood over the threshold, probably looking like absolute hell. "Ava?"

I shuddered as I looked up at him, and I was sure the

tear-tracks on my cheeks were plain to see, glistening in the moonlight, but I made no move to wipe them away. There was no point in hiding them now. "Is—is Rachel in her room?"

"She's not home," Reed said, and dang, even his voice was a compassionate reverberation of concern. It nearly loosened the temporary hold I had on my sanity. "She said something about a sleepover."

A sleepover? No, that wasn't right. *Babysitting.* She talked about it at the game. The memory hit me with startling clarity, enough to make me feel a little crazy for having forgotten it. Now that he'd said it, I realized I hadn't walked past their car in the driveway. Rachel was not here, and she would not be here until morning.

Which meant that I was alone until morning. "R-Right," I whispered, taking a step backward. "Okay."

I hadn't even fully turned around before Reed caught at me, fingers easily circling my wrist. His skin was warm against mine, and a grounding handcuff, pulling me to a halt. "Ava," he said, with the same sort of confused, concerned tone. "What's wrong?"

What's wrong, what's wrong, what's wrong. "Nothing."

"Hey." He tugged on my arm with a pinched expression, scanning my face as if at any moment, an answer would break through. "Come inside."

"I—I need to go back," I told him, but didn't try to pull away. "I left my phone."

"Just for a minute, then." His firmness was enough to draw me into the house, which was as dark as it'd been the Monday I'd padded downstairs for a glass of water. The Monday he found me. The door made a solid clicking sound as he shut it, stepping up closer. "Why aren't you wearing shoes?"

I looked down at my feet, no doubt now grass-stained and dirt-covered. "I wanted to talk to Rachel."

"About what?"

I opened my mouth, but as I looked up into Reed's worried brown eyes, my own started to burn with the familiar pressure again. He set his mug down on a side table and pulled me toward the staircase without hesitation, and this time, I had no fight in me.

We ended up in his bedroom, where the TV that hung from his wall showed a paused episode of some sitcom. I'd never been inside his room before, but I'd gotten peeks from when he'd left the door open as we grew up. The layout was similar to Rachel's, minus the knickknacks and creepy dolls. Instead, his room had a few sports posters hanging from the wall, a white desk near the window with what looked like magazines on the surface, and an overflowing laundry hamper beside it.

He reached for the light switch, but I stopped him, catching his wrist. "Can you leave it off?"

"Only if you tell me what's wrong." He ducked his head. "Talk to me."

I stared at his exposed collarbone. "Can you put a shirt on?"

I half expected the echoed response—*only if you tell me what's wrong*—but Reed looked down at himself the way I'd looked at my toes a moment ago, shocked to find an article of clothing missing. With a curse, he moved toward his dresser. "Sorry. I was turning in early for the night."

He wasted no time pulling on a dark tee, and I stared at him through the whole process, sniffling. "Where's your mom?"

"Already asleep. She worked a twelve-hour shift today." Reed stepped up to me once more, but he seemed more hesitant to touch me now, like his bedroom was different than the foyer of his house, like the shadows in here were more intimate. "What's going on?"

"My mom—" I began, but the words cut off, my throat closing.

Reed's eyes widened. "What happened? Is she okay?"

"She's fine. She's...she's going to sell the house." The words were enough to smash my dam of composure. Once more, the tremors took root in my ribcage, squeezing until my breaths came in short gasps. "She didn't tell me. That's—that's something she should've told me, right? She should've been honest, but they never are. Neither of my parents. No one tells me things."

Reed placed his hands on my shoulders, pressing his fingers in. "Take a breath, Ava."

I knocked him away, advancing further into his bedroom. His room seemed larger than Rachel's without all the clutter, and there was more space to pace in. "Why don't they tell me things? Why don't they talk things through with me? Why is it that I have to find everything out like they're slapping me in the face with it?"

And it'd been with everything, the major life events thrown at me as if they were a baseball and they assumed I'd have a mitt. There was no time to recover from the blow before a new ball hit, cracking me piece by piece. All the while, I'd been shoving everything down, except now there was no *deeper* for things to go. My filing cabinet was full.

Reed's expression crumpled as he stepped forward. "Ava."

But it was a question that had always been in the back of my mind, looping around on the lowest volume setting possible. Barely perceptible, but there. "Why doesn't anyone care how I feel?"

I turned to his desk then, trying to hide my face as I struggled to keep my composure. I couldn't cry, not in front of him. After yesterday, I'd told myself I'd never be vulnerable with him again. And yet as I faced his desk, I realized that the magazines on the surface *weren't* magazines at all—they were comic books. The ones I'd bought for him. One was even laying open, as if he'd been reading it.

And it was like someone threw a boulder at my glass window of self-control.

"I care," he said as he took one more step closer, planting himself before me. There was something so cautious about his movements, like he was trying not to scare me. He reached up and smoothed my hair from my face, his warm palm coasting along my skin and lingering there. "I don't know why they are acting this way, but I care about how you feel."

And maybe that was it. Just someone saying they cared. Just *Reed* saying he cared. Because these words contradicted the painful indifference he portrayed in the car yesterday, once more gifting me nighttime Reed Manning when I needed him most. Either way, his words triggered the waterworks again, and there was no holding back this time.

He wrapped his arms around me as I cried, and all the times I'd wrapped my arms around myself had nothing on this. He eased us onto the edge of his bed, granting my shaking knees the relief from nearly giving out. Reed held me as if I were about to shatter into a million pieces, as if holding me tightly was the only way to keep me whole.

Later, I'd be embarrassed for crying into him, his T-shirt absorbing my tears, but at that moment, there wasn't anything other than the cracking inside me, so intense that it should've been audible.

Five of Reed's fingers smoothed their way up my spine, the thin material of the sleep shirt only marginally numbing the sensation. I melted against him, breathing in the scent of laundry detergent from the freshly washed shirt and the scent of *him*, like jasmine and apple.

"You're not alone," he insisted softly. His other hand came up to coast down the back of my head, smoothing down my hair. "I'm right here with you."

It was hard to imagine that once before, we'd been close like this, but under vastly different circumstances.

I'd wanted to be close again, but I hadn't imagined it being like *this*. I hadn't imagined letting myself fall apart in his arms, hadn't expected him to cradle all the pieces. But here we were, my heart breaking and Reed Manning acting as the duct tape holding me together.

I clung to him tightly, letting his hand continue the circles against my back, crying until I had nothing left in me.

Crying sessions always left me feeling drained, and when sleep slowly receded Saturday morning, it wasn't anything different. My head had a leftover pulse from the crying headache, and I didn't open my puffy eyes, swollen after a night of rest. I remained motionless under the covers, basking in the warmth of a dreamless sleep and the comfort of the sheets for a moment longer. Just a moment.

And it truly was only a moment, because as I laid there, awareness slowly playing peekaboo, I realized I was more than warm. I was *hot*, like someone had slid a furnace underneath my covers during the night. Like I was lying beside the sun.

Like I was lying beside a person.

My eyes flew open and found Reed Manning's face probably six inches from my own, his dark lashes fanning across the tops of his cheekbones, breathing evenly through his nose. Asleep.

I froze. I was underneath his heavy duvet cover, but he was lying on top of it, a thin tie-blanket covering his lower half. We both shared one of his extra-long pillows, and his arm was thrown around my waist, holding me in place.

The window beyond his bed let the sunshine in, hinting that it was not, in fact, nighttime. Confirming that I *had* fallen asleep in his bed. In his arms.

There was panic, for sure, but as I stared at him, something in me quieted. The pain and betrayal from last night felt numb now, distant, and listening to Reed's soft inhales and exhales only seemed to lull me further. Each breath in said "it's all okay" and each exhale out said "don't worry."

You're not alone, he'd said last night, pressing me to him. Now that the tears and crushing weight of emotion had subsided, the words took on a whole new meaning, basking over me like a ray of sunshine. *I'm right here with you.*

I reached out and eased a thin lock of his golden hair behind his ear, one of the few longer pieces, careful not to touch his skin though my finger desperately wanted to. My mind, sluggish with sleep, put up warning sign after warning sign, but I still basked in it. Just for one more moment.

There was no point in listing the reasons dating Reed was not a good idea, but in this moment, I couldn't help but wonder if he's ever done this before. Woken up with someone else in his arms. That thought was what had me pulling away.

As gingerly as I could, I drew Reed's arm off of my waist, laying it in the space between us. *Don't wake up*, I thought to him desperately. *Please do not wake up.* I couldn't even imagine what kind of conversation *that* would be. Even though I wanted to see those brown eyes, I was too terrified of what emotion might be turning over inside them when he realized we'd both fallen asleep. And besides, this was daytime Reed now—he could very well kick me out of his bed. It was better that I sneak out on my own.

The cool air swept across me as I emerged from the roasting blankets, and in my wrinkled pajamas, I padded my way to his closed bedroom door. One last glance proved that he was still asleep, blissfully unaware, perfectly at peace. Thank God.

Without wasting another second, I cracked his door open and escaped into the hallway.

And came face-to-face with Mrs. Manning.

Her hazel eyes widened at the sight of me, and I watched her absorb everything at once. Me, Ava Jenson, emerging from her son's bedroom in the wee hours of the morning. Hair rumpled. Dressed in my pajamas. My wrinkled pajamas.

"Good morning," she said, as if the situation necessitated a nonchalant greeting. As if I wasn't about to pass out at her feet. "Um—is Reed in there?"

"He's—yes. He hasn't gotten out of bed yet." I'd said it to hopefully prevent her from going inside, for whatever reason she wanted to, but when her eyes widened, I realized I wasn't helping my case. "I mean, he—he's—I wasn't—"

"I didn't see anything," Mrs. Manning said, nodding

very quickly, causing her low ponytail to bounce. "I truly didn't."

"Nothing happened," I insisted, desperate for her to believe me. "I swear, Mrs. Manning. I was—"

She raised her hands halfway to her head, almost as if she was going to cover her ears. "I didn't see anything. I'm going to make breakfast."

I could've disappeared into the wallpaper at that moment and would've considered it a blessing. My face was on fire as Mrs. Manning backed toward the staircase, obviously thinking a thousand things at once, and they were all wrong. I had to tell her.

But hang on, were they all wrong? What if she was thinking I stayed here all night in Reed's bed? *That* wasn't wrong. Except it was also a truth that Rachel could never, ever find out. "Mrs. Manning, wait, I can—"

"Ava?"

I stopped halfway down the staircase, but I had a clear view of the Manning's front door and how it was swung wide, letting in a glare of sunlight. Fully high-lighting my best friend standing over the threshold, a pink duffle bag in one hand.

Rachel frowned at me, no doubt rapid-fire looking me over just as her mom had. "What are you doing here so early? Why are you in your pjs?"

Over the course of my life, I imagined in all the ways and places I would die. I didn't quite anticipate it being in the middle of the Manning's staircase with my best friend no doubt bashing my head in with her duffle. Because the excuses I'd been set to give to her mom?

Gone. Poof. My brain emptied like someone pressed the handle down on a toilet.

"She stayed the night last night," a voice sounded behind me, sleepy and low. My hand on the banister spasmed along with my heart as I turned around. Though Reed was clearly awake, the sleep slung to his frame, from his slow blinks to his mused hair. His expression spoke nothing of the night before, like it'd never happened. "Her and her mom had a fight last night, so she crashed in your room."

They say the best lies are masked with some truth, but it was almost scary how easily the lie fell from Reed's mouth. It made me wonder if he'd ever lied in front of me before and I hadn't known him well enough to realize. He didn't look at me as he spoke, as if I weren't even there.

Rachel readjusted her duffle, her expression cloudy. If anyone were to catch him in a lie, it'd be his twin. "How do you know?"

"I'm the one who unlocked the deadbolt." Reed brushed past me and moved down the stairs without turning back, not glancing my way once. He swiped up his *Super Mario Bros* mug from where he'd left it the night before. "Shut the door. You're letting out the AC."

With that, Reed disappeared down the hallway that led to the kitchen, leaving the two of us staring at each other. Leaving me to have heart palpitations all on my own.

"You should've texted me if you and your mom fought," Rachel said to me, kicking the door shut. "I could've come home."

"You couldn't just leave the kid you were babysitting."

Rachel didn't say anything as she shifted her duffle, straightening out its strap.

Last night, that'd been the sole reason for fleeing to her house. In a moment of need, I'd sought out the comfort of my best friend. I'd been fully prepared to tell her everything, to let her hold me while I fell apart. She would be as devastated as me about selling the house, but now the words wouldn't come. After briefly opening the box last night, I couldn't bring myself to do it again. Couldn't risk falling into a hole I couldn't get out of. I guess there was a daytime version of me, too.

"It wasn't anything major," I told Rachel, coming down a step on numb legs. "I just needed space."

"Well, you know my bedroom door is always open. Even when I'm not in it." She pointed at me. "But you better not have cleaned my room because then I'll have to kick you in the shins for destroying my organized chaos."

I hadn't touched a single thing in her room; I hadn't even gone into it.

"Ava!" Reed called from down the hallway, causing me to jump. "Mom wants to know if you're staying for breakfast!"

"I—I can't," I told Rachel, already reaching for the front door's knob. I needed to leave now before I said something wrong. Before my expression gave me away. Before I actually made eye contact with Reed. "I'm going to have breakfast with Dad. I'll see you later?"

"Do you need a ride?" she called after me, but I was

already hurrying down her front porch. "Wait! Where are your shoes?"

I didn't even hesitate to cross the street, and didn't turn back to see if she watched me leave. It was a one-time thing, last night, but I needed the space to sort it through in my thoughts, file it away, and then it'd be fine. I wouldn't think of how safe I felt in Reed's arms. I wouldn't think of them at all.

"Did you know about Mom selling the house?"

It was the first question I asked Dad—demanded, really—as soon as he sat down in the booth across from me, groaning right along with the plastic as he settled in. It wasn't "where have you been" despite him being a half hour late to meeting me for breakfast, nor had it been "hey, Dad, haven't seen you in forever." I wasn't going to waste time beating around the bush.

Dad, though, seemed to not have heard me, livid confusion furrowing his already wrinkled brow. "What on earth have you done to your hair?"

In terms of importance, my pink hair that I'd twisted into two buns on top of my head seemed low on the list. "Mom's selling the house," I repeated, fighting to keep my voice down. "Did you know?"

"Of course, I did. It's still *our house*, after all. Even though she's going to get it in the finalized divorce, she technically can't sell it without my permission." A waitress—not ours—was walking past the table when Dad waved a hand to flag her down. "Can I have a cup of coffee, please?"

"How long have you known?" The answer to the question probably didn't matter much—it wasn't like it changed anything—but I needed to know how deep the betrayal went.

The intensity hadn't left Dad's blue gaze as he went from analyzing my hair to looking me in the eye, and the sudden strangeness of seeing him again after so long struck me hard. "We talked about selling it a little before I moved out."

Ah, the betrayal didn't go too deep. About six feet, which worked, since his words practically stabbed me in the heart. I reeled in the revelation for a moment that, back when I thought things were okay, they were even more broken than I'd thought. "I'm an adult, you know," I told him through clenched teeth. "How could neither of you tell me?"

"It's not something we needed your permission on."

"Not *permission*, but talking it out would've been nice." It was the most I'd gotten to tell either Mom or Dad in ages about the separation. Usually when the S word was used, they shut the conversation down. "Discussing it with me like I'm an adult instead of springing it on me and expecting me to be okay with it."

In a perfect world, those words would've captured Dad's attention. He would've had an epiphany and gone *oh, yeah, we should've talked it through with you.* I needed one of them to hear me.

The waitress chose that moment to stop by our table to drop off Dad's coffee and to pick up our menus. Dad went with his usual—over-easy eggs, bacon, and toast—whereas I kept it simple with scrambled eggs. I wasn't sure I could keep anything more down, anyway.

"You know I hate sitting over here," Dad muttered as he fruitlessly tried to pull his shirtsleeves lower, glaring at the ceiling. "It's right underneath the air vent."

"Dad."

He sighed when dodging the subject didn't work. "Being an adult means dealing with tough things, even when they aren't discussed with you first." He raised his Mexican-flag coffee mug and took a sniff of the black coffee before a long sip. "Have you seen the house she's looking at?"

"No." And I didn't want to. I was sure Mom's idea of a "dream house" was vastly different than mine, since my dream house was the one we currently lived in. Small enough for our family, close to Brentwood High, and forty steps away from my best friend's front door. What else could I ask for? "It probably needs a bunch of fixes. It's my senior year. I don't want to have to worry about a renovation on top of that."

I cringed a little hearing my voice, hearing how complaintive it came across. Dad, too, seemed to pick up on it, and tipped his head to the side. "I'm just saying," Dad said in a distinct way that sounded like *listen to me, because I'm right*. "If you don't go into this with an open mind, nothing's going to be good enough."

"Why should I have an open mind? What does it

matter what I say, anyway? It's not like you and Mom value my opinion."

I'd said the words in hopes of pressing a hot button, to invoke my father's temper—I wanted someone to feel something other than it being just me—but he looked out the window, calmly letting out a breath. "Can we let this go? I don't want it to ruin our time together."

I bit down on my bottom lip to keep from scoffing, slumping into the booth and wishing the food would come faster. Ruin our time together? He had to know that there'd already been a hole blown into this morning, even by him showing up late with no excuse. The disconnect with him didn't seem to register that this went deeper than them selling the house. "Are you finally going to let me see the apartment after this?"

"It's not quite ready for you to see yet, Ava. What if you came over and stayed next weekend?"

My tongue ached with suspicions unsaid, and I couldn't keep quiet anymore. "Do you have a woman there or something?"

Dad closed his eyes a little, almost like a *I can't believe you asked that* sort of face. "Of course not."

"A man?"

"Ava. No. There's no one at the apartment. It's just not ready for guests."

I grappled for a long moment, staring at him. "I'm your daughter, not a *guest*."

I wasn't a daddy's girl the way Rachel had been, but in this moment, I was struck with the cruel irony: Rachel's dad wanted to spend time with her, and my dad viewed me as a *guest*. A visitor. There had never been a question of whether I'd live with Mom or Dad, and maybe that had to do with them assuming my answer, assuming I wouldn't want to leave Rachel, but they'd never asked. He'd never asked.

"You know what I meant," he replied, glancing around the busy diner. I wasn't sure what was making him so uncomfortable: the topic or me. I could probably count on one hand the amount of times Dad and I fought, and never about anything as serious as this. It felt as if we were on a piece of land breaking apart, me on one side, him on the other. "I promise, next weekend, you can come and stay—"

"Next weekend is homecoming."

It was crazy to think that Monday kicked off spirit week and then that Friday was the big game. The first three weeks of school had gone by in a whirlwind, all absorbed by everything going on. My parents' separation, working with Rachel's dad, the Most Likely To list, kissing Reed. The instances had shaved hours away from the week and probably years off my life.

"Maybe I can come over to see you in your dress, then," Dad offered, and I could clearly see him struggling to say the right thing. "It's your last homecoming. We should get a picture together."

It was the right thing, but that was the only reason he'd said it. He didn't suggest taking a picture because he *wanted* to. He said it because it was the right thing to say. Tears burned in my throat, because sitting there in the booth at the Wallflower, I looked at my life laid out in front of me and didn't recognize a second of it. Not a single second. "You know," I began slowly, clenching my jaw to stop the sting from building behind my eyes. It didn't work. "I'm not feeling too good. You can have my eggs."

"Ava." The name came out with an annoyed sigh, one that he tried to mask with a softer follow up. "Sit down, okay? Let's talk about something else."

Like what? I wanted to shout. In a matter of weeks, the man across from me went from my father to a man that was almost entirely foreign. I guess it was fitting. To him, I was a guest. To me, he was a stranger. "Maybe next time," I answered, getting to my feet. Dad didn't try to stop me this time, picking up his coffee and letting me walk away.

Even though it was early in the morning, tiredness swamped through me much like it had Friday night. The fight went out of me like the spotlight of a lighthouse turning into a different direction. It'd come back eventually, but for now, everything was dark.

r. Manning's website was hard to look at. Not because it didn't look good—no, I made sure it was *flawless*—but because the weight of everything I'd done was staring me in the face, as well as the realization that it'd all been for nothing.

Signing a deal with Mr. Manning hadn't saved Mom from following through on what I'd hoped had been a flippant threat—our house was up for sale, and I'd already signed a contract. Despite all of it being for nothing, I still had to complete the site.

Even though I knew Mom wouldn't have been home, I spent the hours since breakfast with Dad camped out at Expresso's, working through the last bit of everything. It'd taken me the entire time to figure out why the mobile version of the site was getting messed up when I inserted their logo, but after I got that down, there wasn't much left to do but send it over for him to review.

It was easy to be hyper-focused on coding and HTML when life was more complicated.

Despite the absence of Mom's car, as soon as I

opened the front door, I heard a soft humming sound from directly up the stairs. Hoisting my duffle bag up higher on my shoulder, I stepped in the direction, careful to dodge the creaking steps.

My bathroom light was on, filtering its yellow glow out into the hallway.

The humming grew louder and louder until I stepped into the doorway, and though I could've glanced at the clutter everywhere else in the bathroom, my gaze went to Reed Manning standing in my shower.

His back was to me, blue T-shirt taut as he reached up and wound a wrench around the shower head. The matte black rainwater one was a fresh sight from the old mildew-ridden chrome one I'd had before.

Maybe later, I'd be embarrassed by the overflowing hamper in the corner, or worried if there were pink hairs stuck in the shower drain, but right now, I listened to him. The diligence of his movements calmed me like watching the sun set on the horizon. From the basic, methodical way he twisted the wrench to the soft noise he made under his breath. If anyone ever told me that Reed *hummed* when he worked, I wouldn't have believed them.

But here he was, going through a tune that sounded suspiciously like a Taylor Swift song.

He pivoted to grab something from his toolbox, spotting me from the corner of his eye, and he jumped with a loud swear. The wrench clattered as he dropped it onto the shower floor.

"Gotcha," I said with a slight smile, watching as he

slumped against the shower wall. A super eloquent response. At least it wasn't *hey, I haven't seen you since we woke up in the same bed together, how've you been?* "Now who's jumpy?"

He closed his eyes, voice breathless. "Your mom said you wouldn't be home today."

"Ah, so you only came thinking I wouldn't be here?"

"I, at least, would've been more prepared for a near heart attack."

My tired lips stretched wider as I ran my fingertips down my duffle bag, eyeing the showerhead. "Fixed it, did you?"

Reed gave me a soft glare before twisting to face his handiwork. "There was a limescale build up in the pipe—that's why it was causing that screeching sound. I could've cleaned it, but your mom wanted to replace it to match the rest of the hardware." He gestured toward the black knobs on the sink before turning to me. "What do you think?"

The last time we'd been together, I'd woken up in his arms, and now he was asking me about a showerhead. As if it never happened. "I'm glad it'll stop screaming when I shower."

"There's got to be a joke in there somewhere."

"Did you know Mom was doing all these fixes because she planned to sell the house?"

I wasn't sure what I expected out of Reed's reaction, nor what I hoped for, but he only let out a long sigh, picking up the wrench from the shower floor. "She said she wanted to up the value of the house. After years of construction with Dad, I know what that means."

Up the value. The *resale* value. After years of listening to Mom talking to her clients, I knew what that meant, too.

Last night, the news of selling the house came like a bomb tearing me apart from the inside out, quaking the ground I stood on. Now, all that was left was the aftermath. I didn't feel like digging in my heels anymore. What was the point, anyway? My tiredness extended to my bones, no fight left in me.

"I'm going to go unpack my stuff," I told him, clenching the duffle strap tighter as I walked out of the bathroom.

I walked across the hall and into my bedroom, dropping my bag onto my bed. I had my pajamas in the bag, as well as all my night routine stuff, and the idea of pulling it all out after being so excited to pack it yesterday left me feeling like I wanted to cry.

"Did something happen?" Reed's voice came from behind me, and when I turned, I found him standing in the doorway with a rag in his hands. He dragged it across his knuckles, but he focused on me. "You seem..."

"What?"

"I don't know. Different."

His words caused my insides to give a complicated twist. *Different from when?* I wanted to ask. *Different from last night when you held me while I cried?*

"It's not like you know me much in the first place," I told him, and then flopped down on my bed, my back bouncing against the firm mattress. "Rachel knows me. You really don't."

The bed dipped as he sat down beside me, his hip level with my shoulder. "I'm Reed. I hate tap water, am terrified of snails, and I'm an Aquarius."

"The food or the animal?"

Reed blinked. "What?"

"Are you afraid of snails, like escargot or the animal?"

He gave his eyes a soft roll. "Escargot, of course. Your turn."

"I'm Ava," I said softly, swallowing hard against the growing ache that wrapped around my throat. The sun filtered through my window, enough to give the room a warm glow. "My favorite color is pink, I love designing websites, and I hate change." I shifted my gaze to where Reed leaned over me, his head partially blocking my ceiling light. "Oh, and I'm a Sagittarius."

Reed smiled like he was only half-listening, but the intensity in his expression told a different story. It was strange, him looking at me like that. Lying beside him suddenly felt much more...intimate. "Now that we know each other better, do you want to tell me what's on your mind?"

I went back to the ceiling. "No."

"Shove over," he said suddenly, and then laid down shoulder-to-shoulder with me, the bed jostling with the movement. The metal frame squeaked, causing my heart to jump just as loudly in my ears. "How about I share what I'm thinking about and then you go?"

"You better not say something dumb, like 'food' or 'girls.'"

He ignored me. "I'm thinking about my dad."

I turned my head toward him; it was the last thing I expected him to say, but it'd come so effortlessly. "Your dad?"

"Mm-hmm. Rachel reminded me...his birthday is in a few weeks. I've been thinking about him."

I didn't look away. His profile looked softer like this, with his head denting into my duvet cover and his eyes relaxed. From this angle, I could see a clear bump in his nose. "When was the last time you two spoke?"

"Probably the day he moved all his stuff," Reed replied. "He didn't fight for custody or anything, so we haven't spoken since. It's hard to look at him."

"I can't even imagine," I murmured, stomach cramping again at the thought of Mr. Manning. Rachel reiterated often how terrible the whole situation was, but I couldn't even begin to understand the depth of it. "You said Rachel reminded you it was his birthday?"

He nodded. "And I've been thinking about it lately. He might've done something stupid—something horrible that hurt all of us—but it doesn't erase the sixteen other years he's been there for us. All of the other birthdays and vacations. No matter how much I wish it would, sometimes."

Reed reached over and laid his hand over where mine was on the bedspread, giving my fingers a squeeze. My insides lurched as if on a rollercoaster, abandoning the landing platform in a sharp jump. After a second of stunned hesitation, my fingers curled around his hand. I wondered if he could feel them tremble.

"Your turn," he said.

His voice was nearly lost in the thundering of my pulse. *My turn, my turn, my turn.* There was so much, and despite it overwhelming me, my cheeks burned at the idea of saying them aloud. But Reed was asking for me to be vulnerable after him, and I could never refuse that.

"I was thinking..." I swallowed hard. "About how embarrassed I am."

"Embarrassed about what?"

"I literally used you like a Kleenex last night. And fell asleep. All of it was a total breech of personal space, and...I'm sorry." *Sort of sorry.* Sorry for how embarrassing it was, but not sorry for getting to experience it at least once.

"Who knew you were such a great cuddler?"

If we were going to get technical, when I'd woken up, *he'd* been the one cuddling *me.*

"In all seriousness," Reed went on, shifting the way his fingers settled against mine. "Don't feel embarrassed. And don't apologize. If anyone needs to apologize, it's me."

Now I looked up at him. I was close enough to see the freckle underneath his waterline. "You? What for?"

"The whole thing with Josh on Thursday. I knew you were going to his house, and I should've given you space. I shouldn't have said yes when Cindy asked me."

It made me wonder: if Reed had said no when Cindy asked him to come over, would things have changed?

Cindy might've gone into her bedroom instead of watching the movie with us, leaving Josh and me alone. And if that had been the case, would he have made a move? Would I have? We'd nearly kissed before Cindy and Reed got there—would I have gone through with it if they hadn't interrupted?

My thoughts slowed to a crawl. "If you knew why I went over there, why did you say yes?"

The air felt too thin when I tried to inhale, my lungs starving for more oxygen. Or maybe I wasn't breathing, not wanting to risk missing his answer. He studied our hands as if we held something precious between our palms instead of just the combined heat from our skin. "I wasn't thinking."

"You weren't thinking," I echoed, and when I shifted, the bed creaked.

"Cindy said Josh was having a friend over, and I knew it was you, and I just...stopped thinking." Almost reluctantly, Reed's gaze traveled to mine, but instead of darting away, we both remained lock on. "I shouldn't have said what I did. About wishing I hadn't kissed you."

I had one question. *Did you mean it?* But I couldn't ask it—there was a high, high chance I wouldn't like the answer.

With his free hand, Reed reached out and allowed his fingertips to trace the skin near my temple, coaxing my hair behind my ear. My breath caught at the touch, at the things it did to me, at the kickstart of my thoughts.

"Ava?"

My name. Not my nickname. "Yeah?"

"I'm worried about you."

The butterflies in my stomach gave an impulsive flutter, but I blinked at him in confusion. "About me? Don't be. I'm fine."

"I think you're trying really hard to be fine. I think things are bothering you more than you're letting on." He tilted his chin down. "Come to me again anytime something like Friday happens, okay?"

My mouth suddenly went dry, and my hand in his definitely felt clammy, but I couldn't move. I should've pulled back. I needed to pull back. "Why?"

"Because you know I'll always be there for you."

Pull back. "As a friend?"

"As whatever you want me to be."

I saw the second Reed's expression changed, when he went from open and honest to wishing he could withdraw the words. The thought was so clear, it was practically written across his face. However, the words had already rooted inside me, impossible to shake. *As whatever you want me to be.*

The edge loomed before me, beckoning me to jump off.

I sat up without warning, tearing my hand from his in the process, shaking it out like I had a hand cramp. Clearing my throat, I said, "I'll come to you first, then. As a friend."

Reed didn't respond. Now I was the one leaning above him, his brown eyes looking up at mine. My heart swelled in a way that was nearly painful, expanding to the point of bursting. God, he was so beautiful. When we were like this, my mind took all the "what ifs" and ran with them. What if he wasn't Rachel's twin brother? What if he wouldn't ask Cindy to homecoming? What if he asked me? What if I kissed him again?

Reed slowly sat up, forcing me to lean back. I looked away, terrified those thoughts had been showing on my face, especially when he said, "I should get my stuff and head out. A few of us are going to the movies tonight over in Hatchfield."

I knew "a few of us" meant the Top Tier, but I couldn't help but wonder if Cindy was involved in that group tonight. Probably. My skin stung, the thought itself not settling well.

We were both quiet as he left my room to go pack up his toolbox of supplies, and I stared at the imprint his body made into my covers. I trailed my fingertips over the spot, tracing the slight difference in warmth where he'd been lying. Once all the work on the house was done, he'd stop coming over. He had to be nearing the end of the list, too. Once he was finished, he'd have no reason to step foot in the house again—all I had to do was wait until then.

I could avoid him at Rachel's house. Heck, I'd been doing it for years. Soon enough, our kiss would fade into a deep corner of my memory, and it wouldn't matter if he was going out with Cindy or the next girlfriend, or the one after that. I just had to wait it out.

Reed stepped into the doorway of my door again and hesitated, his toolbox dangling from his fingertips. He looked on the verge of saying something—lips parted, eyes on me. Ultimately, he gave a soft nod. "Have a good rest of your weekend."

And then he disappeared into the hallway, with only his heavy footsteps and my beating heart echoing after him.

Hey Bobcats! Don't forget that it's SPIRIT WEEK! Don't remember the student-voted spirit days? Well, Babble's got you covered!

Monday — Pajama Day
Tuesday — Twin Day
Wednesday — Country vs City
Thursday — Athletes vs Mathletes
Friday — Blue & Gold!

Send in submissions of your fave outfits. Spoiler Alert—have you seen Madison Oliphant's pjs today? To die for! xx

I had rapidly typed up the blog post before the bell for first period rang. I'd already posted the spirit days on Saturday, but it was good to remind everyone as often as possible—and to remind everyone to vote on their favorite outfit. It wasn't nine o'clock yet and my submission box was full of people wearing their pajamas. Some pictures were mirror selfies, but some were of students who'd snapped pics of others while they walked down the hall. Even from a brief scan, Madison had been the most photographed in her blue and gold nightgown with matching headband.

I loved homecoming week. If not for the excitement of the big game, then for the fact that it was a content goldmine.

"Ava Jenson?" Mrs. Winston called during first period, drawing my attention—and the attention of every other student in the room—to her desk. She had her desk phone pressed to her ear. "They want you in the office."

In the office again? Was this another Most Likely To list intervention? Dear God, I hoped not. I wasn't sure I could sit through another round of *how are you feeling* or *does being voted on the Most Likely To list bother you* questions.

"Oh. To the counselor's office, Ava," Mrs. Winston called once I got to the door.

The counselor's office. Now my guard went up.

The counselor's office was in the same wing as the main office, but a few doors down. I didn't walk there eagerly though, heading down the west wing stairs with my slippers making soft sounds against the linoleum. Going to the counselor's office was probably for something routine. Maybe about my grades, college choices, scholarships. Applications were coming up soon, so maybe they were trying to meet with the seniors about it. That made sense. I could tell whoever that I already had a range of colleges picked out, could tell them that I'd already bookmarked several scholarship applications on my laptop. That had to be what they were meeting me for.

The counselor's office's door was open when I approached it. She didn't have a secretary like Principal Oliphant did, so when I appeared over the threshold, I had a clear view of the middle-aged woman sitting behind her grand oak desk. Her office was filled with a lot of pinks and yellows, from canvases on the walls to throw pillows on the plush chairs opposite of her desk. Even though this office was much smaller than Principal Oliphant's, with one tiny window to avoid a fire hazard, it felt less like a jail cell.

The woman, a petite brunette with a polka dot blazer, welcomed me with a wave. She looked much younger than I'd expected. "Ava? Come, sit! Pick wherever looks most comfortable."

I honestly knew the school counselor wasn't necessarily a psychologist, but right off the bat, it felt like my choice would be scrutinized. The chairs opposite her or the plush loveseat rammed up against the far wall? I opted for the chair with the throw pillow, knocking my knees on her desk in the process.

"How are you doing today?" the woman asked, features still cheery. "I know it's Monday, and Mondays can be a bit of a bummer, but hopefully it's going okay."

"It's fine." I scanned the surface of her desk, finding

the plaque I'd been looking for. "Ms. Murphy, can I ask why I'm here?"

"Direct, I like it. I wanted to check in with you. See how the school year is starting off, chat about you, your goals, your life." Ms. Murphy clasped her hands together and leaned forward, looking like she was unable to sit still. Her expression had this intense sort of sincerity in it, like she was trying to convey something I wasn't quite picking up. "I'll be straight up with you, Ava, and I hope you'll be straight up with me."

"Oh...kay?"

"Your parents asked me to have a session with you. They told me how your home life is changing and how you might need someone to talk it out with. That's why I called you into my office. Just to check in."

My parents had asked her to meet with me? "When? When did they ask?"

"I came in this morning to an email from your mother."

My mother. It would've made more sense for Dad to have sent an email, given our talk at Wallflower Saturday morning. I'd done an efficient job of dodging Mom yesterday, citing a headache and a mountain of homework, and she'd left me alone. We were both experts at cold shoulders. "Can I read the email?"

Ms. Murphy quirked her lips to the side. "What do you think your mother said?"

Jeez, if that wasn't a psychologist question, I wasn't sure what was. I tried not to let myself feel defensive.

"My mom and I don't talk about anything that I thought she'd send me to the counselor for."

"This is just a check in," Ms. Murphy said, lifting her hands in a pacifying gesture. "You're going through some big changes right now and she wants to make sure you have all the avenues possible to talk things through with someone."

"Is that what she said?" I demanded, unable to contain a laugh that rang of incredulity. All the avenues possible. It sounded like something Mom might've said, but the hypocrisy of it all was too ironic. She wanted to make sure I'd have someone to talk to? Make sure I wasn't alone in things? When she was living in the same house and never asked me those questions?

"Your parents are separating, you're moving houses, you're filling out college applications, and being in your final year of high school—those are all stressful things on their own."

And kissing my best friend's brother. Except I'd rather die than admit that to her.

"Talking to someone about what's troubling you isn't a bad thing."

Her words triggered a memory. Reed's voice, clear as day: *You can talk to me, you know. I'm a good listener.* Those words made me remember how quickly he'd pulled me against him Friday night, how tightly he held me, as if he could make me feel better just by squeezing. It was such a painful thing, baring myself, but Reed had accepted it in an instant. No hesitation.

"Thanks for the check in, but I'm good," I told Ms. Murphy, rising to my feet with a plastic smile. The idea of putting myself in that situation with anyone else wouldn't happen. If I couldn't be honest with Rachel, there was no way I could be honest with this woman before me. "But if anything else comes up, I'll come to you."

It was a throwaway promise, and we both knew it. Ms. Murphy let me stand up, though, and walked to the door without calling after me.

By the time Mom got home, the need for confrontation had become impossible to ignore. The brief, intrusive meeting with Ms. Murphy had been in second period, but it left me simmering in the subject for the rest of the school day. I'd been hoping that this Monday would've been one of the rare times Mom beat me home—her normally jam-packed schedule usually meant she didn't get home from work until around six. Surprise, surprise— the garage door started rolling up at 5:05.

I'd made a bullet list in my head, repeating it over and over the course of the three hours I'd been home. *Their divorce, Dad not letting me come visit his apartment, Mom springing moving on me, and now Ms. Murphy.* All the things she didn't talk to me about, and then deciding to let someone else deal with it.

Mom came into the house through the side door in a symphony of jingling keys, clacking heels, and her realtor voice in full blast. "Yes, of course, of course, I'll call the buyers now and see what they think. I'll be honest, I'm not sure they'll swing the price of a replaced water heater given all the other upgrades they've done to the house, but it's worth a shot to ask. Mm-hmm. Yes, I think so."

I was a ghost as Mom brushed by me without even making eye contact, absorbed in lugging her portfolio inside and saying all the right things. I might as well not have been there. "Are you willing to go half on the water heater?" she asked the caller, settling into a seat at the table. "Mm-hmm. Okay, I hear you. I'll call you back with an answer hopefully by the end of the day."

It was against her cardinal rule, but I did it anyway. Trying to talk to her during a phone call. "Mom."

"I think that's a completely valid point," she went on, reaching up to take the claw clip from her hair. "I'll bring that up as well."

"Mom."

"And like I said, I'll call you with their answer." She finally glanced up at me, and it was almost funny how kind her voice was versus how glacial her expression was. "Yes, of course. Mm-hmm. I'll be in touch."

As soon as she lowered her cell to end the call, I jumped. "Mom—"

"You know my rule about not interrupting me during a phone call unless it's an emergency." She looked me up and down. "I don't see blood."

I'd let the comment slide, only because I was going in for the kill. "I need to talk to you."

"I need a few minutes. I've got a client thing to deal with."

"This is important."

"Ava," Mom said as she looked through her contacts list on her phone, her tone already snapping to exasperation. "I *just* got through the door. Give me a second, would you?"

A second? She'd had all weekend in her state of ignorant bliss. She got her second when she was probably in a bubble bath while I cried my eyes out in Reed's bedroom. I opened my mouth to dish it out, but Mom had already placed her next phone call, shuffling through papers from her briefcase. Back on was the realtor voice as she babbled to the person on the other line. She got up and went to one of the cupboards in the kitchen she'd repurposed, pulling out an orange binder.

My anger came out in a burst. "It's funny how you ask someone else to talk me through my feelings instead of bothering to do it yourself."

Okay, so that wasn't the plan—I was supposed to start off small and work my way to my frustrations—but starting off with the strong line was worth it for her reaction. It was the button-pushing I'd tried on Dad Saturday morning, only this time, it worked. Mom turned around so quickly that she lost her balance on her kitten heel, staggering to stay upright. The person on her call continued chattering, their voice an undecipherable stream of words.

"Can I call you back really quick? I'll find those numbers and I'll let you know." Mom's voice was level, expression clear. No indication anything was wrong. "Yes, of course. Give me five minutes."

And then she hung up, and the Jenson household became a warzone with a ceasefire line created by the kitchen table.

"You're talking about Mrs. Murphy?" Mom asked, tapping her fingers against her binder in a *one-two-three* succession. Slow. Methodical. "Why is that so important to discuss while I'm on a call?"

My lungs began to ache as if someone wrapped their fist around them, especially when her expression didn't falter. "Why didn't *you* talk to me, Mom? Why pawn me off on someone else? Because you didn't want to listen to what I'd say? If you were really concerned, you would've talked to me yourself."

"First of all, watch your tone, Ava." It was spoken in that voice all moms had—a feigned calmness so low that it gave me chills. A true sign she was really upset. "Second of all, I figured—"

"Figured you were too busy to talk things through with me, right? Figured it was a waste of your time? All you had to do was say, 'Hey, Ava, your father and I want to talk about something.' Or 'Hey, Ava, let's talk about the house really quick.' You spring things on me and make me deal with everything on my own."

Mom let out a slow breath, but the grip on her binder tightened to the point where her knuckles turned white. She held her chin high, gaze on the refrigerator. Almost like she and it were having this argument. Like I wasn't in the room. "I'm sorry you're taking it so hard, but I have to make these calls before it gets any later."

It was illustrated even further that when, without another word, Mom returned to her files and picked up her cell phone. She tried to hide it, but even from here, I could see her hands were shaking. "Hey, Peter, sorry," she spoke into the phone, once more donning her realtor voice. "I've got those numbers right here for you. Yes, sure, let me know when you're ready."

I could've screamed.

Instead, I stomped over to the front door and slid on a pair of sandals, escaping into the yard. She didn't try to stop me either, but then again, had I expected her to? I pulled shut the door behind me, letting it slam against the jamb, and I knew I might as well have been talking to myself.

As soon as I stepped out onto the front porch, I saw it.

A bright white and yellow For Sale sign, with Mom's smiling face plastered beside the words, staked in the front of the yard like a tacky lawn ornament.

The yellow door of the Manning's house opened, and Reed came out, twirling his car keys. In a split second, our eyes locked. His hair looked extra golden in this light, like he had drops of sunlight in them. Relief was like a small bubble bursting inside me, not fully extinguishing my frustration, but enough that I could breathe a little easier.

Until Rachel stepped out from behind her brother.

"You'll have to text me what she says," Rachel said as she hopped down the concrete steps, holding a poster in her hand. She spoke loudly enough that I could hear her across the street. "Of course, she'll say yes, but I want to hear everything."

She ran into Reed's back, who'd stopped once he spotted me.

"Ava!" Rachel frantically waved her arm. I saw the exact moment she noticed the For Sale sign, her jaw dropping visible even from here. "What is *that?*"

With numb limbs, I made my way across the yard, unable to even glance at the stupid sign as I passed it. My sneakers crunched over the grit of the roadway. "It's exactly what you think it is."

"Is she home?" Rachel craned her neck to glare at Mom's car in the driveway. "Because I'll talk to her. We'll convince her not to sell. Obviously. I'm very persuasive, you know that. She thinks you can move? *Psh.*"

Reed grabbed above Rachel's elbow as she started forward. "Leave it for now, Ray."

"They can't just move away! Did you know about this for a while and not tell me, Ava?"

"I only just found out, too." I bit down on the corner of my lip, trying to channel as much indifference as possible. I could only scratch the surface of the emotion, but hopefully it was enough to keep the tears at bay. "What's the poster for?"

There was a question on Reed's face, but I pretended to be fully engrossed on the poster Rachel unfurled—and then I *was* fully focused as I realized what I was looking at. There was a photograph of our school mascot in the bottom corner, and adorned all around the perimeter were different sizes of pawprints. Words took up the middle of the poster board in a mixture of blue and gold glitter.

IT WOULD BE WILD IF YOU WENT TO HOMECOMING WITH ME

And just when I thought things couldn't get any worse.

"He's on his way to ask Cindy to homecoming," Rachel said, flicking off a stray piece of glitter from the top of the board. "You should've done it at school where everyone could've seen."

"That's exactly why I didn't want to," he muttered. "Everyone would've taken pictures."

The moment was clear as a teenage rom-com. He would've asked her in the hallway before classes. He'd come around the corner, smiling only at her. She would've been standing around all her friends, and of course they would've taken out their phones to snap a picture. They'd have sent it to Babble, giving me the honor of drafting up a post. ***Reed Manning and Cindy LaVore—Brentwood's Next Hottest Couple!***

Still, he was going to her house to ask her. More intimate, more sentimental, more serious. Maybe they'd get Josh to snap a photo.

You were supposed to tell me, I thought as I stared at the board. *You were supposed to tell me.*

"The dance is Saturday, you know," I said instead, unable to tear my gaze from the poster. "You're cutting it close enough as it is—I'm surprised someone else hasn't already asked her."

"Is there anyone you were planning on asking?" Reed asked, slipping one hand into his pocket. From the corner of my eye, I could see his face turned toward me. "What about Josh?"

How could I ask anyone else to homecoming when, just Friday night, I fell asleep in your arms? It was like he'd forgotten about it already—like it'd never even happened.

Reed's words took me back to Thursday on the car ride home, where I said it felt like he was trying to dump me off on Josh, and the feeling resurfaced with a pain behind my ribs. Here my world was, derailed by the idea of him asking Cindy to homecoming, and Reed was offering Josh up to me like he couldn't care less.

And Rachel, glancing between us with a slightly confused expression, was witness to it all. Knowing a quarter of the story.

"You should ask Josh," Rachel agreed, shoving the poster board at Reed. "He might not be your first kiss, but he'd make a great second."

His head turned toward his sister, and for a brief second, I could practically read his thoughts. *How much does she know?* "You had your first kiss, then?" he asked me. "Do I know him?"

Yeah. Seriously not funny.

"He sucks," Rachel told her brother. "He kissed Ava and left her high and dry."

Okay, we were stepping into territory that I seriously

could've died of mortification from. I stepped toward my best friend, trying to convey my desperation in a wide-eyed stare. "Rachel, TMI, okay? Your brother doesn't need to hear this." *Please, please stop talking.*

"He should. A player like him should see what it's like to mess with a girl's feelings." She pointed a finger at Reed and narrowed her eyes. "Next time you kiss a girl and plan to ditch her the next day, think to yourself 'hmm, what if this was Ava? Would I do this to my little sister's sweet best friend?' *No*," she answered for him, "you wouldn't."

So freaking not funny.

"Okay!" My voice came in a loud, squeaky pitch. "This has been an awesome conversation. Reed, best of luck asking out Cindy. Rachel—" I grabbed her wrist without thinking twice, dragging her past her brother and toward her house. I avoided his eye contact as if my life depended on it. "Oh my God, did you have to say all that to him? Really?"

"Maybe your adorable little face will be all he needs to visualize to change his ways." Once the door was shut between us, sealing off Reed from view, Rachel patted my cheek. "As long as he doesn't develop feelings for you or anything. Then we'd have problems."

She started up the staircase, assuming I'd follow her. I did, of course, but with one thought in my mind—we already had problems.

The past two days, my Babble submission box had been flooded with almost nothing other than homecoming proposals. It was tough to wade through them. It seemed that most of Brentwood High followed Reed's example of waiting until the last minute to ask someone to the dance. Once I posted about Reed's hoco-proposal—and shared the beautiful grin Cindy wore in the picture they'd snapped together—Tuesday alone had twelve proposals. By the end of the school day Wednesday, I had a total of nineteen.

This was going to be one heck of a compilation post.

The "cute proposals" coincided with "corny proposals," and I'd seen many of those already. Like Landon Settler's poster to his girlfriend "Let's have a BALL at Homecoming" with little footballs all over the board. Someone else had a poster that read, "We'd make a Sweet couple at homecoming" with little candy bars taped to the surface.

It was corny, but here I was, wishing I'd get a corny proposal.

Then again, I only wanted one person to ask.

Josh was waiting for me by my locker at the end of the day Wednesday. He dug the toe of his cowboy into the tile grout, tracing the line, unaware of my approach. "Hey, stranger."

Josh picked his head up, greeting me with a wave. "Hey, yourself. How are things?"

"Good. Busy." I waved my cell phone a little. "Babble's at its peak this week."

"I know. I've been checking every day to see what the top voted outfits are." He gestured down at his attire. "Is it wrong of me to keep my fingers crossed I made it for Country vs City Day?"

I smiled at his red plaid shirt underneath a pair of worn overalls. The cowboy boots poked out from underneath his tattered denim hem, showing signs of aging in the leather. I took a step back and opened up my camera app. "No need to cross your fingers when you know the editor in chief."

Josh pointed his fingers at me as he posed, his dimple deepening as he beamed. "Brentwood won't forget me now."

"Joshua Geller's name shall never be forgotten," I said with dramatic flourish, causing both of us to laugh. But as I spun my combination lock, I looked at him seriously. "I'll remember you after high school. I promise."

"If it's just one person, then I'm glad it's you," Josh said as he shifted from foot to foot, looking at me with his eyebrows raised. "Cindy took the car today. Would it be cool if I walked with you home? I mean, I know your rode your bike, but maybe you could—well, I mean—"

"I can walk beside it. It'll be nice to have the company."

Josh grinned again, a relieved, dimpled smile that made me remember how much I liked his awkwardness. I hadn't really spoken to him since I'd gone to his house, and seeing him again caused Rachel's words from lunch to bubble up in my head.

"*Maisie, shouldn't Ava ask Josh to homecoming?*" Rachel had asked from my side, nudging her elbow into my ribs. "*She needs to make a sign.*"

"*Do you want to ask Josh?*" Maisie had questioned. "*It's totally okay if you want to go alone, you know. It's not that big of a deal. Rachel's going alone.*"

Rachel had let out a disparaging sigh. "*Thanks for the reminder.*"

The truth was that I didn't really care about going alone. I'd been going to dances alone almost my entire high school career. But there was only one pathetic reason the idea of a date appealed to me—during the slow songs, when everyone would be coupled off, I'd have someone to dance with.

Someone to distract me from a certain couple.

"So, you share your car with your sister, too?" I asked Josh as we made our way toward the bike rack, pulling out my padlock key. "Reed and Rachel have to share theirs, and Rachel absolutely hates it."

"It's the worst," Josh agreed. "Plus, Cindy never fills the tank after she uses it, so it's an extra pain."

I made a soft sound under my breath, kicking a stone. "How long did you say you've been step siblings? Five years?"

"Yep. Our parents met on some online dating site."

"My parents were high school sweethearts. That same old boring love story." *Except for them, it didn't last.* I left that part out.

We walked down the sidewalk away from the school, my bike chain *click-click-clicking* as I walked alongside it. It created a barrier between Josh and me since he walked on the other side of it. Traffic was heavy as we made our way away from the school, and the steady hum of car after car passing us filled the gap in our conversation. I tilted my face up to the sun, the heat glowing on my skin enough to leave me feeling warm despite the slight breeze.

"I've been thinking a lot about Babble since we talked, and I did come up with one cool possibility." Josh turned to me with wide eyes. "So, I went through your posts these past few days, and I noticed that aside from relationships, you post a lot about sport game totals and school events, right?"

I nodded. "Yeah, it works really well to keep people updated. That's originally what Babble was."

"Well, what if you made a blog about that?" Josh tilted his head to the side. "Brentwood doesn't have a school-dedicated blog, and they don't keep their website updated with current events. What if that was what you did? I mean, you would have to get rid of the relationship aspect, but it could be a great way to keep some readership."

I made a soft sound under my breath, running it through my head. He was right—though lately I'd been leaning heavily on the relationship side of things, and this year's Most Likely Tos, most of Brentwood Babble was keeping students updated on current events. "How would I know what to post when?"

"Maybe Principal Oliphant can give you a list of important events or something like that?" Josh shrugged and ducked his head a bit bashfully. "I mean, it's an idea. I'll keep thinking about it. But it could be fun."

"No, I like that," I said earnestly. "It's a great idea. It wouldn't be the exact same, but this way I wouldn't have to say goodbye to Babble completely. That's really smart, you know. I wouldn't have thought of that."

"What can I say? This brain is good for something." His dimples came in full force as he lifted his chin, letting the sunlight catch his cheekbones. Josh cleared his throat, giving me a sidelong look. "Since I helped...can I ask you a weird question?"

"Shoot."

"Do you see me...romantically?"

I forced the bike to a halt, handlebars twisting a little at my sudden stop. "What?"

His smile seemed more boyish, and when he spoke again, his voice was a bit more confident. "Do you see me romantically?"

"I think you're cute," I told him quickly, frantically thinking for the right response. I desperately didn't want to say the wrong thing. "You're really nice, too. And funny."

"But can you see yourself kissing me?" He tilted his head almost curiously. "Being your first kiss?"

If Kissable Josh had been introduced to me before the List, if I'd met him before kissing Reed, who knew what might've happened? But he was just barely too late.

"It's okay," he said when I didn't reply. "Really. I meant it when I said I was looking for friends, you know. I'm not hanging around you because I thought anything would happen between us. I'm only trying to...read the room. And it probably came off super blunt and awkward."

Despite it being blunt and awkward, I smiled. "It's not that I don't think you'd be a good kisser," I told him, which made him chuckle, but it also made my heart skip a beat. "I...I already had my first kiss. The day before I met you. But I didn't tell Rachel."

"Why wouldn't you tell Rachel?" I could feel Josh looking at me, could practically see his turned head from the corner of my eye. It only took him a second to connect the dots. "Wait. Did you kiss *Reed*?"

I nearly had a mini heart attack. Seriously. "How— how did—"

"Why else not tell your best friend?" His expression wasn't judgmental, thank God—it was open, curious, kind. Peak Josh.

I wasn't sure why I wanted to be so honest with him, but the words were drawn out of me like a magnet attracting metal. There was no fighting the pull, nor the strange relief that came from finally being honest with someone. Anyone. "It was the stupid list's fault," I said, and my next words came in a rush. "I hated that I was on it, and I kissed Reed to get it over with. Even though no one else would know about it, I did, and that felt... enough, I guess. Rachel didn't *really* have to know. It was a 'one and done' thing."

"So, you didn't catch feelings?"

"You make it sound like it's a cold."

"It kind of is, though, isn't it? Starts as a tickle in your throat and soon you've got a fever and your stomach hurts every time you think of them?" Josh made a soft *hmm* noise under his breath. "I guess, not that I'd know, but that's how a lot of people describe it, right?"

Maybe Josh wasn't wrong. Liking Reed was kind of like catching a virus, one that was near impossible to shake. Even now, two days without contact, I found myself thinking about him, wondering what he was doing. And it was the single kiss that had spread the germ, one that had gotten me so messed up.

"It happened weeks ago," I reassured Josh now, nodding. "And it was a one-time thing. So don't worry about me stealing him from Cindy or anything. It's—it's not like that."

"I don't think their relationship is as serious as you make it out to be. She invited Ashton over last night for a movie."

"But she's going to the homecoming dance with Reed."

"Dates to homecoming are something that people just

do," Josh told me. "It doesn't mean you're official or anything. It's only so you won't have to go alone."

It was interesting to think that Cindy was talking to more guys than Reed. I couldn't see why she would *want* to talk to anyone else but him. And a guy like Ashton? He was nice, but not on Reed's level. Then again, Reed was the player in this duo, wasn't he? It made sense that this wasn't as serious for him either, given his dating history.

Josh and I approached a stop sign that branched off to our separate roads. I'd continue straight onto my street, whereas he had to walk left to eventually make it to his house. We both hesitated at the crosswalk, turning toward each other. "Do you have a date to homecoming?" I asked him, squeezing my handlebars tighter.

"I do not, in fact."

"Do you want to come with my friends and me? That way, you don't have to go alone?"

Josh stretched his hand to me over my bike seat, offering a handshake like a business deal. It mimicked the way we'd first been introduced to each other, and it made me smile. "I'd love to. Like I said, I'm in the market for friends."

"And we're always in the market for adding more to our lunch table." I slid my hand into his and squeezed it. "We have four empty seats to fill."

"Dang, wait, so am I saddling myself with the loser crowd?"

I gave a mock gasp and squeezed his hand harder.

A car pulled up at the stop sign beside us, and the passenger rolled their window down. "Hey, you two!"

Rachel greeted, frantically waving as if to grab our already-captured attention. "Stop flirting in public!"

Josh waved back. "Hey, Rachel. Hey, Reed."

Refusing to look past Rachel was a futile thing, because as soon as Josh mentioned his name, I couldn't *not* look. Reed sat in the driver's seat, his profile barely visible by the wall his sister created, but he lifted a hand to acknowledge Josh's greeting.

"Ava asked me to homecoming," Josh said suddenly, causing me to turn toward him. "So, it looks like I'll be hanging with you guys Saturday night, if that's okay."

Rachel let out a shrieking sound. "Yes, that's totally okay! You're coming for pictures, then, right? You have to."

"There's a car coming behind us," Reed said suddenly, and he let his foot off the brake. "Roll your window up."

"Wait, I—we're talking later, Ava!" Rachel stuck her head out of the window to call the last bit, because Reed was already pulling away from the stop sign, not giving us time for a proper farewell. Never looking at me once.

Josh patted my upper arm before taking a step toward his route home. "I'll see you tomorrow, then? I'll be looking for my feature on Babble tonight."

"Don't let the popularity go to your head," I called after him, and despite feeling conflicted about Reed, I found myself smiling. Josh may not be the one living rent-free in my head, but he *was* a good guy. A great friend, and I was happy to have met him. Kissable or not.

"Country vs City Day was an abso-lute hit! We had a few ties, but it looks like the amount of Country submissions totally blew City submissions out of the water. Guess we're all a little wild at heart.

Check out these awesome 'fits, though. Never thought I was a spurs gal, but wow! Julia Rodrigo totally killed it with that farmer glam, and did you see Joshua Geller's plaid? Perfection!

Comment below—who wore YOUR favorite fit for Country vs City?"

I smirked a little at my computer screen as I attached Josh's photo onto the post, and then went ahead to link the other most popular photos. Someone even wore chaps —those had to be a Timeless Treasures find. Some people, like me, had only gone as far to get a cowboy hat and boots, but I linked a few that looked pretty.

Instead of closing out Babble, I typed up a draft of tomorrow's post for Mathletes vs Athletes. Afterward, I scrolled down to yesterday's homecoming proposal post and scrolled through the comments, grazing through.

> **HighJumper77: anyone else living for landon and lacey??? They r soooo cute together!!**

> **OraanjeJooce: lol Cameron G has a typo in his poster**

> **LegendaryLila: @OraanjeJooce it's supposed to be spelled like that— it's a pun**

> **Hunt4Bulldogs: anyone else want to place bets on how long Reed and Cindy will last? $5 it's only a week after homecoming.**

I let out a little breath before setting my laptop to the side, dropping it into my bedsheets. My parted curtains let in a bit of the moonlight and the lamplight glow below. It was only a little after ten, and despite it being after my grandma bedtime, it felt good to have everything in order on Babble.

I threw an arm over my eyes, covering my frown.

A little *ding* had me turning toward my laptop, spotting the new email icon flashing in the top corner. I reached over and tapped on the cursor, heart jumping in my chest as it loaded.

Hello Ava,

I hope things have been well since we last spoke. I'm excited to see the final product of the website on Friday. Perhaps we can meet up in person to go through it together, and while we're there, we can discuss some other things. Let's say Expresso's Café in Jefferson around 5?

See you there!
Jacob Manning

On one hand, it was kind of funny, the fact that he hadn't waited for my response to go ahead and set up a meeting, but logically, I knew why he hadn't really given me room to say no.

But it wasn't like I really had a choice. As a client, he wanted to meet up to go over the website in person. A little strange, and I probably wouldn't have done it for anyone I didn't know, but it wasn't like Mr. Manning was going to kidnap me and force me into his trunk. Even though I'd failed in my objective—keeping Mom from selling the house—I had to honor the contract between us. By the time Mom dropped the bomb, I'd already had it practically done, anyway. And heck, maybe if I gave Mom the money, she'd cancel the open house and take the house off the market. That was possible, right? Either way, this would be it. The final time we'd meet, exchange of payment, and then I could mark his email address as spam.

I pulled my phone up and sent a text to Rachel.

Me: Are you asleep?

Knowing her, she probably wouldn't go to bed until closer to midnight.

Reed: Not yet. Want to take a walk?

I'd started to type out my reply—*a walk?*—when I reread the name. *Reed.* Not Rachel.

I dropped my phone, as if that would undo my stupid mistake. How could I text the wrong Manning twin? Was this some sort of like Freudian slip? *Crap, crap, crap.*

I sprang upright, scrambling for an excuse. A walk? At ten at night? That was a bad idea central, and even I knew it. Besides, what would we even talk about? How the last time we saw each other, I cried all over him and passed out in his bed? Or would we talk about the time before that, when he said *what kiss?*

My mind and my heart played tug of war, torn between what was right and what I wanted.

Me: I'll meet you outside in five.

It was chillier than it'd been in a long time when I shut the front door behind me, the breeze sweeping across my exposed legs. I'd worn a pair of shorts to bed and a short-sleeved shirt, and though I'd thrown on an oversized Brentwood Bobcats sweatshirt—an ancient one with tattered sleeves and a makeup-stained collar—I wished I'd thrown on a pair of sweat-pants too.

I wasn't the only one who'd underdressed. Reed had on a pair of sweatpants, but his T-shirt did nothing to cover his arms. He was already at the sidewalk by the time I stepped off my porch, the lamppost reflecting a greenish glow over him. "Hey."

"Hey." I folded my arms across my chest, tucking my fingers into my sleeves. "Uh...which way?"

Without a word, Reed gestured off to the left, and we began our nighttime walk.

Which started off with the heavy air of *awkwardness*. Our footfalls pattered against the concrete sidewalk dully, his sneakers and my flip-flops. I second-guessed all of my potential conversation starters, and Reed wasn't jumping at the chance to say anything either, not right away. Everything that lingered between us stole the conversation before it could begin.

I looked up at the moon and the faint wisps of clouds that ambled past it. The stars were barely there, winking at me in the dark sky as if encouraging me to make the first move.

Reed suddenly pulled up short. "Let's stop here," he said, tilting his chin toward the playground we'd come to. It normally looked fun with all the bright colors, only now the shadowy slides and play gyms seemed a bit more ominous. "Want to swing?"

"Uh, yeah, sure," I replied, but my voice sounded thin to my own ears.

Reed's sneakers crunched over the woodchips as we walked toward the swings, but instead of sitting down, he moved behind one of the swings and grabbed the chains. "I'll push you."

He pulled the chains back, and with it, my insides tugged tauter and tauter. When his hands braced themselves against my shoulder blades, it was almost crazy how I could feel the touch so clearly through the thick material of my sweatshirt.

"So, what has little miss Paparazzi sending late night texts?"

The breeze combed through my hair. "It's only ten-thirty."

"Which is late for you."

Of course, he'd know that. "I didn't mean to text you,"

I admitted softly, biting down on my lower lip as the momentum swung me backward. "I saw R Manning and clicked *send*."

"Ah, the wrong twin." He didn't sound upset as he gave me another well-placed shove, tone more thoughtful. "Why didn't you say so earlier?"

I couldn't come up with an answer that was actually okay to say aloud, so instead, I answered his question with one of my own. "Do you sneak away to the park often at night?" The air was colder as he pushed me forward again, goosebumps beginning to dot along my legs. "Rachel says you take walks at night. I saw you once, you know."

"And you didn't follow me?"

"Hey, I didn't know what you were sneaking off to do. I wasn't sure if it was worth the risk to find out."

Reed stepped to the side of the swing to peer at me, corners of his eyes crinkling. "What was one of your theories?"

Going over to Cindy's late at night. "I thought you might've joined a demonic cult that only met when the sun went down. I was afraid I'd be a human sacrifice."

"We only meet on full moons."

I stared up at the half-circle in the sky. "Phew."

"I do come here sometimes, though," he answered after a moment, coming around in front of me. He was in the direct path for the moonlight to illuminate the high points of his face, eyes bright. "Or walk the block. It helps me unwind, I guess."

"I'm surprised no one's called the cops on you yet." I

lifted my thumb to my ear and put my pinky to my mouth. "'Hello, officer? There's a random man sitting on the swing set across the street.'"

Reed pushed his palms against my knees, shoving me backward with a shake of his head. "You're such a dweeb, you know that?"

Even though the conversation was light, something about it didn't feel right—like we were dancing around a serious topic. One that I couldn't pick up on. "So why are you so wound up at night? Why do you have to leave the house?"

There was something unguarded about him, like this was a new side of himself I'd yet to see. It was then that I realized something *wasn't* right, especially once he opened his mouth. "My thoughts don't really shut down at night. I can't stop thinking. Usually when I walk, I can calm down enough to fall asleep."

"What are you thinking about?"

"A lot of things." Reed watched as my pendulum slowed down, tracing the movement. "My mom, my dad, football, school...other stuff."

"Cindy," I supplied.

He didn't deny it. "And you."

Don't let it get to you, I scolded my fluttering heart. "How many times do I have to tell you not to worry about me?"

Reed caught the chains of my swing and broke my momentum mid-swing, and for a moment, he did nothing but grip me close. "I'll always worry about you."

I wanted to tell him that I hated the idea of him

worrying about me. Thinking about me in that way. When Reed Manning thought of me, I wanted it to be because he *wanted* to, not because he was worried about how I was handling my life drama. I didn't want him to think about me the way he'd worry about Rachel. I wanted to fit into a different category of his life. And I hated myself for wanting it.

Reed brought me forward and eased me back once more, simultaneously saying, "I'm the one that caught my dad cheating."

At once, I slammed my feet down into the sand, my foam flip-flops bending and filling with granules that scraped into my skin. I ground to a halt, inches from Reed, staring up into his eyes. "*What?*"

"I found them," he repeated, reaching out and trailing his fingers down the cold chain. "Last summer. Football practice ended early when it started raining, and I came home to see that my dad had a woman over. Mom was at work and Rachel was with you. They were in the living room." The emotionless way he recited it made me worry, especially pairing with the distant look in his eye. "He tried to lie about it at first, but they were... Well, they were how we were in the kitchen that night, I guess. Obvious."

It was the first time that bringing up that night didn't give me butterflies; they were too stunned by his story. *Obvious.* "Rachel said that he came clean on his own."

"She doesn't know I found them. Neither does my mom. I told him to tell Mom or I would, and he did." Reed didn't look at me, almost as if he wasn't allowed to.

"Sometimes at night, I think about it. Thinking about him. That's why I need to get out of the house sometimes. Just to forget everything."

I laid my hand down on top of his, the warmth of his fingers seeping into the coolness of mine. Desperately, I wanted nothing more than to say the right thing. The thing that would make him smile, make him laugh, that would take this heavy situation off of him. I'd been the shoulder Rachel had to cry on, but did Reed have one?

When had he become someone I didn't want to see in pain? When had he added himself to my collection of special people?

It was a painful moment when Reed pulled his hand away. Almost like he was sheering off a layer of skin. I curled my fingers inward, trying to savor as much of the heat as I could. "Should we head back?" he asked, slipping his phone from his pocket to check the time. "It's getting close to eleven."

"Five more minutes," I said, digging my feet into the sand and propelling myself backward. "Swing with me. Let's see who can go higher."

Reed did not have to be told twice. He fell into the swing beside me and started to build the momentum to hit a higher apex than me. We both pumped our legs, trying to outdo the other, our amusement echoing in the dark air. The swings trembled with the weight of two grown teenagers on it, but we didn't care. We were two kids in that moment, stealing a moment of anonymity that came in the cover of night. He wasn't Rachel's brother in that moment, or the boy who'd asked someone else to homecoming, or even the boy that lived across the street my entire life—he was Reed Manning, and for this moment, he was mine.

We eventually migrated from the swing set to the green jungle gym that was in the center of the play-ground. Reed grabbed ahold of the little pirate wheel screwed into the structure, pretending to steer the ship, while I made my way across the monkey bars, laughing despite the cramp in my upper arms. I'd grown up with his sister, but I'd never gotten a chance to play pretend with Reed like this. It felt like we were pretending in more ways than one.

Reed stood at the top of the tallest platform of the jungle gym, the one that led to the twisting tube slide, and squinted out toward the street. "It's a quiet night on these waters, isn't it?"

I snorted at his roleplay, but started up the stairs toward him. "Is it now?"

"Mmm." Reed turned toward me, and from a few steps below, I looked up at him bathed in moonlight. "Maybe we should put the anchor down here?"

"Do we have an anchor?"

"All ships have anchors."

"Ah." I took another step toward him. "Then go put down the anchor."

"That's the shipmate's duty," he said, and then pointed at his chest. "Not the *captain's*."

My jaw dropped theatrically. "Who gave you the title of captain?"

Reed shook his head as I stepped onto the platform beside him. "We'll be co-captains."

I smiled, turning to peer out at the street. It was deadly quiet, and all the surrounding houses were dark with sleep. It had to be past eleven now, which wasn't *that* late in the grand scheme of things, but it felt as if it were three in the morning. The feeling of adventure clung to the air, the sort of desire born from lack of sleep and lowered inhibitions. As I stood at Reed's side on the playground, examining Walnut Street before us, the feeling closed around me like a jacket.

I glanced over at my co-captain and the first thing I noticed were his arms. "You have goosebumps." Without thinking, I rubbed my hand up and down his skin. The intention was that the friction would warm him up, but my fingers were icer than his arm.

"Jeez, your fingers are freezing," he all but gasped out, jerking away before snatching up my hand. "It's not even that cold out."

"I guess I have poor circulation."

Reed folded my hand between his, letting the warmth of him once more swallow up my palm. Only it didn't stop at my palm. His heat spread from my fingers to the rest of my body, as if traveling through my bloodstream. It was as if I was seeing him for the first time in that snapshot of a moment. With his golden-brown hair tucked behind his ear, his dark eyes on me, rosy lips caught in a half-smile that caused my pulse to hiccup in my chest.

"Reed," I began, a quivering syllable. "I didn't say it before, but thank you. For last Friday."

He didn't brush my words away, but he didn't answer right away, either. He rubbed my fingers between his. For the second time tonight, we were holding hands. "I'm glad you weren't alone. And I'm glad I could be there for you."

"I'm glad it was you."

With his free hand, Reed reached out and brushed a strand of hair away from my face, letting his fingertips trail a path of summer heat along my cheekbone, then to my jawline. The way he looked at me brought me back to that night in his kitchen, after the first four-second kiss. The brightness in his eyes struck me, like he was discovering something he hadn't realized existed. Or maybe it was wishful thinking.

Careful, careful, my thoughts seemed to scream. *Don't play with fire!*

It's too late, my heart whispered, a consoling defeat. *You've already been burned.*

And for a split second, I went down forbidden territory. A dangerous game, but one I played for a moment. I'd say to hell with the risks and repercussions and speak from my heart. In that second, there was no worry about Rachel finding out and hating me, no Cindy drawing away his attention, and there were no houses for sale.

I wondered what I looked like in that moment. Red cheeks and bright eyes. A girl with her heart five sizes too big for her chest. A girl building plans in her head even though they were glass dreams that couldn't come true.

Reed, these past few weeks I've been trying to fight it, but I think I'm starting to fall for you.

And as soon as I had the thought, it all shattered.

"Reed," I said softly, and as I spoke, I could feel my heart thrashing in my chest, beating on the bars I'd put up to keep it protected. But they were iron, firm and fast, and wouldn't dream of budging. "I think we should stop."

"Stop what?"

"Being friends." I stared at his arm, at the goose-bumps lining them, as if that would make this any easier. "I can't lie anymore, and every time that we meet like this, talk like this...I have to lie to my best friend. I can't do it, Reed. There are already too many lies and secrets."

Reed dipped his head to attempt to catch my eye. "Are you talking about the kiss? It was once. One time, weeks ago. I thought we forgot about it."

Except there was no forgetting. There never would be.

"We weren't friends before, and things were fine," I told him, tilting my head to peer up at him for the first time. Even in the dim moonlight, there was no missing the confusion shimmering in his eyes. "I think...I think we should go back to before. You've got Cindy, anyway. You're going to homecoming together. Josh is coming with us, so... This is for the best. Yeah." I nodded quickly, assuring myself that if I said it enough times, it'd come true. "This is for the best."

Reed drew in a breath, and as he did, something changed. He straightened his spine, rocked on his heels, but there was a fundamental change that I couldn't pinpoint right away. The confusion was gone now, replaced by something fiercer, and he reached for my hand. "Listen, I haven't—"

"Reed!"

The name was like a gunshot, splintering apart the moment, and it was one that had me hitting the deck. The area by the slide had opaque partitions, so once I ducked down, I was safely out of view. My knees slammed against the ground hard enough to rattle the structure, reminding me that this was made for kids, not seniors in high school.

"I thought that was you." Rachel's voice carried louder as she came closer. I pressed my palms over my mouth, letting out gasping breaths through my parted fingers. *She didn't see me, she didn't see me.* "What are you doing out here so late?"

"H-How did you know I was here?" Reed asked, and despite the stutter, his voice came off normal. Casual.

"Twin telepathy," Rachel returned, and then the crunching of her footsteps over the mulch stopped. "Is... Do you have someone up there with you?"

Reed didn't even blink. "No."

"I thought I heard another voice."

"Maybe you need your twin telepathy checked."

I shifted my weight on the wooden deck boards, the coolness clinging to my bare legs. It felt like a sliver was trying to embed itself underneath my knee. He was considerably a better liar than me. When we'd been in this situation a few weeks ago, with him hiding behind his kitchen island after the kiss of a lifetime, I'd been much more frantic.

"So, you're just hanging out at a park alone? Like a creeper?"

"I get that a lot." Still without looking, Reed reached down and nudged my shoulder, nearly off-balancing me. "How'd you know I was missing, anyway? I thought you were asleep."

"Please, it's still early. I came to ask you a question about our Physics homework, and you weren't in your room. Are you going to come down or am I going to have to shout up to you? Or I could come up."

"No!" Reed's response was a short shout, one that echoed around the street. "I'll—I'll come down. One second."

He crouched down at the entrance of the slide and turned to cast a look at me now that he was hidden, too. "Ava," Reed whispered, knuckles white as he grasped the bar over the slide.

"Goodnight, Reed," I murmured, my heart giving a left-over *thud-thud* from the situation. *And goodbye.*

He opened his mouth to say something, but the plastic slide echoed as Rachel, presumedly, thumped it. "Come on. What, did you get stuck?"

Reed's eyes fluttered closed for a second before he turned away from me, and without another mumbled word, he disappeared down the slide. I stared into the pitch-black tube, and a few seconds later, I heard him sigh. "All right, let's go."

"Are you going to tell me why you're out here all by yourself?" Rachel asked him, voice suspicious.

No, I thought as his confession came back to me. I wasn't the only one keeping things under lock and key these past few weeks. I knew for a fact that Rachel had no clue Reed had been the one to find out about his father's affair first. She'd always told me that her dad came clean on his own. *Reed won't say a thing.*

I could hear their footsteps crunch over the mulch as they walked away, and without thinking it through, I raised onto my knees enough to peek over the ledge of the play gym. It was risky. At any moment, Rachel could've turned around and seen me—or seen someone's head poking over—but I didn't duck away. Not until they both stepped onto the sidewalk and disappeared behind Mrs. Baxter's overgrown hedges.

With a shaky breath out, I sank to the cold wooden floorboards and rested my head against the edge of the slide, staring through the now dark and quiet structure. Now that Reed left, the magic and fun had gone with him, leaving the playground once more feeling abandoned and empty.

I didn't know how long I sat there, listening to the wind whistle through the structure, but by the time I got up, my legs had long since gone numb.

"Tell me again why you don't want to go to the party tonight," Rachel groaned from her position on her bed.

"It's a Thursday," I replied calmly, using her vanity mirror to twist my hair into a bun. Mom was out with friends, and I'd been at Rachel's house for over an hour now, avoiding the quiet of my own. "I'd rather play it lowkey."

"Lowkey." The word was a muttering scoff. "Ava, the entire school's going to be at this party!"

"Maisie won't be." She was helping her mom out at the art gallery downtown. Her mom was a curator there, and this week was their Brentwood Town Spirit exhibit— or something like that. "Besides, it's not like we could stay long, anyway. You have a ten o'clock curfew."

Rachel cast a sad glance toward the digital clock on her desk, the numbers 8:44 staring back unforgivingly.

Every Thursday before the big game, someone from the football team threw a party to celebrate. Last year, Connor had been the one who hosted the party, filling his fancy house on Bleeker Avenue to the brim. This year, the responsibility fell to one of the defensive linemen, Ashton. I'd already gotten a few submissions through Babble about how big his house was—small—and how many people had shown up—many—so I was staying firm to my objection.

"This is so not like you, you know," Rachel said. "You love parties!"

The statement was technically true. Or, at least, it had been. Last year, if anyone at Brentwood threw a party, I did nearly everything I could to get an invite. Even to the parties reserved for football players only. This schoolyear, though, the idea of squeezing myself into a house and mingling almost had me feeling... panicked. Suffocated. I couldn't imagine pulling on a party face, holding it in place the whole night. There was too much going on that the idea of even attempting to be social had me feeling thoroughly exhausted.

"It's homecoming week," Rachel said. "Maybe Mom'll extend curfew just this once."

"No, she won't." Mrs. Manning pushed Rachel's door from halfway open to fully wide, peering at her daughter with a basket of laundry on her hip. "Especially not on a school night."

Rachel raised her eyebrows. "You could be the cool mom for once."

"She's already a cool mom," I added lamely, trying not to wither under the brief look Mrs. Manning then gave me. It was a neutral acknowledgement, but it was near impossible to look at her and not remember our last interaction. Me, stumbling from her son's bedroom at eight in the morning, wearing my rumpled pajamas. *Kill me.*

"A cool mom who is collecting towels." With a stab of emphasis, Mrs. Manning whipped a cream-colored towel off the floor by Rachel's closet. "No matter how many times I tell you two, you and Reed both leave your laundry lying around. Rachel, how do you have piles of clothes *everywhere?*"

"It's a science, Mom." Rachel leaned over the side of her bed and picked up another towel from the floor, shooting it into her mom's basket. "Is Reed home yet?"

"Should be soon. He said he'd be home around nine."

I turned to study my reflection in the mirror, pulling a few pieces out of my bun to frame my face. Eyebrows down, lips relaxed, eyes not squinty. *Channel the nonchalance.* I ran through my bullet list of facial features for one reason: I knew Reed was out with Cindy. Apparently, according to Rachel, it was *date night.* Jealousy was a sick emotion.

Before Mrs. Manning ducked out of Rachel's bedroom, we locked eyes in the mirror. I wondered if my mask was compelling enough or if she could see right through.

Once her mom's footsteps disappeared down the hall, Rachel sprang off the bed and crossed her bedroom toward me, tripping over a sneaker she'd left on the middle of the carpet. "Ava," she whispered, casting a furtive look at the open door. "What if we snuck out?"

I raised an eyebrow at her. "You think your mom won't check to make sure you're in bed?"

"I can stuff my covers. You know, like they do in the movies."

My expression didn't budge.

Accepting her defeat, Rachel flopped down in the corner of her room by her closet, her head landing on a wadded-up sweater. "Has there been any offers on your house yet?"

My stomach gave a sharp twist. "I don't know." I hadn't talked to Mom since Monday, our longest string of the cold shoulder in a while. Then again, it was mostly on my end. When I wasn't in my bedroom, I was at Expresso's Café, trying to be home as little as possible. It hurt to look around the house and to know that all of those walls holding my memories would someday belong to someone else. Someday soon. "I haven't even seen the house that she wants to buy."

"I can't believe you're moving," she said softly, almost like the words didn't compute. "And I can't believe you don't want me to try to convince her."

"If she doesn't listen to her daughter, I'm sure she won't listen to her daughter's friend."

Rachel kicked her feet a little in the air, letting out a groan. "Why did your parents have to get a divorce? Or, at the very least, couldn't they have waited until we went off to college?"

I stared down at her, a surprising urge to snap spreading out from my chest. "You'd rather they be unhappy so I can live closer?"

"I mean, it's not like they're at each other's throats or anything," she said, tapping her fingertips on the hardwood floor. "Things weren't *that* bad between them, you can't lie. It's not like your dad cheated or anything to make things awkward."

The heat surrounding my ribs stretched out further, squeezing my throat.

Rachel, oblivious to my dissolving patience, had to add one more thing. "You're lucky it wasn't like that."

And that one more thing turned her bedroom into the blast zone. "You keep saying that," I bit out, voice breathless with confrontation. "That I'm so lucky. Explain it to me, Rachel. I'm lucky my parents are divorcing? I'm lucky that I have to move away?"

Rachel tipped her chin so she could look at me, exposing the surprise sitting in her wide eyes. She rose onto her elbows, never breaking the stare. When she spoke, her words came slow. "You have to admit that compared to our situation, you—"

"Who's comparing? Why do we have to compare who has it harder? Why can't it suck for the both of us?"

"Because it doesn't suck the same."

"Says *who*?" My voice cracked. "Just because you don't think my time is as tough as yours, you can't hear me out? Sympathize just a *little*?"

Rachel didn't move from her half-sitting position, and she didn't look away from me either. I couldn't read her expression. It was like she'd read my mind earlier, and was creating a mask of her own. Eyebrows down, lips relaxed, eyes not squinty. The only sign that she was upset was the rapid rise and fall of her chest.

I closed my eyes and let out a breath through my nose, frozen in the thick tension in the air. Fighting with Rachel sucked, but I'd never left her house mad before. Now, I couldn't imagine sitting there a second longer.

"I have a website to finalize," I said stiffly, standing from the vanity seat and curling my hands into fists. "I'll see you tomorrow."

Rachel didn't call after me as I walked out of her room, nor did she call after me as my footsteps clomped down the stairs. Each step I took caused unease to cramp inside me. My brain screamed *go back, tell her you're sorry, don't let her be mad at you!* and I wanted nothing more than to listen. But what would I be sorry for? Finally confronting her about something that bothered me? For keeping it bottled up for so long?

I signed myself up for this, though. The confrontation had been brewing for a while, the things I'd bottled up rebelling against the lid. How could I fight with Rachel? But then again, how could she *not* see things from my side? When had our friendship become so skewed?

As I wrapped my hand around the front doorknob, a soft voice did register, and I stopped in my tracks.

"I'm just saying," the warm voice began, and I recognized it as Cindy's. "Josh told me you kissed her."

No, no, no. The front foyer turned wavy as my pulse skyrocketed. I knew I should've opened the door, effectively silencing that conversation, but cowardice rendered my legs numb. The blood rushing in my ears was so loud that it was a wonder I heard Reed's reply. "*Josh?*"

"I asked him if she ever said anything about you. Guess how shocked I was when he said *that*." She didn't sound angry, but then again, it was nearly impossible to gauge emotions from a whispered voice through a thick wooden door. "I don't get why you didn't tell me. Were you trying to keep it a secret?"

"Rachel doesn't know," Reed said. "She *can't* know, okay? Can you keep your voice down?"

"Why kiss her if you knew it'd get you in trouble with your sister?"

The world dipped beneath my feet as everything hung in place, waiting for his excuse. It'd been a question I'd wondered for a while—*why?* What made him stop me that night? What changed his mind? Once rooted to the floor, I free floated now, stuck on the verge of insanity.

When Reed finally responded, I knew, then and there, that I should've walked out to stop the conversation. Before my heart shattered. "It was a pity kiss," he said, and God, even through the door, I could hear the indifferent tone in his voice. "She came up to me and asked to get her first kiss over with. It was before you and I were even really talking. That's why I didn't say anything."

Boom. All along, I'd known it was true, but I hadn't expected the dropping bomb to hurt so much. I hadn't expected so much nuclear fallout. *A pity kiss.* And I *knew it*—that was the worst part. My brain had told me, over and over, that he hadn't felt the same as I felt about him, but my heart... My heart had been too stubborn to accept the truth when it'd been right in front of me.

Stupid hope.

I didn't realize I hauled the front door open until I found myself staring at the equally shocked faces of Reed and Cindy, both standing on the porch. I couldn't look at either of them, but there was no dodging the absolute all-consuming humiliation that settled over my skin like mud. "Didn't mean to interrupt," I said with a false tone of politeness, and without another word, I brushed past them, trying to keep my head up.

Pity kiss, pity kiss, pity kiss.

Who knew I'd be running away from both of the Manning twins, heart broken into so many pieces that I knew I'd never find them all?

The most wonderful time of year in the city of Brentwood was not the Christmas season—it was home-coming. A certain amount of insanity clung to everyone in the community during the week leading up to the big game, but Friday? If a surface didn't look like blue and gold threw up on it, it was considered a felony.

Not a single person at Brentwood High was *not* wearing school colors to some extent. Maybe they wore a different shade of blue, and maybe the gold was cele-brating a different brand than the Bobcats, but the two colors were prominent on every single student that crossed my path. Even me. Though I felt like someone had stuck their hand into my chest and ripped out my heart, there was no chance of me *not* dressing up.

So, I was this: A girl wearing a blue and gold Bobcats jersey she'd purchased at the spirit shop, blue shorts with gold glitter along the hem, and her pair of yellow shoes laced up tight. Looking merry, feeling miserable.

"I want you to see the house," Mom said from the driver's seat as she twisted the steering wheel around a round-about. As soon as I'd gotten home from the half-day at school, she'd corralled me into the car, not even letting me drop my backpack off in my room. "It's in Jefferson, but closer to the border of Brentwood. You'll still be eligible for the Brentwood school district, so don't worry about that."

I didn't know what to say, so I just stared out the windshield, turning my cell over in my hands.

"Two bedrooms, two bathrooms," Mom went on, leaking into her realtor realm. "The backyard is a bit small, but we're not much for outdoor people anyway, are we? But I think this could be a good fit for us."

My phone chimed, but instead of the Babble staccato I'd always come to expect, it was the chime of a text message. Wildly, I yanked my phone up within inches of my face, holding my breath as I checked the sender.

Rachel: **Don't forget to send Maisie and me pics of the house!!!**

Disappointment swamped me before annoyance took its place, and then guilt for that annoyance. Less than twenty-four hours ago, Rachel and I had our first fight in nearly three years, and yet here she was, pretending like it didn't happen. Pretending like I hadn't left mad. Like our friendship didn't have a rift sliced down the middle.

"Not who you were expecting?" Mom asked, glancing at my phone.

Again, I didn't answer. What would I have said, anyway? If I told her about my fight with Rachel, she'd surely ask me why. If I told her about *who* I was hoping it'd be, that would be opening another can of worms.

I found myself looking for Reed today at school. I couldn't help it. It was like pressing down on a bruise, slowly at first, waiting for the tender pain. I'd only seen him in Physics class, and even then, we hadn't made eye contact. Head bent down over his textbook, golden hair in his eyes.

The driveway of the house Mom pulled up to only fit one car, and the attached garage looked like it could barely accommodate her SUV. But there was street parking, and for the time being, Mom slid up along the curb. "It's cute, right?" she asked, leaning to peer out my side window. "What do you think?"

What did I think? *Cute* and *quaint* could've been synonymous in this case, but even though the house was smaller than our current one, she was right, I guess—it *was* cute. It gave me cottage vibes, with a grand bay window in the front and a wide door set on a small porch. There was a dormer on the roofline with three windows.

"The yard's nice," I told her, eyeing the manicured green grass. "Is there a sprinkler system?"

"There is," she answered excitedly, popping her door open. "One less thing to worry about, yeah?"

It was funny that sprinklers were on Mom's list of must-haves. She loved the look of green, healthy grass. I hadn't even stopped to think what might've been on my list throughout this; I'd been too determined that I wasn't moving that I hadn't stopped to think about what might've been fun in a new house.

The porch creaked a little as we stepped onto it, but in a way that felt homey rather than treacherous. Mom keyed in the combo to the lock box and pulled out the door key, letting us inside. "It has central air, new hardwood floors. Like I said, it's practically a dream home. It's a steal at this price, too."

"Have you put in an offer already?"

Mom shut the door firmly behind us, letting me look around the foyer before she responded. It was small, but someone had built a collection of locker-looking racks for coats and shoes. It would've been the perfect place to hang my backpack when I got home from school every day. "Well, we should talk about that," she said, voice firm, like we were about to discuss business affairs instead of personal ones.

But standing in a stranger's house, I wasn't really in the mood. "Where would my room be?"

She forfeited the subject with an inward sigh. "It's upstairs. It's the only room up there, so you'd have to come down to use the bathroom. I think it used to be a loft, and they converted it into a bedroom."

I ventured deeper into the house without another word, eyeing the living room space as I passed it. Or I assumed it was a living room space—there was no furniture in the house, and the blank canvas made the area feel empty. Didn't make it feel like someone was living in it. It made it less awkward to roam around in.

I took the carpeted steps slowly, pressing my hands to either side of the enclosed staircase. The tight space was one that made me feel at ease, because even though it was dark with the lights off, it felt cozy. The stairs deposited me on the landing with one oak door at the top. It was propped open, and I poked my head inside.

The room was small, about the size of Rachel's room, actually, but the dormer windows letting in the west facing light in made it feel so much larger. I stepped up to it, placing my hands on the sill and peering out at the street. Years of looking out my bedroom window and seeing the Manning house left me shocked at the view, or maybe it was the view itself. There was a one-story house across the street, but since I was on the second level, I could see over its roofline. Behind that house was a large expanse of trees, a small forest within Jefferson limits, with the sun's rays shining through the branches. It was beautiful.

I curled my fingers against the sill, nails scratching at the section of peeling paint. As I turned back to the room, I could almost begin to see where I could put my furniture, imagine what the closet would look like with my clothes hanging up.

I could imagine myself living here. And for the first time since Mom dropped the bomb...I didn't hate it.

Mom was waiting for me when I came downstairs. "How was it?"

"It was nice." The compliment felt a bit pulled out of me, but I didn't want to lie just to be petty. Dad's words resurfaced then. *If you don't go into this with an open mind, nothing's going to be good enough.* It wasn't like I wanted to make her life more difficult, but something in me wanted to dig its heels in, refusing to go further. "Can I see the rest of it?"

We went through the rest of the house in relative quiet. The kitchen looked a lot like ours, with updated cabinetry and a subway tiled backsplash. The guest bathroom was also updated, and the white marble vanity put the one I had at home to shame.

If I were to put my sadness to the side, I could see how this could be Mom's dream house. Even more, I could see that this house would be Mom's fresh start. A way to separate the life she'd lived with Dad, to start a new one for her. Just like Dad had done with his apartment. It just sucked that I had to leave my life behind, too.

We made our way outside, once more bracing against the wind, and Mom locked the house up. The porch creaked its farewell, and we went to the car. I tugged on the door handle, but it didn't give. "Can you unlock it?" I asked Mom, giving the passenger door another useless pull.

But she eyed me over the roof of the SUV, the wind tugging at her hair. If my pink locks hadn't been tied back, it would've been flying like crazy. "I've been doing this all wrong."

"Doing what?"

"Making these big decisions. I've been treating you like a child instead of nearly an adult."

Her words felt a little like too little, too late. "Ironically, I'm not in the mood to have this conversation now," I told her, tugging the door again. Broaching the topic caused a flurry of heartbeats in my chest, a tickle of anxiety.

Mom drew in a slow breath. "They don't teach you how to break these sorts of things to your children. There's not a book on it."

I was sure there was, somewhere. There was a book about everything nowadays. "It doesn't change the other things, though," I said, because fine, if we were going to have the conversation now, we were going to have it. "You still asked Ms. Murphy to talk to me instead of talking to me yourself."

The car suddenly beeped as Mom pressed the button on her key fob, and she nodded her chin toward the SUV. "Hop in."

At first, I thought that it was another subject change, at least until we were both in our respective seats and she let out a deep breath. She trailed her fingertips along the steering wheel, taking a moment to think through her words. "I know it may not seem like it, Ava, but every-thing that's been going on…it's been really hard."

For who? I wanted to ask her, because it seemed like it was troubling me more than it was bothering either of them. But I thought about the tissues I'd seen on Mom's nightstand, and I even thought of something Reed had said. *That's why I need to get out of the house sometimes. Just to forget everything.* It made me think of all the times Mom had stayed at work late, went out with friends, did anything other than be home.

Kind of how I was at times, camping out at Expresso's or at Rachel's.

"Learning how to navigate life differently has been a lot harder than I thought it'd be. I don't want you to blame your father, Ava, I truly don't, but I was…caught off-guard." Mom spoke slowly, and for the first time in a long time, I could detect sadness in her voice. She usually bottled the emotion up, put on her realtor voice, but things were starting to slip through. "It's been hard to wrap my head around it myself, to accept everything, and I didn't even stop to think of a way to talk to you about it."

The pain of the situation had my lungs in a vise grip, and looking at my mother now, struggling to keep her composure, caused something in me to crack. But her explanation, though it made sense, didn't make me feel any better. Not really. The phantom pain of navigating everything on my own still hurt. "I know it would've been hard, but I wanted to hear it from you, not a stranger."

"Talking with Ms. Murphy wouldn't be a bad thing, but you're right, I should've talked to you first." She hadn't quite looked at me yet, but that was how I knew she was affected, too. "Your father and I both should've talked to you about everything. We should've explained *why* we decided it. I was just afraid, I suppose. Not knowing what to do, how you'd react. Talking about things before I know a concrete outcome is hard for me."

I could understand that. I was kind of the same way, not wanting to talk about it until things were less tumultuous. It was why I hadn't told Rachel about kissing Reed while my feelings were still in a whirlwind of chaos. It made sense to be nervous about it, but the bone-chilling fear of coming clean was more than normal. I didn't know what her reaction would be, and the realm of not knowing was too scary for me to venture into.

"Do you wish you hadn't gotten married so young?" It was a question that I'd always bounced around. Before, when they'd sprung the separation on me, I'd forced myself to deal with it, to bury everything down deep. Now was time that I could scratch a bit of the surface. "Do you wish you hadn't been high school sweethearts?"

Mom looked thoughtful for a moment. "Sometimes you grow apart as you grow older, but it doesn't mean I'd change it. Do I wish I had dated others before settling down?" She smiled a little. "I don't. Do I wish we'd made our love more of a priority as we lived life? Do I wish we put each other before work? Yes. But I don't regret any of it, Ava."

I swallowed past the tightness in my throat. "I think I'd be afraid of falling in love too young."

"Oh, don't be afraid of it, sweetie. Don't ever be

afraid of falling in love, at any age. You know what they say—it's better to have loved and lost." She didn't say it, but I filled in the rest of the quote. *Than never to have loved at all.* "You can't live your life afraid of what could happen. You can't hold yourself back from living because you're afraid of the consequences. Love is always worth any risk. Even now, where I'm at, I believe that."

I looked into her eyes, pressure beginning to build behind my own. She was braver than me. That was why I wasted my first kiss, why I almost kissed Josh even though I didn't have feelings for him. I was afraid of falling in love too quickly, too young. Afraid of repeating her history.

Love is always worth any risk. I wanted so badly to believe that, but I wasn't sure that I did.

"I've been struggling these past few weeks," I told her, and though it might be tough, I knew I needed to get it all out. I couldn't let anything sit unsaid between us anymore. "It's got a lot to do with Rachel and school and...Reed."

Mom didn't react to hearing his name, but she did lean her body against her door, facing me as fully as she could. "Go ahead," she said, patting my hand where it sat on the middle console. "And don't leave anything out. My full attention is on you."

Without hesitating, I told her everything. From the Most Likely To list to kissing Reed, from butting heads with Rachel to even talking about Josh. We sat in front of the house with a For Sale sign in the yard for what seemed like hours, finally pulling back the curtain and letting her know what had been on my mind. She listened to me the whole time, and even though she got a few text messages, she never even checked them. Her full attention was directed toward the passenger's seat, toward her daughter, who shared everything for the first time, and it finally felt like how it was supposed to.

had a bad feeling the second I walked into Expresso's Café. There was nothing outwardly alarming about the coffeeshop—the tables were full, the baristas were smiling, and they were playing Top 10 Greatest Hits over the speakers—but the lingering feeling of dread was impossible to shake. I should've taken the tension in my throat as a sign then, should've hightailed it back out the door and given Mr. Manning an excuse as to why I couldn't make it. I should've listened.

Instead, I did what I did best—shoved down the feeling and urged forward.

The first ten minutes of my meeting with Rachel and Reed's dad went by without hiccup. I walked him through the website page by page, clicking on each link and triggering each animation. I held my breath throughout the whole ordeal, especially with his eyes raking over every inch of my work.

In its full glory, Manning Construction's website was, objectively, so much better. Before, everything had been kind of jam-packed with small fonts and a boring color-scheme, but now, the rich maroon, gold, and silver would catch the eye of anyone scrolling through. The animations on the homepage popped up just as they were supposed to, and I'd even tweaked the mobile site enough times until the loading sequence ran smoothly for each tab. It took me longer than my normal web designs, but I was proud of each small facet of HTML code.

Proud, but sick to my stomach every time that I looked at it.

Once I got to the last link, Mr. Manning sat back in the metal chair, giving it a satisfied nod. "This looks great, Ava. Especially for someone of your age."

Something about the compliment didn't quite feel right to me, but I thanked him anyway. "I'm glad I was able to help you with this, Mr. Manning."

"I'm glad too. And don't worry, I'll be passing your contact info along to that start-up company I talked about before." He gave me a businessman's smile. "And now for the exciting part for every teenager, right? Reed would always get so excited when he got his paycheck."

The money. The main reason I'd accepted this job in the first place, threw my morals to the wind, and agreed to work with the enemy of my best friend. Before, I'd needed it. Now, with nothing imperative for it to go toward, this money felt dirty.

I looked at the frosted door of the café, almost as if I was about to bolt through it.

"Speaking of Reed and Rachel," Mr. Manning went

on as he rummaged through his things, "do they have dates to the homecoming dance?"

I tried to tell myself it wasn't weird that he was being nosy into their love lives—a lot of parents were. "Um, Reed has a date, but Rachel doesn't."

"Oh, I saw her out with a boy the other day and just assumed."

My eyebrows slammed together. "Rachel was with a boy? When?"

"Hmm...a few Saturdays ago? Not this past Saturday, but the one before it." He pulled out an envelope, and from the brief flash as he turned it over, I saw my name scrawled along the front. "I was driving past the town park up near the school and I saw them walking along the sidewalk."

I wasn't dumb enough to ask him if he was sure—if it was his daughter, he'd know. But what boy would Rachel have been with that night? Whenever she hung out with a guy, she always made sure to tell me. No, she made sure to *gush* about them to me. And yet she was out Saturday night, walking around with a guy, and she never said anything? In the past few weeks, she never even talked about a guy except Josh.

A slow, confusion-riddled realization crept over me. "Was he blonde?"

"I couldn't really see. He wore a Hawaiian print shirt, though. I do remember that."

A Hawaiian printed shirt. Saturday, at Wallflower, that was what Josh had been wearing. After he dropped me off, he went on a walk with Rachel? Why wouldn't she have said anything?

"I hope it's okay if I email you from time to time," Mr. Manning said, interrupting my train of thought with that sly smirk. "You can be my informant of sorts on my kids, right?"

I wasn't sure if it was the lingering confusion of the whole Rachel and Josh thing, or the dread swamping through me about the money, but the graciousness I'd been carefully holding in place for all of our interactions cracked. "No."

It wasn't what he'd been expecting. "No?"

"I don't think they'd like it if I talked to you about them." It was what I should've said from the beginning, because even though Rachel and I were technically fighting—even if she pretended that we weren't—she was my best friend. "I think...maybe you should be the one reaching out to ask."

"Well, what about just Reed?" He leaned across the table. "Can you tell me a little about him? I've tried reaching out to him, but we haven't spoken since—well, everything."

There's a reason for that, I wanted to say, a protective urge swelling up. The door to the coffeeshop chimed as a stream of people filtered in, and along with them came a soft chattering of their voices. "Mr. Manning," I began, ready to lay it all out. I wasn't going to be his spy anymore. If he wanted to know about them, he'd have to work on mending the relationship—and respecting their wishes. How I was going to manage to say that nicely, though, I had no clue.

In the end, it didn't matter. When I raised my head from the envelope in my hand, my gaze snagged on the group of high schoolers that walked in, all sporting Brentwood's signature colors.

The first face I recognized was Cindy's, with her gorgeous hair and spirited Bobcat apparel. And then I looked past her by a few inches, landing on Reed Manning.

I jerked my head down, fanning my hair across my face in a reflex I couldn't fight. *Please*, I begged, and in that split second, my heart jumpstarted into a race it could never win. *Please, please.*

Mr. Manning's voice dashed any trace of hope. "Oh— Reed, is that you?"

If I didn't open my eyes, I could've pretended everything was okay. I wasn't sitting across from Mr. Manning anymore, with Reed no doubt already looking at us with widening eyes. I could pretend that he wasn't with Cindy right now, that this wasn't about to go down with an audience. I could pretend that Reed couldn't recognize me, despite my pink hair being a beacon of *Ava Jenson*.

But that bubble of bliss only floated around for a moment before it popped.

"Ava?"

I slowly moved my palm away from my eyes to reveal Reed.

In the past few weeks, I'd seen a side of Reed I'd never

noticed before. The vulnerable side. The softness behind the player exterior he always flaunted. The fears behind what drove his actions. I'd learned more about him in these weeks than I did in all the years I'd known him.

Which was why I knew, from the tightness in his brown eyes, that I'd royally screwed up.

Reed looked at me and only me, as if I sat at the window table all alone, but Mr. Manning wasn't going to give up in gaining Reed's attention. "How have you been, son? My God, look at you. It's crazy how much older you look in just a year."

I watched as Reed took in the iced hot chocolate in my hand, the one that was growing increasingly slick from the condensation pooling on the plastic. He then looked at my laptop, closed in front of me, finally settling on the envelope with *Ava* scripted in thick black ink. "Reed," I began, but his name didn't get further than a soft whisper past my lips. I wasn't sure he could even hear me.

Mr. Manning got to his feet, chair scraping on the tiled floor. The people Reed came in with—which, upon a closer look, was Landon, his girlfriend—all went up to the counter to order except for Cindy. She lingered behind Reed, shifting uncertainly. "Is this your girl-friend?" Reed's father asked. "I'm Reed's dad. It's nice to meet you..."

"Cindy," she offered, leaning around the wall of muscle in front of her to offer her hand. "We're going to homecoming together."

The way Mr. Manning laughed, with total lack of

awareness of the situation, made my skin crawl. "Nice to meet you, nice to meet you. I see you don't have a jersey on, Reed. So, it's true? You quit the football team?"

It was the taboo subject that never failed to cause Reed to falter. Reed's expression darkened, the way the sky dimmed once the sun dipped underneath the horizon. It left the atmosphere several degrees cooler.

"Ava," Reed said, looking straight at me. "Can I talk to you outside?"

There was nothing else to do but to gather my things and follow Reed out the chiming door, not letting my eyes stray to either Mr. Manning or Cindy.

As soon as we got out onto the sidewalk, Reed grabbed my wrist and pulled me away from the coffeeshop, away from any prying eyes peering out the windows. I went with him willingly, clutching my laptop bag to my chest. *Think. There has to be something you can say to diffuse this situation.*

But when Reed ducked into a narrow alleyway, turning toward me, all of the possible excuses slipped through my fingers like water.

"Why were you with him?" he demanded, the intensity in his eyes enough to turn anyone to stone. "Why were you *getting coffee* with him?"

"I wasn't *getting coffee.*" I mimicked his emphasis despite the desire to deescalate things. My whole being swelled with the confrontation in his voice, throwing up the defense. "We were just...talking about things."

"About how I quit the football team? You told him everything I said?"

"No! I didn't tell him anything about you quitting." That, at least, was true. I danced around the issue as much as I could when Mr. Manning had brought it up. "It's not like it's *not* public knowledge, Reed. You haven't been playing. You're not wearing your jersey on homecoming."

Reed turned to peer across the street, as if he couldn't look directly at me. "What were you talking about, then?"

"I...redesigned his website. We were going over the final things."

There. One of the secrets I'd been keeping for weeks was finally out there, right in the open. I'd been so caught up in imagining what would've happened if Rachel found out everything that I hadn't stopped to think about what Reed's reaction would be. Rachel would've rained hellfire. Reed, however, just looked betrayed.

And it cut deeper than I thought it would've.

"When did you start that? Have you been working on it this whole time?"

The definition of "this whole time" was hard to nail down, but I knew what he meant. *Since our kiss?* "He asked me the day after the list came out."

"And you said yes? Just like that?" That distrust returned to his gaze as he looked at me. "This is one of the secrets you were talking about the other night, right? Jeez, Ava, I didn't realize I was included in the list of people you kept things from."

The words themselves weren't designed to be piercing, but they cut through me anyway, mostly it's because he was the one person who'd been able to see practically everything these past few weeks. "I'm sorry," I got out, swallowing hard. "I thought I could use the money to help Mom out and keep her from selling the house. I—I thought if I could pitch in, it'd take some of her stress off. And then your dad said he'd recommend my work to his friends, and I—I figured that I could work on the website and then be done with him."

"You figured that you could do it and never say anything, right?" Reed blinked quickly, chest jumping with a sudden breath in. "You knew what he did. You knew how it hurt my family. And yet you worked with him anyway? After what happened between you and me?"

"You were the one who pulled me aside and said the kiss was meaningless to you," I shot back, my desperation spinning into something that resembled anger. The left-over frustration that'd come from the argument with Rachel had been yet another emotion I'd buried, and here it was, resurfacing at the worst time. It was too much to think around. "You said so yourself—it was a *pity kiss*. I didn't realize what I did would matter to you."

Reed flinched, the wince knifing across his expression. He had to have known that I overheard last night, since I practically walked in on Cindy and his conversation, but then again, after waiting all day for a text from him, it never came. Babble after Babble submission, sure, but no text. "Ava," he began, in a slow way that made my cheeks hot.

"Don't try to make me feel less embarrassed," I told him tightly, squeezing my laptop with knuckles that began to ache. "Because it's true, no matter how much I wish it weren't. No matter how it felt to me."

Reed's voice was lower than before when he asked, "How did it feel to you?"

Like a pencil under pressure, I felt something snap inside of me—not anger, not the defensiveness that'd swamped through me moments ago. No, this was something in my chest, something suffocating. "It doesn't matter, because you and me... We began and ended with that kiss."

And everything else after the fact was just a bonus chapter.

I brought the strap of my laptop bag over my head and rested it against my hip, lifting my chin up. "I have to go. I'm supposed to be at Maisie's house in ten minutes."

Reed reached out for my wrist again when I moved to step past him, eyes wide. "*Ava.*"

I once more pulled from his grip, looking him square in the eye. "I'm sorry for working with your dad. I'll come clean to Rachel, so you don't feel like you have to keep it from her."

I brushed past him, holding my breath like that would hold back the tears that burned my eyes. They hadn't fallen yet, which was a feat in itself, but I had to be seconds away. It was frustration and pain that raged inside me, as unforgiving as a storm.

"I liked it." The words came from Reed in a rushed breath, like he was desperate to get them out before he lost the nerve. They rang in the air, and I was grateful he couldn't see my face, because my eyes widened like they were about to pop out of my head. "It wasn't a pity kiss—I didn't mean that when I said it. The kiss... Our kiss. I liked it."

This was a moment I'd wondered about—worried about—on a near constant level. The situation, though, had always been reversed. It was me calling out to Reed, confessing the thoughts that'd played on a loop. It was Reed who had his back to me, and Reed who ultimately turned me down.

But here we were, with Reed saying things that did the exact opposite of what I'd always wanted. They didn't comfort me. They didn't make me smile.

Maybe he did think about the kiss, but he didn't think about *me*.

"We should stop here, then," I said without turning. "Before it gets worse."

"You're saying that because you're afraid." Reed's shoes crunched over the gravel in the alleyway as he took a step closer. "You told me yourself, you wanted to get the early relationships out of the way. The meaningless ones. Like Josh. You're afraid to fall for something *real*."

"What about you?" When I whirled around, I felt a hot tear track down my cheek. "You don't like me." The sentence came out with a soft scoff, one that made the pain blatantly obvious. "Not like that. You, Reed Manning, are always the one to walk away first. You're just afraid of someone walking away from *you*."

Reed clenched his jaw, and if I hadn't known any better, I would've thought his eyes were shining too. His hands hung at his sides, fingers loose and letting the breeze tickle them. I'd never seen him with such an expression on his face, and it stung, knowing that it was all my fault. *What a mess*, I thought with a woeful sigh, looking around at the tatters of this moment sadly. *Indeed, what a mess.*

"I'm not walking away," I told him, hastily swiping at the tear that made its way to my chin. Later, I'd be humiliated for crying again in front of him, but right then, it was the last thing I cared about. "I'm stopping before someone gets hurt." *And before my heart breaks more than it already has.*

I expected Reed to grab me again. It was a secret, shameful hope. Even if he had called after me, I would've kept walking, because I couldn't give in. Reed didn't say my name again, though. He didn't call after me.

I walked out of the alley with stiff shoulders and tears running down my cheeks, leaving behind the boy I never should've fallen for.

The bleachers for the homecoming game were filling up fast, and though excitement coursed through everyone like they shared a consciousness, I couldn't bring myself to tap into the energy. Tonight, of all nights, when my school spirit meter should be off the charts, that part of me felt totally empty.

"I can't believe you missed the homecoming parade," Rachel said as she nudged her elbow into my side, bouncing like a toddler who'd eaten three pixie sticks. "Madison's and Jade's dresses are to *die* for. Seriously. Jade wore gold and Madison wore blue. Gorgeous, right?"

Nothing in her tone belied our fight from the night before. As if it didn't happen at all. As if she couldn't tell that her best friend was practically catatonic.

Since today was a half-day at school, Rachel and I didn't have lunch together, which made it easier for me to stew in my feelings. A few hours ago, when Maisie had summoned us both to her house, she had seemed perfectly normal too. And it was easier for Rachel, apparently, to assume that everything was fine.

I would've been frustrated if I didn't feel like someone had flicked the lights out inside my body. Everything felt dark.

"Hopefully Maisie ends up coming tonight," she went on, slipping her hands into her pockets. "I know it's not her thing, but it's the *homecoming game*."

"Think about what she told us," I said to Rachel, voice flat. "Would you want to come?"

The bomb Maisie had dropped still shook me to my core. For the past two weeks, she'd been tutoring Connor Bray in secret, and last night, they'd *kissed*. Kissed. Like, her lips touched the lips of the most popular boy in school. And yet...nothing came of it. It was one of those moments that I couldn't possibly comprehend, especially the fact that he seemingly chose popularity over my best friend.

If I ever got him alone, we were going to have *words*.

I'd done a good job at keeping up a happy face earlier, but it was getting harder and harder.

"Is Josh still going with you to homecoming?" Rachel asked, tilting her head to peer down at me.

"Going with *us*," I corrected. "He's coming with all of us."

"Wait, why not as your date?"

"Because I don't want him to be." I squinted at the bobbing heads of people around us, all chattering away to pass the time. We had fifteen minutes until the game started, but we'd shown up early to snag the best seats. Front row in the student section. "Why didn't *you* ask him?"

"*Josh?*" Her voice turned up with confusion. "Why would I ask Josh?"

"You were out walking with him Saturday night."

From the corner of my eye, I saw her shoulders square as if she was about to go off to battle. "Did he tell you that?"

No, your father did. But she did confirm—it *was* true. "Who cares who told me? The fact is that you, my best friend, didn't."

Rachel forced her attention toward the field, losing all traces of her giddy, pixie stick-induced attitude from a moment ago. It was then that I realized it'd all been forced. She smoothed her palms down her bare knees, her skirt coming to her low thigh, but it was easy to see her goosebumps. "I guess neither of us has been fully honest lately."

"What's that supposed to mean?"

"When are you going to tell me who you had your first kiss with?"

I stiffened, the suggestion causing my skin to crawl. I wanted to take the secret with me to my grave, especially after knowing for certain that Reed liked our kiss but didn't end up liking me. Would I be able to lock it up? Shove it down, pretend it didn't hurt like a knife to the heart? That's what I did with my parents, and I ended up lashing out at both of them. If I kept this secret, would it be the unraveling of Rachel and I's friendship? The end of us? "I don't know."

"You don't know?" Rachel's voice came out clipped. "Isn't *that* something you tell your best friend? Seeing as I was the one to find you a guy to kiss in the first place."

"I never asked you to."

"Rachel, Ava—hey." Maisie walked up to us in the front row, looking a bit like how I felt. I couldn't tell if she'd heard us bickering or if the chatter of everyone around us had drowned it out. She was probably the least decked out in spirit gear, though she did wear an old Bobcats sweatshirt that must've been her sister's. "You guys snagged a front and center seat."

"Sit with us," Rachel encouraged, squeezing into the boy beside her to pat the bleacher. "We'll make room."

"That's okay," she said with a wave of her hand. "I think Jozie's getting popcorn, and I'll sit with her." Something in my expression caught her attention. "You okay?"

"Of course I am." My lips stretched into a smile. "It's homecoming."

At that moment, the Bobcat football players took to the field, wearing their rich blue jerseys with gold shimmering numbers. The bleachers, which were already nearly full, erupted into cheering at the sight of them, ringing bells and calling out the Bobcat chant. Rachel jumped to her feet and cheered along with the crowd, and I watched as Maisie shrank away from the railing. "I'm going to go find Jozie," she told me—or really mouthed to me, since most of her volume was cut off by the chants and the rattling bells people rang. "I'll catch you in a bit."

"You should be taking pictures," Rachel told me. Her voice was neutral, backing down from the severity we'd peaked at. "This is our last homecoming—Babble should be flooded with them."

She was right, of course. In all honesty, I should've been going around now and snapping pictures of seniors in their spirit gear. It was what I'd done last year, and that post had been a big hit. Now, though, it was all I could do to pull out my cell and point it at the field. I snapped picture after picture of each football player. I snagged a shot of Connor stretching his legs on the grass and a picture of Landon pulling his arm back to throw a football. Out of all the players, their names generated the most clicks.

"How about I come over tonight after the game?" she asked, looking down at me. Her expression wasn't as serious as it'd been moments before, but the ice hadn't thawed between us. "We can lay everything out. Both of us."

"You have more?" I squinted at her. "What, are you and Josh secretly dating?"

"It's not like that," she assured, adding an eye roll for good measure. "But...yeah, there's more. Just like you have more, right?"

There was a ton more. We hadn't even scratched the surface of everything that'd been piling up. But tonight, we were going to lay everything out in the open. Despite the weight of it, the fact that it was so freaking terrifying, I found myself nodding.

"Reed, my man!" a boy boomed from somewhere in the student section, and everyone around us rallied at the figure who stepped up the bleachers. He wore the same clothes he'd been wearing at Expresso's, only now accompanied by a light jacket to fight off the late September chill. Brentwood Bobcats spirit gear, of course. He smiled at the people who greeted him, who commented on the fact that he should be on the field and not in the stands, but he didn't say anything.

My heart squeezed at the sight of him, and it hurt even worse when his roaming gaze locked onto mine.

"I thought you weren't coming," Rachel said to Reed as he walked past us, putting her foot out as if she meant to trip him.

He stepped over it, stopping in front of me. "I thought I should come and support the guys."

I pinched the material of my jeans, studiously focusing on Landon as he launched another football. Reed's arm was in the frame of my vision, but as long as I stared at Landon, it didn't matter.

"Are you sitting with us?" Rachel didn't sound overly fond of the prospect; she didn't scooch down like she'd done for Maisie. "Because I don't think you deserve front row privileges, since this is the only game you've been to so far."

"I think I see Cindy up near the top," he replied, and my heart squeezed a little more. "I'll sit with her."

The football player who caught Landon's pass threw it back to him, but it'd been too hard of a throw, and Landon couldn't back up in time to catch it.

"I'll see you two later, then?" It was a hesitation of a question, like he wanted to linger for a moment longer.

"Wait!" Rachel shot from her seat and latched onto

Reed's wrist, dragging him to a halt. She turned her brown puppy dog eyes to me. "Can you take our picture? Mom would love it if we got a homecoming photo of us."

I sucked in a breath as she passed over her phone, wasting no time. Moments like this were rare between the Manning twins, but I didn't question it. I guess even if it seemed out of character, it made sense if Rachel wanted to commemorate one of their final events together.

Rachel tugged Reed to lean against the railing with her, and she wrapped her arm around his back while he draped his over her shoulders. "Would've been a much better picture if you'd stuck to football," she grumbled. "Y'know, with your jersey instead of some lame Bobcats sweatshirt."

Reed jostled her. "Cry a river."

"Smile," I told them. I tried not to, but I lingered on one twin more than the other, at the way his smile was wide, but it wasn't the same one I'd gotten used to seeing. It wasn't the one that caused butterflies to fill my stomach, or the one that crinkled around his eyes. "*Really* smile."

"I *am*," Rachel said through her teeth, and it was true —she was.

Reed's half-hearted grin faltered before it stretched wide again, wide enough to crinkle around his eyes, but still not wide enough to *really* touch his eyes. Not enough to feel real.

It was like we were looking at each other through the phone, and as I snapped the photo, I was transported to a few hours earlier. *You're afraid to fall for something real.* He'd spoken it so easily, like he hadn't had to think about it. Or like he *had* been thinking about it for a while.

But even if what he said had been true, what I had said had been true, too. *You're just afraid of someone walking away from you.*

"Your mom will probably tape it on the fridge," I said stiffly as I passed the phone back. "Send it to me. I'll post it to Babble."

Reed only lingered for another moment, but ended up being shuffled down the aisle when more students joined the fray. I lost him in the sea of blue and gold, and forced myself to drop my gaze.

As he walked away, and the football players were beginning to huddle on the sidelines, waiting for the buzzer to tick down, it hit me. The rest of my life would be filled with these moments. Falling silent when Reed walked past Rachel's bedroom door, or not being able to properly pipe up during their sibling banter. When Rachel talked about her brother, a bundle of confliction would come along with her words. Family parties, birthdays, holidays—it was going to be a lifetime of learning how to stop thinking about him.

I guess we were both afraid, and there was nothing to do but let it go.

My phone chimed as Rachel sent the photo over. "Don't forget to save some battery for the halftime show," she told me when the players took to the field, leaning onto the balls of her feet as the starting players moved to kickoff. "Hopefully, since it's our senior year, it's epic."

I hugged my closed laptop to my chest, which trapped my racing heart inside. In a matter of minutes, Rachel would walk into my room, and then it was time. Coming clean was terrifying, but I couldn't avoid it anymore. All I could hope for was a lesser sentence in the court of Rachel Manning.

My bedroom door was open, and I could hear the soft hum of the showerhead pump out water. I also heard when, in an anxiety-inducing second, the water shut off.

I'd gone back and forth an insane amount of times whether or not to tell Reed what I was about to do. Most of this did involve him. I even got as far as pulling out my cell, drafting the text, and then...throwing my phone onto my duvet. What did I expect from him, anyway? To show up and help me tell the tale?

Yeah, Rachel, it all happened when I went downstairs to get a drink of water. Your brother walked in shirtless, and we just decided to kiss.

And what would Reed say? *Yeah, we did.*

No, better to face this on my own. It was my mess—it

was my job to clean it up. Rachel shouldn't be mad at Reed for any of this. It was all on me.

"Your showerhead is *divine*," Rachel called in a singsong voice as she opened up the bathroom door, and even from where I lounged on my bed, I could see the steam billow out. "Like, seriously. I remember it being much worse."

"You can thank your brother for that," I called back, stretching my legs out on the mattress. My pajama bottoms had little coffee mugs on them, and I traced the outlines. "He was my mom's little construction worker for the past few weeks."

"Yeah, he said something about that." Rachel walked into my bedroom with her own silky pajamas on, rubbing at her brown hair with one of our towels. Instead of sitting on the bed beside me, she went to where her overnight bag was by the window, sifting through it until she pulled out a hairbrush. "Which makes me want to pummel him even more. He's over here, helping your mom get ready to sell."

"She was going to do it regardless. Without or without his help."

"Without his help would've taken longer."

I thought of the bills and the shutoff notices, knowing she didn't have time to take too long.

Rachel combed through her hair, peering out the window as she did so. Wetness was already starting to gather on the silk of her top, darkening the blue. I could see her somewhat in the reflection of the window, a pale face against the dark. "What do you have your laptop for?"

I hugged it tighter, like she was going to rip it from my fingertips. "It has to do with...coming clean."

While Rachel was showering, I'd gone ahead and loaded up the newly redesigned Manning Construction website. It would be the first page that it opened up to. Kicking it off with a bang. But after debating and debating, working with her dad seemed like the lesser of the two evils I needed to confess about.

She turned around to face me, wielding her hairbrush. "I'm sorry," she said.

I blinked. "Sorry?"

"For last night." Her gaze drifted to the side. "You're right. I shouldn't have been comparing my experience to yours. Our parents splitting up isn't a trophy that only one of us can win."

I hadn't expected my eyes to sting so early on into our conversation, but here I was, fixing on the lamp near my bed in hopes of drying them up. "I know it probably brought up hard stuff for you."

"It did." Rachel padded slowly across the floor, sitting on the opposite edge of the bed than me. She continued to brush her hair, using it as a lulling motion. "But you were there for me when I went through it. I should've been there for you. I just—" She let out a harsh breath. "I was jealous."

"Jealous?" I echoed. "What was there to be jealous of?"

"Your dad walked out, but it wasn't like you were cut

off from him the way I was cut off from mine. It wasn't like—it wasn't like you weren't allowed to miss him."

I tried to duck my head to catch her eye, but she turned away. "Did you miss your dad?"

"Every day. I could never show it, though. It was obvious Reed and Mom were angry—which, I mean, I get that they were—so it felt like I had to be angry, too. Which...it was easier to be angry than to miss him. Like, it wasn't *wrong* to be angry, but it was wrong to want to talk to him." She gave a sharp shrug, forcing out a chuckle as if to brush everything off. "So, I guess that's why I was jealous, that you could talk to your dad and it wasn't that big of a deal."

It suddenly felt too exhausting to sit upright, so I nestled against my array of pillows, curling my legs to my chest. I set the laptop off to the side. "I've only seen him once since he left, and it was only for ten minutes."

It turned out that the weight I started with ended up being the one I carried the longest. As I told her about my father, and how things had devolved into a text message every few days, I could practically physically feel the tension easing off my chest, especially when she reached over and picked up my hand. Tears were shed on both sides of the bed, but when I finally talked about the divorce, I could tell she was actually listening. Not comparing. Not judging. Just being there for me.

"You should've told me," she said with a sniffle, patting her tears off her cheeks. "You must've felt so alone."

In my head, I could picture Reed lying in his bed, my

body tucked up against his. The steady pulls of his breathing echoed in my ears, along with his voice. *I'll always be there for you. As whatever you want me to be.* "I had someone I could talk to."

I expected her to dig more on that since I'd left the door wide open, but she didn't. Instead, she almost looked fearful, setting the hairbrush down. "There's something else. One other thing that I've been keeping from you."

Her words caused anxiety to shift through me. She only had one thing left, but I had two major things. The playing field felt totally unfair. "Go ahead."

I'd always thought I'd been able to read Rachel's mind. It'd been something I'd prided myself on as we grew up—that I, more than her twin, could guess what she was thinking. Like what movie she wanted to watch, or which boardgame she wanted to play. What she wanted. However, I never would've guessed what she said next.

"I know you were working on my dad's website," she said, voice small. "I know, because I was the one to tell him to work with you."

It was like I forgot to compute the English language for a second. *I was the one to tell him to work with you.* Meaning she'd been in contact with him. Slowly, realization dawned. In all of the emails, his focus had mainly been on Reed, not Rachel. How was Reed coping with high school? Why wasn't Reed playing in the game? When he asked me to be his informant, he asked me about Reed, not Rachel.

Because Mr. Manning was already talking to Rachel.

"I kept waiting for you to say something. I figured there was no way you'd work with him without asking me about it. But you didn't. You never said anything."

There wasn't a hitch to her voice when she spoke, but something in her eyes had my heart picking up its pace. "I needed the money to help Mom," I told her quickly. "I was afraid to ask you, because if you said no...I wasn't sure if I'd have been able to pass it up for Mom's sake. But —that wasn't the only thing that convinced me. I tried to tell myself that he wasn't your dad, but it still—I still felt *terrible*." Rachel nodded as I spoke, but something else hit me. "You never told me you were talking to him again."

"It's like I said." She sighed a little. "It didn't feel like I was allowed to miss him. I guess we both felt guilty for not coming clean. I should've told you everything from the beginning instead of...testing you, I guess. Seeing if you'd tell me. That was crappy."

"It was crappy of me not to tell you," I reaffirmed. "But Reed...he isn't talking to your dad?" I knew the answer before I asked; Reed's expression upon finding us in the café today was answer enough.

But Rachel shook her head. "And he doesn't know I see Dad on the weekends. Maybe one day, he'll come with me."

I thought about what Reed had said about Mr. Manning's birthday, and how he felt bad for his father, in a way. Hopefully Rachel was right, and that Reed could meet him—and hopefully that day was soon.

Even though the shame lingered like an aching

bruise, the sharp pain at the idea of telling Rachel the truth had disappeared. The fear that I'd never been able to shake was gone. Now there was one item left.

Except when I opened my mouth, Rachel cut me off. "Let's talk about Josh."

"Josh." I let out a little breath, because it was like a reprieve in all the heaviness. Even thinking about his dimpled face made everything lighter. "I don't like him, you know. Not like that."

"I know you don't."

"So, it's okay if you *do.*"

She gave her head a slight shake, expression thoughtful. "I don't know if I do or don't. I do like being around him, though. I know that, at least."

"You should go for it, then. Test the waters." I lightly nudged her arm. "Find out if he really is Kissable Josh."

That made her laugh, and in an instant, she was moving. She pulled away from me so she could reposition how she sat on the bed, leaning forward to put her elbows on her knees. "So, it's time for you to tell me."

I sucked in a breath. "Tell you?"

"Who *your* kissable guy is."

Things seemed to slow down. *Lie,* my brain encouraged, because it knew the consequences to follow. *Lie, lie, lie.*

Lie, my heart urged, because it knew that it couldn't handle any more breaks. *Lie, lie, lie.*

She sat down beside me, pulling her legs underneath her. I could see where her hair dripped onto my duvet cover. "You can tell me who it is. I promised you earlier that I wouldn't be upset. As long as you're honest, it'll be okay."

Still, I hesitated. This was the deepest heart to heart we'd had in a while, but kissing Reed—would telling her about that be the straw that broke everything? She forgave me for working with her father, but could she forgive me for kissing her brother? And really, that wasn't even the worst part. Yes, I kissed him, but I also fell for him. Josh was right—I let him invade my thoughts like a virus, one that I couldn't shake.

Every possible scenario shuttered through my mind. Rachel yelling, Rachel leaving, Rachel calling off our decade-long friendship—all of it was a massive bundle of *terrible*, and I couldn't even bring myself to take the first step of opening my mouth.

"God," Rachel said with a light eye roll. "I'll rip the bandage off for you—I know you kissed Reed."

I jumped away from the headboard so fast that my head spun, or maybe it spun from the bluntness of her words, of the shock that pummeled through me like a wave. It knocked the breath out of me, and I literally gasped like she gave me an electrical shock. "I—you—*you knew?*"

She raised her eyebrows as her mouth curved up into a small smirk. "I didn't know for total certain. Not one hundred percent. Not until right now."

And now I was breathless once again, feeling like she'd smacked me in the face.

She took advantage of my silence and went on, tapping her chin. "After you told me you kissed someone,

I thought to myself, 'Who would Ava kiss on impulse? Why would she regret the kiss? Why wouldn't she tell me who it was?'" She pointed her hairbrush at me. "And then I come home one Saturday morning to find you in your pajamas, claiming you spent the night without me there? You've never done that."

I wanted to deny it, but the horror of everything settled thickly inside me. I had to admit, though, she did have a point.

"Also, c'mon. If I couldn't tell you were crushing on my brother, looking at him with total googly eyes earlier at the game, what kind of best friend would I be?"

I hugged my knees closer, relief pouring through my veins. A strange emotion for the moment, absolutely, but it was like I'd been walking a great distance with a heavy backpack weighing me down, and, after being desperate to do so for so long, I was finally able to let it drop. My feet hurt from walking, and my shoulders ached from the journey, but the weight of the secret was gone. "You're not mad?"

Rachel looked up at the ceiling, as if she were really thinking about it. "I might've been freshman year, but I'm not fourteen anymore. I think it's mega gross to think that you like the slob that is my brother, yeah, but...no, I'm not mad."

My breathing became pinched then. I curled my fingers, but it didn't stop them from trembling—didn't stop *me* from trembling. "It just happened," I told her, words rushing together. "It—it wasn't supposed to mean anything, but then it did, and I didn't know how to stop it.

I tried with Josh, but then Reed was over all the time, and I wanted to tell you *so badly—*"

My words cut off as Rachel wrapped her arms around me. The scent of my strawberry body wash smelled differently on her skin, but still comforting. "Ava, it's a wonder you didn't explode these past few days," she murmured, rubbing her hand in circles on my back. The action only made me burrow deeper, trying to choke down a sob. "Shh, shh. I'm not mad. You're not mad at me, are you?"

I shook my head.

"See? Everything's okay."

I leaned my head firmly against her shoulder, not caring that her hair was wet and cold. "If you thought I kissed your brother, why did you ask me about Josh?"

"I love Reed," she said at once. "He's got a big heart, but I know how closed off he's been since Dad. I didn't want to see either of you hurt, but I didn't want my best friend's first heartbreak to come from my brother."

It's too late, I wanted to say, but I drew away, looking into her eyes that looked so much like his. "It wasn't like we were going to be together, though. Him and me."

"Why not?"

"He's not exactly the boy next door," I said. "He's with Cindy now, but just the first week of school, he was talking to someone else. And last year was worse. What if I'm just next on a list?"

"Ava." She reached out and wiped my cheeks with her fingers, and then moved to clasp my upper arms.

"That's the whole point of liking someone. You have to put yourself out there."

But if I had doubts in the beginning, what was the point of going forward? What was the point in risking it all if it wouldn't work out? Sure, Mom said that she wouldn't have changed her relationship with Dad, but would Mrs. Manning change hers with Rachel's dad? Was avoiding any potential heartbreak better than not falling at all?

Even more than that, a different fear nagged at me. "What if he doesn't like me?"

"I don't think he would've kissed you to begin with if he didn't like you—which, I'll have you know, I haven't forgotten about, so you can go ahead and explain—"

"What if it doesn't work out?" I whispered, cutting her off with wide eyes. "What if it's strange and messes everything up? Like you said, your parents split up. Mine split up. What if something happens? What if it affects our friendship?"

"Then we can bubble-wrap his bedroom and replace his shampoo with bleach or something." She pinched my leg lightly. "Girl, I think we can be mature enough to not let a guy get between us, even if he is my brother, can't we?"

"But what if—"

"Ava." She pulled her head back to stare at me. The determination in that stare was all my best friend, so much so that it nearly made me emotional again. "Enough with the what ifs. You're never going to know if you don't go for it. It's okay to be afraid, but you can't let that stop you from living."

Liking Reed had been risky at first, fearing any anger that Rachel might've had. Now that Rachel gave the green light, a new set of risks came into the play. What if he turns me down? What if we find out that being together is awkward? What if we fall out of love? Any of those could happen if I took the step forward, if I stepped past liking Reed and doing something about it.

"Don't overthink it," Rachel said, and hugged me once more. "I can see the hamster wheel spinning in your brain. Whatever happens, I'm right here, just like you'll be there for me. No matter what."

She was right. No matter what happened, we had each other. "I love you," I said into her hair.

"I love you, too." She patted me on the back once more. We stayed like that for a moment, listening to each other's breathing, before she said, "So, uh. When *exactly* did this first kiss even happen?"

"Smile," I said cheerfully, snapping a flashing shot of another couple. This girl's dress was to die for—a brilliant green with dark sequins sewn into the fabric. The boy had suspenders to match. "Perfect! Keep an eye out for it on Babble, okay?"

To the beat of music that probably wasn't appropriate for high schoolers, I went around taking photos. I flitted around, going from couple to cute couple, taking a few candids and asking for poses. I would have time to dance later, and I'd rather take the photos now, when the dance first started, before everyone got sweaty from the heat of the gym.

The current fast-paced club song melted into a slow song, and I watched as groups of people broke off into pairs, beginning their slow-dance. *Perfect.*

I found Connor and Maisie first among the couples, and though she'd given me a rule about *not* overexposing their relationship, surely a moment like this one was allowed, right? They were close enough to the strobe lights that I flicked off the flash, hoping to fly under the radar.

I sought out Rachel and Josh next, but stumbled upon the quarterback instead. Landon was standing near the outskirts of the dancefloor, expression totally caught in thought. I held up my cell, but as if he had a sensor for it, the redhead lifted his head and spotted me.

Landon's expression was light. "Work never ends, huh?"

"Haven't you heard the phrase 'a blogger never sleeps'?" I replied with a smile, walking closer to hear him better over the music. "Where's your girlfriend? Lacey, right?"

"Not here yet." His smile was soft under the lights that blinked with the soft beat. "How about you? Did you have a date?"

"Unless you count this baby." I waved my phone.

"A lot less complicated." Something flitted across his expression, almost like he regretted speaking.

"Come find me when Lacey gets here," I told him, giving him a friendly smile. "I demand a picture of the two of you together for Babble."

Landon nodded, but his lips fumbled their upturned tilt just a little. "Yeah, will do."

I ventured once more into the fray of couples, and the first slow song switched into the second. The lights dimmed even lower for this one, the deep purplish blue making it tougher to navigate. I edged around a girl in a beautiful pink dress when a hand wrapped around my wrist, tugging me backward.

And I found myself pressed up against Reed Manning's chest.

His beautiful, suit-clad chest.

"Dance with me?" he asked, releasing my wrist to rest his hand at my waist.

It was such a surprise that I found myself standing stock-still for a moment. My fingers landed on his smooth black tie, and I was close enough to be able to see the paisley-printed pattern on the black material. It was only a shade lighter than the tie itself, but beautiful. "Where's Cindy?"

"She's dancing with Ashton." His other hand came up to rest on my other hip, firm enough for me to feel every single point of pressure through the material of my white dress. "And I wanted to dance with you."

I swallowed past the thickness in my throat—swallowed the thoughts screaming at me to put distance between us—and allowed my hands to smooth their way up his suit jacket, resting at the tops of his shoulders. The top two buttons of his collared shirt were undone, but the fabric laid in a way that I couldn't see his collarbone. It was weird to feel the firmness of the jacket, because once upon a time, I'd touched the bare skin here.

"You look stunning, you know. I thought I was imagining you when I saw you."

"Because Ava Jenson couldn't possibly look stunning?" I tried to sound teasing. I sounded tense instead.

Reed acted like he didn't notice. "Because I didn't think you could be real."

I forced myself to look everywhere else but at him

and the buttons that were undone at his collar. The butterflies, though, had already burst into action in my stomach, his words giving them life. "I told Rachel the truth."

"About my dad?"

"About everything." And then I added, "About the kiss."

His fingers loosened their touch at my waist. "What—what did she say?"

I explained to him how she said she already had a feeling, but she wasn't mad. I conveniently, though, left out the part where she said she was rooting for us. He didn't need to know that. "I guess we worried for nothing."

Reed's left hand slid around my waist, creating a path of warmth as it settled on my lower back. The embrace became more personal, the fraction of a difference in where he put his hands. It fogged my brain. "Ava?"

"But it doesn't change what I said yesterday," I rushed, hating that my gaze returned to those buttons. "I meant it when I said we should stop."

"Stop what?" Reed's voice slipped lower as his head ducked toward me, and his voice filtered into my ear. "Stop caring about each other?"

"You only think you care about me," I whispered, more because my voice disappeared as the slow song rose to its bridge. "It's all because of that stupid kiss."

Reed looked down into my eyes, the brown swimming with the multicolor strobe lights. They flickered wildly as the beat rose to a crescendo, casting glowing rays across his skin. "I think," he began, hand giving my waist a gentle squeeze, "that you should stop pretending that the kiss meant nothing."

It was a pity kiss. Reed's words to Cindy echoed like a shout in a tunnel, distorting with every second, and the only thing that lingered was how they made me feel. I dropped my hands from him. "You shouldn't say those things when you're here with someone else," I told him fiercely, bitterness seeping into my words. The song was almost over; it was on its last line. "You should go find her."

Without waiting for him to respond, I threw myself into the crowd, trying not to knock into any couples but hardly managing it. My heels scraped across the floor as I hurried across it, uneven, like I was drunk. After several seconds, I burst from the dancefloor, gunning for the double doors that led out of the gym.

Watching from afar was enough. Pulling away from him was the smart idea. Minimal risk. I wasn't sure I had it in me to give any more.

Except apparently the universe didn't want me to stay in my comfort zone.

"Ava!" Reed's voice followed me out into the hallway, and a second later, he was there, squinting under the bright lights. Students lingering in the hallway all turned to listen. "Listen, I—"

I grabbed his wrist and tugged him away from the kids around us, shoving through a set of doors that led out into a courtyard. There wasn't anyone out here, despite the reprieve of the music and heat. The crisp air chilled me, icing the sweat on my skin. "Reed—"

"You know what I want to stop?" he demanded, spreading his arms wide in a way that would've made him appear defeated if it weren't for the fierce look in his eyes. "I want to stop pretending like you're just my sister's best friend. I want to stop pretending like I don't have feelings for you. Stop acting like the idea of walking away from you doesn't rip my heart out. And you know what else? I want to stop acting like that kiss wasn't the best one I've ever had."

Each sentence was a punch that winded me more and more until oxygen was completely out of the question. Poof. Gone. Stolen by Reed Manning and the frosty air.

"Maybe I am afraid," he went on, cheeks beginning to deepen with color. "Like you said yesterday. But I know I'm more afraid of letting you go than I am of you walking away. I'm afraid of looking back on this moment in ten years and regretting it."

I wrapped my arms around my waist, more in an attempt to keep myself together than to keep warm. An ache began to form in my chest, so severe it felt like I'd crack apart. "But Cindy—"

"She came to the dance with me, that's all. We haven't even danced together—she's been dancing with Ashton the whole night. Which is completely fine, because the only person I wanted to dance with was you."

I closed my eyes then, because he was going to

completely drive me crazy. It was like the things he said were perfectly designed to tear down any of my defenses, to rip me apart until there was no way I could push him away anymore. *You can't be like your parents*, the old insidious thought whispered. *You can't fall for him. You can't risk that kind of heartbreak.*

Almost like he could hear the voice, Reed asked, "Do you like me?"

"Reed—"

"Yes or no, Paparazzi. Easy as that."

I let out a breath, pulse thrumming higher. "I—I do, but I—"

He didn't even let me finish. Much like he had for our first kiss, Reed surged forward and cut me off, pressing his mouth to mine in the most perfect way to shut me up.

One of his hands wrapped around the back of my neck, and five of his cool fingers pressed into my hot skin. I tipped my head back, a shiver wracking its way through me as it pressed us closer. His other hand came up to cup my face, thumb sliding along my cheekbone in a gentle caress. The scent of him was everywhere, the taste just as intoxicating.

My own hands slipped up his chest, fingers catching on the undone buttons, easing the fabric of his shirt aside to feel the skin at the base of his throat. I kissed him with a ferocity that'd built inside of me ever since that Monday night in his kitchen. I hadn't known what I was getting into then, but I knew now. Everything I'd been wishing for, thinking about—it was finally happening again.

Except this time there was no fear. No hesitation.

We parted with a soft gasp, both of us breathing as if we'd run a mile. Reed smoothed my hair out of my face, trailing his fingers through the pink locks with an almost mesmerized gaze. "You can't tell me you want to stop now."

"I'm scared," I found myself whispering again. I reached up and hung my hand off his wrist. "I don't want either of us to get hurt."

"What if we agree not to hurt each other?" His thumb once more began its smooth path down my cheek. "Agree that there's no running away, and no giving up. No regrets, not with us."

No regrets. It was something Dad couldn't get past with mom, wondering the what ifs. I knew, with one-hundred percent certainty, that this would be my moment. My what if. I squeezed his wrist, feeling his pulse tremble underneath the skin. "I'm scared," I repeated.

He let out a soft, ghostly-sounding laugh. "It is scary. Terrifying. But maybe we can be afraid together."

The swelling pressure reached its breaking point, popping and letting a rush of conviction ride its way through me. And that was what it came down to. Which what if could I live with? *What if we break up* or *What if I'd allowed myself to really fall for Reed Manning?*

"Afraid together," I echoed, reaching up and touching my fingertips to his golden-brown hair. The locks were soft—exactly how I remembered them feeling. "Deal."

To seal it, I stepped up onto my tiptoes and gently

pressed my lips against his, a savoring kiss when our previous two had been filled with desire and need. This was a different sort of need, one that burrowed itself into my bones and created a blanket of warmth. It calmed the nerves, the anxiety, and as soon as I made up my mind, peace came with it. *Good choice.*

Reed wrapped his arms around me and pulled me into his chest, cocooning me in the warmth of him. I nestled in deep, threading my arms underneath his jacket and tightening my grip around his waist. "Can you get me more comic books?" he asked, smoothing his hand down my hair. "I've gone through the ones you bought already. Maybe we can read them together."

I smiled, closing my eyes. "As long as you bring the chocolate cake this time."

Reed pressed his lips to the top of my head, giving a contented sigh. In the background, there was the faintest sound of music playing from inside the dance, and there might've even been students peering through the courtyard windows and snapping photos to send to Babble, but in that moment, I didn't care about anything but being in Reed's embrace.

A good choice, indeed.

"I know it's not much," Dad said as I stepped into the guest room, lingering in the doorway while he rubbed his knuckles. The nervous energy he'd exuded the second I stepped over the threshold had simmered down now, but he still fidgeted back and forth. "I tried to decorate it how I thought you'd like it. If you want, we can paint the walls like how we did in your old room. Something to make it feel more...homey."

I glanced around the sparsely filled guest room and could see where he'd tried to channel me. The bedspread covering the twin mattress was a light pastel pink, and I wasn't sure if he knew that was my favorite color or took a guess based off my hair, but it was pretty. The room wasn't large enough for two end tables, but he'd squeezed one wicker one against the wall with the window. A small work desk was in the other corner, next to the slatted closet doors.

"I like it," I told him, trailing in deeper into the room and running my fingertips over the duvet cover. "I think it'll be perfect for when I stay here."

"Which is next weekend, right?" Dad dropped his hands, guilty expression deepening. "I never meant for you to feel like an outsider here, Ava. I wanted you to see this when everything was finished. *Furnished.* It's a terrible excuse for putting off our weekends, and if I'd known how you felt—"

"Dad. It's really okay." It wasn't the first time he'd apologized for that. Last weekend, when he stopped by the house for homecoming pictures before I left for Maisie's, he'd expressed that sentiment. That he was embarrassed for me to see the apartment when he only had a mattress and a few cardboard boxes for end tables. He didn't want me to see the apartment—*him*—like that. And even today, when I walked into the two-bedroom flat, the first thing he'd done was give me a set of keys to put on my lanyard. "I wouldn't have cared either way, but I'm glad I could come over now."

When Dad returned the smile, his seemed watery. "I hope this can become like a second home to you."

This was such a huge transition period of my life, and as we made our way back to the living room, I couldn't help but reflect on all of it. My parents' separation. Dad moving out into a new space. Mom selling my childhood home to move to the next town over. All that happening while transitioning into my senior year, the last year of high school. It was almost too much.

Which was why I should've listened to Reed sooner when he said I should talk to a therapist, and why I shouldn't have gotten so upset with Mom for asking Mrs. Murphy to speak with me. We met two times a week, now, for a half-hour after school, and it really was nice to just talk. About anything. Everything.

My cell buzzed in my pocket, and when I fished it out, my chest began buzzing, too. "My ride's waiting for me," I told Dad. "Do you have those leftover moving boxes?"

That'd initially been what I'd stopped by for—more boxes for Mom. We'd underestimated how many we'd actually need to pack up the house, but then again, they'd been accumulating stuff for over twenty years. We probably weren't going to have enough boxes, but with two months to gather everything, we had more than enough time. Especially since we had help.

"I'll see you next weekend," I said as we collected the boxes and headed toward the elevator. Thank goodness, too, since he lived on the fourth floor. "For sure."

"For sure," he repeated, waving at me when the elevator doors slid apart, revealing the lobby. "Get home safe, kiddo. Text me if you ever need anything, okay?"

It wasn't quite how things had been between us, but it was better than before. The month we'd spent not seeing each other had left things different. Especially given the circumstances. But we'd get back to where we were eventually—we just needed time.

Though the sun was out, the October air was chilly, and I would've tugged my cardigan tighter around myself if I weren't juggling the folded cardboard. I did an awkward shuffle-walk across the parking lot. They slipped in my grip, to the point where my knees kept hitting the ones about to fall.

"Here." Two hands came to the rescue, closing on the cardboard right underneath mine. "Let me take them. I texted you asking if you needed help."

I huffed out a breath. "I wanted to be strong and impressive."

Reed took the folded boxes from me with much more ease than I'd had a moment ago, and he quickly tucked them under his arm, pressing them against his body. Then, with his concentration free, he turned to me with a glimmer in his eyes. "You already are strong and impressive."

"Except when it comes to cardboard boxes."

He winked. "We all have our Kryptonite."

"Hey!" It wasn't hard to find the location of the voice. Rachel, sitting in the backseat of their shared silver sedan, rolled her window down. "Put the flirty eyes away and come *on*! Or this technically is going to count as your guys' alone time."

Despite the scowl on her face, I laughed. After the homecoming dance last week, Rachel declared her new rule, replacing the "no dating my brother" one. The time I spent with Reed had to be matched with the time I spent with Rachel. She wasn't going to let her twin get everything this time, especially when she had me first. Her words.

It'd been a funny conversation, listening to them work out the semantics while I was taking off my makeup from the dance. Rachel had started it. "So, *school gets out at three—*"

"*And she goes to sleep around ten,*" Reed had interjected.

"*Which leaves seven hours of free time,*" Rachel had nodded. "*So, I get three and a half hours, and you get three and a half hours.*"

I'd tried asking them what about my own free time to work on Babble posts and other web designs, but my words hadn't even broken the barrier of their strategizing.

Now Reed frowned as we got closer. "How can it count as alone time for us if you're here, Rachel?"

"I'm helping you, you know," she said as we moved toward the car. Reed went to the trunk to put in the boxes. "If you two would've run this errand on your own, it would've deducted from your time together. It would've been lame to spend it on *errands*. At least since I'm here, it cancels each other out."

"Very selfless of you," I told her as I slid into the passenger's seat. I angled the vents toward me, letting them puff warm air onto my fingertips.

"Except maybe I would've preferred to have run this errand with just Ava," Reed said as he climbed into the driver's seat, casting me a sidelong glance. "At least then I could've held her hand on the drive over without you nearly having an aneurism."

Rachel huffed. "They say 'hands at ten and two' for a reason, Reed."

"I thought you said you were cool with us being together," Reed said, looking up at the rearview mirror. "I distinctly remember a whole 'I want you two to be happy' line in that speech you gave after the dance."

"Yes, but *my* happiness comes first, of course. You'd think with our twin-telepathy, you'd understand that." Rachel let out a satisfied sound. "Besides, she was my friend first."

They bickered about it, but it made my chest feel so light. This was another transition period, learning how to navigate the Manning twins without too many hiccups. Of course, hiccups would happen eventually. Rachel had to learn how to let her brother and her best friend have couple time, and Reed had to learn how to share his girl-friend with his sister. Until then, we'd keep having bick-ering contests, with me happily letting them hash it out.

Reed rested his head against the headrest and looked over at me, and despite the sibling squabble, his expres-sion was amused. "We should walk home and let her drive the car."

And maybe more importantly, Reed and I both needed to learn how to give up the desire of control and let things *be*. In any aspect of our relationship. I had to say, though—we were doing pretty great at that so far.

I lifted my eyebrows at him. "Should we?"

"No, no!" Rachel slapped her hand on the console between us. When I turned around to look at her, she was pressing her palms over her eyes, angling into the backseat door. "You have five seconds. Five seconds and I *swear to God*, I better not hear a sound, or I'll hurl in the backseat. And you, Reed, will have to clean it."

I thought Reed would brush it off, but he wasted no time in leaning across the console and pressing his lips to mine, and I had to swallow the gasp to keep Rachel satiated. My toes curled as Reed touched his fingertips to my jaw, and I hung my hand off his wrist, holding him there.

"Okay, that's five seconds. I'm looking now. Hello? You better not still be—" Rachel let out a sharp sound. "You two! I swear! Stop kissing!"

Reed's lips curled up into a smile against mine, and I knew I needed to pull away—to be considerate of my best friend who was probably trying to keep down her lunch—but I just wanted to memorize the feeling of him smiling against me. I wanted to remember how the tingling sensation felt forever.

Rachel wiggled her hands between us to shove us apart, and Reed's laugh was a musical sound as he fell back into his seat. I bit down on my lip to keep from grinning, pressing a hand to my cheeks to cool it off.

"I'm deducting that from your day," Rachel muttered, and the car rocked as she wiggled to the far side of the backseat door. "You get five less seconds of Ava time than me. And you know what else? I'm going to deduct the time it's going to take to burn the image from my mind, too. That's going to be, like, fifty years. Hope you look forward to dating when you're sixty-seven."

"It was worth it," Reed said, and in front of the console, out of Rachel's view, he offered his splayed hand to me. "Don't you think?"

I pressed my palm against his, insides warming as his fingers curled around my hand. My cheeks were hot from the kiss, my lips still buzzing with it, but I'd never been happier in that moment. With my best friend behind me and my boyfriend beside me—my *boyfriend*—I was utterly and perfectly content. I looked at Reed, at the freckle beneath his waterline, at the sliver of skin where his collarbone was exposed, and smiled. "Totally worth it."

Thank you so much for reading!

Order Book 3 in the Most Likely To series, *Rebelling With the Bad Boy*, today and fall for Brentwood High's bad boy! Keep reading to see a bonus scene from Reed's point of view!

After everything that happened with my dad, I learned that I hated the quiet. My thoughts had the opportunity to get too loud in the quiet, too suffocating.

Which was why the TV hanging above my dresser was on, automatically playing the next episode of some sit-com it switched to, but I didn't actually listen. Instead, I just let it be background noise as I flipped another worn page in the comic book. I pressed the pad of my finger against the staple holding the pages together, wiggling it back and forth as my eyes scanned the page. There was so much to take in—from actions to character expressions to the surrounding setting—that each page easily kept my thoughts focused, alert, leaving no room for wandering. The colors were a bit dull from age, but it made it more interesting. Thinking about who held this before me, what their favorite sections were, when they first bought it.

The best part? Dad hated comics.

Though my TV was on, I had the volume turned down in case the noise reached Mom's room. I didn't have to worry about Rachel complaining about it tonight, thankfully. She came home after the game to collect an overnight bag, citing a sleepover, which I hadn't questioned at the time. Now, though, I debated texting her asking where she *really* was. She only had two friends, and they always came over here for sleepovers. She took the car, which meant she didn't go to Ava's. Ava didn't go with her, which meant she probably wasn't going over to Maisie's.

Not that I paid attention to Ava going into the house and not coming back out, of course.

And just like that, the pink-haired shortie popped into my mind and refused to see herself out.

Train of thought interrupted, I dropped my head back against the headboard, letting out a groan. An idiot. I was a total idiot. The way we'd left things—the way *I* left things—yesterday still made me uneasy. Anxious. A part of me wanted to blame Ava, because it was like the jerkiest things came out of my mouth whenever I got close to her. It was like she just pulled them out of me. *The kiss didn't mean anything to me* and *What kiss?*

The bigger part of me, though, knew it was just because all of it freaked me out.

It was dumb. I tried to push her to Cindy's brother, but whenever I thought about Josh kissing her, I about lost my mind.

I tried to separate everything in my mind, like I could

put it all into little boxes. Ava Jenson—Rachel's best friend. She fit perfectly into the *platonic* category.

But then, our *kiss*...

For probably the billionth time since it happened, I thought of that night in the kitchen, the comic book before me morphing from a radioactive dump site to Ava's big eyes looking up at me in the darkness of the kitchen. The second she mentioned having her first kiss, just getting it over with, there was no looking away from her lips if I tried. It took her out of the box I'd been perfectly content to keep her in, introducing thoughts I'd never had before.

And then—

So, after that pep talk, you're not going to follow through?

I groaned again, hating the way my blood warmed at the memory. *Stupid, stupid, stupid.* How she couldn't read that as desperation was beyond me.

Focus on the comic book, Reed, I scolded myself, gripping the pages tighter, wiggling the staple. *Stop thinking about Ava Jenson.*

Now, comic bubbles and facial expressions did nothing to draw me into the moment. Reading was an effective way to blot out any thoughts of my father, but apparently thoughts of Ava were stronger. So, setting down the comic book on my desk, I made my way to the kitchen for a glass of water.

Because I was thirsty. Not for any other reason.

It wasn't the first time I'd wandered in here for a

"glass of water" since everything happened. Though before, it'd been almost like a test. *See, I can be in this kitchen and not think of Ava Jenson.* That didn't work, though. Then it was a test of *See, I can think of Ava Jenson, but I won't think of* that *moment.*

Now, with my *Super Mario Bros* mug cradled in my grip, I looked at the exact spot she'd stood when I pressed my mouth to hers, wondering why I was fighting a losing battle.

I asked myself—*why her?* Though I'd flippantly told Ava I'd kissed twenty-one people, I truly had no clue what the number was. Either way, I never thought about kisses past the in-the-moment desire, never really thought about it lying awake at night. It was like I was able to separate life as Reed Manning and the dating life of Reed Manning. Like, if I wasn't with the girl, I'd be too focused on everything in my own life. But with Ava, it was like she invaded my brain at every waking second.

But she wasn't just any girl.

A sudden sound had me jumping, and for a moment, I struggled to place it. It was a hard thump, like something had struck the front door. Or like someone tried to open it against the deadbolt.

I was ready to tell Rachel to use her key—had I really missed hearing the car pull back into the driveway?—but when I opened the door, I realized it wasn't Rachel at all.

My thoughts had done a wonderful job at copying and pasting Ava before my eyes, standing right there on the front porch, except she was wearing different pjs from that night. Her pink hair seemed to glow in the porchlight, but another thing that glowed were two little tracks running down her cheeks, as if tears had put them there. Her voice, though, seemed too calm to have been crying. "Is Rachel in her room?"

As soon as I told her, no, Rachel wasn't home, Ava took a step backward, glassy eyes seeming to fill. I caught her by the wrist before even thinking twice, pressure clamping down on my chest at the thought of her walking away. I tugged her gently, hating that I could feel her resistance. "Come inside."

"I need to go back," she said quietly. "I left my phone."

Yeah, not totally sure how that correlated, but I finally managed to ease her over the threshold, heart strangely pumping fast. It was the sort of feeling I got right before a play started, staring down the eyes of the opponent ready to plow me into the grass. I appraised Ava quickly, looking for the unknown adversary of the situation. She looked okay—she was obviously ready for bed, dressed in her pajamas. Her hair was loose around her face, which was rare for her ever since she dyed it. She must've been a bit cold walking over, with no jacket on, and no—

The pressure in my chest surged tighter. "Why aren't you wearing shoes?"

"I wanted to talk to Rachel."

You're worrying me, I wanted to tell her, but I was afraid she'd take it as more of a burden than the excuse I intended it to be. The excuse she needed to unload whatever she needed, whatever was making her voice sound so detached and her eyes look so glassy.

I didn't know Ava well enough to know how to coax it out of her, but that was all I wanted to do. Whatever was eating at her, I wanted to take it instead. But I knew if I was going to get her to talk, it wasn't going to be in the foyer. Holding her hand, I drew her up the stairs and into my dimly lit bedroom, where she asked to keep the light off. I threw on a shirt while she ventured deeper into the space, looking at the posters on my wall.

I'd known Ava for over ten years, and I'd probably only saw her cry twice. She wasn't like Rachel, who cried about almost anything, whether she was happy or sad. No, Ava seemed much more reserved than that, determined to take it all or go down with the ship trying.

That was why I was so concerned for her now as her eyes filled. That had to be why.

"My mom... She's going to sell the house." Ava let out a shaking breath, pressing her palm to her damp cheek. "She didn't tell me. That's something she should've told me, right? She should've been honest, but they never are. Neither of my parents. No one tells me things."

Her words were alarming, but the way she was breathing caught my attention more. Her breaths were too close together, like she was starting to hyperventilate. I didn't want to touch her at first, but grounding her to the moment seemed more important than whatever would've been considered proper. "Take a breath, Ava."

She just knocked me away and turned back toward my room, giving me the view of her back. I didn't know what to do, and the helplessness gripped me hard. When Rachel cried, it was like she was trying to cry the house down. Now, though, it was as if Ava was the house, and she was desperate to keep standing. To ignore the quakes and tremors.

When she spoke next, the broken quality of her voice reached into my heart and shattered it to pieces. "Why doesn't anyone care how I feel?"

Instantly, I was transported back to yesterday in the car and her frustrations that I brushed off. I'd attempted to dam up the feelings that'd been welling inside me with my words—*what kiss?*—but now I could see the truth of them. They hadn't helped me stop thinking about her, but they'd been yet another blow to her, striking into her without mercy. *Why doesn't anyone care how I feel?*

I reached up and laid my palm against her damp cheek, the coolness of the tears contrasting against the flame of her skin. I'd imagined touching her a million times since the kiss, but the thrill of the moment was dulled now, replaced by the gnawing desperation to make her feel better. "I care," I whispered to her, ducking my head to bring her eyes to mine. "I don't know why they are acting this way, but I care about how you feel."

The girl before me, with pink hair and parted lips, seemed to deflate at the words. Once again, her eyes filled with tears, and I couldn't tell which of us reached for the other first.

Ava wrapped her arms tightly around my waist and clung to me, muffling her cries into my shirt. I could feel each hiccupping breath shudder through her, and I pressed her even tighter to me, smoothing my palm up and down her back. My own eyes stung the harder she cried, and I held her in place, hoping to keep her heart from breaking.

I wasn't sure how long we sat on my bed—or, really, how long *I* sat on the bed, holding her up. I just knew I would've sat there forever if that was how long she needed me for.

"You remember that time I skinned my arm?" I murmured into her hair, almost like a kiss, but not quite. I wasn't sure that she heard me over her cries, but I spoke anyway, hoping that, like me, the background noise would help calm her racing thoughts. "Mom had just gotten Rachel and me that electric scooter, and we were all taking turns riding it down the block. I turned around too quickly, and I ended up crashing against the curb.

"Rachel, the little devil, just picked up the scooter and took it down the street. She couldn't have cared less. You, though, do you remember what you did?" I smoothed my palm down her back, picturing it in my mind. "You screamed for my mom like I'd cracked my head open. Like it was the worst thing in the world, scraping all the skin off my arm. My twin took off, but you were right there with me. Do you remember that?"

She didn't answer, but she did fist my T-shirt tighter.

I wasn't sure how old we were. Was it the fifth grade? Sixth? I couldn't even remember what month it'd been, but I could remember how her voice sounded. Could remember her panic, and how strange it'd seemed. In a good way. "You were there for me then," I whispered, resting my chin against her head, drawing in her scent. "And I'll always be here for you."

I let those words linger in the air, hoping they'd echo in her. They solidified in me, and I knew that no matter what happened, I wasn't going to push her away again.

Her cries had soon died off to sniffles, and from there, she fell quiet. I still coaxed my fingers through her hair or traced a path up and down her spine, any sort of lulling gesture I could think of. After a while, her hands around my back slackened, her body leaning against mine in full force. I hadn't realized she'd fallen asleep until I pulled away enough to look at her, and her damp lashes were stuck to her cheeks.

My heart squeezed painfully in my chest.

I laid her down on my bed, careful as I propped her head on my pillow. As gently as I could, I smoothed the tears from her skin, easing the strands of hair from her face. Her lashes never even flinched. I should've probably taken her to Rachel's room, but all I could think about was Ava waking up in the middle of the night, feeling abandoned again. Embarrassed. Hurt. I never wanted her to feel that way again.

It was in that moment that I realized I was on a train quickly running out of track. There was no ignoring the feelings anymore, no pretending they meant anything different—I liked Ava. Our kiss was great, but it wasn't just that I liked it. I liked seeing her smile, liked watching her eyes light up with a Babble submission. The kiss had merely been a light flipping on. Ava had never been on my radar in that way before.

And now she was the only one on it. The only one who'd ever be on it again.

I covered her with the duvet before lying down beside her, propping my head on the same pillow, listening to her breathing. *I'll be right here*, I thought to her, closing my eyes. *I'll always be right here.*

ACKNOWLEDGEMENTS

I've never had a crush on my best friend's brother, but living vicariously through Ava and Reed has been such a fun experience. Thank you, dear reader, for coming on this journey with me! I hope you fell in love with Ava's quirks and Reed's smirks as much as I did. It's so fun to share the stories of my heart with you all, and I can't thank you enough for giving these books a chance.

Thank you to my amazing editing team, especially Esperanza! This book was stubborn when it came to its ending, but your support, encouragement, and suggestions really helped flesh this baby out to what it needed to be. I couldn't have gotten here without you!

Thank you to my proofreading team, especially Vivian, Marissa, Caitlin, and Stephanie for being awesome extra sets of eyes!

Thank you to my dad, who, when I explained the situation between Reed and Ava and then told him the title, teasingly pointed out, "But he lives across the street, not next door." You always know how to make me laugh.

Thank you to my mother—you always believe in me, and for that, I can never thank you enough.

And thank You for this incredible journey. Thank You for guiding my steps, for being there for me when I feel discouraged, and for this glorious plan of Yours. No matter what, all the glory is to You.

What Are Friends For?

Who said falling for your best friend was a good thing?

Out of My League

Fake dating the captain of the baseball team is all fun and games until someone catches feelings.

If the Broom Fits

How do you move on from someone you never fell out of love with?

CAN'T CATCH MY BREATH

Can't Catch My Breath

Can she break free of the past and find true love?

Two Kinds of Us

Diamonds meet rock n' roll and secrets meet their end.

Christmas As We Know It

Meet me underneath the mistletoe.

Teaching the Teacher's Pet

Tutoring sessions in both algebra and love...which one will get schooled?

www.ingramcontent.com/pod-product-compliance
Lightning Source LLC
Chambersburg PA
CBHW060947190726

48286CB00005B/1467